Chapter One

'God, I feel sick.'

Corinne Marchand's dark eyes dimmed with pain. It was too hot. So horribly oppressive. Mid July, and despite the air-conditioning she was sweltering in a black linen suit in the executive bathroom at her father's office, making last-minute touches to her make-up.

'So do I.' But Yolande, standing beside her, still looked infuriatingly cool even at this moment of crisis. 'You're smudging your mascara. Let me.'

Corinne obediently stood still while her younger sister skilfully repaired the damage. Her stomach had been invaded by a squadron of butterflies, her hands wanted to shake. But she had her speech ready. In her head. Word perfect. She was here to fight. And she was going to win.

'What if they vote against me?'

'They won't.'

'But everybody expects Georges to take over.'

'Why? Papa certainly didn't want him to, and he doesn't even want it himself.'

'What about you? You're perfectly entitled to stand against me.'

'Oh, Corinne, *really* …'

And they both had to grin. As if. Yolande had never been interested in anything other than modelling and enjoying herself in Parisian night spots where Corinne always felt out of place.

'Had to read you your rights, *petite fleur*.'

Yolande smiled sadly. That had been their father's endearment for her. 'Yeah, I know. But no thanks. Oh, I

1

miss him so much.' She turned into her sister's arms, clung on, choked back the tears.

'Me too. Me too.' Corinne held her close, struggled to keep her control. 'Don't start me off. I'll look like a complete Goth if this mascara runs again. We're already late.'

It was quite a change after the high-rise steel and glass of the bank's office on London Wall – a boardroom in exquisite Second Empire style, with all the gilt and glamour befitting the headquarters of a major fashion house on the chic Avenue Montaigne. Miles Corsley was at last beginning to enjoy his secondment to Paris. He briefly checked his tie in one of the huge mirrors and laid out his papers on the polished walnut table, tuning his ear in to the various conversations in French going on around him. There was Marchand Enterprises' finance director, Georges Maury, a well-built man with thinning grey hair combed back neatly from his forehead, in ponderous discussion with a sharp-featured junior: business school clones. Then a couple of leisured looking gentlemen, more interested in their golf handicaps than the fact that they were here to vote on the future of one of France's most prestigious companies. Non-executive directors up from the provinces, Miles guessed. Probably from Burgundy, where the late Jean-Claude Marchand had started his business empire as producer of one of the finest wines on the Côte d'Or before branching out into exclusive cosmetics and fashion.

Miles had met the legendary Jean-Claude only once, four weeks previously, and had been almost knocked out by his sheer zest for life. He was every inch the tycoon – tough, shrewd, and charming, with penetrating green eyes and a sharp wit. That he had found time in his crowded diary to try to lick a young banker from London into shape was a tribute to both his generosity and his energy. And,

2

Miles was sure his Uncle Rupert would say, to his incurable optimism. Now he was dead. It was a sharp reminder that one should always seize the day.

An impeccably dressed young man with a shock of black hair was pacing the other side of the room. That had to be Yves de Rochemort, one of the major shareholders. Miles noted his height because it was unusual for him to meet a Frenchman at the same eye-level as his own six feet two inches. He was a baron, if Miles remembered correctly, though of course the title was of no account in the French Republic except in certain circles where the old nobility still concerned themselves with such things. He kept looking anxiously at the panelled double doors.

Clearly the Marchand sisters were unused to business, and didn't realise they should have been here fifteen minutes ago. They probably wouldn't stay long. All Miles had heard was that their late father had been wildly indulgent and that the youngest, Yolande, who intermittently pursued a modelling career at Hervy, the ailing couture house he had rescued from oblivion a few years before, filled the gossip columns with her escapades. Twenty-nine-year-old Corinne was something of a mystery. An airhead like her sister, his colleague James had said, but without the looks. She worked for her father in some senior role, but seemed very good at keeping herself out of the limelight. No, they would be gone quickly. Georges Maury was sure to become the new managing director, and then Miles could have a long hard chat with him about the huge sums that Marchand owed Corsley First European Bank.

The boardroom doors swung open. So the Marchand sisters had finally decided to show up. Miles glanced up perfunctorily; and was sure he heard the thud as his jaw hit the floor. The taller of the two had the grace of a dancer and a beauty that was searing and vital – tumbling chestnut hair, luminous green eyes under arched brows, high cheekbones, full mouth, and a surprisingly firm chin. Aristocrat and sex goddess all in one. He wouldn't have believed her to be real if she hadn't cast him a curious half-smile as her eyes swept the room. Obviously used to making an entrance, he thought. And bloody terrifying; the sort of girl who could eat a man for breakfast and two more for lunch and dinner. That had to be Yolande. He would have recognised her anyway by the strong resemblance to her father. Yves de Rochemort bounded over to her and circled her waist with his arm, then kissed her lips. He escorted her to a seat, while Georges Maury went over to Corinne. After the formal cheek-kissing, he gave her an affectionate hug.

Miles watched in growing appreciation as Corinne was led to the head of the table. James needed to get his sight tested. Though her looks were more reticent, she was every bit as easy on the eye as her sister. Curvier, but still slender, her legs and hips were swathed elegantly in black. She wore a pale pink silk blouse and minimal jewellery. Dark hair was swept back from a classic face, with the same arched brows, high cheekbones, and uncompromising chin as Yolande. He realised that smouldering black eyes were trained on him warily but he just stared back. Couldn't help it. A man could drown in molten eyes like that. And when he caught the spicy notes of her perfume, he felt as though he'd been punched in the gut.

'Who the hell is that?' Corinne whispered to Georges.

'He's representing the lenders. He'll go when we've discussed the figures – first item on the agenda.'

Corinne resented the way the man stared at her, and not just because of his want of manners. It was the fire of arousal in his eyes, the hungry way they raked over her and laid her bare. It infuriated her because for a millisecond she felt a responsive shiver, desire she thought

4

she had killed entirely during the past few years. And surprised her because outwardly he seemed like a gentleman. An attractive one too if it weren't for that insolent gaze. He had an air of unmistakable authority, with piercing grey-blue eyes that gave intensity to a rugged face. The nose was aquiline, the mouth stubborn. His light brown hair was closely cropped like a soldier's. There was nothing soft about him, she thought. Well, maybe a gentleman who played hard ball. His pin-striped suit was decidedly English, and if she wasn't mistaken, so was he. She resolved to conduct the entire meeting in French.

She took the chair and called the meeting to order. A secretary began to take minutes. There was one empty seat – it belonged to Antoinette Brozard, one of the non-executive directors. Corinne looked questioningly at Georges.

'I'm afraid Toinette is unwell and sends her apologies. She nominated me as her proxy.'

Corinne quickly extinguished a flicker of annoyance, and then fixed her eyes on the stranger.

'We haven't been introduced,' she said, her voice as icy as her expression.

'Miles Corsley.' He stood up, tall and straight. 'From Corsley First European Bank. May I offer our sincere condolences on your father's death.'

Oh, the boss's son, thought Corinne. And though his French was good, the accent was definitely Anglo-Saxon. They had a damn nerve sending some junior family member to check on her company and apologise for driving her father so hard he had dropped dead of a heart attack. Fifty-eight, no signs of illness. No warning that her wonderful father, so full of life and love, would be lying on a mortuary slab instead of chairing this meeting with his customary verve and good humour. She felt tears come to her eyes, and forced herself to block out the image of his body at the hospital, that last kiss on his cold forehead.

'Thank you,' she said curtly. She turned to the secretary. 'Sylvie, please note that Monsieur Corsley will be in attendance for agenda item one only.'

It wasn't so difficult when Corinne hit her stride. The butterflies fluttered away, her voice gained in confidence, she engaged everyone in the meeting with a look, a smile, as she hoped they would approve her presentation of the latest company figures. She'd watched her father do it so well, so many times. It was in her blood. And it soon showed.

'As you can see from the spreadsheet, Marchand-Beauté profits show a seven per cent quarterly increase, with a projected twenty-five per cent for the full year – our sales peak comes at Christmas. We have increased turnover and reduced costs, and I expect further cost savings of twelve million euros for this year to come through once our rationalisation of production is complete. Our mid-range products are doing well in retail, but we have had rapid growth from the web boutique. It will be one of my priorities to continue the work my father started in this area. Hervy couture is finally showing a profit – modest, but very encouraging – while the accessories have really taken off in China and Russia, and I expect continued profits growth as we roll out in other global markets. We are spending a considerable amount on launch of the *prêt-a-porter* range and perfumes, but if anything I feel the profits forecast for this sector is conservative. My recent trips to London, New York, Beijing, and Tokyo have convinced me we have the right designer and product range to bring this great brand back to the glory days when Hélène Hervy established the company in this very building so many decades ago. Now, on the second page you'll see projections for our holding in Elegance Hotels …'

Miles lost his air of amused superiority during the

second sentence. He even forgot how sexy Corinne's voice sounded as coolly and swiftly she shredded all his preconceptions with her expert financial summary. He'd throttle James Chetwode when he got back to the office for giving him such inaccurate background information for this meeting. This was no brainless bimbo living at Papa's expense in a job where she couldn't do any damage, but a highly competent, intelligent professional who knew her company and her audience inside out and was about to subject him to ritual humiliation. He could see it as she turned those megawatt eyes on him with a charming but deadly smile and flipped over another page.

'Monsieur Corsley, I'd like to draw your attention to page six, where you will see that although Marchand's gearing is still substantial, we made two additional debt repayments during the last quarter and are well on target to meet our obligations for the rest of the year. I have outlined plans for further cost reductions across the group, which when combined with our increasing turnover and profits, should comfort the bank that despite a change at the top, Marchand will remain a well-managed and profitable business for decades to come.' He felt the chill sweep across him as she switched back to ice queen mode. 'If you have any questions, I'm sure Georges will be happy to discuss them with you offline. I'll get this report emailed to you this afternoon.'

And that was it. The regal dismissal. She didn't give him a second glance as he gathered up his papers. He strode out of the room, fuming.

'Well, that busted his ego,' said Yolande, earning a reproving glance from her sister. She was quite unused to meeting protocol.

'Was it altogether wise?' Yves wondered aloud.

'He had no right to be here,' Corinne shot back. 'Who invited him?'

Georges cleared his throat. 'Your father, my dear.'

She paled and felt a little sick.

'He's new to Corsley's Paris office and is taking over the Marchand account, and Jean-Claude thought it would help him to get his bearings if he sat in on one of our board meetings.'

'Oh joy.'

'Your father was also going to invite him to tour some of our operations, but I'm not sure how far he got with that.'

'All set up, *monsieur*,' said Sylvie. Then she looked at Corinne. 'I've already put them in your diary.'

By the time Corinne was ensconced in an armchair opposite her sister in their late father's office she was the new head of a global luxury goods company with, as Georges kindly informed her, a great deal to do to persuade the markets that Marchand's board had made the right choice. The first thing she did was to take the clips out of her hair and let it fall free, then slip off her detested high heels with a sigh of relief and curl her legs up beneath her.

'I told you they'd vote for you,' said Yolande.

'Considering that in the end I was the only candidate, it was hardly a triumph. But thanks for your support, darling. I really appreciate it.'

'You'll be brilliant.'

Yolande wasn't gushing. She was absolutely convinced her clever older sister could handle anything. Corinne had waltzed through her degree at Oxford with a First, and had improved results at every department of Marchand she had ever worked in, from the shop floor up. Yolande herself had undertaken a few fairly calamitous placements with the firm in her summer vacations during a protracted spell of higher education on both sides of the Atlantic, before kicking off her modelling career at Hervy at the grand old age of twenty. She'd had countless agents trying to sign her for years, but hadn't taken the idea seriously until it became clear she would never graduate. Her father had indulged her, always hoped that one day she would wake up and become more like Corinne. And when that failed to happen, he had pinned all his hopes on her engagement to Yves – one of those on-off affairs that kept the paparazzi happy, if no one else.

It would be the wedding of the season if it ever took place. The Rochemorts had a large Burgundy estate neighbouring the Marchands' vineyards, and the two combined could dominate the market for *grand cru* red burgundies. Other business alliances could also be strengthened. Yves was both a major shareholder and director of Marchand Enterprises, and his father and Jean-Claude had been close friends and business partners. He was the perfect choice. Too perfect. Perhaps that was why Yolande seemed to be doing her best to scupper the match. Rows and reconciliations had followed a predictable pattern over the past few months. Corinne looked at her and let out a deep sigh. How was she supposed to cope with her adorable, irrepressible little sister now their father was gone? She needed someone she could rely on, and all she had was a headstrong girl she'd fished out of trouble more times than she could remember. Without his encouragement and support, a Rochemort-Marchand marriage now appeared to be doomed. It shouldn't have been Yves and Yolande, anyway. It should have been her and Philippe. She forced her mind back into focus. It was never a good idea to start thinking about Philippe.

Sylvie provided a welcome interruption when she tripped in with a tray and cups. 'I thought you might like some coffee, *madame la présidente.*'

Corinne almost choked. 'I hope you're not going to make a habit of calling me that.'

A discreet and very polished senior PA, Sylvie had worked for Jean-Claude for over two decades and had known Corinne as a girl, but she was a stickler for etiquette. She looked a little pained. 'But ...'

'Corinne is fine.'

'But ...'

'Please.' The tone was final. 'And you shouldn't be bringing us coffee – I usually get my own. But thanks very much. It's been a long day.'

'It's so kind of you, Sylvie,' added Yolande, gratefully taking a cup and dropping in more sugar lumps than any girl her size had a right to eat.

Sylvie melted as two smiles exactly like the late Jean-Claude's beamed up at her. 'It's no trouble. Can I do anything else for you?'

'You could tell me why Papa arranged all these visits for Monsieur Corsley,' said Corinne. 'I don't remember him ever paying such attention to our bankers before.'

'He genuinely liked him, I think. You know how he used to take a fancy to certain people. But he always had his reasons for a charm offensive.'

'Exactly. If we were in a tight spot with them I could understand, but actually we're not. Did he mention anything else to you?'

'Not really. But he seemed to want you to handle most of the visits.'

Sylvie left the room and Corinne frowned. Now she would have to be nice to the sexist pig. What on earth her father had seen in him she couldn't fathom. She looked up and caught a glint of amusement in Yolande's eyes.

'What?' she demanded in English, just in case they could be overheard.

'Maybe Papa was trying his hand at matchmaking.'

Corinne spluttered on her coffee.

'Think about it.'

She did. And was horrified to conclude that Yolande was probably right. Miles Corsley was exactly the kind of man her father would have considered an appropriate suitor; a dead boring banker with a superiority complex. Despite his own tangled private life, Jean-Claude had always held peculiarly antiquated views on relationships when it came to his daughters.

'What a bloody cheek! He should never have accepted the meeting.'

'I don't suppose he has any more idea that was what Papa had in mind than you did.'

'I'll make damn sure he never does.'

'But he's seriously cute, even if he is a bit stuffy. And he's definitely got the hots for you.'

'Oh really?' Corinne wasn't sure whether to be exasperated or amused. Yolande's requirements of men were seldom the same as hers, but her radar for the basics was usually infallible. 'Wouldn't he be more up your street?'

'Absolutely not. He's far too old.'

Corinne decided to be amused. Anyone over thirty was ancient as far as her sister was concerned, and she doubted that Miles Corsley was more than thirty-five. She chuckled.

'Anyway, he doesn't want me,' continued Yolande. 'But he certainly noticed you, although that put down you gave him probably pissed him off a bit. He was simply drooling over you when you walked in.'

'Look who's matchmaking now.'

'Oh I'm not suggesting you go that far! Just have a bit of fun. I bet he's good in bed.'

'Yolande!'

'Oh, like you didn't notice.'

'You really are insufferable.'

'That means I'm right.'

Fortunately for Corinne, who found annoyance getting the better of her humour, Yolande's mobile rang. 'Patrick? Yes, the meeting's over. I'm with my sister. Of course, darling, I'd love to. The Bar des Théâtres? I'll be about an hour. See you.'

It wasn't the 'darling' that alerted Corinne. Yolande was always lavish with endearments – on a good day even their dour old concierge Monsieur Boniface could be 'darling'. But the gleam in her eyes boded only one thing if she knew her sister – she was planning to have sex, and it clearly wasn't going to be with Yves.

Yolande just looked at her, all innocence.

'You can't fool me. Is this Patrick someone I need to worry about?'

'No. He works for you, actually – modelling at Hervy. He's great fun. But he's an actor. He only models when he's resting.'

'You know that isn't what I meant, Yolande. I thought there was something up with you and Yves.'

'I was going to talk to him today, actually. But he's gone straight back to St Xavier, and I can't do it over the phone.'

'Promise me you won't keep stringing him along. It isn't fair. You know it isn't.'

'I just don't want to hurt him.'

'You think screwing around behind his back isn't going to hurt him?'

Yolande's expression hardened, and she seemed about to lash out with a retort but thought better of it. 'You're right. I must talk to him. I will, promise. He'll be fine. He's not in love with me, you know.'

Corinne shook her head. 'You silly girl.'

'God, you sound just like Papa.'

'And you're acting just like him!'

Yolande looked a little shamefaced. She said nothing.

Corinne had adored their father, but his dizzying parade of female companions had been proud testimony to his inconstancy. Mystifying, really, when their mother was so beautiful and charming and had been very much in love with him when they had married. But the marriage hit the rocks soon after Yolande was born. Grace Albury had bitterly resented Jean-Claude's philandering, and after one particularly blazing affair was talked about all over Paris, she walked out and went home to England. A protracted and acrimonious divorce followed. When Grace remarried five years later, she settled with her American banker husband in New York, but Jean-Claude retained custody of their daughters. Eventually they reached a messy compromise whereby the girls spent term time with their English grandparents in London and attended the French Lycée, with holidays divided between France and America. It had hurt so much. Corinne loved both her parents. She had hated taking sides, the rows, the court battles, the long tearful goodbyes every term. Now her father was gone, and she hadn't had him to herself nearly enough. And Yolande seemed bent on continuing a most undesirable family tradition.

'Be careful, Yolande. Please. I'm not going to say any more about it. You're a big girl now. But I love both you and Yves, so it's quite hard for me to sit on the sidelines while you two tear each other apart.'

Yolande went over to perch on the arm of Corinne's chair and put an arm round her. 'Don't say anything to Mummy, will you? Not until I've spoken to him.'

Corinne tugged her down and gave her a fierce hug. 'Monster! Of course not. Now let me up. I'm going back to the Avenue Foch to start clearing out Toinette's stuff.'

Yolande got to her feet. 'Damn, I'd forgotten. I'll come with you. I'll put off Patrick.'

'It's OK, she's not there. She's at her own apartment. But we'll have to cope with her at the funeral.'

They both looked grim. Immaculate, elegant, steely Antoinette Brozard had been Jean-Claude Marchand's mistress for over twelve years. Though she'd never been unkind, she'd been hell to get along with. Nothing could ever be out of place or less than perfect. It was like living in a TV commercial. The girls had tolerated her, but could never pretend they liked her – which was doubtless why they hadn't thought of her before. They always tried to airbrush Toinette out of their lives as far as possible.

Corinne winced as she pushed her feet back into her high heels.

'They look really fab on you.'

'Pity they don't come with an insurance policy to pay for the corrective foot surgery I'm going to need.' Corinne started to pack up her laptop. 'How *do* you wear them all the time?'

'Years of practice. And ...' Yolande pulled out a pair of glittery flip-flops and some Hervy jeans from her bag and proceeded to throw off her suit, '... emergency relief supplies.'

Corinne laughed. 'You are such a fraud.'

With her blouse hanging loosely over her skinny jeans and the flip-flops on, Yolande didn't even look her twenty-three years, more like a fresher at an Ivy League campus. She shook out her hair and fastened a huge belt around her hips to complete the look.

'That's better. I'll probably see you later tonight.'

Corinne raised an eyebrow.

'Or maybe not. Bye, darling.'

Future of Marchand Enterprises in doubt as Madame Brozard threatens lawsuit.

Corinne threw the newspaper down in disgust. There was a pile of them, all with similar variations of the story. Only two days after his funeral. Poor Papa. How Toinette must have fooled him all those years! And the way she had wailed at his grave – just a disgusting sham.

Yves bent his long frame down to gather up the papers, then sat back at the large cluttered desk by the window of his office. Outside, the vineyards and gardens which made the Château de Rochemort one of the most celebrated estates on the Côte d'Or were bathed in hot summer sunshine.

'Do you really think she'll sue us?' asked Corinne. 'Can she?'

'Probably not,' he said, scanning the reports rapidly. 'Look, this piece is by Laurent Dobry, and he and Toinette go way back. It's just to frighten the Bourse.'

He tossed the paper aside and poured Corinne a glass of red wine. One of Château de Rochemort's classic years; she sipped it appreciatively.

'You shouldn't waste your best vintages on me, you know.'

'I'm sure you'll reciprocate,' he said. 'So what are you going to do? Marchand shares have already depreciated eight per cent. You could buy them in.'

'Can't afford to.'

Yves drummed his fingers on the desk. 'Well, someone will make a killing, and it could be Toinette. Don't forget that holding company she has an interest in – the one that bought Philippe's stake.'

Corinne flinched. Philippe. Yves' older brother. Breathtakingly handsome, clever, sexy. The love of her life. The ten months they had been together had been the happiest she had ever known. But he had left her, his family, and France one fine day three years before without a word of explanation. Marchand-Rochemort companies almost collapsed when Philippe sold his holdings in both family businesses to UVS, a private equity company with an address in Paris and not much else. Yves had eventually recovered the Rochemort shares by taking out a hefty bank loan, but a heavily indebted Marchand had been unable to do the same. Months of silence and heartbreak followed before word came that Philippe was in Australia. But even his redoubtable mother Marie-Christine knew little of his activities. He sent only the occasional postcard or noncommittal e-mail to show he was still alive and nothing at all to show that he cared.

Corinne rubbed her eyes, tried to, had to focus on business. 'You don't think UVS will launch a takeover bid?'

'Doubt it. You and Yolande are majority shareholders. They can't get overall control. It could just make life awkward for a while.'

'You really think Toinette is behind all this?'

'She's the sort of woman who has to get her own back.'

Corinne bridled. 'But Papa left her five per cent of the company! Not to mention a drawer full of Cartier and some rather collectable paintings.'

Yves gave her a wry look. 'Corinne, look at it from her point of view – twelve years with your father, taking so much care of him – don't look like that now, you know she did.'

'So?'

'She hated it because she couldn't call herself Madame Marchand. When a woman has enjoyed that kind of lifestyle she's sure to view a five per cent shareholding and a few diamond necklaces as a pretty poor pension.'

All Corinne remembered were the times she'd been forced to attend Toinette's famous parties, how she had detested the superficial chat and hordes of strangers who had left her feeling an outsider in her own home.

'Let's leave it for now. Perhaps you'd come over for lunch tomorrow? We can talk then. I've got so much paperwork to get through.'

'Great. I want to talk to Yolande too. We really must discuss the wedding. I've hardly seen her lately.'

He sounded confident, as he had every right to be. He had inherited his mother's imposing features, with intense blue eyes that sometimes reminded Corinne too much of Philippe. But at twenty-eight, Yves showed no signs of developing Philippe's deadly charm. He was still the same direct and down-to-earth guy she had grown up with, though perhaps a little cool for some tastes. But he had always been her friend and she was very fond of him. She was tempted to warn him about Yolande, then thought better of it. There had been Patricks before. If Yves was willing to turn a blind eye to what Corinne sincerely hoped was just another of her sister's regrettable lapses, there might still be a wedding to talk about after all.

His mind was still on business. 'Do you mind if I give you some advice, Corinne?' He leaned forward in his chair. 'Let the world know that Marchand Enterprises has a new boss, and stop these rumours before the shares fall any further.'

'Georges will sort it out.'

'But it's your company! Georges is a great accountant, but he has absolutely no flair. I assume he'll remain vice-president, but make sure he dances to your tune. Jean-Claude always did.'

She rose to leave. 'You are, as usual, absolutely right. I'd better get on with it.'

Corinne returned home to Le Manoir de St Xavier, the Marchands' mellowed seventeenth-century mansion with shuttered windows and a high mansard roof, to find Yolande glumly contemplating a sheaf of papers. She waved it at her sister as she entered the salon.

'Corinne, thank God you're back! Georges gave me this while you were out. What does it all mean?'

'That you're rich and powerful.'

'But what about my allowance?' wailed Yolande. 'This is all in bonds and shares.'

It took an hour to convince Yolande she wasn't a pauper, and only a few minutes more for her to decide that Corinne was the best person to deal with her affairs. A salaried non-executive directorship on Marchand's board without the inconvenience of work seemed a good deal overall. Afterwards Yolande went off to finish removing

Toinette's personal possessions from the house and Corinne went into her father's office.

Small and comfortable, it couldn't have been more different than his imposing quarters on the Avenue Montaigne. It felt so odd to be sitting behind the desk instead of in the armchair at the side. Wine charts were fixed to one wall, whilst a Fragonard adorned another. Just the style of painting her father had most enjoyed – the frivolous, erotic side of the eighteenth century. On the desk beside the computer there was a framed photo of Yolande and Corinne as children with their mother, and stuck to the monitor, a holiday snap of Toinette, laughing and happy. Corinne ripped it off and dropped it into the bin, then picked up the telephone and opened her father's large business address book. He had never really got to grips with his personal organiser. Yes, all the numbers were there, neatly listed under newspapers.

'*Les Echos*, can I help you?'

'This is Corinne Marchand. I'd like to speak to your editor, please.'

Then *Le Monde*, *Le Figaro*, Reuters, Bloomberg, and the *Financial Times* in London. A press release from Marchand's communications director would have been sufficient, but Corinne felt the personal touch would work better this time. Her husky voice sounded appealing in both English and French, and reporters were duly tasked to write up articles for the following day's editions.

'Do we have a picture?' asked one senior editor.

A researcher tracked down a photo of Yolande in one of hot young designer Franco Rivera's creations for Hervy. 'It's her sister.'

The editor whistled. 'Just make sure we run it.'

Marchand shares rally under new chief executive.

'Well done, Corinne,' Yves said over lunch the following day.

Georges looked amused. 'It was classic Marchand PR.' He turned to Corinne, who sat quietly next to Yolande, rather disconcerted by their praise. 'You're more like your father than you know.'

She was astounded by her own success. The share price had recovered, rumours of a lawsuit had ceased that very morning, and Yolande's beguiling smile had cheered many a businessman's dreary commute to work. The crisis was past. Soon they were in animated discussion of the marketing plans for Hervy's new ready-to-wear collection which was being launched in Europe and the States in the autumn.

Yolande was remarkably quiet throughout the meal. Yves, sitting opposite her, tried to read her expression, but her eyes were distant and unfathomable. When they rose from the table, he took her by the arm and steered her outside into the garden. They walked aimlessly across the lawn until they reached the welcome shade of a poplar tree. He stopped and pulled her into his arms.

'Yolande…'

She let him hold her, but he could feel the resistance in her muscles.

'We need to talk about the wedding.'

'It's useless, Yves. It's over.'

'*Over*? You don't mean that.'

She broke away from him and took a few steps backwards. Then she tugged his diamond and emerald engagement ring off her finger and held it out.

Yves was shocked, but he played it cool. She was feeling fragile. There was no need for a scene. 'I'm so terribly sorry about your father, darling. Perhaps we should talk later, hmm?'

He moved close and stroked her cheek gently. Yolande's patience snapped. She hated the way he treated her – like a child, a small recalcitrant child. All she had ever wanted was Yves. She had adored him – hopelessly, it seemed – for ever. He'd had a string of girlfriends while she was away at school and university, and then suddenly he'd opened his heart to her, told her he loved her and proposed. She'd walked on a cloud of happiness for weeks, and then came the slow, bitter awakening. He never shared his plans, discussed their future, made her feel necessary. Worse, he never made her feel like a woman. He held her as though she were a priceless porcelain vase and pressed tentative lips against hers, and she wanted to scream at him to take her, to love her with the same fierce desire she felt for him. But he never did. If she tried to arouse him he would draw back, smile that truly sweet smile of his and stroke her cheek or kiss her hand; and make her feel as though she were five years old again, grateful that he had come to her birthday party and admired her new dress.

'I told you – it's over. I know you think it's only because of Papa dying ...' Suddenly she desperately wanted to cry and she paused for some moments, fighting back the tears. 'But it's not that, Yves. I don't want to marry you, that's all.'

'I thought you loved me,' he said, looking straight at her.

It was harder than she had foreseen. She didn't hate him. It was impossible to hate Yves. She'd loved him so long that he would always be part of her life, and anyway he was the sort of man you simply had to like. His blue eyes seemed to be boring right through her, but it had no effect. She could only think of Patrick. She needed him so badly. Soon she would be with him again and everything would be all right.

'I don't love you,' she said. 'Not that way. Not enough to marry you.'

Yves was stunned. She seemed determined. So beautiful. So unaware of how much she meant to him, how much he wanted her. He seized her in his arms, crushing

20

her against him. 'I'm sorry I haven't been around much lately. I've neglected you. But once we're married it will all work out. Yolande, please …'

His lips brushed against her neck, his words came in hot breaths on her skin. She tried to break free, but he held her fast and forced his mouth down on hers with a passion that was entirely unexpected. But it was far too late now. He'd had his chance and he'd blown it. She pulled away.

'Let me go, Yves! I mean it.'

'Have you met someone else?' he asked, his voice quivering slightly.

'Surely you guessed a long time ago?'

'But I love you!'

'Let me go!'

He bent his head to kiss her again, but she struggled and he released her. Yolande didn't want to see the wounded look in his eyes and ran back into the house, wiping her lips with the back of her hand. He'd get over it. His pride had taken a knock, that was all. Men didn't suffer heartache in the same way as women.

As soon as Yves entered her office Corinne knew the inevitable had happened, but she hadn't expected him to look quite so upset.

'It's over?'

He nodded.

'I'm so sorry.'

He sat down opposite her, staring at the ring which Yolande had tossed at him as she turned away. 'Why did she wait so long? Now she says she doesn't even love me!'

'I'm afraid she doesn't tell me all her secrets.'

'Who is he?' demanded Yves savagely.

There was no need to stoke the fire. Corinne didn't answer.

He was silent for several moments, then put the ring in his pocket and said goodbye. As he crossed the hall on his way out, he heard a movement on the staircase and looked up. It was Yolande. She stopped and leaned on the carved balustrade.

'I'm really sorry, Yves. But you know I'll always be your friend.'

He didn't see the cool, poised woman she had become, those spellbinding siren eyes, but the little girl he had played games with, the teenager he had laughed and danced with, the Yolande he had loved for as long as he could remember. He turned on his heel and left. She sauntered into the office a few moments later looking quite puzzled.

'Do you know, Corinne, he won't even speak to me now?'

Her sister glanced up from her e-mails with a despairing expression, then the telephone rang. It was another business call from Paris.

Jean-Claude Marchand's legacy wasn't going to be an easy one.

Chapter Two

'What the hell are you doing here?' Franco Rivera, small, sleek, dark, and harassed gazed at Yolande in surprise, then turned and bellowed to the stylists and semi-clad models behind him. 'Catherine, that belt's too slack! Kim, do I have to tell you *again*? It's the *red* shawl!'

'You've given Catherine my outfits!' exclaimed Yolande. 'Didn't you get my voicemail? I called you yesterday to say that I'd still do the show.'

'Here, *carissima*, come where we can talk.'

Franco led her to the relative oasis of a clothes rail loaded with numbers for Hervy's autumn collection. The Rivera style, instantly recognisable – colourful materials cut daringly, yet with the innate classicism that characterised all his work. He hugged her close and kissed her warmly on both cheeks.

'Sorry, I've lost my mobile again. Catherine very kindly stepped in at the last minute, and I can't really send her away now.'

'I see.' Yolande's lips puckered slightly.

'I thought – well, with your father's death. I was sorry, truly sorry to hear of it. He was such a lovely man.'

She looked at him sharply. 'You think I'm a bitch, don't you? Doing a show only a week after his funeral. But I couldn't bear it at home another day. My sister's taking over the business, so I'm back here where I belong.'

Franco gave a shrug – he had too much to do to have time to attend to the cogs turning the wheels at the House of Hervy. 'Well, you've done some brilliant PR for me with your picture in all the papers.'

'Where's Patrick?'

'Back there,' he said, jerking a thumb over the rail. 'Look, Yolande, perhaps you'd do me a favour now you're here? I have some very influential people out there today. One in particular – he may get me the backing I need to set up on my own.'

'You're leaving Hervy? But why?'

'My contract runs out next year, and Paul Dupuy's already recruiting my replacement.'

Paul was always terrified that Hervy would lose its reputation for dressing the discreet and discerning. Franco had been considered a daring gamble when appointed by Jean-Claude Marchand straight out of fashion college in London, but he had succeeded in maintaining the 'Hervy look', albeit at the expense of his natural flamboyance. Yolande fully understood his desire for independence, though as an owner of Hervy's parent company it ought to have worried her.

'So what do you want me to do?' she asked.

'Just look gorgeous and tell this guy how wonderful I am.' He cast a critical eye over her figure-hugging dress, flatteringly cut in dark grey jersey, then dashed off to a table nearby, returning with some chunky costume jewellery which he draped around her neck.

'But Patrick …'

'He's all yours after the show. Come on, Yolande – there isn't much time.'

A tangible air of expectancy could be sensed amongst the occupants of the hard gilt-framed chairs arranged in a semi-circle beneath the grand chandeliers in the Hotel Intercontinental's Salon Opéra. Fashion editors and buyers, film and television celebrities, a couple of European princesses, a few sports stars, and a battalion of photographers. Only a few of the seats still bore place-cards, a fact that clearly pleased Hervy's operations director, Paul Dupuy, sitting next to his wife in the front

24

row with a self-satisfied smile on his face. The fashion writers were impatient for something, *anything* to liven things up. The shows had been predictable this season. No earth-shattering new trends, no dramatic sackings of erratic designers. Juicy copy was at a premium. Had any of them known that Franco Rivera was presenting one of his last collections for Hervy, there would have been uproar.

But the lights dimmed and music began, so few people noticed Franco discreetly ushering Yolande to a chair next to Count Ulrich von Stessenberg, who was chatting quietly to Althea, sociable wife of the dull but exceedingly rich American entrepreneur Hank Pedersen. Stessenberg stood up, bowed slightly, and kissed Yolande's hand as she was introduced, greeting her in one of those hard-to-place international accents – English with American undertones, yet occasional hints of European stress. Althea Pedersen looked at her quizzically when she heard her name.

'Rikki, you're flirting with a girl who's just become president of a big company here. Am I right?' she asked Yolande.

Yolande sat down while Franco hurried away. 'I'm afraid not. My sister's the new president.'

'Marchand Enterprises, Althea,' said Stessenberg. 'Didn't you know they own Hervy?'

'Well I saw your picture in the paper, so I thought it must be you,' continued Althea doggedly. 'Who can figure out all that French? Are you French?'

'Half. My mother's English. She's married to an American now – Tex Beidecker. Perhaps you've met him?'

Althea raised her well-manicured hands in a comic gesture. Didn't the whole of New York know Tex Beidecker? He was a great guy. They knew Yolande's mother too, and Stessenberg made some flattering remarks about her which drew a volley of giggles from Mrs Pedersen. Yolande noticed that he still kept cool appraising eyes on Franco's collection as the models started strutting down the catwalk. Remembering Franco's brief, she was enthusiastic in her praise of the designs, and the count was keen to get her opinion.

'Is this the Hervy look according to Franco Rivera, or Franco Rivera according to Hervy, mademoiselle?'

A tricky question, thought Yolande, surveying the lean contours of his face. German or Austrian? She wasn't sure, but it was a patrician face. Keen, slightly sardonic, but inscrutable; a closed book. He was perfectly dressed, faultlessly polite, and altogether chilling.

'Well, Franco tries to do his own thing, but there are limits. We have a strong brand to promote.'

'He's under exclusive contract to Hervy, isn't he?'

'Yes – until next year.'

'Hey, I go for that one,' whispered Althea, as Catherine fluttered past in a revealing crimson ensemble.

Yolande didn't think it would suit her at all, but remained quiet.

'What do you think of that?' Althea asked, as another, more restrained dress appeared on the catwalk.

'Elegant and timeless,' remarked Stessenberg, turning to Yolande. 'That's Hervy rather than Franco Rivera, eh?'

Before the show ended, she found herself invited to have dinner with them both at Le Grand Véfour that evening. Franco was delighted when she told him, hugging her with Italian verve as he promised to make her look fabulous.

'You are coming with me, Franco? I can't go alone, and you want to speak to this guy, don't you?'

'Not yet, Yolande. Paul Dupuy has spies in every restaurant in Paris. If I'm seen with Stessenberg ...' He drew a finger expressively across his throat. 'All you need do is a little discreet advertising. Take Patrick – I'll lend him something to wear. He always looks so hungry.'

'*Merde*!' Patrick Dubuisson surveyed his reflection dismally in a mirror propped against a wall of his studio flat in the Marais. 'I actually look respectable. It's gross.'

'You look marvellous.' Yolande danced round him, straightening the collar of his loosely cut Hervy evening jacket. 'I wish you'd dress like this more often.'

He put his hands around her waist and gave her a serious look. 'Yolande, don't try to change me. I'm an actor, remember – and tonight I'm playing a part just for you. So, what does Franco want? Mean and moody?' He fixed his heart-throb features in a gangster's glare and looked terrifying. 'Sweet country boy up to see the sights?' Yolande struggled with laughter as he adopted a vacuous smile. 'Or simply irresistible.' The lust poured out of his eyes into hers.

'You're just supposed to wear the clothes,' she got out before she collapsed with giggles. 'Idiot.'

'My talents are wasted on you,' he said in mock disgust.

She caught his face in her hands. 'Oh, I wouldn't say that, Mr Irresistible.'

'God, you're so beautiful.'

She met his lips eagerly, desire erupting through her whole body. Patrick always had this effect on her. His arms tightened around her, his mouth feeding greedily on hers. She could feel him hard against her as his fingers moved unerringly to the concealed zip at the side of her low-cut dress.

'No, darling, later. We're supposed to be there at eight.'

But her impatient tongue in his mouth was telling him the exact opposite. He pulled the dress down to the floor and rubbed his thumbs over her nipples, teasing them until they were aching with expectation. Then his tongue followed, while his fingers moved down to stroke between her legs. She was already wet, swollen, begging for it. He liked making her beg. She whimpered and started to move rhythmically against him, her hands tugging away his clothes.

'Two weeks without you …' he groaned. 'I thought I'd go mad.'

He had her naked and on the bed in a matter of seconds, pulling her gorgeous long thighs apart while he freed himself from his trousers. He couldn't hold it much longer. Crushing his mouth to hers, he simply plunged into her. Yolande arched up to receive him, feeling at last that she was home. It wasn't making love. Patrick thought *making love* was for wimps. It was raw sex, visceral need, possession, pain, ecstasy. Fast, breathless, merciless. She screamed out his name as they shuddered to climax, her nails digging into his buttocks. Afterwards he lay still inside her while she kissed him over and over again.

'I love you,' she murmured.

'Didn't you love me before?'

'Yes – but I kept thinking it would have to end, that it was all wrong.'

Patrick rolled off her on to his back, his hazel eyes anxious. 'So you're not going to marry your baron now?'

'No.' Yolande smiled, then bent her head and kissed him lingeringly on the lips. 'Aren't you pleased?'

He didn't know how to react. He hoped she wouldn't propose to him. She was beautiful and passionate and he couldn't get enough of her, but long-term commitment wasn't on his agenda.

'Patrick … is everything OK?'

He grinned and pulled her back towards him. They were more than half an hour late leaving for the restaurant.

'Do you think we ought to order, Rikki? She's obviously not going to show.' Althea Pedersen enviously eyed the guests at a neighbouring table in Le Grand Véfour.

'Fashion's such an exhausting business, isn't it?' said Stessenberg. 'I take it you've ordered something from

Hervy?'

'It means staying here for the fittings, but Hank's tied up with his bid for Brenton so I might as well enjoy myself.'

'The pharmaceuticals group?'

'Yeah. He's really after their cosmetics subsidiary but they won't sell it off. Somehow I don't think you've got any fittings lined up.' She gave him a canny glance. 'What are you up to, Rikki?'

Stessenberg leaned back in his chair. 'I'm simply soaking up the history. Do you know that revolutionaries used to meet here two hundred years ago?'

'Should I be bothered?'

'Only if you believe in ghosts.'

'It would take more than some old French ghosts to scare me. Well, here she comes at last!' exclaimed Althea, as Yolande breezed in and heads swivelled. 'Who's the hunk with her?'

'I don't know, but he reminds me of someone.'

Althea took Patrick in from head to toe as he and Yolande were ushered to the table. Twenty-four or twenty-five. Five-eleven and slim. Tousled short brown hair, sexy eyes, luscious mouth. Decidedly French. And a very cute butt. Yolande's profuse apologies left no one in any doubt as to what had delayed them.

'I hope you don't mind me bringing my boyfriend? Patrick Dubuisson – he's an actor.'

Althea liked the gallant way he kissed her hand, and registered something in his eyes that said he wasn't impervious to her thirty-eight-year-old charms. Though not beautiful, she had a very good figure, an attractive face, and knew how to make the most of herself. Stessenberg called for the menu, and was rather put out by Patrick's broad smile when he ordered a bottle of Château Lafitte.

'Don't you like Bordeaux?' he enquired.

'Yolande is from Burgundy. She 'as 'er own wine.'

'Really?'

'Yes,' said Yolande. 'My father … I mean, my sister and I have a vineyard at home in St Xavier.'

'St Xavier!' exclaimed Althea. 'Not *the* St Xavier?'

Yolande nodded. 'It's been owned by the Marchands since 1792.'

'What did I tell you about ghosts, Althea?' whispered Stessenberg.

But she didn't hear. 'You mean you actually *own* it?'

'One of my ancestors bought it when monastic property was confiscated during the Revolution.'

Yolande would have been glad to leave the subject there, but Althea kept at it throughout the entrées. It transpired that Mr Pedersen, as well as owning a global corporation with interests ranging from petrochemicals to toiletries was also a wine connoisseur.

'He's thinking of buying a winery in California, you know, but he only wants the best. They don't come on the market very often.'

Patrick raised his eyebrows in disbelief. 'You know, in Paris very few bars 'ave the American wine. Sometimes I go to 'Arry's Bar to see the film producer there. But is not possible to 'ave good discussion without the French wine.'

It was the longest continuous speech he had ever managed in English, and he looked round triumphantly.

'If you want to cut it in Hollywood, you'd better restrain your chauvinism,' said Stessenberg in fluent French.

'Hollywood? I asked Yolande to help me with my English so I could do a screen test, but you see how far I've progressed. Do you know any producers who want French actors?'

'Not off hand.'

'Hey, what's all this about Hollywood?' interrupted Althea, annoyed at being unable to follow the conversation.

She soon found out, and the main course was punctuated by a discussion of the American film industry. Patrick's polite interest became real as the names of famous stars were mentioned casually as neighbours or friends of the Pedersens.

'I'm from California, and we have a beach house at Malibu,' explained Althea. 'We don't use it much, I guess. Hank's mostly in New York, and I'm often some place else. But I suppose I know all the big names. Vic Bernitz, for example.'

Patrick was impressed. 'The director of *Night Below Zero*? One of my favourite films.'

'He's a neighbour. A real nice guy.'

Yolande felt ill at ease and suspicious. They were baiting him, teasing him, dangling the Hollywood carrot in front of his nose; and he had fallen for it completely. She wished she hadn't come, and feeling cross, departed for the ladies' room. Althea gave Stessenberg a sly smile, then asked Patrick for his telephone number.

'I'll pass it on to Vic when I get back home. You've been in some movies already?'

'Yes – French. One film of Jacques Bertin I am in won two awards at Cannes this year.'

'Not bad,' remarked Stessenberg. 'I thought I recognised you.'

'So you 'ave seen *Souvenir Amer*?' asked Patrick eagerly. 'What you call in English … *Bitter* …'

'*Bitter Memory*? I don't think so.'

'I know I haven't,' said Althea. 'I don't get it. I was sure I'd seen you somewhere before too.'

Patrick lapsed into silence, and when Yolande returned the conversation dwindled into meaningless small talk. She was glad when at last she got him away from the seductive atmosphere and outside into the warm Parisian night. They started to walk.

'Aren't we going to the Avenue Foch?' he asked.

'I don't think so. Corinne said she was coming up to town this evening.'

'My place then. Let's get a taxi.'

Back to a narrow seventeenth-century street, up the breath-snatching stairs to the top floor, into a dark studio. There was enough light from a dim lamp to reveal the unmade bed and Patrick's usual domestic discomfort – minimalist furniture and dirty laundry strewn haphazardly on the floor, film posters on the stark white walls. It couldn't have been more unlike Yolande's luxurious abode at the other end of town, but she liked it.

'I hope you're not pinning your hopes on Mrs Pedersen and Vic Bernitz,' she said, as Patrick took off his jacket. The air was heavy, and he opened the window before lighting a cigarette.

'Of course not.'

His shoulders and head stood out in relief against the night sky. Yolande was anxious, wondering what Althea Pedersen had said to him during her absence. His mood was quiet and reflective. She had a horrible sensation of not being party to his thoughts, not counting in his plans. He seemed absorbed by ambitions she neither shared nor understood.

'What did you think of her?'

'Mrs Pedersen?' he asked. 'Quite an amusing woman. Vain, likes admiration, has spent a fortune on her teeth. That's why she smiles so much.'

'I hadn't noticed.'

He moved over to the bed, sitting down beside her. Yolande took the cigarette from him and inhaled deeply before handing it back.

'What's wrong?'

'It's you, Patrick. Sometimes I feel I don't know you at all.'

He fell back on the duvet, looking at her a little warily.

32

'Are you worried because you've got no work? Surely your agent will come up with something soon? Especially after *Souvenir Amer* did so well.'

'I didn't win the awards, Yolande – the director did. He's working on a new film, but he won't tell me about it.'

'Did you fall out with him?'

Patrick snorted. 'Who doesn't fall out with the delightful Jacques? He's such a shit. Don't worry. He's not the only director in the world even if he thinks so.'

Sometimes she amused him, fussing him like a baby, looking so hurt when he recounted his setbacks. She couldn't see it was all a game. Jacques would call him next time, and he would make him crawl. Althea Pedersen, now, she knew the game. Vic Bernitz might even give him a chance.

'Still, Franco needs you,' said Yolande. 'There's the Hervy gala in New York in October, and he'll want you to go. Will you?'

'If I've got nothing better to do.'

Patrick had had enough of the conversation. He pulled her down beside him. She didn't understand, she wasn't the right woman for him, but her body acted on his like an addictive drug. That amazingly beautiful face, lit up with desire for him. Her smooth silky skin, her eager caressing hands, her creative and insatiable sexuality. He took her slowly this time. No restaurant to hurry to, no important strangers to entertain. Just the two of them in the enveloping darkness, heat on heat.

'Why are you jealous of Althea Pedersen?' he asked, when she lay quivering beneath him.

Yolande ran her hands down his back, her legs clamped around him, then pulled his head down so that her lips brushed his cheek. 'Because I couldn't bear to lose you, Patrick. I just couldn't.'

He shut her up with a kiss, and not until much later did Yolande realise she had let him know how far she depended on him. How had he guessed she was jealous? Was she? Not of Althea Pedersen, surely, but of that plausible Hollywood talk that made Patrick's eyes light up in a way they never did for her. Talk which smelt of greasepaint and rolling film cameras, actors and scriptwriters – talk that excluded her. For the first time in her life she felt insecure. It wasn't a sensation she enjoyed.

'So how's your new boss, Georges?' asked Toinette Brozard, pacing tigress-like in the pristine salon of her small apartment near the Invalides. 'I hope she appreciated my flowers.'

'She was rather surprised to get them after your little sabotage effort in the press. But she asked me to thank you and said she's sorry to hear you're still ill.'

Toinette gave a short laugh, then coughed. 'This wretched flu. Can't seem to shake it off. Have a Scotch.'

She motioned him to an armchair and stepped over to a sideboard to pour him a drink. 'Ice?'

'Please.'

Still lithe and slim at forty-nine, neither flu nor a loose gown pulled in carelessly at the waist could lessen her appeal. Her small, pretty features were skilfully made up, and her hair, Viking blonde and a little flyaway, was tailored neatly to the contours of her head. She handed Georges a glass and sat down opposite him.

'What's this about Yolande? Is it really over between her and Yves?'

'So it seems. She's mad about some actor.'

'I met him. It won't last.' Toinette fiddled with a ring on her finger. 'Jean-Claude invited him to dinner a couple of months ago, and one could tell it was just sex – well, for Patrick anyway.'

'Yolande has other ideas,' said Georges. 'She's practically living with him.'

'Silly girl! Throwing away a fantastic guy like Yves for

some egocentric young actor who will dump her once he's successful.'

'I had a chat with him at the Hervy show to try to get some information for Corinne, and it was as though we'd met before. Very odd.'

'Do you know, I felt the same thing? There's something about him, but I just can't pin it down. He wouldn't reveal much about his background.'

Georges smiled. 'So you did ask? He told me Jean-Claude never mentioned it.'

'Did Jean-Claude ever look into things like that? It was always left to me.' She got up and poured herself a drink, which she gulped down. 'I shouldn't, but I must.'

'How are you managing?' he asked gently.

'OK, I suppose. It's horrible without him. I hate it here. No one to talk to, nothing to do.'

'What about your friends?'

'They're a bit thin on the ground.' She resumed her seat, giving an expressive shrug of her shoulders. 'Let's face it, Georges, most of them only cultivated me because of Jean-Claude. I don't suppose Corinne will do much entertaining.'

'I shouldn't think so.'

'How could she be so dull at such an early age? I've never exactly seen eye-to-eye with Yolande, but at least we usually agreed on parties and clothes. But Corinne ...' She sighed at the hopelessness of her elder step-daughter.

Georges gave her a penetrating look. 'Why did you threaten to sue, Toinette?'

She took a cigarette from a silver case, and tapped it two or three times against the lid engraved with her monogram before lighting up. Only after she had inhaled did she answer him.

'I was his wife in all but name for twelve years. I did the best I could in difficult circumstances. But those girls treated me like a pariah. And the legacy was an insult.'

'But a five per cent stake in Marchand, as well as a seat on the board …'

'I earned that directorship a long time ago!' she snapped. 'He would have lost control of the company if I hadn't stepped in when Philippe sold out.'

'You hardly helped matters by encouraging Philippe to sell his shares to UVS.' He leaned back in his chair.

'Jean-Claude couldn't afford to buy them. You know that. I thought it would be better having them owned by a firm over which I have some influence rather than letting our rivals buy them on the open market.'

'Possibly.' He grimaced. 'But UVS is such a secretive little outfit, isn't it? Nobody had ever heard of it. We did a lot of research, but all we uncovered was a foreign private equity firm in which you have a thirty per cent stake.'

'So. Would it kill you to thank me?' she asked. 'If Jean-Claude hadn't overstretched himself buying Hervy, none of it would have happened.'

'True.' Georges drummed his fingers on the arm of his chair. 'But we could never get Philippe's shares back afterwards. I always wondered why.'

'How should I know? I don't make the investment decisions for UVS.' She took a long pull on her cigarette. 'Look, Georges, I know what you're driving at, but if you really think I'm about to stage a bid for Marchand you must be paranoid.'

'Then why threaten a lawsuit? Why force down the share price?'

'I told you – I was very upset over the will.'

'So it was simply spite?' he persisted.

Toinette considered the question carefully. 'Not at all. I wanted to remind Corinne and Yolande to treat me properly in future. I could still make things very awkward. They shouldn't forget that. They've hardly been sympathetic so far.'

'But they were extremely hurt.'

'So am I. I *loved* him.'

Georges began to look very uncomfortable, as though he'd had his fill of broken-hearted females lately. He seemed relieved when Toinette stood up and stalked over to the sideboard to pour another drink. She turned to face him, glass in hand.

'I'll see you around, Georges.'

He moved across to her. 'We must do lunch soon.'

She kissed him lightly on each cheek. 'Give Corinne my love, won't you? I'll continue to support her for the moment, but you know me – I can easily change my mind.' They walked towards the door. 'And tell Yolande I hope she'll invite me to her wedding.'

After he left, Toinette rested for a while on a sofa, chain smoking in the grey light grudgingly admitted by the half-shuttered windows. When she felt sufficiently calm, she picked up the telephone and called Ulrich von Stessenberg's suite at the Crillon.

Chapter Three

'So where are you off to today, monsieur?'

Miles Corsley looked up from his map as Madame Lebrun approached the table with steaming coffee and croissants. The aroma was delicious. Already the warm August sunshine streamed in through a small recessed window, casting a pleasant brightness over the rustic Burgundian dining room.

'St Xavier,' he said, pushing aside his guidebooks to make way for the breakfast tray. 'I have an invitation to Le Manoir.'

Well, one given through gritted teeth. He smiled as he recalled Corinne Marchand's frosty confirmation of her father's open-ended offer to show him all of the company's operations, and the way her eyes had flashed as he asked if he could visit the vineyard. Fitting a wine tour into what would otherwise have been a fraught business trip had been a stroke of genius as far as Miles was concerned. It gave him both a holiday and the opportunity to observe Corinne in her natural habitat. A lesser man would have run by now, but Miles didn't scare easily, and her formal politeness since that appalling board meeting only fuelled his curiosity to discover if a real woman lurked somewhere beneath the alluring, but glacial façade.

'Only the best for you, eh?' Madame Lebrun was suitably impressed. 'Vosne-Romanée, Vougeot, Gevrey-Chambertin – there won't be a *grand cru* village you haven't visited.'

'That was the whole idea.'

'Well, St Xavier is one of the prettiest. You must look

at the church. And the Château de Rochemort is magnificent. Of course, you can only see part of it, but they'll certainly let you have a tour of the cellars.' Baron Yves' place. He might as well squeeze that in too. 'Will you want a packed lunch today?'

'No, thanks. A colleague recommended the *coq au vin* at a restaurant in St Xavier. Le Tastevin? But I'm sure it can't be as good as yours.'

Marie Lebrun shook her head reprovingly and trotted back to her kitchen. A large, practical, middle-aged farmer's wife, she was usually dismissive of compliments, but praise of her culinary skills never left her unmoved. She was also, as a rule, proof against masculine charm, but there was something about her young English guest that, had she been twenty years younger, would have led her into serious indiscretions. Tall, tanned, and toned, his long legs stretched out under the table in thigh-length shorts and his chest was hard and muscular beneath an open-necked polo shirt. She wondered how many girls had been burned by those easy manners and that open smile, but as he pored over a map and made a few pencil notes, she almost expected him to turn and order a sergeant to fall in or out, or do whatever soldiers did. He was like a commander planning his battle strategy. The head was held high, the chin jutted out uncompromisingly. He'd stopped off at the farm guest house for one night but had now stayed three. As he drove off in his Range Rover, she wondered if he would bring back any more wine. He had several cases stacked in one of her outhouses already. Still, he'd hardly be able to afford St Xavier or Château de Rochemort. They ranked among the most expensive and sought-after wines on the Côte d'Or, and were almost sold on the vine. Not what one would find in a *coq au vin* at Le Tastevin, of that she was certain.

Miles was going with the flow. No rush. He wanted to

relax and enjoy the summer landscape, threading his way along winding back roads flanked by some of the most illustrious vineyards in France. It was only since the Paris secondment that he'd begun to take a serious interest in wine. Of course he knew his Champagne, the standard brands with which he had toasted the memorable events in his life; getting his degree, winning the Queen's Sword at Sandhurst, being awarded a gallantry medal for service in Afghanistan. Only a few years ago, yet it seemed like an eternity. It had been a huge shock to his colleagues when he decided to leave the regiment. Everyone said he had a brilliant future in the army. His father, Brigadier Peter Corsley, would certainly have been dismayed. But Miles' father had died along with his mother on a minor country road when a lorry smashed into them while they were returning from the supermarket run. Miles and his younger sister Caroline were away at school. It was far too banal an end for Peter Corsley, who'd survived bombs in Northern Ireland and snipers in the Falklands. His brother Rupert, a merchant banker in the City, had other ideas for his nephew's long-term future. At thirty, Miles exchanged his uniform for a suit and spent three years at Corsley First European's London headquarters before being sent to the Paris office.

The bank had a solid client base and a fearsome reputation in European takeovers and mergers. Miles loved the job, found his company apartment on the Ile St Louis the perfect bachelor pad, and took every opportunity he could to escape the confines of the city – which was why he was happily motoring down this enticing Burgundian road in the rising temperature of an August day, looking forward to a gourmet lunch, more wine-tasting, and another run-in with Corinne Marchand.

A car horn sounded loudly behind him. He pulled over to let a sleek black MG streak past and whistled at its speed. An old coupé, it had obviously been expertly reconditioned. It was also expertly handled, taking the bend ahead in consummate style. He hardly saw the driver. The rest of his leisurely progress to St Xavier was punctuated by reflections on why anyone should want to hurtle through such beautiful countryside, and in an MG of all cars.

'Well we're closed, monsieur,' barked a surly cellar man at the Château de Rochemort. 'Can't you see? It's the weekend.'

'Couldn't you possibly show me round? I'd like to buy …'

'*Buy*?' The man was incredulous, and pushed his grubby denim cap a little further back on his head. 'We're sold out. Viewing only, and as I said, not at the weekend. *Monsieur le baron* insists on his privacy.'

He scowled threateningly, and Miles decided there was nothing for it but to leave. Damn the baron and his privacy; damn his bloody rude minions, too. He started up the car and reversed down the track which led back to the main road. Things were not going according to plan. Le Tastevin was fully booked, the Château de Rochemort closed, and the sun was now unrelenting. Glancing back, he saw the cellar man, brawny arms folded across his chest, still standing outside the *cuverie*, which housed the vats and press, and cursed him again. He should have accepted Madame Lebrun's offer of a packed lunch.

Le Manoir de St Xavier was three kilometres away, on the other side of the village. Well, at least they would have to let him in. But when he reached the imposing wrought-iron gates they were shut and locked. Built of stone in Baroque style, the building had an inviting air. Unlike Rochemort, this was elegance on an intimate scale, complemented by the formal French flower beds and miniature box hedges along the drive. Just visible at the side of the house was a car he recognised with surprise – a black MG. Miles was pulling out his mobile to call Corinne when he heard a dog barking. She was coming round from the rear of the house with a golden Labrador at her heels.

He sprinted up to the gates. 'Mademoiselle Marchand!' he shouted.

She looked in his direction, paused, then walked slowly down the gravel sweep towards him. He was glad to see that for once she was dressed casually. The change out of corporate armour was all to the good. Those long legs of hers were encased in navy pedal pushers, while her arms were bare and swung gracefully by her sides. A short striped top clung to her breasts. Her hair was loose and ruffled by the breeze. She looked relaxed and free. Until she recognised him.

'Oh, it's you, Mr Corsley,' she said coolly, stopping some distance away. 'You're very early.'

Perfect English, perfect indifference. He wondered how she had got so fluent, without even the trace of a French accent. Still, it was a sign of progress that she was letting him speak his own language for a change.

'I know. I'd made up my mind to taste a few wines, but never on a Saturday seems to be the motto here.'

Corinne swiped a card by a small post, and the gates swung open. 'You'd better come in. I'll see if my manager will show you round.'

'I tried the Château de Rochemort, but it was shut,' said Miles, bending down to make friends with the dog, who was introduced as Marius, 'and Le Tastevin wouldn't even offer me a seat at the bar.'

'Oh, they wouldn't. Their *maître d'* has become intolerable since they acquired their last Michelin star. Is that your car?'

'Yes.'

She glanced at him mischievously. 'Well, I've heard of cautious bankers, but you're the first I've known to bomb along at thirty miles an hour.'

Miles fell into step beside her, inhaling the fresh spicy notes of her perfume, wondering if she had decided to be friendly at last or was softening him up for a killer blow. Marius, having satisfied himself that the stranger meant no harm, followed them into the house through a side door that opened on to a passage to Corinne's office. Miles studiously examined the wine chart on the wall as she picked up the telephone, then turned his head and was captivated by the Fragonard. He heard a rapid volley of French, then Corinne hung up and told him that her manager had agreed to forego a fishing trip to come and show him the *cuverie* and the cellars.

'There's absolutely nothing Gaston Leclerc doesn't know about wine,' she said as they made their way outside once more. 'His father and grandfather were both managers here.'

They were soon in a neat courtyard, flanked by buildings that were completely invisible from the front gates. A few barrels stacked in one corner gave a patch of shade where Marius flopped down on his belly and stretched out for a sleep.

'Could I buy a case?' Miles ventured.

'I expect so,' said Corinne as they sauntered across the cobbles. 'We don't usually have much left to sell, but my father always liked to keep a small stock here for passing enthusiasts.'

'Do you sell through a merchant?'

'Not any more. We used to sell to a merchant in Beaune, but there was some suspicion that our wine was being diluted with a cheaper variety. Nothing was ever proved, but we decided to go independent. We store all the wine here, of course, but the bottling is done jointly with the Château de Rochemort.'

They stood together in the afternoon sunshine, for once at ease in each other's company but finding it difficult to direct the conversation to a more personal level. He was far too conscious of her beauty, and she felt strangely nervous and exposed.

'Your English is flawless,' Miles said. 'I'm surprised you've put up with my French for so long.'

'My mother will be pleased. She's English, you know.'

Miles saw the sly smile flicker across her face and was tempted to slap her. 'You could have told me before.'

'Why? It was more fun this way.'

And because it was easier, he just let the laughter out. 'God, you're obnoxious.'

Corinne found herself laughing too. 'It's incurable, I'm afraid. Look, I'm sorry we got off on the wrong foot, Miles. Friends?'

He shook her proffered hand, tried not to get lost in the depths of those bright eyes alight with warmth and humour. 'Friends. If I offended you in any way, I'm truly sorry too. We met at a very bad time.' His expression was suddenly very gentle and sympathetic. 'It must be tough without him.'

She tried to remember that he wasn't someone she could possibly trust with her deepest feelings, despite his unexpected kindness. 'It is. He was so full of life. Such fun.'

'Yes, he was. He made me feel old.'

'You? Old!'

'Oh, I've knocked around a bit.'

She looked him over, the picture of health and fitness. Bad idea. She couldn't avoid noticing that he was utterly gorgeous. He was looking at her in a way that sent a shiver through her again. Just what had she let herself in for by dropping her guard with Miles Corsley? But he smiled so genuinely, she had to smile back. He had an intelligent face and his voice was pleasantly deep and warm. A man you could respect, she thought, a man who knew his own mind. Suddenly she sensed that he was also assessing her, and she looked away, slightly embarrassed.

'I'm sorry for the delay. Gaston's probably having lunch.'

'Lucky bugger,' remarked Miles.

'Haven't you eaten at all, then?'

'No.'

'Perhaps you'd care to stay for lunch here?' she asked quickly. 'It will be rather late, I'm afraid. The Rochemorts are coming, but Yves has been held up with business.'

Miles accepted the offer with alacrity. He'd be mad to turn down lunch with the owners of the two St Xavier *grands crus* on their home turf. And any chance to get closer to the intriguing Corinne Marchand was extremely welcome. He felt in serious danger of being bowled over by his good fortune.

Gaston Leclerc was a short dynamo of a man who blew in like a whirlwind and was passionate about his job. He kept pressing Miles to taste more vintages as they toured the long, welcomingly cool vaulted cellar which ran beneath the entire length of the house. It had been part of the original medieval abbey, and appeared to have changed very little. Miles almost expected to see a monk pop out from behind a pillar. There were rows of oak casks in which the wine was matured for three years, racks of dusty bottles, and a small alcove that served as Gaston's library, containing piles of tasting notes and a board on which he had pinned newspaper and magazine clippings. Several featured pictures of Jean-Claude Marchand.

'Mademoiselle Marchand doesn't seem much like her father,' remarked Miles, as he slowly absorbed the rich texture and flavour of a three-year old St Xavier .

Gaston watched him cautiously. 'In four years' time that will be marvellous, monsieur. It hasn't fully matured yet.'

'One can already tell the genius who made it.'

The Frenchman raised his glass in acknowledgement. 'Did you mean Mademoiselle Corinne?' he asked, reverting to Miles' original comment. 'I think she is – well, certainly when it comes to business. She's very sharp. But she takes after her mother in looks. Mademoiselle Yolande is more like her father.'

'I sense that you enjoy life here.'

'I wouldn't work anywhere else,' said Gaston emphatically. 'After all, Leclerc and St Xavier are synonymous. My eldest son is studying at the wine college in Beaune, and he'll take over when I retire.'

'Do you have shares in the business?'

'No. But I get a percentage of the profits, so it's in my interest to see we stay top of the league. Now, come this way. I thought you might like to see the old press. We don't use it now, of course, but it's an interesting machine.'

'Has Gaston quenched your thirst, Miles?' asked Corinne as they finally reappeared at the door of her office.

'He certainly has. He even sold me a case. Shall I pay for it now?'

Corinne rose from her desk as the doorbell sounded. 'That will be the Rochemorts. Gaston, would you see to Mr Corsley's invoice? And don't forget,' she shouted as she disappeared down the passage, 'our wine should be treated with the greatest possible care. You'll have to stick to fifteen miles an hour on your way back.'

Lunch was a lengthy affair, served in a handsome panelled dining room overlooking sloping vineyards which stretched away into the distance. Miles was greeted warmly by Baroness Marie-Christine de Rochemort, Yves' very aristocratic mother. She walked slowly, in obvious pain, leaning heavily on her son's arm and a stick, though she didn't seem particularly old.

'Arthritis,' whispered Corinne as they followed her and

Yves to the table. 'She doesn't like to talk about it.'

Perhaps it was this hint, or more likely the effect of the wines he had already tasted, that brought Miles' powers of entertainment to the fore. Marie-Christine soon extracted his life story, and even Yves managed to show some interest in his army career, although often his eyes focused mournfully on the seat Yolande usually occupied when at home.

'Do you know, I've never spoken such fluent French in my life before?' said Miles, as the meal drew to a close. 'It must be this superb cooking,' he glanced across the table at Corinne and the baroness, 'and the delightful company.'

Marie-Christine smiled. 'I know whose *beaux yeux* have improved your French. Not that she'll let you say such a thing.'

Yves sensed Corinne's embarrassment and quickly switched the subject to the Range Rover, since he was thinking of buying one. It was a good move, and within a few minutes he and Miles left the room so its finer points could be demonstrated.

'I'm afraid he's suffering terribly,' said his mother when they had gone, 'but he won't talk about it. Where is Yolande, exactly?'

'In Dorset – with our grandparents.'

'Ah yes – at their country house? I stayed there years ago with your mother. We had a great time.' She paused, her fingers tracing the carved head of her stick, then fixed fierce blue eyes on Corinne. 'Has she taken that actor with her?'

'Yes.'

'So it's serious. I thought she'd come back to Yves but … oh well. He's so reserved, that's the trouble.'

Corinne didn't know what to say and twirled her wine glass absentmindedly.

'She'll regret it, Corinne,' continued Marie-Christine. 'I know she will. Yves would give her anything she wanted.

He adores her. This Patrick sounds like a gold digger.'

'You've made enquiries?'

'Naturally. My son's happiness is at stake. But what's the use?' She shrugged her shoulders resignedly. 'No one seems to know where Patrick Dubuisson comes from. I suppose it's his real name?'

'I hadn't really thought about it.'

The baroness was astonished. 'Just like your father! Never thinking people might do you harm. Look how he was caught off guard when Philippe sold his shares in Marchand.'

Corinne's heart lurched. It had all happened only a fortnight after Philippe had asked her to move in with him. But he had left without explanation, without even saying goodbye. It had been a painful episode for them all.

'Have you heard from Philippe lately?'

'Not for several months,' replied Marie-Christine, her expression betraying her pain. 'The last postcard was from California. Does it still hurt?'

'It annoys me when I realise how naïve I was.'

Corinne sounded braver than she felt. Oh yes, it hurt like hell. More than anyone would ever guess. But the baroness was ill, and she too had suffered a great deal because of Philippe. It wasn't fair to burden her with additional misery, particularly now Yves was clearly causing her concern.

'Well you'll never be short of men, anyway,' said Marie-Christine with a smile.

'I'm not interested – which is a good thing, as I simply don't have time for a boyfriend.'

'Corinne! *Really*. What about Miles – didn't you invite him to lunch on a whim? I must say, I admire your taste. You've made a conquest, darling.'

'You mean he's been vanquished by Françoise's *boeuf bourgignon*. And don't you really fancy him yourself?'

The baroness laughed loudly and the conversation

49

shifted to less dangerous topics, but when Miles and Yves returned, the warm smile the Englishman gave Corinne produced a provoking *'What did I tell you?'* look from Marie-Christine. Corinne wasn't so put out as she would have been over anyone else. Somehow during the past few hours the entire dynamic of her relationship with Miles had changed. No longer the priggish banker she had been determined to dislike, but an interesting man she wanted to know better. In fact he was beginning to feel like an old friend, and as they all said goodbye outside an hour later, she wasn't surprised when he kissed her.

'I can't tell you how much I've enjoyed this afternoon,' he said, holding her for a fraction longer than was polite. 'Perhaps I could reciprocate in Paris?'

'I won't be back until September.'

'That's a date, then.' He smiled. 'I'll call you. Goodbye, Corinne.'

'Goodbye, Miles.'

She watched him climb into his car and waved until he was out of sight. Of course he wouldn't ask her out on a date. In Paris they would be constrained by their business relationship and it would be impossible. It had been a very pleasant afternoon, all the same. But Corinne didn't expect to see Miles Corsley in anything other than a professional capacity again, and the thought mildly depressed her.

Miles took his time getting back to the Lebrun farmhouse. He needed it to cool off, to forget how she had felt in his arms, and how instead of politely brushing his lips against her cheeks he had had to exercise all his self-control not to taste her mouth, drag her off somewhere and ravish her. The woman was trouble. He'd known it the second he set eyes on her. But she was in his system, and he was going to have to deal with it. It would, he decided, be interesting to find out whether the ice queen or the warm and lively Corinne Marchand he had met at St Xavier would be the one he eventually got into his bed.

'What did she say about Yolande?' Yves asked his mother as they sped off through the village.

'She's in England with that actor. Darling, I'm sorry, but I really think it's hopeless.'

His jammed his foot down on the accelerator.

'Yves, for God's sake, do you want to kill us both? I may be half-crippled, but I'd like to try to enjoy the years I have left.'

He slowed down at once. 'Sorry.'

She sighed, hating feeling so powerless. She could do nothing to help, and even commiseration upset him. When they reached the château, Yves left her to read a book while he went for a swim in their pool. But no amount of energetic front crawl could ease the torture. Yolande was gone. She didn't love him. The more he thought about it, the more he felt he had only himself to blame. He had handled everything the wrong way – put her on a pedestal and worshipped her as a goddess, and not let her know how much he loved her and needed her as a woman. Her absence was like a physical wound, gnawing away at him from the inside. But it was too late. She was in England with Patrick Dubuisson, being screwed out of her innocence and her money. It was driving him mad. And there wasn't a damn thing he could do about it.

Chapter Four

Just after 6 a.m. Half-asleep, Patrick leaned across Yolande to pick up the telephone, bleeping shrilly and insistently on the floor beside the bed. She stirred and snuggled against him as he groped for the receiver.

'Allo?'

'Is that Patrick Dubuisson?'

An American voice, female, just audible on an echoing line. It took him a while to register the words.

'Speaking,' he replied, summoning up all Yolande's lessons on answering the phone in English. 'Who is it, please?'

'Well, I don't know if you'll remember me. It's Althea Pedersen …' the echo was louder. Patrick sometimes hated cordless handsets. 'Althea Pedersen,' she repeated. 'We met over dinner at Le Grand Véfour back in July.'

Vic Bernitz. Hollywood. His mind switched into top gear. 'Mrs Pedersen! How could I forget? It was such a delightful evening. How are you?'

'Fine, just fine. Your English has certainly improved.'

'I've been practising all summer.'

'Still the same teacher?'

'Yes. In fact she's here now.' Patrick shifted his weight so that Yolande could move, but she was now awake and slid her arms around his waist. 'We were asleep.'

'I'm sorry, I should have realised. But I'm throwing a party in Malibu, and Vic Bernitz is here. I mentioned your name to him and he was interested. Shall I put him on?'

'Yes please. It's very kind of you.'

Patrick could hardly believe it. He heard her shouting 'Vic!', and mentally rehearsed what he would say.

Yolande kissed his shoulder. 'Who is it?'

'I'll tell you afterwards.' Mrs Pedersen was still calling 'Vic', and he could hear the buzz of voices in the background.

'Hi, this is Vic Bernitz,' came a deep, laid-back Californian voice at last. 'Althea tells me you're the hottest property in France since Alain Delon. Are you?'

'Hotter,' replied Patrick, deciding in a flash that an over-the-top approach would score on a long distance phone call. He had to sell himself – fast.

Bernitz laughed. 'I can't go into much detail right now, but I've been offered an intelligent thriller that requires an exciting new male lead. Have you much experience?'

'Two films and some television work.'

'Good, good. Well, this is the set-up. The financing isn't fixed yet, but I'm looking for a cast anyway. Shooting couldn't begin until next February at the earliest. I'll send you the script, and we can take it from there.'

'Yes, yes. *Merveilleux*. Perhaps we could meet to discuss it? I'll be in New York in October.'

'Sure. You could audition for me then. I'll be in touch.'

'Thank you, Mr Bernitz, I …'

'Don't thank me, son, thank Althea. I'd never even heard of you. Goodbye.'

'So is it all fixed?' came Mrs Pedersen's breathless voice. 'What do you think of him? Isn't he a real nice guy?'

Patrick said he was and thanked her extravagantly. She rang off after extracting a promise that he would visit her while he was in New York. He put down the receiver, wondering if it had all been a dream.

Yolande groaned as he moved back to his own side of the bed. 'Who was it?'

'Vic Bernitz.'

He pulled her into his arms and stroked her hair; long silky hair which felt good as it floated in thick bunches across his bare chest. He wanted to thank her for introducing him to Althea Pedersen, for taking so much trouble to improve his English, for giving him the break he needed. Patrick Dubuisson, mega-star ...

'Who's Vic Bernitz?' asked Yolande. She vaguely recalled the name, but it didn't interest her. All she was conscious of was Patrick's caresses and the beating of his heart beneath her head. He wasn't often tender, and she liked the gentle movement of his hand across her cheek and through her hair. Her thoughts drifted to a white wedding in warm Burgundian sunshine, with Patrick leading her out of the *mairie* at St Xavier.

'He's only the best director in Hollywood.'

Yolande's bubble burst instantly. That Pedersen woman must have called. That's who he'd been cooing to down line. She suddenly felt excruciatingly jealous. She knew she had no right to block his career, but the thought of losing him to some American film set made her angry. He had her. Why did he need the adoration of a fickle public too? She pushed his hand aside and rolled away.

'Yolande – what's the matter?'

'I'm tired.'

'I might get a starring role. Vic Bernitz is sending me a script. Aren't you pleased?'

'Of course,' she muttered into her pillow.

'He's promised me an audition when I go to New York in October.'

'So you're doing the Hervy gala after all?'

'I might as well.' Patrick leaned over and pulled her back towards him. 'Come here. Don't be such a baby.'

'You don't give a damn about me. All you really care about is acting.'

He kissed her, but she was unresponsive.

'Let me go back to sleep.'

'I want you.' He kissed her again, harder, forcing his tongue between her lips. His hand moved over her breasts to the smoothness of her midriff, firm and possessive. Then lower. She groaned and began to respond to his mouth, and he pushed her hand down to his groin.

Patrick had to get control. She needed to know who was boss. He wanted her desperately, but she was going to want him even more before they were through. He liked issuing orders, making her pleasure him, giving her a small reward to keep her going but never enough to make her come. She'd have to beg for that. He almost ejaculated just thinking about it. She'd been dynamite in bed the first time, but a bit too demanding. The most important lesson he'd taught her was that he *always* came first.

'Come on, Yolande ...'

She shook off her drowsiness as he pressed her fingers around his smooth, stiff cock. It was useless. She could never resist him. He settled back for the ride as she began to please him in all the ways she knew so well. The woman was pure sex, and she fuelled a need in him that never seemed to end. It wasn't until much later that he dragged her off, kissed her savagely and lay between her thighs. They were both hot, sweaty, grunting. He pushed her knees right up until her legs were draped over his shoulders and drove up inside her. Deep, slow thrusts. Yolande moaned as she felt the heat work through her craving body. *Faster, harder. More, more, more.* Then he stopped.

'Patrick, *please* ...'

He pulled out although it was killing him. It was worth it to see the alarm in her emerald eyes. 'Had enough?'

'No!'

'Oh, so you want it now, do you?'

'Don't tease me,' she gasped.

'On your knees,' he said, and flipped her over.

Then he gripped her hips, rammed his full length into her and it was fast and exhilarating and she wondered why she had been so jealous about the call from Los Angeles.

Of course it was good news. It was marvellous. He was wonderful, he deserved to do well.

Afterwards she lay wrapped in his arms in the dark, and Patrick repeated the telephone conversation in detail. Yolande soon had suggestions to make. She would help him rehearse for the audition; they could stay with her mother in New York and make a holiday of it, she'd show him Manhattan …

'You won't have time for all these things once you're famous, darling.'

'What makes you think I will be?' he asked.

'You want to be, don't you?'

He was silent.

'Don't you?' she insisted.

'Yes.'

'Well, Althea, I thought you said this French guy didn't speak very good English?'

'He didn't in July.'

'Learns fast, then,' said Vic Bernitz, picking up his Piña Colada and heading for a large wickerwork armchair positioned with a view to the garden. Beyond lay the Pedersens' private beach.

Althea occupied an identical chair nearby. It was quiet now. The guests had gone, and some of the inevitable party debris was already being cleared away by Juanita, her maid. Peace and plenty reigned along this small stretch of the Malibu coastline. Althea kicked off her shoes and curled her toes to relax the aching muscles in her feet.

'Do you have any pictures of Dubuisson?' Vic asked. 'I'd like to get an image before I mail the script.'

Juanita was sent to fetch the pile of magazines Althea kept at her bedside. She never slept for more than five hours a night, and the combined efforts of journalists the world over were insufficient to keep her amused. There were the usual glossies and then more solid journals. When she was in a serious mood, she would skim through a political or economics article over breakfast. She liked to be considered well-informed.

'Here,… this is a still from a movie he made last year – *Souvenir Amer*. It picked up a couple of awards at Cannes.' She indicated a picture of Patrick wearing tight jeans and a sulky pout.

Bernitz took it in slowly, then turned to her. Fiftyish, his jet black hair and beard were liberally streaked with grey, lessening somewhat the devilish effect of his smile. 'Now I know why you were so keen to promote him.'

'I liked him, that's all.'

'Whatever. He's sure got the looks.' He fumbled in his jacket pocket for a pair of horn-rimmed glasses, then studied Patrick's picture more closely. 'If he can act as well, I think he'll do … Strange, but he doesn't look unfamiliar. And there was something about his voice I seemed to recognise.'

'Not you too!' exclaimed Althea. 'Rikki and I both thought we'd seen him before.'

'Oh, so you met him with our dear friend Rikki?' Bernitz took off his glasses and dangled them over the side of his chair.

'Why don't you get along with him anymore?'

'He pulled out of my last picture.'

'I see. Who's backing this one?'

'I can't say yet. Belco has the rights, but I'm not sure they've got the cash. But it'll be good, Althea. This is the movie I've always wanted to make.'

Althea smiled. 'You almost persuade me to ask Hank to sink a few bucks in it. But he won't hear anything except Brenton these days.'

'I thought that business burnt out weeks ago.'

'Are you kidding? When Hank buys a company he really takes over – the whole shooting match. Until the next acquisition, that is.'

'And he's not sold on the movies. What a pity.' Bernitz

gave a comical sigh. 'You really ought to knock a little culture into him, Althea. It would relax his corporate mind.'

'Believe me, Vic, I've tried.' Sipping her cocktail slowly, an idea suddenly hit her. She picked up an old copy of *Vogue* and thumbed through the thick, shiny pages. Then she passed it to Bernitz, pointing to a photograph featuring the Hervy show at the Hotel Intercontinental.

'Look.'

'You and Rikki and some stunner,' he remarked. 'So?'

'Look again.'

'She's extremely beautiful. Why don't I know her?'

'I'll introduce you. She's Dubuisson's girlfriend. Very rich, and totally nuts about him.'

'Hmm … I get the scenario. She pays me to give lover-boy a big break?'

'Something like that,' said Althea. 'She'll probably come with him to New York for that fashion gala at the Met next month. They both model for Hervy.'

'You mean this girl has to *work*?'

'It's only a hobby.'

He grinned, rubbing his beard while he examined Yolande's delectable profile. 'How rich is she?'

'Well, she part owns Hervy for a start. Then there's Marchand-Beauté, the cosmetics firm … tens of millions.'

'Marchand-Beauté? Oh yeah, – *la belle Nature*, and no animal experimentation. My daughter insists their perfume is the best around. Won't buy anything else.'

'I suppose Marchand fragrances are special. They don't grab you head-on, but creep up on you. Seductive – slow and seductive.'

'You've been seduced by their publicity, Althea.'

'I take a professional interest in it. After all, we're in the same market.'

Bernitz gave a short laugh. 'No disrespect, but the stuff

Hank sells just isn't in the same league. It's got no cachet – and that you *can* smell.'

Althea wasn't pleased. The subject was dropped, and Bernitz soon took his leave. She wandered outside onto the terrace, letting her hair flow in the warm Pacific breeze. A balmy night, the sound of the sea and swaying palm trees, even stars to complete the backdrop. But she was alone. It was just another pretty tableau in the monotony of her success. On nights like these she wanted to be young again, running barefoot along the shore at La Jolla with suntanned Californian kids who never went home, always laughing, having fun, making love, dreaming of impossibly gilded futures and never thinking the life they already had outdid all their dreams.

Althea had realised her dream. It enclosed her, locking her tight in its opulent embrace. If she felt like it she could go anywhere she wanted – right then. The limousine was waiting, a private jet was always at her command. She could exchange her Malibu cage for one in London or New York. Or she could roam around, staying with friends whose activities fuelled the gossip columns. Her husband indulged her every whim, but he wasn't there to share this beautiful night. He was almost never there. Big blond Hank, with his unromantic corporate mind; he would call soon and say how sorry he was to have missed the party, and she'd answer, 'Oh, that's OK'. Then they would talk awhile before she went to bed. Alone.

Juanita appeared at the French windows. 'Mr Pedersen's on the line, ma'am.'

Althea sauntered back into the house, by-passing the Art Deco telephone in the lounge for the more functional white extension in her bedroom. She lay back on the bed.

'Hey, Althea, what kept you?'

'The sea and the stars, darling.'

'Had a good time?'

'Divine.'

'Sorry I missed the party, but you know how these guys tie me up here. If I didn't keep an eye on them – you know how it is. …'

'It's OK, Hank. So how rotten is the Big Apple today – tonight, rather? And what are you doing up so late?'

'I got caught up with paperwork.'

'Bad boy. Did you take your ginseng and that new vitamin supplement?'

'Sure. Who came, then? Did Brett Gallway show?'

'Yes – and with Mrs Gallway too. She's a real cutie. He's not so bad either, considering he earned ten million bucks for his last picture. By the way, I think I've found Vic Bernitz the lead for his next movie. There's a business tie-in which might interest you.'

'Really?'

'It might just add Paris as a province to your perfumery empire.'

Hank whistled.

'I told you, I'm keeping it on ice for now.'

'You're so mean.'

She laughed. 'I knew that would wake you up.' Then a pause. 'I went to the clinic this morning.'

'Yes?' he said eagerly. 'You got the results? What did they say?'

'There is positively no reason why I shouldn't be able to conceive a child.'

He didn't answer for some moments, but a sigh indicated how deeply the news had affected him. 'So it's me, then?'

'Looks like it, Hank. They'll have your results through next week.' Suddenly she longed to hold him, to comfort him, to tell him it didn't make any difference to the way they felt for each other. 'Don't beat yourself up over it. You can't help it.'

'Surely we could do something?'

'If you were home more often, didn't work so hard.

61

We're never together at the right time.'

'It must be more than that, Althea. Damn it, we've been married six years. I thought it would work out. I'm sorry. I always wanted kids.'

'Me too.' She tried to rally, sound optimistic. 'There's treatment available. You could …'

'Let's talk about it some other time, hey, honey? I don't feel like it right now.'

'Tired?'

'Very.'

'Goodnight, sweetheart. I love you. I love you very much.'

'I love you too.' He was about to ring off, then thought better of it. 'Althea?'

'Hmm?'

'Will you fly over here tomorrow? I really miss you, and it doesn't look as though I'll be able to get away.'

'OK. Send a car to the airport.'

'See you tomorrow.'

She put down the receiver, then told Juanita to prepare for the journey. The house seemed horribly empty. Time for bed. Althea was tired, but she hated that bed. A big, plush, springy bed, just for her. No one to make love to her, no arms to hold her. Nothing to distract her from the thought that she was never going to have a child. She could leave him, find someone else. No, she couldn't. Walk out and leave him with his failure? Poor Hank, who had everything but the power to get her pregnant. She loved him. They were often apart, but they always missed each other, kept saying it was bad and next year they would do something about it. But somehow they never did.

Althea quickly undressed and showered, then slipped between the sheets, flipped on the bedside lamp, and picked up a magazine from the pile. Couldn't focus, couldn't be bothered to read. She tossed the magazine onto the floor and buried her face in the pillows. When Juanita looked in half- an hour later to see if she wanted a nightcap, Althea was still sobbing.

A grey September morning was breaking over Central Park as Tex Beidecker sprinted across the gracious drawing-room of his Fifth Avenue apartment to answer the telephone.

'It's Yolande for you, Grace!' he shouted.

There was a torrent of words from the other end of the line.

Tex smiled. 'How are you, baby? I'm good. Of course it's early here! You're coming over? That's great – yes, we'd love to. Patrick? Of course it'll be fine. He's the actor, right? He's going to audition for Vic Bernitz? Wow, that's impressive. Look, your mother's here. Give my love to Corinne, won't you?'

Grace Beidecker emerged from the bathroom wrapped in a towel and took the receiver. He kissed her cheek, then went off to finish sorting papers for his briefcase.

'Hello, darling. No, it's all right. Tex has a board meeting this morning. You're coming to do the Hervy gala? That's wonderful! Of course you must stay here. So you're bringing him? Is it serious? Well, I'm still sorry for Yves. We'll talk about it when you get here. How was Dorset? Granny wrote me a long letter about it all …'

'I'm glad Yolande's coming,' remarked Tex when they sat down to breakfast. 'I thought she'd forgotten us over here.'

'Did she tell you she's bringing her new boyfriend?'

'Yes.' He laughed, and his lined face looked boyishly attractive. 'The one your mother doesn't like.'

'That's the understatement of the year.'

'A free language course with sex thrown in, didn't she say? Sounds like a smart guy.'

'It's not funny, Tex.' Grace's dark eyes were reproachful.

'I'm sorry, darling. Are you still feeling bad because you didn't go to Jean-Claude's funeral?'

'I couldn't have gone with Toinette Brozard there. But I do so wish Yolande hadn't broken up with Yves. They're made for each other. She was always absolutely crazy about him.'

Tex sipped his strong black coffee. 'Puppy love. She's just grown up, that's all. Yves is a great guy, but if she doesn't want him anymore, there's nothing you can do.'

'Marie-Christine is really upset.'

'Ah yes, the baroness … Hell, I was terrified when we first met. And that château!' He looked rather wistful. 'That was a fantastic holiday, Grace. We ought to go again sometime. What about Christmas?'

'Are you free?'

'I ought to be when I've wound up all this Brenton business for Hank Pedersen. The guy's a nut. Buys a company everyone thinks has sunk without trace and then goes for a rights issue straight away. Still, it'll probably work. Stamp Pedersen Corp. on any piece of paper and it's sure to sell. I've never known him back a loser yet.'

'He just rips the heart out of someone else's company and sacks people as far as I can see,' she said seriously. 'It's not right.'

Tex laughed. 'Grace, my sweet – all these years I've tried to corrupt you, and you will stick to your principles. Pedersen did his hard work years ago. He built up the myth. Now he's trading on it. Besides, he usually comes up with the goods. The man's a genius.'

She raised her eyebrows quizzically, and Tex smiled. Eighteen years of marriage, and he still thought he was the luckiest man in the world. She had wafted into his life one sunny afternoon in London, walking with her daughters in Kensington Gardens. Nice kids, lovely mother. He had released Corinne's kite which was caught in a tree and they had started talking. Just his luck to fall for a married woman. He had tried to forget about it. Good-looking, fit and almost forty, a bruising divorce had made him swear never to risk another trip up the aisle. His ex-wife had walked with his son, a Manhattan penthouse, their summer place in Maine, and his self-respect. She'd remarried within six months. Then he met Grace again. A formal introduction this time, at an American Embassy reception. Grosvenor Square hospitality, more talk, smiling dark eyes that seemed to understand what his were saying. He found out she too was a divorcee, and proposed to her two weeks later. They had been inseparable ever since.

He moved around the table to her. 'What are you doing for lunch?'

'Is that an invitation?'

'Yes. I should be through by one. Will you book somewhere?'

They kissed lingeringly. Grace smoothed his hair. 'You're such an old romantic, darling.'

'Is that so bad?'

'No. In fact it's a damn good thing for overpriced Manhattan restaurants.'

'Well someone has to keep them going.'

He was leaving, but she pulled him back by the sleeve of his jacket. 'Tex, did you really mean it about Christmas?'

'Sure. I thought we could meet the whole family. Either in France or England – or both. You fix it. I'll make the time.'

'Promise?'

'On the book.'

She kissed him again. When Tex Beidecker made a promise like that, it was rock solid. Christmas in Europe – the first for four years. She might be able to find out what those beautiful daughters of hers were really getting up to now they had no father – however indulgent – to keep an eye on them.

Chapter Five

From the window of her office on the Avenue Montaigne, Corinne looked down wistfully at the street below; serried ranks of chestnut trees, just starting to turn an autumnal shade; purposeful taxis heading for the Hotel Plaza Athénée, ferrying serious shoppers with their seriously expensive designer bags, the sort she had spent her morning wooing with a new marketing campaign. Doubtless quite a few of them had visited the Hervy boutique below to snap up the latest must-have – the Hervy trenchcoat, based on the original wartime design by the great Hélène Hervy herself, but given a modern twist by that genius Franco Rivera, with daring colours and luxurious fabrics. Corinne had ordered a limited pre-release of stock ahead of the main *prêt-à-porter* launch, despite Paul Dupuy's reservations. And as usual had been proved right – rave reviews in *Vogue* and *Harpers*, with a *Vanity Fair* spread to come. She sighed and returned to her desk.

It was a lovely September day, and Corinne longed to be outdoors in jeans and a sweater with the wind in her hair and nowhere in particular that she had to be. She dragged her attention back to the latest company figures Georges Maury had just sent through. All profits were up for the month, and the trend for the year was very positive. Not a cloud dimmed the business horizon – so why was she so depressed? She didn't need a shrink to spell it out. Too much work, no chance to recharge her batteries over the summer, not enough fun. And no time to grieve. There was her father's estate to settle and her presence as the new head of Marchand to establish with the employees and the markets. People seemed to welcome Corinne's personal approach, though her managerial style was somewhat different from Jean-Claude's. He had always been a strategic head in the Paris head office, whereas she made a point of visiting all her managers to explain her ideas personally. Had Georges nursed any ambition of becoming head of the company, he would have been sorely disappointed. But although her style differed from Jean-Claude's, Corinne shared his tactical approach to the business. Ultimately she was in charge, and a Marchand continued to run Marchand with characteristic astuteness.

Corinne missed her father far more than she had ever thought possible. He had always been the fun parent, the one who made silly jokes, the extravagant Papa who had celebrated her every success with copious amounts of Champagne. Only now was she beginning to realise that he was also the one she had relied on, whose advice was always sound even though he appeared to be the last person to turn to for common sense, the one who could really comfort her when she was upset. She just longed for him to walk in with that glorious smile of his and tell her to snap out of it, because how could he take his daughter out to lunch with a frown ruining her beautiful face?

'Corinne, darling, they'll think I'm a slave driver.'

'You are, Papa,' and she would already be smiling. *'An absolute tyrant.'*

'In that case I order you to eat, drink, and be merry with me, unless you'd prefer a week in Accounts.'

They used to lunch together once a week. It was sacrosanct – he never missed it. Neither did she, which was why she had tears in her eyes now as she saw the recurring appointment in her electronic calendar. It should have been today. Sylvie hadn't taken it out, and Corinne didn't have the heart to do it either. If only she could talk to him about her plans for Marchand, see if he approved. And ask him what to do about her sister, who seemed to have found a unique way to channel her grief by a gratuitously public and passionate affair with Patrick Dubuisson.

Yolande was a problem – the entire family was agreed on that point. Her Dorset holiday with Patrick made waves on both sides of the Atlantic. She had turned down several modelling jobs, started going to all-night parties, and snubbed all her old friends. Her ungracious and thoughtless behaviour with Patrick at her grandparents' house had upset even their very indulgent grandmother, who adored her.

Now Yolande was back in Paris for a few weeks, but Corinne hardly saw her. Just as well. That way she didn't have to lie to Yves about what her terrible little sister was up to, although there was enough coverage in the gossip columns to give him the general idea. It was painful to see how much he still loved her. He'd flirted valiantly with a couple of girls his mother invited to Rochemort during the summer, but neither wanted to play second fiddle to Yolande Marchand. They flounced back to Paris with the dubious honour of not even having had to pretend to resist the advances of a sexy Baron de Rochemort. Instead of long August afternoons of multiple orgasms and cocktails, it was tennis, swimming, and country walks. Standards at the château had slipped appallingly now Philippe was gone.

Corinne herself was very relieved to escape from Burgundy when that great French convulsion, *la rentrée*, commenced in September. At least in Paris one could try to evade the ghosts of happier times. But even as she forced her attention to the launch of Hervy's new perfume range, she found her thoughts full of her father and Philippe. The two men she had loved – both gone. And here she was, selling love and romance to other people.

She almost jumped when the phone rang.

'Monsieur Corsley for you, Corinne.'

'Miles? Hello. How are you?'

'Fine. I would have called before, but I've been in Frankfurt for a couple of weeks. I seem to recall that we have a date. Would you be able to join me for lunch today? I've got a table booked at the Plaza Athénée.'

Corinne almost laughed. Was this her father's idea of a weird joke?

'One o'clock,' she said. 'I'll meet you there.'

It was extremely short notice, but Miles never dragged his heels with women. If she liked him, she would come; if she didn't, he would have to forget that he had been thinking about her far too much since their encounter at St Xavier.

She looked as breathtaking as the day they first met when he saw her heading towards the table in Le Relais Plaza, dressed in a navy two-piece suit that showed off her curves and drew wolfish glances of admiration from fellow diners. There was slight embarrassment initially. A polite business-like handshake, both sheltering behind formal small talk for the first ten minutes, a formality reinforced by the historic dining room, its design based on that of the famous 1930s liner the *Normandie*. Then they began to relax, and Miles toasted Corinne's success with the new Hervy trenchcoat.

'You certainly don't read fashion magazines,' she said matter-of-factly. 'So you must have been checking up on me.'

'Haven't you paid me the same compliment?'

Their eyes met; mutual recognition and amusement. She raised her glass, smiling. 'Here's to Daniel Lemoine. I assume we engaged the same man.'

'How did you know?'

'He advertises your bank as one of his clients. Otherwise he's very discreet as private eyes go. So how did I rate?'

Miles looked grave. 'Rather worrying, I'm afraid. Highly intelligent, beautiful, sound business brain, no known defects.'

What had most interested him was the gaping hole where there should have been information on her private life. Just a sentence that said she had been single for several years. It seemed impossible. Now he knew why. 'How much did you pay him?'

'More than you did, possibly.'

'Don't I get to know what he found out about me?'

Corinne was thrown by the steadiness of his gaze now. She noticed the dark rings around his irises that accentuated the flecks of grey and blue and made them look like gleaming flint. Sharp, piercing. Looking straight into a part of her she never let anyone see. This was no longer a joke. No man but Philippe had looked at her like that. Philippe, who had broken her heart. She began to wish she hadn't come. Why had this relative stranger made her admit she'd been interested enough to check his background? All Daniel had come up with was a pristine record of achievement – which was exactly what one would expect of someone like Miles Corsley.

'Why don't we exchange the reports?' she said.

'Deal – next week?'

'Next week?'

He leaned back in his chair, smiling once more. 'Of course. You are coming out with me again, aren't you?'

Corinne didn't remember saying yes, but they met the following week, the deal over the reports by then in oblivion. Miles was such good fun. She agreed to meet him again after that, and tried to convince herself she enjoyed his company simply because he was discreet and detached from the French business network which could threaten her – divorced from the rumour mill by his Englishness. But it was his job to keep a finger on the pulse of Parisian commerce and after all, he was her banker. Somehow it soon seemed irrelevant. They seldom talked shop and their telephone calls and emails increased in length and frequency with no apparent purpose.

On their fourth date, Miles asked her back to his apartment after an evening at the theatre. Corinne admired the neatness of the place – a stark contrast to the clutter she remembered at Patrick's studio, where she had been invited to meet her sister's new boyfriend before they left for the Hervy *prêt-à-porter* launch in New York. Patrick and Yolande had been living it up in Manhattan for barely a week now and her mother was already sending frantic emails. It was pleasant to relax in this quiet, neutral room, which betrayed little about its bachelor occupant. There were two heraldic shields mounted on the wall, a few sporting prints, and on the mantelpiece a large photograph of a dashing Guards officer in full dress uniform. She looked again and realised it was a very young, ridiculously handsome Miles.

'How could you give up all that for a bank?' she asked as he handed her a glass of wine.

'The thrill of polishing one's kit and being shot at wears off after a while, you know. Besides, if I hadn't given it up I wouldn't have met you.'

Corinne sipped her drink, too conscious of his presence next to her on the sofa. She could feel his warmth spreading across her, smell his aftershave. Dior – she recognised it at once, and admired Miles for not trying to win points by wearing Hervy. He would be within a few days, though. She never let a customer get away. And then she was focusing on that magnificent physique ... Was his body as muscular as it looked through his clothes?

Damn, he was fit. Any other woman would have got him into bed long before now; but the last thing she needed was more heartbreak. She'd never found it easy to detach herself emotionally from sex, and it would be foolish to try with someone like Miles. If she slept with him, Corinne knew she'd fall in love with him, and then when it was all over she'd have to try to pick up the pieces. And she didn't think she could do it again.

'What are the shields?' she asked, snapping her thoughts back to safer topics.

'Winchester and my regiment. I suppose you think I'm immature having such things around?'

'No, not at all. We all have our icons. Whatever made you say that?'

Miles edged a little closer, his arm resting along the back of the sofa. 'I'd like to know what you think of me. I can't work it out. You're so reserved.'

'Am I?'

'Aren't you?'

'You tell me.'

'I just did.'

They both laughed. She felt his fingers running through the ends of her hair. His eyes were trained on her face. 'In fact, I think you're the most secretive person I've ever met.'

'Oh come on.'

'But it's true.' He took the glass from her hand and put it on the floor. 'You're a beautiful enigma, Corinne Marchand.'

He leaned in towards her. Lips parted, eyes intense. She knew what was coming and moistened her own lips in readiness. A kiss couldn't possibly hurt, couldn't really complicate things. Then his arms were wrapped tightly around her, and his mouth was on hers. His chest was hard, immovable – his lips urgent and warm. She was surprised to find that she was pressing him to her, giving way to those delicious, firm lips. The kiss began to vibrate through her whole body. It was just wonderful to feel a man's body again, the slight scrape of stubble on her skin, the rapid breathing, the rush of desire. She didn't hear herself moan, didn't realise she was the one who took his mouth and plundered.

Miles wasn't expecting the explosion of desire that ripped through him. How could she kiss in so many ways – with tenderness, innocence almost, then greed, passion, heat. She was like a volcano, pouring liquid fire into him. She coaxed his lips apart in a slow seductive dance with hers, and then her tongue was caressing his, and he simply had to have her. He eased her back against the cushions and began to explore her body. He felt her stiffen slightly as his hands cupped her breasts, teased her nipples until they were hard. She was moaning something, but he didn't hear. Quickly he unfastened his trousers. Then his hands were underneath her dress, on her thighs. Shocked, she submitted as his mouth took hers in a searing kiss.

'Corinne … I want you so much. You're so lovely …'

'Miles, please don't.'

His lips were against her throat, his hands pulled her legs apart, probing, caressing. She gasped with pleasure as he found her core and stroked, and began to strain towards him with low murmurs of pleasure. She hadn't thought she could feel like this again. It felt so good.

And then, from nowhere, came a wave of blind panic and fear. She felt suffocated, trapped, horrified by her own body's betrayal. She writhed furiously when she felt him, rock-hard, move up between her legs.

'No, Miles! Get off me!'

'But you want me. I know you do.'

'Get off me! Now!'

There was no arguing with that tone. He released her and slumped back, angry and frustrated. He had felt the woman, as hot and hungry as he was – and then the ice queen had returned.

'What the hell's wrong? I thought you liked me.'

Corinne jumped to her feet. 'Not that much, Miles. Just forget it, will you? I'm going home.'

He stood up and zipped himself back in, but the

erection refused to die. Corinne averted her eyes, feeling completely stupid. How could a harmless snog have turned so quickly into such a disaster? She shouldn't have let herself get trapped like that. Silently Miles picked up his car keys and escorted her out. Their drive back to the Avenue Foch was equally silent, but he held her by the arm before she could get out of the car.

'Look, Corinne, I really am sorry. I suppose you like me only as a friend?'

'Yes.'

'I see.' He let her go. 'Goodbye then.'

'We are still friends?' she asked.

'Oh right, let's be friends, ...' he said mockingly. 'After the way you kissed me! You should think a bit more before you stick your tongue down a guy's throat like that. What do you think I'm made of? I always thought you French were meant to be better at sex than the rest of the planet.'

Was *that* how he saw her? A trophy conquest to be clocked up to his Paris assignment? Hating him and herself for having so misjudged him, Corinne got out of the car and slammed the door. It sped off before she even reached the entrance to her apartment block. So it was over. No more lunches, no more friendly calls and emails – all just a ploy to get her to bed. Still, he hadn't lied and pretended he loved her, and for some inexplicable reason that made her feel worse.

Miles could have kicked himself as soon as she was gone. He drove about for a while at high speed to work off his temper, but when he got back to his flat, the lingering smell of her perfume immediately recalled their kiss. A kiss that had promised everything – warmth, tenderness, passion. And more. He poured himself a drink and sat down. Then everything fell into place. Why hadn't he realised that she meant so much to him? He had mauled her like a horny teenager desperate to get laid. Then he'd insulted her. And now she probably hated his guts. He picked up his phone and speed dialled her apartment. It rang for some while before she answered.

'Hello, Corinne?'

The line went dead. When he tried again, the phone was off the hook. A grovelling apology he sent by email the following morning was returned undeliverable. He tried her office, and was brusquely told by Sylvie that his calls would no longer be accepted. Her mobile number became unobtainable. She didn't appear in any of their usual restaurants for lunch that week. His colleagues at the bank noticed his sluggish performance, and he soon got a rocket from London.

'What the fuck's going on, Miles?' Rupert Corsley barked into the phone, as loud as a sergeant-major. 'I've had complaints about you that can't be ignored.'

'It's nothing, Rupert.'

'That's not what I've heard. You can forget Corinne Marchand. I'm handing the Marchand account over to James Chetwode, and I've told him to think with his head and not his prick. You bloody fool. You should know better than to try to get into a client's knickers. I've been apologising for you all over Paris. So get your head down and keep out of trouble. There's that bid for Masson's coming up soon, and I must have a preliminary report.'

'Of course. I'll get it to you as soon as possible.'

'And if you need some action, why not look about while you're home for Christmas? I'll see if your aunt can find someone to take care of you.'

Typical Uncle Rupert; crisp, cold, factual. He had always prided himself on the bank's staff benefits, but Miles thought trying to cater for their sexual needs was going too far. Work on the Masson report commenced that very day. Miles didn't contact Corinne again.

'The homeless of New York join me in thanking you for your magnificent generosity on this occasion …'

The list of thanks for contributions continued, interspersed with sporadic applause from the thousand or so guests at the Metropolitan Museum of Art in New York. Club Met. One of those chic charity affairs where the indebted and notorious could buddy up with the rich and famous, and all in a good cause – thousands of dollars to the museum, a fair slice to the organisers, a fraction to the homeless of New York.

Philippe de Rochemort leaned indolently against a pillar, thoroughly bored. He had seen the same mix of socialites, celebrities, and wannabes too many times before in Paris, and a fashion gala ranked lower with him than most. It attracted a clientele of surgically-enhanced middle-aged women accompanied by their trendier daughters, dutifully squeezed into formal party dresses for the evening and trying desperately hard to fly the flag for Manhattan in the face of a Gallic invasion. The French Ambassador and a bevy of attachés were present, together with prominent French businessmen and a host of assorted Europeans who constituted Hervy's fashion team.

Of course the House of Hervy was very proud to be associated with New York City in a new venture to support the homeless. It was also delighted by this opportunity to launch its first *prêt-à-porter* collection in such a distinguished setting. When Paul Dupuy had mentioned his goal of bringing classic fashion to the people, Philippe had almost choked on a canapé. Haute couture for the masses? At over three hundred dollars for each separate, it was hardly the bargain basement.

Philippe wondered why Hervy had bothered to ship itself across the Atlantic to display a collection of street wear. But then Paul Dupuy was given to the occasional fit of lunacy. There was even a rumour that Franco Rivera's contract wouldn't be renewed at the end of the year. Still, the fashion editors and buyers seemed to like what they had seen, and Hervy's understated foray into ready-to-wear would probably be hailed as an important supernova in the fashion galaxy.

Philippe felt that his boredom and his contribution to the homeless of New York might well be rewarded now the catwalk was empty and drinks were being dispensed by the high-speed waiters. Though he looked insolently handsome and lazy, very little escaped his deep-blue eyes – least of all a tall, graceful brunette who was drifting in his direction looking slightly lost.

He straightened himself up, parked his wine glass on a plant stand, and headed purposefully towards her. The reward had come.

'Yolande!'

She stopped short, stared at him, and just managed not to scream.

'Well, don't I get a smile?' he asked, moving close to her side and slipping an arm around her waist. 'How about a kiss?'

'Philippe! What *on earth* are you doing here?'

He kissed her quickly on the lips and propelled her to a quiet corner. When they were seated, he clasped both her hands tightly in his and just drank her in.

'God, it's so good to see you again! You look wonderful, my darling. How's my mother? And Yves?'

Yolande's green eyes were fixed on him in silent incredulity. The same charming, brazen Philippe, who had walked out of the Château de Rochemort three years ago and broken his mother's heart, calmly asking for news as though nothing had happened. She could hardly believe he was actually holding her hands, smiling in that affectionate way that brought back memories of the long hot summer days of her Burgundian childhood.

'Yolande?'

'I'm all right. It's just the shock. You haven't changed at all.'

'So you thought I'd be a decrepit old man after three

years in the wicked wide world?'

Laughing, he released her and casually swiped two glasses of Champagne from a passing tray. She took one and leaned back in her seat, gazing at him thoughtfully. She could have killed for a cigarette. He made her feel strangely nervous, gazing at her with those keen blue eyes which reminded her too much of Yves and her own unkindness.

'So how's my mother?' he asked again.

'She really misses you. Why don't you call her?'

He shrugged his shoulders. 'It's not that easy. We parted on rather bad terms.'

'That's hardly surprising, the way you disappeared with half the family fortune.'

'It was my money! Anyway, Yves has surely paid off that loan by now. I've seen what he's charging for the wine. He must be clearing a handsome profit.'

'I wouldn't know about that.'

'I thought you'd be the first to know.'

'I'm not his girlfriend,' said Yolande.

'Oh? What happened?'

'We got engaged. I broke it off. I haven't seen him recently. But your mother's ill. She can hardly walk.'

'What!'

'Arthritis in her hips. She won't have an operation.'

'I see.' He looked gloomy. 'I ought to go home and talk some sense into her.'

'Why don't you?'

He laughed a shade too loudly, then leaned forward and hugged her close. 'Oh, Yolande, I've missed you. You're so funny, do you know that? You have such a wonderful, simple view of life. And you're utterly ravishing.' He rested his head against her shoulder and kissed her neck. 'You don't know how good it is to hold a Frenchwoman again.'

'Philippe!'

Embarrassed, Yolande pushed him away. No, he hadn't changed at all. He was drop-dead gorgeous, flirtatious, and definitely explosive. 'People are watching us.'

He sat up and stared round the gallery. 'They're really people? I was confusing them with the statues – not that there's much comparison from an aesthetic point of view.'

Then he took her hand once more, his expression suddenly sombre. 'So Maman is very ill? Why won't she have surgery?'

'She's frightened of having the anaesthetic, because her sister died during that heart operation. We've tried to persuade her things have moved on since then, but she won't budge.'

'I see. By the way, I was sorry to hear about your father. Extremely sorry. It must be tough. Are you OK?'

'When I don't think about it.'

There was a silence while he swung her hand to and fro mechanically, deep in thought.

'What are you doing in New York, Philippe?'

'Management consultancy. Sounds grand, doesn't it? A general dogsbody for Americans who think it gives them class to have a baron on the payroll. I do a lot of work with European clients, smoothing over the language barrier. It's not exactly challenging, but they pay well. I lost rather a lot of money in Australia, you know – hoping to break into the wine trade. But I just couldn't stand it out there. Then I went to California. Hated it there too. So I came to New York, flaunted my title and my pretty face, *et voilà*! Instant success. Listen and learn, my darling – don't ever try to be anything but shallow. You and I are both doomed to triumph through our overpowering beauty and sexual magnetism.'

Yolande couldn't help giggling, but there was something she simply had to find out. 'But why did you leave France in the first place? All those terrible rows when you left … My father had a hell of a time trying to get back your shares, and I know Yves still owes a lot of money on Rochemort.'

He gave her a wry smile. 'That answers your question about why I won't go home. I'd hardly be welcome.'

Yolande squeezed his hand, looking at him seriously. 'Please get in touch with your mother. She'd be thrilled to see you.'

'If she knew everything, it would only confirm my role as the family's black sheep.'

'Don't be idiotic.'

It was a quiet, firm remark, and Philippe seemed to draw some comfort from it. His face brightened, and he restrained her when she tried to get up to join Patrick, who was visible in a distant part of the gallery earnestly engaged in conversation with Althea Pedersen and Vic Bernitz.

'Stay here and talk to me. I want to know what's been going on. What really happened between you and Yves?'

She decided it was worth holding on for a while, if only to persuade him that he ought to attempt a reconciliation with his family, though admittedly she was equally keen to discover the unexplained reason for his abrupt departure from France. He also seemed anxious to ask her something, and eventually the words came out, too careless to be as casual as intended.

'You haven't told me about Corinne. How is she?'

Yolande looked at him sharply. 'Fine. She's become head of Marchand.'

'I know. Do you think she's forgiven me?'

'Corinne doesn't wear her heart on her sleeve.'

'No, she never did,' said Philippe after a pause. 'She's so controlled. So lovely, too. And I treated her appallingly. I'll always regret it, Yolande. Always. Tell her I'm sorry.'

'But why did you leave her?'

'Because I was unfaithful and I lied to her. She was far too good for me.'

Yolande was mystified. A minor fling hardly seemed sufficient cause for the family crisis precipitated by his departure, nor grave enough to warrant a self-imposed exile from France. He caught her expression and his eyes twinkled.

'So you want to know what was really at the bottom of it all, my inquisitive little cat? Well, I'll tell you. It involved a certain government minister – or more precisely, his wife.'

Yolande leaned forward expectantly.

'Not to mention official skulduggery,' continued Philippe. 'By the way, this is strictly *entre nous* – and Corinne, if you want to tell her.'

'Well? Who was the minister?'

He shook his finger reprovingly. 'You know I can't tell you that. He was a very busy man. His wife was much younger and bored to tears, so I helped her while away the time. Unfortunately she became pregnant – just before Corinne and I were going to move in together. So you see I was in a bit of a fix. The minister's wife felt obliged to tell him everything, and he not only refused her a divorce, but made it impossible for her to terminate the pregnancy. Religious grounds or something.'

'But the baby? What happened?'

'In a minute. I'm not finished with the minister yet. He wanted to bring me down. I think it was more to punish his wife than me, because she loved me. I had a visit from two tax inspectors with a warrant to search my apartment. The first time I thought it was a warped joke. The second time it wasn't so funny. I went home one night to find the place ransacked. They really were trying to pin something on me – perhaps even plant evidence. You can imagine what it would have meant – the family name dragged through the mud, the image of Château de Rochemort ruined, everything we stood for discredited. So I decided to get out. Of course my mother wanted to know why, but I didn't dare tell her the truth – she would have killed me. And as for Corinne ...' he waved his hands despairingly. 'I couldn't bear her to find out what I was really like. Now I live in Manhattan, my daughter doesn't know I exist, and she's being raised by a pious arsehole in France.'

He took his wallet from his breast pocket and extracted a snapshot which he handed to Yolande. 'She's called Isabelle.'

Yolande gazed at the picture of a chubby, smiling two-year old with the Rochemort blue eyes and black hair. 'She's absolutely adorable, Philippe!'

She was surprised by his proud paternal smile. 'Isn't she just? My pretty baby. And I don't suppose I'll ever know her. Her mother sends me news now and then. She was trying to find an excuse to bring Isabelle to New York, but with her husband, it's extremely difficult.'

'She must still love you.'

'How can she? I've been a total shit.'

'There's no accounting for taste, darling.' Yolande stared at the photograph a while longer. 'So your mother has no idea she has a granddaughter?'

'No. And don't tell her – please. It would only make matters worse. You can tell Corinne if you think it will help her to understand. But no one else.'

'OK.' She handed back the photograph. 'Please come home. Surely you could now?'

He stood up abruptly. 'Perhaps.'

Then he helped her to her feet, put an arm around her waist, and steered her off towards the other guests, wearing one of his best party expressions. 'Now come on and introduce me to everyone I don't know. Is that your new boyfriend over there?'

'Yes.'

Philippe gave Patrick a long appraising look. 'Having trouble with your eyesight these days, my darling? How the hell could you have dumped my brother for him?'

Chapter Six

It was only a few blocks from the Metropolitan Museum of Art to the Beideckers' building, but too far for high heels. Patrick and Yolande emerged into the brisk evening air and got into a cab. They were dining later with her parents, and he wanted some questions answered while they were alone.

'You weren't engaged to *that* baron, were you?'

'Of course not – to his younger brother.'

Yolande was gratified that he seemed jealous. So he did love her, after all. She had been tormented by doubts since their arrival in New York. The run-up to his audition for Vic Bernitz had almost driven her mad, and in the four days since he had been moody and offhand. The temperamental switch reminded her of that evening in Paris when they had first met Althea Pedersen – when she had realised that his career was by far the most important thing in his life.

'Do they look alike?' Patrick asked.

'Yes. But they're totally different in character. Philippe's a dreadful flirt.'

'So I noticed.'

'You weren't at all interested in Yves when I was still engaged to him.'

'I thought he was just a boring aristo. But if he looks as sexy as his brother ...' He paused. 'I can't understand why you jilted him for me.'

Yolande grimaced. 'Looks aren't everything, you know.'

'You never slept with him?'

'No.'

'Didn't you want to?'

'Of course I did.'

'So he didn't want to sleep with you?'

'Look, I don't know, really. We just never did.'

It was too embarrassing to admit that Yves hadn't found her attractive enough to want to make love to her and had never tried once to get her into bed, even after they got engaged. And she had wanted him to, desperately.

'Must be gay,' said Patrick. Or blind. Or both. He couldn't understand it; he seemed to have a permanent erection whenever he was with Yolande.

She pondered for a second. 'I don't think so. It would be against his religion.'

'What's religion got to do with it?'

'Yves is a committed Catholic. Just because he didn't sleep with me, it doesn't mean that he's gay. He's very – … very – …' She struggled to find the right word. 'Very *proper*.'

Couldn't get it up, was Patrick's conclusion. 'I see,' he said.

She could tell that he didn't even begin to see. How could he, not having visited Rochemort and soaked in its atmosphere of romantic chivalry and centuries of strong moral fibre?

But Patrick's mind was on more immediate concerns. He scowled as he recalled Philippe's arm around Yolande's waist, the lordly way he had kissed her lips when he said goodbye, his dazzling and sophisticated performance. Patrick recognised the act for what it was – a bravura display from a man who looked extremely able to claim his *droit de seigneur*. Somehow he had been insulted even by Philippe's mocking blue eyes. They had excluded him, raising a barrier between him and Yolande. He suddenly realised that in his effort to keep his own background obscure, he had failed to take proper account of hers.

In Paris, she blended easily into his chaotic existence, happy to leave the formality of the Avenue Foch and the Hervy salon for his studio and his friends who congregated in a café near the Place des Vosges. But in New York, the realities of her life were highlighted all around him. Her mother and stepfather for a start; they obviously preferred that impotent fiancé. Patrick had been thrown off guard by the established opulence of their apartment. Even Yolande's stepfather turned out to be old money, a descendant of one of New York's city fathers, with tastes and lifestyle to match. Tex Beidecker's great-grandfather had built the large classical townhouse as a retreat from the noise and pollution of Lower Manhattan in the mid-nineteenth century. The family had lived in the whole house then; now the Beideckers occupied the top two floors, with the remaining storeys leased to suitably discreet and well-heeled tenants with their WASP wives, who doubtless were on the committee that had organised the Hervy gala and did a great deal of socialising for charitable causes. Having Philippe de Rochemort appear to remind him of his status as an interloper was just too much.

'Patrick, what *is* the matter?' asked Yolande, after she had paid off the cab.

'Nothing.' He followed her sullenly into the building.

'Thank you, Javier,' she said, smiling at the burly doorman as he called the lift for them. 'How did the game go?'

'The Giants rule!' He grinned. 'And I had twenty bucks on it. You had a good evening, Miss Yolande?'

'Terribly dull,' she said, stepping into the lift. 'We weren't allowed to throw any balls around.'

Javier laughed uproariously as Patrick followed her into the lift. When they were inside, he pulled her into his arms and kissed her passionately.

'Do you still love me?'

'Darling, whatever made you think I don't?' Yolande kissed him back, her hands clasped round his neck. 'Has Vic Bernitz turned you down?'

He smiled. 'No. In fact, I've got the part. As soon as the backing is arranged, we start shooting.'

She couldn't take it in for several moments. 'You're not joking?'

'No. I just have to get the contract finalised with my agent.'

'Oh, that's marvellous! Fantastic! Oh, Patrick, I'm so happy for you ...'

It was exactly what he wanted to hear. Soon he would really put her to the test. She would have to choose between him and her hidebound family, which, he sensed, sneered both at him and his profession.

Hank Pedersen stared in astonishment at his wife, then walked across to the window of his Central Park West drawing-room to look out at the rain, pouring down on a dark October evening.

'You're nuts, Althea. It won't work.'

He thrust his hands into his trouser pockets, and turned to face her. Tall and blond, his physique had suffered from years of desk work. His face was gaunt. He'd been up nearly all the previous night, sorting out a problem with one of Pedersen Corp's Far East subsidiaries. Though Hank always insisted on recreational facilities for his staff, he himself was never to be found working out in the corporate gym housed in the basement of his company headquarters in Midtown. A guy didn't get rich pulling weights.

'So you're not really interested in buying Marchand Enterprises?' asked Althea. 'I wish I'd known before. I've almost fixed everything with Rikki von Stessenberg.'

Hank joined her on the sofa, frowning. 'Well, it's a great opportunity. ... But Jesus, Althea, I couldn't. Tex

Beidecker is a good friend of mine.'

'Tex Beidecker doesn't own Marchand.'

'But the girl's his step-daughter. He's fond of her.'

'Well, well.' Althea leaned back and surveyed him cynically. 'I never thought you of all people would let sentiment get in the way of the bottom line.'

'I thought Rikki and Vic Bernitz had fallen out. How are you going to convince Vic that Rikki won't pull out of this movie like he did the last?'

'I've taken care of all that. Rikki will be our agent. He won't be openly involved in the deal at all. Neither will we. We just step in at the end and buy his shares in Marchand – that gives us 35% of the company. We could soon put in a bid for the rest.'

'I just don't like this emotional stuff, Althea.' Hank gave her a piercing look. 'You're banking on the girl's feelings. Suppose she dumps Dubuisson? We lose the deal.'

'But we can't lose anything by trying, darling.'

He was struck by the remark. 'No, I guess not.' There was a pause. 'You really have fixed it?'

'Rikki's keen – he wants to offload his Marchand holding anyway. All we need to do is get Patrick Dubuisson to persuade his girlfriend to back the picture. Vic is desperate now it looks as though Belco is going bust. I've spoken to him. He'll make the initial approach, then Dubuisson will turn on the sweet talk.'

'Then what?'

Althea picked up a file from the coffee table and handed it to him. 'I've checked her out. She's very rich, but it's all tied up in Marchand equity. If she agrees to back the picture she'll have to sell out. Rikki will buy her shares. And we'll buy them from him. Couldn't be simpler. Vic gets the finance for the movie directly from her. That's nothing to do with us at all.'

'What about her sister? Surely she won't let this Yo –

how the hell *do* you pronounce it?'

'Yo*lande* – as in bond.'

'Surely she won't let Yolande sell outside the family?'

'She can't stop her. I don't think she can buy her out, either. Marchand may have a high profile, but they have huge borrowings.'

Hank ran his eye down the company's latest figures. Yes, Althea had certainly done her homework. The profits were good, the potential was phenomenal, but they were over-leveraged and had few capital reserves. He smiled in anticipation.

'Well, count me in. I'll back you one hundred per cent.'

'What do I get?'

'How about a yacht?'

'I get seasick.' Althea leaned towards him, her expression serious. 'The only thing I want is you, Hank.'

They kissed, but she knew he wasn't in the mood. A sweet, meaningless kiss which meant he was tired and wanted a good night's sleep. She rested her head against his shoulder and playfully pulled his tie. 'What an awful colour. I hope I didn't buy it for you'

'Damn, I used to wear this when I was in college! Must have grabbed it this morning without looking.'

Althea swiftly removed it, then unbuttoned his collar. 'That's better.'

Hank hugged her and kissed her forehead. Outside the rain continued to pour. Althea kicked off her shoes and stretched out on the sofa, her head in his lap. He stroked her hair.

'There is one thing,' he said. 'How can Rikki be sure Yolande will sell the shares to him?'

'She won't – not directly. But he's got a French nominee company. She'll sell to them. Actually, her stepmother has a stake in it.'

'Oh.' He sounded wary.

'Now what?'

'Too many women. Too many feelings.'

'Look, Marchand wouldn't be in business at all if people didn't give way to their feelings. Glamour, fashion, romance – they sell the stuff. If you want to muscle in on their market, you've got to play ball their way.'

'Sure you can handle it?'

'I'm a woman, aren't I?'

He ought to have caught her up in his arms and devoured her with kisses, but it didn't happen. He just murmured 'hmm' and stopped stroking her hair. Althea could have cried with frustration. Nothing could drag him away from his balance sheets, his board meetings, his eternal conference calls. He said he loved her, they still wanted children, but even now on a perfect night for passion, he was too hung up with business. She sat up, and he seemed glad to release her.

'Tell me about the movie, Althea. Is it good?'

She raised her eyebrows. 'You aren't thinking of bailing Vic out, are you?'

Hank laughed. 'No way. I swore I'd never back a picture after I lost five hundred dollars to a pal of mine at Harvard who was supposed to shoot a promotional video. He blew it.'

'I guess the experience traumatised you,' she said frostily.

'Honey, what's wrong?' He stretched out his hand and caressed her cheek. 'I'm tired, OK? Tomorrow, I promise.'

'Put it in your schedule in case you forget.'

'Althea, please don't get like that. I do love you. I'm just very busy right now. Hey, come here. '

He pulled her back into his arms as the tears welled up in her eyes.

'I always come last, always. Hank, what's really wrong? Don't you want me anymore?'

'Come on, don't cry …'

He held her close and kissed her – quick, halting kisses

on her lips and cheeks. Althea knew it was hopeless, and allowed herself to be pacified. He needed time. Ever since he had learnt that his sperm were sluggish he'd been even less interested in sex. A man's prick was an inalienable part of his ego, she realised. It was too bad when it was on the droopy side.

'Did you read that stuff about treatment they sent you from the clinic?'

'Yes.' He kissed her again. 'It'll work out, darling. Just be patient. I've got to sort out this Singapore problem.'

'Then there'll be a storm brewing some place else. Can't you *ever* relax?'

Hank smiled knowingly. 'Relax for five minutes in this town and you can kiss goodbye to a few million bucks. This is no kindergarten, Althea.'

It was an unfortunate remark, and he fell silent. She looked over his shoulder at his latest acquisition – a Monet. Bright blue, green, red; a riot of colours depicting a Norman cornfield. It had to be worth thirty minutes' relaxation. The silver candlesticks on the sideboard standing beneath it represented a mere few seconds. The Turner canvas hanging nearby: ten minutes? Fifteen? She wasn't sure, but she knew that she'd gladly give them all up in return for a bigger percentage of her husband's time. He stifled a yawn, and she loosened her arms around his neck.

'Do you really want to know about Vic's movie?'

'Yes.'

She stood up and held out her hand. Hank smiled and got to his feet. He was sound asleep before she had even half finished outlining the story that would make Patrick Dubuisson a worldwide sex symbol and bring Pedersen Corporation control of one of the most prestigious companies in France.

Gianni's on West 44th Street didn't usually figure on

Yolande's list of places to eat out in New York. Too kitsch, far too many tourists, too much noise. She generally preferred the restaurants that Tex and her mother frequented on the Upper East Side, but today was different. Vic Bernitz had invited her to lunch in the Theater District to chat about Patrick's film. He had brought along his assistant, Ethan Casavecchia, whose jaw dropped when she sauntered in with a distinctly Parisian élan.

'You haven't thought of going in for movie-acting yourself, have you?' he asked as she joined them at their table.

'No. Why?'

'Can't you see you've got them all rubbernecking?'

Yolande surveyed the clientele with cool green eyes, then shrugged her shoulders.

'I can't act.'

'That's not necessarily a problem.'

'Where's Patrick?' asked Bernitz. 'This was meant to be a celebration.'

'He's got neuralgia. He got soaked going to Liberty Island yesterday. I've asked Franco Rivera to make up the four. He should be here soon.'

Bernitz didn't seem unduly surprised, and promptly ordered drinks. Franco showed up ten minutes later, cursing New York traffic in rapid Italian, French, and English.

'Yolande, how does your adorable mother get around in this city? Magic carpet?'

'You need a drink, Franco.' She poured some wine.

He sank gratefully into a chair and took the proffered glass. The mood mellowed, and soon all four were discussing the film. Yolande asked how far casting had progressed, and was staggered when Bernitz informed her that so far Patrick was the sole actor with whom he had agreed terms.

'By the way, tell him the contract won't be ready for another three weeks at least.'

She caught a guarded look in his eyes. 'Why the delay?'

'We have a funding situation,' said Ethan.

'Do you mean you've got no backers? And you've already given Patrick the role? But it might never come off!'

'Don't panic,' said Bernitz, waving his hand. 'We have a few problems, that's all. I had everything set up, but my main backer is in a bad way.'

'He just got arrested for fraud.'

Yolande looked at Ethan uncomprehendingly, uncertain whether his deadpan remark was serious or not. He gazed at her owlishly from behind large round spectacles.

'It's true. You've heard of Jason H. Bronckmann? He's been pulled in for insider dealing, corporate tax fraud, embezzlement. I forget the rest.'

Franco raised his eyebrows as if to say that's exactly what he would have expected. 'You have a big problem, Mr Bernitz?'

Vic Bernitz never got agitated about anything. It was not his way. He thrived on a calm, laid-back approach which matched his deep, lazy voice and imperturbable cast of features. But insofar as it was possible to deviate from this carefully cultivated image he gave Yolande and Franco the impression that yes, indeed, he had a very big problem.

'Bronckmann owns Belco Pictures, which has the rights to the movie. Do you remember *Night Below Zero*? Belco backed that. It was my first success. Then I didn't do so well with *The Far Coast* and Belco lost interest for a while. After *Dreaming of Youth,* which I made for Zelden, Bronckmann asked me back. He was really hooked on this script, and believe me, a lot of other guys will be now he's in the can. Belco will go into liquidation soon unless someone steps in, and bang goes our movie.'

Yolande was very worried. 'So Patrick would lose the role?'

'Pretty much,' said Ethan.

'What's the film called?' asked Franco, to break an uncomfortable pause.

'*Fast and Loose* – a thriller set in the Balkans. It's a brilliant script. Really intelligent. Great locations too.'

'Any women?' said Franco, unimpressed.

'We're in talks with Jayne Herford's agent.'

Jayne Herford was a Hollywood bombshell with a string of successes to her name, but Franco nodded unenthusiastically. Yolande sensed that he didn't like Bernitz, the film, or the restaurant. He tore his bread in a determined fashion.

She picked at an olive, looking at Bernitz. 'How much would it cost to buy Belco Pictures?'

'Probably less than twenty million. But they have quite an impressive back catalogue, even though they are a small company.'

'Couldn't you just buy the rights to the script?' she asked.

Not as dumb as she looked, thought Bernitz. But that would be far too easy, and it wouldn't require her to liquidate all her assets in Marchand.

'Not possible. I've tried already. They're hanging on to it to try to make the whole company more saleable.'

'What would you expect to make on the film?'

'With worldwide theatre and cable release, DVD, and merchandising – and if we get Jayne Herford – a minimum three to four hundred per cent profit.'

'And your projected budget?'

'Thirty million dollars.'

'What, with Jayne Herford? I would have thought she'd ask for that just for herself.'

Definitely not as dumb as he had been led to believe.

'She's very keen to do this script. There's awards potential. Her last two movies haven't really done much for her reputation.'

'You must be a very persuasive man, Mr Bernitz.'

He grinned. 'Oh, I am.'

'It's a winner,' said Ethan. 'Believe me. The script is superb. Ross Ballard is writing the score. It's got everything.'

There was no mistaking the look in Bernitz's eyes now. He was asking her for the money. He knew she was rich and Patrick was her lover – it was logical. Suddenly Yolande didn't feel hungry. A horrible sense of foreboding overcame her, and she wished she were somewhere else.

'How long have you got before Belco goes into liquidation?'

Bernitz rested his elbows on the table and slowly pressed the tips of his fingers together, smiling at her like a reassuring dentist. Franco shot him a venomous glance.

'Pretty soon. The wolves are prowling already.'

'I see,' said Yolande, thinking of the dreadful effect on Patrick if the project fell through. 'How soon is soon?'

'Three weeks maximum.'

'Three weeks!'

'Without a rapid capital injection, it's a no-win scenario for us.' Ethan relished the phrase, his eyes fixed imploringly on Yolande's face.

She was beginning to think he had scripted the whole scene. He and Bernitz seemed to be acting in tandem; slowly letting out the information, testing her reaction, pulling her their way. Millions of dollars? Yes, she had them. Not in hard cash, but she could raise it. Patrick would surely be grateful – very grateful. And she was assured of a handsome profit.

'Yolande, don't forget the Hervy cocktail party at three,' said Franco. 'You'll have to change.'

She was jolted back down to earth. Bernitz treated her

to another reassuring smile. 'It'll work out, I'm sure. Are you in New York long?'

'We return to Paris this Saturday.'

Ethan looked crestfallen. Did he expect her to stand up there and then and announce how much she could give them?

'Can I have your phone number, Mr Bernitz?' she asked, as Franco grew ever more pressing to leave.

'Patrick's got it. I'll be in L.A. And call me Vic.'

'Can we give you a lift?' asked Ethan.

Franco looked horrified.

'I've got a car,' said Yolande.

Bernitz shook her hand, Ethan kissed her cheeks, and the farewells were made.

'What a convenient cocktail party,' Yolande said to Franco as they drove off. 'You have a very fertile imagination.'

'I had to get out of there. They would have talked all afternoon.' Franco was preoccupied, and stared ahead moodily. 'These streets are too long.'

'Where do you want to go?' she asked.

'Can we drive around? I want to talk.'

She headed up Sixth Avenue towards Central Park.

'Don't do it, Yolande,' he said.

'Do what?'

'Put money into that film. I've never seen such a calculated act. They would have liked a blank cheque on the spot.'

'I didn't give them one.'

'No. But you will.'

'It's none of your business.'

He turned towards her, his expression concerned. '*Carissima*, listen to me. Don't think you'll hold Patrick through underwriting this film. If he wants to go, he'll go. Spend all your millions, but it won't make the slightest difference.'

97

'So you think he doesn't love me?' she asked sharply.

'He's just a sex machine. That's how he caught you in the first place. But has he got a heart?'

She was cross. How dared he analyse her relationship with Patrick? Tell her what to do? Just because he was a good friend it didn't give him the right to lecture her.

'Yolande, don't sulk. It spoils your expression. Can't you accept friendly advice? I'm only trying to warn you. Go ahead and buy Belco Pictures – but *only* if you're going to make a good profit. Not for Patrick. He really isn't worth it.'

'Thank you, Franco,' she said icily. 'I'll remember that.'

They turned eastwards and drove on in silence. Franco sighed. She was such a baby – a charming, beautiful, spoilt baby. And she was going to let Vic Bernitz pull the silver spoon from her mouth.

'By the way, *carissima*, I've got some news too. I'm leaving Hervy next year. Paul Dupuy has signed Guy Monthély.'

'Monthély! He's a total nightmare to work for.' She grimaced. 'What will you do?'

'Do you care?'

Yolande said nothing until they were back in the Upper East Side, then she turned off down a quiet tree-lined side street and parked the car. She faced him, her expression conciliatory.

'Of course I care. You've done so much for Hervy – such a lot for me, too. I'm sorry if I was sharp with you.'

'I'm launching my own label.'

'So that's why that count turned up at the homeless gala. I wondered. What's his name again?'

'Stessenberg. It's not absolutely settled yet, but we have an agreement in principle. He puts up most of the money and finds me a financial director, and I devote my energies to the clients and the designs.'

Yolande suddenly realised it was very bad news. Franco had boosted Hervy's sales and image enormously – now he would take his expertise elsewhere. Possibly Hervy's clients too.

'Does my sister know of Monthély's appointment?'

'I suppose so – but she's never taken much interest in couture. Paul seems to have *carte blanche*.' Franco pressed her arm. 'It's not the end of the world. I ought to branch out now before I get typecast.'

'Will you stay in Paris?'

'I might move to Milan, but I'm not sure yet. I'll really miss you, Yolande.'

He was very close, his huge brown eyes soft and warm under thick black eyebrows. Without another word he leaned over, cupped her face in his hands, and kissed her lips. Yolande was too surprised to resist. She stared at him, perplexed.

'Why?'

'Because I want you.' He pulled her into his arms.

'But aren't you gay?'

'Not all the time. I'm bi. How could any man be gay when you're around?'

He nibbled her earlobe. She was at a complete loss. She had assumed that because he designed clothes he had to be gay – but now she thought about it, she'd never seen anything to indicate that he particularly fancied men. She suddenly felt acutely embarrassed, remembering all the times she had stood semi-naked while his hands roamed over her body with a tape measure.

'Does *this* feel as though I'm gay?' He kissed her again, more urgently, and placed her hand over his crotch.

Yolande tried to push him off, but he was pressing her into her seat. 'Franco ... no. I like you ... as a friend ... but Patrick ...'

'Fuck Patrick!' He drew back angrily. 'He's using you, and you're too blind to see it!'

'And what do you think you're doing now?'

'Saying goodbye.'

'You're not leaving Hervy until next year, and it's hardly the usual way of saying goodbye.'

'I might not get another chance,' he murmured, kissing her again, while he slid his hand beneath her top. 'Don't be cruel.'

'Franco, for God's sake stop it.'

She wasn't angry, didn't try to fight him off. How could she when his lips were making love to hers and he was whispering soft Italian words in her ear? Then came the thumping on the windscreen. He swore, hastily getting back into his seat and tucking in his shirt. Yolande straightened her clothes before winding down the window. A traffic cop peered in with a knowing leer.

'Move it, miss. You can't wait here. And make it snappy.'

She smiled disarmingly and turned the key in the ignition. When they had moved off down the street, she burst out laughing.

'What's so funny?'

'Your face, darling!'

He scowled. 'Let's go to my hotel. Please, Yolande. You'll enjoy it. Satisfaction guaranteed.'

'No. It would be very wrong.'

'Good sex is never wrong, *carissima*.'

She laughed. 'That rather depends on who it's with. I'm going home.' She was firm now. 'Do you want me to drop you off at the Pierre?'

'I suppose so.'

'Oh do cheer up, Franco. I give you full marks for effort and ingenuity, and credit for all the rest. Still friends?'

He smiled ruefully, and they parted on the best of terms. Not until she was back in her mother's apartment, relaxing with a remarkably un-neuralgic Patrick, did

Yolande begin seriously to think about her conversation with Vic Bernitz. It was worrying. She was a multi-millionaire, and she hadn't the foggiest idea of how she was going to get hold of her own money.

Chapter Seven

Grace Beidecker emerged from the walk-in closet with an armful of hangers and clothes. 'Are you leaving these here?'

'Might as well,' said Yolande, looking up from her suitcase. 'I want to ask you something.'

'Shoot.' Grace disappeared again.

'Do you like Patrick?'

There was an ominous silence. At length Grace faced her daughter. 'Not much.'

'I see.'

'Well, you did ask. Is it that important, darling?' She moved some clothes waiting to be packed and perched on the edge of the bed.

Yolande leaned against the lid of the suitcase, her fingers hitched into the pockets of her jeans. 'I want you to like him. Because I love him – very much.'

Grace looked sceptical. 'I seem to have heard all this before.'

'I know how you feel about Yves, but it was a mistake for us ever to have got engaged. I only thought I was in love, because he's so nice and I'd known him so long, and everybody thinks he's charming.'

'He is. I couldn't have hoped for a better son-in-law,' said her mother firmly. 'Tex thinks so too.'

Yolande sighed. 'Well I know it was a mistake.'

'Let's hope Yves feels the same way. You've treated him atrociously. And though it may hurt, Yolande, Patrick just isn't in the same league.'

'But he's such fun, and he's amazingly talented.'

'In bed? I'm sure he is. But I don't trust him.'

Yolande looked sulky, and began to fold a dress.

'I may be your mother, but I'm not completely over the hill. You've just let sex get the better of you.'

'I haven't! I do love him!'

'Look at it sensibly, darling. Does he love you? What exactly has he offered you? A home? Children? A future?'

'We've got ages to think about all that. There's his career to consider first.'

It was all coming out too pat, and Yolande knew it. Patrick had never offered her anything but half his bed – wherever it happened to be – and she was too proud to admit that her mother was right. She did want commitment, she would love to have children. Instead she was being asked to part with nearly all her fortune to promote his career. But that was something best kept strictly to herself.

'And another thing,' said Grace, who was now on a roll. She'd been aching to talk to Yolande about Patrick, but had been afraid to bring the subject up first. 'Where does he come from? Have you met *his* family?'

Yolande unfolded the dress and carefully laid it out again, her face concealed by her hair. 'God, you're such a snob.'

'You don't seem to realise that you're extremely rich and as far as I can see he's broke.'

'Well, he's never asked me for anything, if that's what you think. Honestly, you make it sound as though I have to pay him to go out with me!' Yolande was starting to get cross. 'And Patrick *does* have a family. I met his mother once when she came to visit him. She lives in Provence.'

'What's she like?'

'Like most people's mothers, I suppose. She was an actress years ago.'

'Like most people's mothers!' exclaimed Grace, her dark eyes flashing. 'How elegantly you put it. Perhaps I should phrase the question differently. Is she like Marie-

104

Christine?'

'Oh no.'

'Or me?'

'No.'

'Or anyone else's mother you know?'

Yolande shrugged her shoulders. 'Mummy, don't quibble. She was nice. About fifty. Quite chic.'

'So you don't care about Patrick's background, then. You haven't a clue about his real feelings for you, and I suppose you'll cling to him until he dumps you. He's that type.'

'He isn't! You haven't even tried to get to know him!'

She looked as though she was about to cry. Grace stood up and put an arm around her. 'I'm sorry, darling. Can't you see it's because I can't bear you to get hurt? You're too trusting. Yves would have taken care of you. He really loves you.'

'No he doesn't.'

'Because he didn't ask you to sleep with him?' Grace gave her a serious, searching look. Yolande lowered her eyes. 'You should never confuse sex and love. With Patrick, it's only sex. It's no good staring at the floor, don't you think we know what's going on? We'd have to be deaf not to. With Yves, it was love. But there would have been sex. He wanted you, but not just for an affair. For life. For a family. And you couldn't see it.'

'But he never even *talked* about it.'

'Couldn't you read his eyes? Perhaps he is a little old-fashioned, but believe me, he's still a man, and from all I've heard, a pretty hot one.'

'Yeah, right.'

Yolande didn't believe her. She knew exactly what her mother was trying to do, but no one could be less passionate than Yves. Who would want to be with a man who was colder than a mid-winter day in Alaska?

Her mother shook her head. 'You're so much like your

105

father – throwing away something wonderful for the first pretty face to pass by.' She deftly folded the clothes to go in the suitcase. 'We'd better get on with this. By the way, did your father meet Patrick?'

'Yes.'

'What did he think of him?'

Yolande placed the now satisfactorily folded dress on top of the pile. 'He still wanted me to marry Yves.'

'Well I must give him credit for that. And Toinette?'

'She had a strong impression she'd seen Patrick somewhere before.'

Grace straightened up, struck by the comment. 'Now isn't that odd? I feel the very same thing.'

'She's not the only one,' added Yolande, 'but I can't see it. He doesn't remind me of anyone.'

'You're not as ancient as we are. Perhaps he's like his mother. Was she well-known?'

'She did a season at the Comédie Française once.'

'Really? And his father?'

'He never mentions him.'

'Hey, come on you two, aren't you ever going to be through with that packing?'

It was Tex. He sauntered in and looked aghast when he saw how much remained to be done. 'What have you been getting up to? Girl talk, eh? Let's hear it.'

'Mummy's been giving me a lecture,' said Yolande. 'And you're just about to sit on a couture gown from Hervy.'

Tex bounded up, holding a garment bag tenderly in his right hand. 'Will it survive?' he whispered falteringly.

They burst out laughing. Grace threw a scarf at him. 'Get out, you pest. And if you must know, we were discussing men.'

'Oh,' he drawled. 'Where do *I* fit in?'

'At the top of course, *mon ange*,' said Yolande, smiling. She adored Tex.

106

'OK, baby, what's the deal this time? I'm such a sucker for compliments.'

'How about a limo to the airport tomorrow? And dinner tonight? And just one good word for my poor Patrick?'

'You've got the car. You've got the meal. Patrick now – well, I guess my French isn't so hot, but I'd say he was *pathétique*.'

He grinned, and was gone before they could correct him. Grace collapsed into laughter again, but Yolande pouted for a whole five minutes.

Yolande only remembered it was All Saints' Day when she found Paris resolutely closed for the holiday weekend. It was extra bleak in that huge apartment on the Avenue Foch, with a cold late autumnal wind sweeping in from the Bois de Boulogne. Corinne was in London until mid-November on a trip to promote the new Hervy perfumes, and Yolande didn't relish the prospect of a fortnight alone. She invited Patrick to stay as soon as they arrived by taxi from Charles de Gaulle airport.

'Are you sure?' he asked.

'Of course. Please, Patrick – otherwise I'd rather stay with you until Corinne gets back.'

Patrick decided to sample life on the Avenue Foch. It wasn't difficult to adapt to the luxury; he had already clocked up some experience whilst in New York. There was a maid to do his laundry, no one to criticise him, and Yolande had an inviting four-poster bed. But he was disconcerted when the first thing she did was to pick up the telephone and announce that she was ringing the Château de Rochemort.

'It's private. I must speak to the baroness. Give me a few minutes.'

He went off into her bedroom and quietly closed the door, then kicked off his shoes and stretched himself out on the bed. He wondered why she didn't have a photograph of him on her bedside table. There was a studio portrait of her father, whom she greatly resembled. And a telephone extension. He leaned over and prised the receiver carefully off the hook, eager to hear the conversation.

It was some while before anyone answered the telephone at Rochemort, but that was by no means unusual. The place was so rambling, with extensions rather arbitrarily scattered through the splendid, empty rooms.

'Hello, is Marie-Christine there, please?'

'Yolande!'

Yves. Damn. She ought to have remembered he would be there.

'Hello, Yves. Is your mother at home?'

'No. She's dining out.'

'How is she?'

'Not too bad in spirits, but the arthritis isn't improving.' He sounded put out by her coldness. 'How are you? Corinne told me you were in New York.'

'We – I just got back today. I'm rather jet-lagged. Are you all right?'

'Not really.' There was a pause. 'Darling, I miss you so much. Couldn't we …'

'I don't want to talk about it.'

'Are you still with that actor?'

'Yes.'

'It won't last,' he said. 'Yolande, listen to me, please. It's been hell all summer without you. I still love you. Won't you give it another chance? I'll do anything you want.'

She was tempted to hang up, but perhaps it was better to clear the air now. They would have to meet some time, and she didn't want to have any awkwardness between them. It was a bloody nuisance that he was so closely connected to the family.

'Please, Yves, don't ever mention it again. It's

embarrassing for both of us.'

'*Embarrassing*? Is that all you think of me?'

'Of course not. I'll always care for you – as a friend. You know that. But I made the right decision when I broke off the engagement and I'm not going to change my mind now.'

Patrick was enjoying the dialogue. He settled back on the bed, waiting for further intimacies, but Yves decided he would grovel no longer.

'So what made you call?' he asked coldly.

'I wanted to tell your mother that I've seen Philippe.'

'What! Where? When?'

'In New York, at the Hervy gala. We had a long talk.'

Patrick frowned, and hooking the receiver under his chin, lit a cigarette. He had taken a strong dislike to Philippe.

'What did he say? How does he look? Is he coming home?'

'I think he might eventually. I can't tell you everything. There are a lot of complications. But he's very well and as handsome as ever. I'm sure he misses you both.'

'Have you got his address? His phone number? Hold on, Yolande, I'll get some paper.'

'It's no good, Yves. He wouldn't tell me. But I'm sure he'll get in touch.'

'I see.' He was very disappointed. 'Well, thanks for telling me, anyway. Will you ring Maman tomorrow? She'll demand an eyewitness report.'

'Of course.'

'Don't worry, I shan't bother you about my feelings again. Give my love to Grace and Tex.'

'They're coming to St Xavier for Christmas.'

'That'll be nice,' said Yves. 'Goodbye, Yolande.'

She was so taken aback by the abruptness of his farewell that she held onto the receiver for some moments – long enough to hear a tell-tale click on the line. Furious, she sprinted out of the salon and along to her room. Patrick, unconcerned, smiled at her from the bed.

'You were listening!'

'So?' he said. 'Why shouldn't I? You're mine.'

'That's no excuse.'

Then her anger evaporated. *He says I'm his. He must love me. I'm his.* She joined him on the bed.

'That's better,' said Patrick. 'Didn't you think I might be jealous? I knew you were going to speak to him.'

'I didn't mean to.'

'Perhaps not, but he didn't mind. But I'd prefer it if there were no encores.'

He kissed her and began to undress her, though she was very tired and too preoccupied for sex. But Patrick seemed happy, although she couldn't orgasm. She snuggled against him afterwards, her arm across his midriff.

'Don't go to sleep, Yolande.'

'Hmm? I'm exhausted.'

'I want to talk to you, darling. And we haven't had anything to eat.'

She patted his stomach. 'You're always hungry. Go and get something from the kitchen.'

Patrick moved her and got to his feet. 'What do you want?'

'Pâté, bread – anything.' She propped herself up on her elbow. 'For God's sake put some clothes on! If Françoise sees you like that she'll have a fit.'

'She should be so lucky.'

'Show-off. Here.' She threw him his jeans. 'Don't get lost. It's left at the far end of the passage.'

Yolande was now wide awake, too conscious of everything, her mind echoing with the conversation with her mother in New York and Yves' voice at the end of the telephone.

I still love you. Won't you give it another chance? I'll do anything you want.

No! It had to be Patrick. She stumbled from the bed and pulled on a dressing-gown, trying to forget. Why should it affect her now? When she and Patrick were so happy together? If only he had let her go to sleep.

He returned with a trolley laden with cold meats, bread and side salad, wine, glasses, plates, gleaming cutlery, and two artistically folded napkins.

'Mademoiselle, room service! Perhaps you'd care for the chicken – the finest Bresse, mademoiselle. Or our pâté? The chef insists on the best ingredients. Or the *jambon persillé*? Wine? Red or white? Burgundy, naturally.'

A perfect waiter, straight out of a comedy. She laughed, and all her doubts vanished. Gorgeous, wonderful Patrick. How could she ever live without him?

When they had eaten, she asked him what he wanted to talk about.

'The film,' he said, pulling her into his arms. 'What did Vic Bernitz tell you at Gianni's on Wednesday?'

'He more or less asked me to back the whole thing.'

Patrick whistled.

'Don't pretend to be surprised. You weren't at all ill when I got back.'

'Yolande, I'd never even dream of asking you for any money. But I had heard rumours about the backing being shaky. Someone went bankrupt or something.'

'Convenient, wasn't it?'

'What's the matter?' he stroked her cheek. 'Should I refuse the part? Whatever you want, darling. ... Just say so, and I'll ring Vic Bernitz this moment and tell him.'

She gazed at him thoughtfully. His hazel eyes were open, honest, loving. It was nothing to do with him. Bernitz had been trying his luck, that's all. But if he couldn't find another backer, Patrick would suffer. And it would be her fault. She had his future in her hands. Three weeks – no, less than two and a half now.

'Is it really important for you to make this film?' she asked. 'I mean *really, really* important?'

'It's the only chance I'll ever get to break into Hollywood.'

'What would you say if I decided to back you?'

He seemed astonished. 'You wouldn't! Would you? But it's impossible. They need millions.'

'But what would you say? Patrick, I'm serious.' She held his face in her hands. 'Serious, *mon amour.*'

'Yolande! You'd be an angel. Of course, you'd come on location with me, wouldn't you? It would be fantastic being together. And it *will* be a success, I know it will. You can't lose! You'll make millions too. We'll have such a marvellous time.'

He began to kiss her and her body throbbed under his slightest touch. She knew then she would back him. They could be together all the time. Forever. No drowsy fumbling this time. Raw desire and burning need, gasps, screams, moans.

'I'm going to fuck your brains out,' he said as he entered her.

And that's exactly what he did.

'There's one big problem,' said Yolande much later, the telephone call to Los Angeles made and everything fixed. 'I'll have to sell my Marchand shares.'

'Oh, let's think about it tomorrow. Everything's so marvellous. Don't spoil it by talking about money.'

She was drifting into the luxurious sleep of the sexually satiated and was soon breathing quietly in his arms. Patrick slipped from the bed and removed the trolley from the room. Françoise was rather surprised to find the glasses rinsed clean when she wheeled it back to the kitchen.

Patrick was delighted with his performance, though ashamed they had needed a little help. He carefully placed

112

his small stash of pills back in an inside pocket of his bag. It wouldn't do for Yolande to find it. She was firmly against drugs. But an actor had to know how to use props. And she'd certainly enjoyed the sex. It would all be for the best. She would make money from the film, and he would keep her happy for as long as necessary.

'Better check your inbox, Miles. According to Jacques, Corinne Marchand's in trouble.'

Miles looked across at James Chetwode, his colleague in Corsley European's corporate finance department, then found the email from Jacques Daubigny, head of the research section, who was adept at sniffing out stories before they reached the press. A few lines suggested that it might be worthwhile to investigate Marchand Enterprises' takeover potential now that half the family holding in the company had been diluted.

He put a call straight through to Jacques' office, two floors below in the bank's Paris headquarters near the Bourse.

'I thought you'd be interested.'

'Is it true?'

'Absolutely. But it's not widely known yet. I got onto it at lunch yesterday. Friend of a friend – you know how it works. I followed it up with Georges Maury, the vice-president, this morning. He would neither confirm nor deny the rumours, but my information is that Yolande Marchand has sold her entire stake, resigned her directorship, and slipped out of the country while the storm gathers. Charming girl. Met her once at a party, but she didn't fancy me.'

'She held twenty-seven per cent of the equity, didn't she?' asked Miles.

'That's right. That leaves her sister Corinne with twenty-seven per cent. Maury has only ten per cent. Yves de Rochemort has fifteen per cent. It doesn't look very healthy for your girlfriend.'

'She's not my girlfriend.'

'Excellent. You won't be worried then if we advise Marchand that an agreed takeover might work better for them than trying to fight a hostile bid.'

'Have you any predators in mind?'

'Several. Two French. Three, maybe four, foreign. I haven't got the whole picture yet. As far as I know, Yolande sold her stake to a private equity firm.'

'Why didn't she sell to her sister?'

'Don't quote me on this – I believe she's going to bail out a company that's producing a film starring her boyfriend, and the money was needed fast. Obviously her sister couldn't raise the cash in time. As you well know, Marchand's gearing is extremely high.'

'Thanks, Jacques. Keep me posted, won't you?'

Miles rang off, then dialled Marchand's offices on the Avenue Montaigne. No, he couldn't speak to Corinne. She had only just arrived from London. Besides, calls from Monsieur Corsley would not be put through. He slammed down the receiver and swore loudly.

'Temper, temper,' chided James, wagging his finger. 'You're still crazy about her, aren't you?'

'It was strictly a business call.'

James raised his eyebrows. 'Well, I shouldn't worry. She'll just have to hold onto her knickers and fight off the vultures. Think of all the lovely money there could be for us if she loses.'

'Oh, bugger off.'

Miles tried to contact Corinne later that afternoon, but was outlawed again, and when he called the Avenue Foch in the evening the telephone was off the hook. By then the whole affair had reached the press, and Corinne was under siege.

Corinne sat in an armchair at Georges Maury's Neuilly

home, her eyes almost black with anger. She was furious with herself. She should have returned to Paris as soon as Yolande called to say she wanted to sell her stake in the company. Georges should never have been left to handle the negotiations alone. But she had been extremely busy in London, and it had seemed quite straightforward – desirable too. By buying her sister's shares Corinne would have commanded the powerful position her father had enjoyed before his death. Yet it had all gone staggeringly wrong. Now she was in danger of losing his company altogether.

Georges paced up and down the salon, a glass of whisky in his hand, hardly able to look Corinne in the face. He'd done everything she had asked; discussed the proposition with Yolande, offered her the market price for her shares, then set about raising the money to pay for them. But before he had secured the capital, Yolande rang him to say she had accepted a higher offer. The treachery of it all was breathtaking.

'Who made Yolande this offer she couldn't refuse?' asked Corinne in a hard voice.

'I don't know. They're bearer shares as you know, and the buyer hasn't come forward yet. Someone mentioned a private equity company. I've got people working on it. We ought to be able to buy them back.'

'It's going to cost the earth now. Surely you could have asked Yolande who she sold them to?'

'I was too busy trying to persuade her to hold on for a while. But she was adamant. She said she needed the money at once, and anyway our offer was too low. I just couldn't talk sense to her, Corinne. I tried so hard. Believe me, I tried.'

'I'll kill her! It's because of that bastard Patrick. It must be. And where the hell *is* she?'

'I don't know. She's stopped answering her phone.'

Corinne just sat, clenching and unclenching her hands.

Georges went over to the sideboard and poured her a Scotch. 'Calm down, Corinne. I'm sure we'll be able to get the shares back. After all, what use is twenty-seven per cent to anyone?'

'A seat on the board for a start. A strategic niche from which to lever us all out of the company.' She sipped the drink. 'We're well and truly screwed. That plan to increase our holding in Elegance Hotels is dead for certain. And you must realise that I can only remain PDG now if you and Yves support me.'

'We still love you,' he said, smiling. 'Come on, try to be positive. As soon as we know who's bought the shares, we'll buy them back. It'll all be settled by Christmas.'

'I don't see how we can afford it. Our gearing is unsustainable now – who's going to lend us any more money? I wouldn't if I were a bank.'

'But our profits are rising all the time. I'll get a report out tomorrow. Now, how about London? Did the launch go well? Paul Dupuy reports excellent reactions from New York.'

Corinne managed to give a rational account of what had, in fact, been a very successful trip to London, but she kept returning to Yolande's treachery.

'I still don't understand, Georges. Why did she need so much money? And so soon? She only told me it was for something important.'

He stared at his feet, afraid to look her in the eye. 'She's buying an American company that's producing a film starring Patrick.'

'*What*! She's mad! I don't believe it. I just don't believe it!'

'I'm afraid it's true. She told me herself, and I've never found her out in a lie.'

Corinne rose to leave. 'I'm going home. See you in the morning, Georges.'

As he kissed her goodbye he asked what she intended

to do about Yolande.

'I never want to see her again. I hate her!'

'But St Xavier and the apartment – she still owns half of everything.'

'I'll buy her out as soon as I can drag her out from under Dubuisson for five minutes. And after that, as far as I'm concerned I have no sister.'

Chapter Eight

'I really don't know why you're so upset, Corinne,' said Toinette Brozard, lighting a cigarette. 'It's just a storm in a teacup.'

Corinne was struggling to keep her cool. Toinette was so calm, so self-assured, sitting in the salon of the Marchand apartment on the Avenue Foch with the unshakable ease of one perfectly at home. Dressed in classic Hervy, with black-stockinged legs and dainty feet neatly encased in black court shoes, she looked every inch the society hostess who had reigned there so magnificently when Jean-Claude was alive.

'I'm glad you haven't changed anything,' she remarked. 'I always loved this room.'

'Perhaps you were fonder of it than you were of Papa,' suggested Corinne icily. 'Otherwise I don't know how you could threaten the very existence of his company.'

'Don't be so melodramatic.'

'How *could* you? I know you don't like me, but …'

'That's not true,' interjected Toinette.

'It was a perfect opportunity for revenge, wasn't it? Buying Yolande's shares behind my back, breaking the family control of Marchand'

'Really, Corinne, if you haven't anything reasonable to say, I'll go. I thought this was a business meeting.'

'What price do you want for Yolande's shares?'

Toinette drew on her cigarette. At length she sighed and settled back in her armchair. 'There's a slight problem. They aren't for sale. You see, Corinne, I don't own them. I received a telephone call instructing me to buy Yolande's shares for UVS – and I haven't been given instructions to sell them again. You aren't the only person who's approached me, you know.'

Corinne glowered at her. 'Who gave you your instructions? How did anyone know Yolande was looking for a buyer?'

'I'm sure you'll find out. You seem to run a very efficient pack of bloodhounds. I was astonished at how quickly they tracked me down.'

'Laurent Dobry was the first to break the story. You ought to rotate your friends now and again, Toinette.'

So Yolande had sold her stake to UVS, the same company that had acquired Philippe's shares three years before – and presumably still owned them. As with all bearer shares, it was sometimes impossible to ferret out the owner. It was a minor miracle that Corinne had managed to trace the threat this far, but she had a gut feeling that Toinette wasn't her real enemy. Of course she'd be in on the action for some personal gain, but she would hardly want to take control of Marchand – that was too much like hard work. Corinne was left with a chain of businesses to run on a high amount of debt and ripe for a hostile takeover. Deadlock.

'You own thirty per cent of UVS, don't you?' she asked Toinette.

'Yes. And we're private, so if you were thinking of a reverse takeover, it's not going to happen.'

'Perhaps you'd tell me what UVS intends to do with its holding in Marchand?'

'Well, it's not up to me,' said Toinette, stubbing out her cigarette and immediately lighting another. She wasn't enjoying herself; her nerves were shot, and sitting here brought back too many memories of Jean-Claude. 'I only manage the Paris end of things, and we operate on a very loose basis. I just buy and sell as instructed. As far as I know, UVS has no plans to lobby for a seat on your board, but I'll attend the next meeting as usual. On my own account, of course.'

Corinne bit her lip, wishing there were some way Toinette could be removed from Marchand's board for good.

'Will UVS give me first option on Yolande's shares if it decides to sell?'

'They aren't Yolande's shares now,' corrected Toinette. 'But I'll certainly ask for you.'

'Do you have to be so friendly?' snapped Corinne.

'Darling, I rather think you're the one who's being hostile. I've just told you I'll help if I can.'

'You could have helped by not buying the shares in the first place. And *don't* call me darling.'

Toinette stood up and approached her. 'Corinne, really! No one can take Marchand over with twenty-seven per cent, and I can assure you that I have absolutely no desire to step into your shoes. Just relax and enjoy Christmas.'

'Christmas!' Corinne shuddered. 'With everyone looking over their shoulders for predators, it's going to be simply wonderful, isn't it?'

'You don't care what happens to me. This will be my first Christmas without Jean-Claude.'

'You're not the only one.'

'I miss him so much.'

'So do I.' Corinne was annoyed that the conversation had taken this turn but her voice was gentler. She was surprised that Toinette seemed to be genuinely upset.

'May I look in his room?'

'Of course – we haven't touched a thing.'

As though he was going to come back and put everything right, she thought. They went quickly down the hall. Corinne waited at the door to her father's room while Toinette looked around, touching odd items on the dressing table; his hairbrush, cologne, cufflinks. She lingered some while, her back to Corinne. The slight movement of her shoulders suggested that she was crying.

'What do you really want, Toinette?'

'Him,' was the muffled reply. 'God, I want him!'

Corinne swiftly moved across the room, and involuntarily put an arm around her. Toinette leaned against her for a moment, wiping her eyes.

'Is there anything of his you'd like?'

Toinette sniffed loudly. Corinne moved away. 'Could I – would you let me have that photograph?' She pointed to the mantelpiece.

'Of course. Haven't you got one?'

'I didn't have much time when he died. I only have snapshots. And memories.'

Corinne handed her a large fiftieth birthday studio portrait of her father which had claimed pride of place on the mantelpiece. She and Yolande both had copies in their rooms. Toinette tucked the photograph under her arm and walked slowly to the door.

'Thank you very much, Corinne. Are you spending Christmas at St Xavier?'

'Yes.'

'I'm going to my brother's in Strasbourg. Perhaps I'll give you a call?'

She expected a definite answer. Corinne couldn't understand what was going on, or how the ground had shifted. They had met to discuss business. Toinette had bought Yolande's shares and refused to sell them back, yet somehow Corinne found herself comforting her and promising to accept a call at Christmas. It was crazy.

'Don't worry,' said Toinette, as they said goodbye. 'Your father wouldn't have let it get him down.' Then she leaned forward and kissed Corinne on both cheeks. 'Take care of yourself, darling. *Au revoir.*'

'I don't get it, Yves. What on earth is she playing at?'

He shrugged his shoulders. 'She absolutely refused to sell you the shares?'

'I don't think she can. It seems to me she was a very conveniently placed agent for someone else who targeted us for takeover some while ago and was on the lookout for an opening. Whoever it is also knows about Yolande's involvement with Patrick Dubuisson and this bloody film.'

Yves winced at Patrick's name. 'Someone in the States?'

'Has to be.'

They were in his office at the Château de Rochemort on a cold late November afternoon, a tray of coffee on the large, venerable walnut desk between them. It was their usual venue for business talks, where the atmosphere seemed to encourage constructive thinking. Like the whole château, Yves' office exuded an air of confident grandeur.

'We traced the parent company, by the way,' continued Corinne. 'It's a very elaborate set-up. It's registered in London, but that's only a decoy. I'm having it investigated at the moment to see if we can unmask the villain of the piece by Christmas.'

'Toinette must know.'

'She's not telling. I wish I knew what she really wants, then she'd help. But that's obviously part of her little game.'

Yves stuck his hands behind his head and stretched out his long legs. Stylishly cut jeans, a plain cashmere sweater – he was a living advert for Hervy's new menswear range, and Corinne thought he looked fabulous in it. How could Yolande have dumped him for a louse like Patrick Dubuisson?

'I should give it a rest until the New Year, Corinne. Whoever this predator is, he's obviously waiting for the share price to fall once takeover fever has died down. Nothing will happen for several weeks now.'

She smiled. 'Don't bank on that. I could do a deal with Toinette.'

'Is she ready for one?' he asked.

'I think so.'

'Just how much Marchand equity does UVS hold?'

'Well, twenty-seven per cent for a start. Plus Philippe's stake, unless it's been resold – thirty-five per cent. Even more if they've bought on the Bourse as well.'

'It doesn't look promising,' he said gloomily.

'No. Why don't we talk about something else? Wine, for example.'

'I suppose you want me to handle all the marketing for this year's vintage?'

'Could you, Yves? I know it's asking rather a lot, but I really have my hands full. You'll get the usual commission, of course.'

'What an easy way to earn money. It's been a fantastic year, one of the greats.'

'Mummy and Tex are coming over for Christmas, so it should be lively.'

'I know. Yolande told me.'

She stared at him in surprise. 'When?'

'I spoke to her on the phone – by chance – when she was just back from New York. She rang to tell my mother that she'd seen Philippe.'

'What!' Corinne nearly shot out of her seat. 'Philippe! How? Where?'

He poured her some more coffee, but as she picked up the cup her hand was shaking.

'He's living in New York. Yolande ran into him at the Hervy gala. He's homesick. She said he'd be in touch, but we've heard nothing.'

'I wondered why your mother keeps getting jumpy when the phone rings.' She sipped her coffee slowly, trying to keep her hand steady. How stupid to get worked up about Philippe after all this time. 'So you might have a reconciliation with your brother, and I've just fallen out with my sister. Must be karma or something.'

'Won't Yolande come home for Christmas?' he asked,

a shade more eagerly than he should now he was seeing the daughter of a marquis who lived near Beaune.

'I haven't heard from her since the beginning of the month, and quite honestly I hope I never hear from her again.'

'Corinne!'

She gave him a piercing look. 'I would have thought you'd be glad not to see her. Aren't you serious about Gabrielle d'Emville?'

He just shrugged his shoulders. 'How about coming to see our new puppies? Geraldine had a litter last week.'

Marius, who had been lying motionless at Corinne's feet, suddenly pricked up his ears. Geraldine was his mother. He stalked across to the door, wagging his tail. As they followed him out of the room, Yves admired his tactful way of putting an end to the conversation. It wouldn't do to be forced to admit that for all her faults he was as deeply in love with Yolande as ever – particularly now his mother was desperate to see him settle down and start a family. And if he couldn't have her, Gabrielle d'Emville, he supposed, would do as well as anyone else.

It was hardly the happy family Christmas Grace and Tex had planned. Of course they brought over a mound of presents to place around the large decorated tree in the salon at Le Manoir de St Xavier and were determined to be cheerful, but the festive spirit was lacking. Yolande's absence left a gaping chasm everywhere – no laughing, silly pranks, or sheer unbridled enthusiasm. She always loved Christmas and used to spread her joy around. It was a shock to realise how much they all missed her, but Corinne wouldn't admit it, even to herself.

Yves looked ill-at-ease when he appeared for dinner on Christmas Eve with Gabrielle clinging desperately to his arm. A slip of a girl, clearly out of her depth. Conversation flagged, so everyone drank more than was good for them and woke on Christmas Day with crashing headaches. Then it was time to visit the Château de Rochemort, where Marie-Christine did her best to liven things up. She and Grace had always got on well, and Tex's blunders in French helped create some much-needed mirth. At least Gabrielle found them funny. Barely turned eighteen, she was bearable if she kept her mouth shut. But she would keep talking, and her high-pitched voice and constant giggling so irritated Corinne that after lunch she left the others in the draughty drawing-room to take a stroll in the gardens with Marius.

It was much worse with her mother and Tex here. She felt she should be as lively as they were trying to be, despite the difficult circumstances. She wandered aimlessly where Marius led, eventually reaching the château's open gates. An Aston Martin was parked just beyond them, and in the driver's seat was Yolande. Corinne stopped dead.

As soon as she saw her sister, Yolande jumped out of the car and ran towards her. Corinne remained immobile as she was hugged and kissed.

'Darling, what's wrong? Haven't you forgiven me?'

'No.'

'Please, Corinne.'

Why did Yolande look so appealing, so much like the baby sister she had always loved? But it was different now. She was a woman, and she should have known what she was doing. Corinne pecked her cheek coldly, and looking downcast, Yolande let her go.

'I can explain everything. It was the time factor, you see. Otherwise Patrick would have lost the role.'

'I'd rather you didn't mention his name to me.'

Yolande bent down to make a fuss of Marius, who much to Corinne's disgust, seemed overjoyed to see her.

'What are you doing parked out there?'

'Well, I went home first, naturally. Françoise told me

126

you were all here. I just got cold feet when I reached the gates.'

'If you're worrying about Yves, don't,' said Corinne, as they started to walk back to the château. 'He's seeing Gabrielle d'Emville. I've had to put up with the stupid girl for the past two days.'

'Gabrielle! But she's so young.'

'He seems to prefer virgins. Or hadn't you noticed?'

Yolande shot her a reproachful look, and ramming her hands into the pockets of her thick navy jacket, marched on. 'Corinne, please listen. I know I should have explained it all to you before. I tried to call you in London again, but all I could get was voicemail. I was sure you'd be able to buy the shares back. After all it's only a holding company, and it's French.'

'You idiot!' Corinne stopped and faced her. 'You bloody idiot! I've had it all out with Toinette, and she's just an agent. UVS is foreign and hostile. Why didn't you wait for Georges to firm up our offer?'

'I had to have the money urgently. The film company would have been sold off otherwise and Pat ...' Yolande stopped herself just in time. 'I was offered a much better price than yours and immediate access to the capital. I was sure you'd be clever enough to sort it out afterwards.'

'Bollocks. All you were thinking about was jumping into bed with your precious Patrick.'

'Well I love him, so you'd better get used to him!'

'Yolande, if you think you'll ever get me to welcome Patrick after what he's done to my company, you must be mad.'

They didn't go straight back to the château, but turned off down a gravel path to the fountains, Yolande biting her tongue. She was no closer to Patrick now than she had been before the film.

'And where the hell have you been all these weeks?' demanded Corinne. 'If you were so sure you acted in good

127

faith, why did you run and hide?'

'I – I had to arrange the backing,' said Yolande, faltering a little. 'We went straight to London to finalise the deal with Vic Bernitz. He's producing and directing the film. Then we went skiing. I thought that everything would be settled by now.'

'Well it isn't – and you bloody well knew it wouldn't be. You didn't even have the guts to face the music, did you? Whatever's happened to you, Yolande?'

'Patrick.' She grasped Corinne's arm. 'Please, do try to understand. I *know* he's right for me. I had to choose between him – and all this.' She waved a hand at the château.

'You really are mad.'

'You're just sour and jealous because of losing Philippe. Oh God, I didn't mean that.'

'Go to hell!' Corinne ran ahead, trying to stop the tears.

'Corinne!' Yolande followed her and gripped her arm so tightly that they had to stop. 'Darling, I'm so sorry. It was wrong of me to say that. Please!'

'Just leave me alone!'

'He gave me a message for you.'

'I'm not the slightest bit interested in Philippe.'

'But he's got a child. That's why he left France.'

Corinne heard out the whole unedifying story in silence as they crunched over the gravel, and it made her feel even worse. It was just like Yolande to gloss everything over with emotion. She and Philippe were exactly the same – living at the expense of everyone else's feelings. Selfish and deceitful, dangerous and unreliable. She wished neither of them had been part of her life.

'Are you coming in?' she asked coldly when at last they reached the entrance to the château's west wing, where the family lived.

'Just to say hello.'

They went inside. A far from pleasant visit ensued,

during which Yolande tried to explain herself to her mother and avoid Yves' piercing looks. She drove off an hour later without even handing out the Christmas presents she had brought with her. Back to Patrick, back to love. It had been a mistake to try to put things right so soon. He had warned her against coming. She stopped off at the churchyard to lay flowers on her father's grave, then swept past her own home and headed for the A6. Thank God Patrick's mother was so understanding. Her Provençal villa was small but comfortable, and Yolande had been made very welcome. After the New Year they would fly out to California. Perhaps she would have to strike a deal with Corinne over Le Manoir and the apartment on the Avenue Foch, but that could be done through a lawyer, not face-to-face. And once her mother and Tex were back in New York, they could surely be won round.

Yolande comforted herself with this thought all the way down the autoroute, but that night she broke down sobbing in Patrick's arms.

'Yolande, don't let them ruin your life. You've got me.'

But how could he understand? She had alienated her whole family for him, and now the enormity of it all hit her, she felt more miserable than she had ever been in her entire life. From being everyone's favourite she had become an outcast overnight.

'I'll take care of you, Yolande.'

She had to believe him. There was no other choice now.

'It's for you.'

Corinne took the receiver from her mother without much enthusiasm. Since the row with Yolande on Christmas Day her mood had been even blacker. It was December 27th now, and they were packing to leave for England to spend the New Year with her grandparents.

129

'Corinne? Please don't hang up. It's Miles.'

'Hello,' she said, not unfriendly.

'I just rang on the off-chance that you wouldn't have some dragon there to cut me off. Happy Christmas.'

'Happy Christmas. How are you?'

'All right.' He sounded subdued. Obviously he hadn't enjoyed the festivities either.

'Where are you?' she asked.

'At my uncle's place near Salisbury. He's invited some horrendous females down for me to entertain.'

Corinne laughed for the first time in a week. 'I hope you're doing your duty.'

'I've been sneaking off to the pub. But they pursue me in full cry and drive out all the locals, so it's not made me too popular.' He paused and cleared his throat unnecessarily. 'Corinne, can we be friends again? Please. I miss you.'

'Yes.' It was so good to hear his voice. 'Oh yes, that would be great. I wanted to speak to you, actually.'

'About your sister selling out?'

'Yes. James Chetwode doesn't seem to appreciate how serious things are.'

'I've got some ideas. I called you when it happened, but your PA wouldn't put me through.'

'Well, I'll be in Dorset in two days' time. Will you still be at your uncle's? We could meet.'

'Terrific. Give me the number – or can we fix something now?'

They exchanged English addresses and found they would be staying within twenty miles of each other. A meeting was rapidly arranged for New Years' Eve, at the home of Corinne's grandparents, and Miles sounded noticeably more cheerful by the time he rang off. Corinne had a smile on her face for the first time in ages. She hadn't mentioned that the Alburys always held a big New Years' Eve party and that he could expect to dance rather than talk business. But then they could get down to hard work once they were back at their desks in Paris.

'Who was that?' asked her mother, alert to her change of mood. 'Are you sure he can withstand an Albury party?'

'Should be able to. He's ex-army and very fit. Miles Corsley – as in the bankers.'

'And?'

'He works in their Paris office.'

'And?' insisted Grace.

'We went out for a few weeks.'

'Oh.' There was a pause. 'He's got a nice voice,' said Grace at last. 'I'm sorry, darling, I've rather neglected you since this upset with Yolande. I suppose I should have known about Miles.'

'Well now you do,' replied Corinne.

'Do you fancy him?' asked her mother hopefully.

'I haven't got time for all that nonsense.'

'That means he fancies you.' Grace was warming to the idea of Miles Corsley. It was about time her eldest daughter got herself a new man.

'Mummy, shut up. I don't want to get involved. Miles is a good friend and I want it to stay that way.'

Grace was unconvinced. 'But when you and Philippe …'

'Why does everyone assume that my life must have ended because I broke up with Philippe?'

'Everyone?' said Grace, rather alarmed by Corinne's angry expression.

'Yes. I'm absolutely fed up with all this commiseration.'

'Marie-Christine told me this morning that she'd just had a call from him, and he's more or less threatening to come home.'

'I can take it.'

Corinne headed for the door to put an end to the conversation. She was still raw from Yolande's disclosures, still not sure whether her anger over Philippe's deceit outweighed the heartache of losing him. Still wondering if it had been some inadequacy on her part that had driven him into the arms of another woman. It would be interesting to see the reactions of Marie-Christine and her mother when they found out about his love-child. But he would probably be welcomed back to the fold with open arms. Philippe could get away with anything when he switched on the charm. How could he have had the gall to send her an apology through Yolande – three years too late?

'Corinne, don't go for a minute.'

'What is it now?' She returned to her chair in the dainty, very feminine salon, which had a fine painted ceiling framed by beautifully wrought cornices. The walls were host to eighteenth-century family portraits and Italian landscapes.

'It's Yolande. I know she's behaved very badly, and caused you a great deal of trouble.'

'If that were all.'

'Please, don't let it become a vendetta. You've every right to be angry – but do try to make it up with her soon. After all, she's your only sister.'

'Don't you mean she's already convinced you that she's acted perfectly within her rights and I'm the one being difficult?'

'No, I don't. She's been very stupid. But I don't think she *meant* to hurt you. It wasn't deliberate.'

'That's beside the point. She's damaged the company, not just me personally, and I'm still not certain I can put it right. How can I ever trust her again?'

Corinne stood up, not enjoying this discussion either.

'So you won't speak to Yolande again?'

'No.'

'What about all the property? Please, be reasonable.'

'That can all be arranged. I'll make sure I have a

binding legal contract this time.'

'Suppose she won't agree to sell you her share? And it's rather a lot of money ...'

'What's a few million between sisters? I've got a plan. Crédit St Honoré will probably give me a loan to settle the real estate. We'll just have to divide up the furniture and fittings.'

Grace was horrified. 'You wouldn't! But you'd ruin the whole character of the place! I never thought I'd hear you sound so hard, so bitter.'

Corinne turned on her heel, her eyes filling with tears. Grace watched her helplessly. 'Darling, what *is* wrong?'

'Papa's dead,' she said in a choked voice, then fled up to her room, almost colliding with Tex who was ambling downstairs. When he entered the salon he found his wife staring grim-faced out at the garden, so cold and bare in the pale winter sunlight. She ran across the room and flung her arms around his neck, then burst into tears.

'Oh, Tex. Everything's falling apart.'

'Don't be silly. It'll blow over. Calm down.'

He was so understanding, so kind. But Tex hardly ever quarrelled with anyone. He didn't realise that Grace had just relived years of her life she had thought entirely dead. Jean-Claude was everywhere. In his daughters, who resembled him far too much. In this house, which he had made so beautiful. In that small plot of earth in St Xavier churchyard, which seemed hardly big enough to contain his exuberant, vital personality. Grace could almost feel his presence in the room, a charming salon he had created specially for her on their marriage. Nothing had changed. But he was dead, their love had ended in bitterness, and their daughters were now enemies.

'Let's get out of here, Tex. Shall we go for a walk?'

'Anything you say.'

He put an arm around her waist and they wandered outside. She had forgotten to put on her coat, and soon began shivering.

'Do you know what, Grace? Next Christmas we're staying at home.'

Chapter Nine

Claire Garnier-Dumont zipped up her waterproof jacket and tied a silk scarf around her neck before climbing up on deck. Hervy, naturally. One could hardly go sailing off Monaco wearing a lesser label, and her husband, for all his fine rhetoric about social exclusion, was a terrible snob. The trouble was that Henri's short, ungainly figure didn't lend itself at all to the role to which he aspired. He was one of the least charismatic government ministers imaginable, but he displayed great political flair and had a certain crumpled charm – at least that's what people told Claire. She wondered which of these attributes had secured an invitation to spend this first weekend of January aboard the magnificent yacht of leading French industrialist Didier Lamarche.

'I'd much rather see my parents,' she had said when Didier rang unexpectedly just before Christmas. 'And what about Isabelle? She might not be up to it.'

Henri had been cross, as always when Isabelle's needs had to be considered. 'You can go to Le Mans afterwards. And Isabelle will be perfectly all right.'

End of conversation. The invitation was accepted, and the few days' rest Claire had promised herself after a claustrophobic Christmas with her in-laws in Picardy were devoted to grooming herself for Monaco. Not that she wasn't usually chic, but Henri had given her a large cheque for new clothes, so it was clear she was expected to impress.

Claire was utterly weary of playing his beautiful wife. Who was he trying to fool, anyway? Surely it was obvious that the heart had been ripped out of their marriage long ago. Now she had Isabelle she was even less interested in his career, his ambitions, and his friends. But Isabelle was the bond – or rather the weapon – which kept them together as a vote-winning double-act; adorable little Isabelle, who looked so much like her father Philippe de Rochemort. Although Claire had been very reluctant to go through with the pregnancy, given the circumstances, she now wondered how she had ever managed to live without her daughter.

Henri had hounded Philippe out of France, made divorce impossible, threatened to create a horrible scandal, so Claire had submitted to the marital charade and presented him with her lover's daughter. To give her husband his due, he didn't remind her of his magnanimity more than once a week; sometimes he even played with Isabelle, especially if there were photographers about. She would be another valuable asset in time, just like her mother.

'So you don't want to come sailing today, Claire?'

She was jolted out of her reverie. It didn't do to think too much about Philippe. Didier Lamarche sat beside her in the cockpit, dressed in well-worn yellow oilskins that contrasted embarrassingly with her pristine outfit. She felt like the *arriviste* she was, and wished herself back in her twenties, a pretty, unknown provincial research assistant, unencumbered by a husband with a position to maintain. Didier smiled reassuringly. He was a friendly man, and had the gift of making people feel at ease.

'I thought – if you really didn't mind – that Isabelle would enjoy a day ashore. She isn't a very good sailor, I'm afraid.'

'Nor are you,' he said.

Claire looked at him questioningly. With her small, delicate features and slender frame, she seemed lost, and entirely unconscious that her vulnerable beauty could fell a man in seconds. He admired her blue-green eyes – changeable, like the sea.

'Don't worry. I'll arrange everything with Henri. We'll be back about three this afternoon. If you like I'll book you a table for lunch at the Hôtel de Paris.'

'That's extremely kind of you.'

'Not at all.' He moved closer. 'Claire, I can't help noticing how unhappy you seem. I hope I haven't offended you?'

'Oh no, really. You've been so hospitable. So good with Isabelle.' She smiled. 'She likes being spoilt.'

'Well, I must say her father doesn't pay her nearly enough attention. Such a beautiful child, too. I wish I had a daughter even half as lovely.'

Claire felt uncomfortable. It was a perfectly innocent remark, he was just flattering her, appealing to her maternal pride. But he was too near the truth. She caught a rakish glow in his warm brown eyes, and moved away.

'I always wondered how Henri managed to marry someone like you,' said Didier.

'It was easy. He only required a mayor and a ring.'

'That sounds rather bitter.'

Claire shrugged her shoulders. 'I presume you married your wife the same way?'

He laughed. '*Touché*. All right, I give up. Shall I fetch Isabelle?'

There was no need. She had somehow scrambled up a companionway, and was treading purposefully towards them clutching her teddy bear.

'Darling, how did you get up here?' Claire scooped her up in her arms and kissed her.

'Sarah brought me. *And* James.'

Sarah was Isabelle's English nanny, and James, her equally English teddy, was a Christmas present from Sarah. He was already in danger of losing one eye. Isabelle showed him to Didier, giggling as he asked her questions about his age, and whether he spoke French yet, and if he liked sailing? Claire held her daughter close, laughing at her answers. She was so like Philippe, it hurt; his black hair, those deep-blue eyes, his smile, his charm. Philippe had adored the photograph of Isabelle that Claire had emailed to him in New York. Did he really love a child he hadn't even wanted, or was it just extended narcissism? She would never know. Henri made it impossible for Philippe to have any contact with his child.

Sarah appeared on deck, and ran forward to rescue James, who was now being dangled perilously over the back of the boat. Leaving Isabelle in her capable hands, Claire went below to change. Sarah beamed at Didier when she learnt they were to be spared another day's buffeting at sea. They started to chat about the yacht's name – *Vol-au-Vent* (Didier liked puns), but it began to rain, and, she scurried for shelter with Isabelle. Didier sighed. Not his lucky day. He too went below to talk to his skipper, who had planned a leisurely cruise along the coast. Now all the ladies were abandoning ship, the trip could be replaced with some speed trials. *Vol-au-Vent* had done extremely well in competition the previous year, and he was keen to race her at Cowes in the summer.

Claire wore a bright smile as she entered the cabin she shared with Henri and told him of the change of plan.

'Are you sure Didier doesn't mind?' he asked.

She quickly threw off her waterproofs and slipped out of her jeans and sweater. 'He's quite happy. You go ahead and enjoy yourself.'

He watched her coldly as she rifled through her clothes for a skirt and blouse. Her beauty had long ceased to arouse him, and she was acutely conscious of his lack of interest. She felt as inanimate and unappreciated as the paintings he had acquired for their Versailles home. But what else could she expect? He'd been too old when she married him, and even before her affair with Philippe they had seldom made love.

'Don't you like sailing?' he asked, as she buttoned up her blouse.

'You know I don't.'

'You could at least pretend to enjoy it – for my sake. Why are you always so hostile towards my friends?'

'Stop lecturing me, Henri. Didier has even booked us a table for lunch. And you'll be better off without us if you want to discuss anything important.'

'This was supposed to be a social occasion, Claire,' he said in his most pompous ministerial manner. 'You have no consideration for me whatsoever. It's hardly polite to snub someone like Didier Lamarche.'

She zipped up her skirt and thrust her arms into the sleeves of her jacket, gazing at him pityingly. 'Really, you're pathetic.'

'Claire!' He stepped forward angrily, his eyes bulging. He always looked ugly when he was cross. She shrugged her shoulders and sat down to powder her face. 'All you think of is yourself and that wretched child,' said Henri, pacing up and down. 'I've protected you, I prevented a scandal. You might at least have the decency to do as I ask now and then.'

'You prevented a scandal! You bastard! All you've done is make me unhappy. And how *dare* you insult my daughter?' Claire got to her feet, eyes blazing. 'She's already had a miserable time with your family at Christmas, and I suppose you'd like her to die of sickness on this stupid boat, wouldn't you? Well, I've had enough. I'm going to have a gorgeous day with Isabelle. We're going to lunch at the Hôtel de Paris and do a little shopping, and forget all about you for a few hours. Maybe you'll be in a better mood by the time you get back.'

She snatched up her coat and handbag and walked out of the cabin, trying to calm herself down before she had to face Didier again. Why did Henri always make her want to cry? She'd been happy for a few moments with Isabelle in her arms and the prospect of a day's freedom. Now he had spoilt it. He spoiled everything.

But he couldn't change her daughter. Back on deck with Isabelle, Claire was soon smiling again. Didier complimented her on her appearance and handed her an umbrella, then pushed some money into Isabelle's eager hand. 'Get yourself something pretty, *ma petite*. How about a little kiss?'

She kissed his cheek enthusiastically, far more enthusiastically than she did Henri's when he suddenly stumbled up towards them, anxious to convince Didier that he was on excellent terms with his wife and child. Claire was silent as Henri brushed his lips against hers and playfully patted Isabelle's face. 'Have a wonderful time, darling,' he said.

'You too, Henri. Isabelle, say bye-bye to Papa.'

'Bye,' was her only response. She turned her head as he kissed her, holding up the teddy bear. 'Kiss James.'

Smiling, Henri obeyed, to Didier's evident amusement. Claire felt that he guessed far too much of the real state of affairs, and was relieved to be going ashore. The charade complete, she and Isabelle were followed down the gangway by Sarah, and not long afterwards *Vol-au-Vent* cast off and was being steered out of the harbour. They waved from the quay until the figures on deck were mere blobs, then set off to enjoy themselves.

Sarah appreciated the free time, and Claire was happy just being away from Henri and at liberty to spoil her daughter, wandering in and out of the shops, acquiring ever more toys for a delighted Isabelle. She hadn't felt so relaxed for months. Sarah joined them for lunch, a lingering affair which Isabelle enjoyed to the full. She seemed decidedly smitten with the young waiter, insisting that he have some of the sweets she had bought with Didier's present. As there was an admiring audience, she redoubled her efforts to gain his undivided attention. Yes, she was certainly like Philippe.

They were eating dessert when Claire felt a sudden hush descend. The hotel manager had entered the restaurant, and was conferring in a low voice with the *maitre d'*. After a few moments he made his way swiftly to their table.

'Madame Garnier-Dumont? Could you please come to my office to answer the telephone?'

She stared at him, automatically stretching out a hand to prevent Isabelle from tipping cream onto the table cloth.

The manager looked solemn. 'It's urgent, madame.'

Claire rose from the table and followed him. The call was from the police commissioner in Nice. It was with extreme regret that he had to report that *monsieur le ministre* her husband had drowned at 2 p.m. after being knocked unconscious into the sea by the boom of the yacht *Vol-au-Vent*. Death must have been almost instantaneous, since his body had been recovered within minutes by the *Vol-au-Vent*'s crew, who had radioed immediately for assistance. Helicopters were on the scene, and the deputy commissioner was already on his way to the Hôtel de Paris and could give her further details as information came in.

'May I express my deepest condolences, madame, on this sad loss – not only for you and your daughter, but for the whole of France. Madame? Madame?'

The receiver crashed to the floor. Claire had fainted.

Philippe collapsed onto the king-size bed in his 30th floor Manhattan apartment and loosened his tie. It had been an unusually tiring day. After a few minutes' relaxation and a cigarette he began to feel human again. He'd skipped the trauma of after-work karaoke with colleagues for a little peace and quiet. Must be getting old. Could probably have got laid too – there was a blonde from marketing whose chat-up lines had been getting more explicit every week.

But Philippe longed for a French meal and a conversation about the latest French books and films, anything which took his thoughts from this eternal wheeling and dealing. He made himself some coffee and ripped open the copy of *Le Monde* he had grabbed from his pigeonhole as he left the office.

Henri Garnier-Dumont drowned off Monaco: The president mourns the tragic death of his trusted ally

Oh God. Claire. Claire and Isabelle. He rifled through his address book for Claire's mobile number, which he'd purposely not stored on his own phone lest he'd been tempted to call or text her. He knew her phone was tapped, but he couldn't think who would be at all interested in her love affairs now. He quickly punched in her number.

She sounded overwhelmed to hear him after such a long time. 'Philippe! Is it really you? I never thought I'd speak to you again.'

'Are you all right? Is Isabelle safe? What happened?'

She managed to give him an account of the accident, details having been sketchy in the paper. Henri had apparently ignored instructions to remain seated in the cockpit, and in moving forward on the deck he'd been caught by the boom as it swung round when they tacked, instantly fracturing his skull as it pitched him into the sea. Conditions had been squally. He was dead by the time the crew hauled him back on board.

'Thank God you were ashore,' said Philippe feelingly. 'Isabelle's all right, then?'

'She doesn't really understand what's happened, and I suppose that's for the best. I want her to meet you.'

'I'm just as keen to meet her. But it will be rather awkward at the moment.'

'The funeral's next Tuesday. The president's attending. All the publicity – I don't know how to face it. I need you.' She paused, hoping he would respond. 'Philippe, I love you.'

142

Silence.

'Do you – have you found someone else?'

'No.'

Well, it wasn't exactly true. He had been planning to marry Corinne, and he didn't even count his transient American girlfriends.

'Don't you think we should discuss this when we meet? Listen, darling, I'm going to come home. But I have some business deals to tie up first. I'll see you when everything's fixed.'

'But I was hoping you'd come soon.'

'Claire, be sensible. It won't do you or Isabelle any good at all if I appear now. You're in the media spotlight, and I want to see you privately. It will be soon, but not just yet.'

'I see.' She sounded unconvinced.

'Henri won't be able to spy on your emails now, will he?' he asked, trying to cheer her up. 'I'll write as often as I can. And we can talk anytime.'

It was more than she had dared hope for. He had to be serious, he must want to see her. And once he had held Isabelle in his arms she was sure – as sure as she could be of anything in her present uncertainty – that he would stay.

After she rang off, Philippe drained his coffee and gazed at Isabelle's picture on the wall. He'd had the snapshot blown up into a poster. He hadn't told Yolande that. He hadn't told her how homesick he was, how much he missed his family and all the things he had taken for granted when he was in France. Now he could go back and they were his for the asking. So was Claire; sweet, graceful, forgiving Claire, whom he had ill-treated the most. He didn't know if he was man enough to accept her love. What could he offer her in return? His heart? Surely not. Most women he slept with concluded that he didn't possess so vulnerable an organ, and on reflection he was inclined to agree. But when he looked at the smiling face of his daughter, something stirred. When he thought of his mother, he had sharp twinges of shame and regret. When he thought of Corinne – but he made a point never to think of her. Their love, so unexpected, so brief, so intense, could have no place in the superficial cocoon he had woven for himself over the past three years.

His next call was to Rochemort. His mother was ecstatic when he announced that he would be coming home. Philippe received an express package from her later that week, containing a silver St Christopher with the Rochemort arms engraved on the reverse. The prodigal son was forgiven.

To her surprise, Corinne returned to Paris in early January in a reasonably cheerful frame of mind. The New Year wasn't the disaster she had feared, though the weather in Dorset was foul. But her grandparents were, as usual, unfailingly good-humoured, and with the house full of uncles, aunts, and cousins she hadn't seen for some time, the atmosphere defied gloom. Everyone ignored the fact that Yolande should have been there. Lady Albury actually seemed relieved by her favourite granddaughter's absence. The long stay with Patrick over the summer had temporarily dampened her enthusiasm for Yolande.

Miles turned up on New Year's Eve with a breezy smile and some papers he intended to discuss with Corinne, but was immediately pounced on as good party material. Sir John Albury had been stationed with Miles' father in Germany, and treated him to some hair-raising army stories, whilst Tex had a few questions on banking issues. Corinne's teenage cousins, Fiona and Annabel, then hauled him off with knowing smiles and wicked giggles.

'Corinne, you must kiss him,' insisted Grace.

'Mummy, don't be mean,' laughed Corinne as she was propelled towards the library, where Miles had been manoeuvred into an inescapable trap under the mistletoe.

'I didn't invite him here to be assaulted.'

'Oh, I rather think he's enjoying it.'

'Absolutely,' agreed Fiona, keeping him firmly in place as Grace had instructed.

He was laughing, but he looked embarrassed as Corinne drew near. She tried to joke it all off. 'Perhaps I should have warned you that we have a female hit squad here too.'

'But they kiss much better than they do at my uncle's,' he said. 'Now girls, why don't you beat it so I can be seduced in style?'

Protesting loudly, they were hustled out of the room by Grace, who closed the door as she left with a wink. As soon as they had the library to themselves, Miles moved away from the mistletoe. Corinne retreated to a window seat flanked on either side by huge bookcases, their shelves crammed with volumes old and new. Jane Austen was just as likely to be found next to the latest thriller and Wisden. It was an elegant room rich in oak, with extensive views over the gardens. She stared out, suddenly feeling rather foolish.

'This is a lovely house,' said Miles, joining her. 'Late Georgian?'

She faced him, trying to regain her confidence. '1770, actually, designed by Robert Adam. Of course, we've not had it that long. The first Baronet Albury bought it in the nineteenth century. He had a smaller place down on the coast before.'

'How did he get the title?'

'Nothing glamorous, I'm afraid. We didn't get round to fighting until the Boer War. I think he helped with some loan for the Crimean campaign.'

'So you have banking connections too?' he asked. 'It's uncanny, really. We're linked in so many ways; finance, the army, same part of England. And yet we wouldn't have met if I hadn't been seconded to Paris.'

Corinne smiled. It was a train of thought that would definitely appeal to her mother, who had obviously been matchmaking since his arrival.

'It's so good to see you again,' said Miles, wanting to edge closer, but resolutely sitting two feet from her. 'I've missed you, Corinne. You were right – about being friends, and all that. I was completely out of order and I'm sorry. I've brought some stuff over if you want to talk business.'

Corinne stood up, disappointed that it had come to this. Just business. Before they used to have fun, they used to talk about so many different things. Now there was a barrier, and she felt it within herself.

'I don't think we'll have much time for that, Miles. Lunch is any minute now, then some neighbours will come over. And tonight you'll be danced off your feet if Fiona and Annabel have any say in the matter. Not to mention my grandmother.'

'And you?' he queried, also rising.

'Oh, I can dance too, you know.'

'Save me a slow one?'

'All right. We can talk shop when we get back to Paris.'

'So you'll come out with me again?'

Corinne took his hand and drew him back under the mistletoe. 'Yes,' she said, putting her arms around his neck. 'I'd love to. Now, if you don't want your reputation shredded, you'd better pay your dues. They're probably looking through the keyhole.'

His lips were cautious at first, his arms hanging free, but as her mouth responded to his, he clasped her waist. Her lips parted and she took his tongue in, teased and caressed it, made love to him with her mouth. Again. Blood and sense drained from his head, straight to his groin. Did she have any idea of what she was doing to him? Her kiss was as lethal as it had been before. His

146

desire was as strong. But his love was stronger. He pulled her body tight against his and felt the tandem thumping of their hearts. A perfect fit. When their lips parted they remained locked together, Corinne's head against his shoulder, her fingers playing idly with his hair.

'That wasn't too painful, was it?' he murmured.

It was so good to be in his arms again. Her legs were a little shaky, her breathing rather too fast, but she wasn't afraid this time and she didn't want to run. No threat now, no convenient bed for casual copulation; just a warm, loving embrace which she enjoyed without reservation. She sighed and nibbled under his jaw. Miles felt her relax and turned up her face.

'We've missed an awful lot of kissing since October – which is a tragedy, since you are spectacularly good at it.'

'It's not the kissing I mind.'

It was the way she said it. At once he knew there was someone else. Someone who had really messed her up and smashed her heart. He wanted to tell her how he felt, but it wasn't the right moment. She would have to learn to trust him completely first.

He kissed her again, tenderly, then loosened his arms and smiled. 'Didn't you say something about lunch?'

The rest of Miles' visit passed off as well as it had begun, and he was certainly high in Grace's favour by the time he returned home. Corinne, however, eluded all her mother's queries and meaningful suggestions, saying goodbye to her and Tex at Heathrow after the holiday without revealing anything of her plans – business or emotional. She returned to Paris an hour after their departure for New York.

Paris was cold and the atmosphere sluggish. There were no communications from potential bidders for Marchand Enterprises, no sign in fact that anyone was interested in acquiring the company. Yves was right. Whoever had fuelled takeover speculation when Yolande sold out was obviously prepared to play a waiting game. Corinne had nevertheless devised her own strategy, of which Georges Maury greatly approved. He also approved of Miles' report on the affair, which she presented to him as soon as she got back to her office on the Avenue Montaigne. It identified the likeliest predators and outlined a takeover defence – demerging and de-listing the group – which Corsley European would, of course, be only too pleased to handle.

'This is good, Corinne, very good,' said Georges, as he cast his eye over the report's conclusion. 'He's clearly done his research. But we can't afford it.'

'I know. And it would weaken our control over the business.'

'Really, it's a banker's dream. Think of all the money he'd make if we let him put this plan into operation.'

'Think of what we might lose if we don't.'

He took off his glasses and rubbed his eyes. 'Are you seriously considering this option, Corinne?'

'Not yet. It depends on Toinette. We spoke at Christmas and I've fixed a meeting for next week.'

'Shall I come?'

Corinne grimaced. 'I'd rather you didn't, Georges. It's going to be a very emotional chat.'

'I see.' He looked thoughtful. 'So you're going to appeal to her love for Jean-Claude? But she's sure to want something solid in return.'

'I've thought of that. Just leave it to me. Everything will be all right.'

'I hope so. Perhaps you understand her better than I do. But if you do succeed in acquiring her stake in UVS, what then? There will still be trouble.'

'That's why I'm having lunch with Miles Corsley today. I rather think that whatever happens, he could be very helpful.'

She sounded so like Jean-Claude, Georges thought it

was uncanny.

'By the way,' he said as she was turning away. 'About Yolande.'

She jerked her head round sharply. 'What about her?'

'Is she really going to sell her share of the apartment and St Xavier? Yves mentioned it to me.'

'I've had a letter from her lawyers. But she's stated conditions. She's only selling her share of Le Manoir, not the vineyards. And she wants all the pictures and furniture valued independently, so that when she comes over they can be divided up fairly.'

Georges shook his head. 'I don't like it, Corinne. You two shouldn't be speaking to each other through lawyers.'

'That's how she wants it,' she said coldly.

'Don't you mean that's how Patrick Dubuisson wants it? You're just playing into his hands. He's cut Yolande off from her family. Now he's got her completely under his spell. Quite frankly, I'm deeply concerned about her. Can't you stop this feud before it really damages you both? I hate to see it continuing.'

Corinne had a momentary twinge of conscience. Georges had watched them grow up, when they had been their father's joy and devoted to each other. Yolande had been very much everyone's baby, and easy to get along with until she met Patrick, even though she had always been volatile. But what she had done was unforgivable.

'Please don't tell me how to conduct my personal affairs,' she snapped.

'All right, all right.' He waved his hands despairingly. 'Have it your own way. But I'm quite sure if your father were alive it would break his heart.'

Corinne left the office. He would have to mention Papa and make her feel bad about it all. When Miles met her for lunch she looked as though she'd been crying, and it took her several minutes to persuade him that he was not the cause.

149

Chapter Ten

An agreement was struck between Corinne and Toinette on a cold mid-January evening at the Avenue Foch. Toinette sold her holdings in Marchand and UVS to Corinne at a discount, in return for a generously salaried directorship at Marchand and a free lifetime tenancy of the splendid apartment. Georges was baffled when he heard the details, but both women got what they wanted. Corinne made a leap forward in regaining control of her company and Toinette was fully reinstated into the life and perks that Jean-Claude's death had abruptly terminated. All in all, Corinne thought it a very satisfactory deal.

Toinette smiled rather sadly as they toasted their new *glasnost* over a glass of champagne. 'You remind me so much of your father.'

'Papa usually got what he wanted. I'm only just beginning to learn how he managed it.'

'I'm sorry for the way things have been between us. We should have talked more.'

'I didn't understand. You see, I never realised ...' Corinne broke off, embarrassed.

'You never thought I really loved him, did you?'

'No. I'm sorry.'

'You don't have to apologise. I must take some of the blame. I never felt obliged to convince you or Yolande, only your father. You were away so much, and when you were home I sensed the hostility. I never tried to overcome it, so we never got to know each other properly. That was my big mistake.'

'Why didn't you take more time to sort things out after Papa died?'

'Have you forgotten the packing cases you sent me so soon afterwards?'

Corinne lowered her eyes, ashamed. But Toinette was determined to let bygones be bygones, and was anxious to catch up with all the family news.

'So Yolande's actually living with Patrick now?'

'As far as I know they're both in California prepping for this film,' said Corinne.

'I'm afraid she's going to get badly hurt. I thought it was a harmless infatuation and she'd still marry Yves. How is he, by the way?

'He's trying to fall in love with Gabrielle d'Emville.'

'Oh dear.'

'Quite. But you know Marie-Christine is desperate to see him settled. He'll probably marry Gabrielle just to please her.'

Toinette raised her eyebrows expressively. 'And what about you?'

'Oh, I'm fine. Well, I will be once I've got the company straightened out.'

'No boyfriend?'

'No.'

'You really will have to put that affair with Philippe behind you one day.'

Corinne looked surprised.

'So you think I didn't know how serious it was?' continued Toinette. 'You kept everything to yourself, but I saw the pain. I don't know if your father realised quite how badly it hit you – he was too busy trying to deal with the business fallout.'

'But I'm over it!' said Corinne defiantly. 'Philippe means nothing to me now.'

'There you are, on the defensive at once! You see, he's still there – like a ghost. Exorcise him, Corinne. Why let him ruin the rest of your life? I was besieged by men at parties here asking to be introduced to you. And you didn't even know they were alive.'

Corinne was silent, thinking of Miles. Strange that Toinette had put it like that. She was absolutely right. Philippe's shadow hung over her all the time. He'd satisfied desires and needs she'd only tentatively explored before they got together, then made her hate herself for letting him use her, afraid of intimacy in case it wounded her again. But Miles had somehow wormed his way through her layers of armour, gained her trust. Perhaps he could help her with an exorcism.

'What's this?' asked Toinette, picking up a folder from the coffee-table. 'Corsley European? They're British, aren't they?' She flicked over a few pages of Miles' report. 'Hmmm … a takeover defence. My God, you couldn't possibly afford this!' She put the folder down, feeling guilty. 'I'm sorry, darling. I've put you in a terrible position.'

'It won't be now we've reached an agreement. But I'd like to know something – did Yolande tell you *why* she was selling her stake in Marchand?'

'Of course not. Otherwise I would have done everything to stop her. I was simply instructed to buy her shares for UVS. Yolande only wanted to know how quickly she could have the money.'

'Who instructed you?'

'Count Ulrich von Stessenberg. He's based in New York.'

'UVS,' said Corinne, as it dawned on her. 'That simple and we didn't pick it up. Christ.'

'I should have told you before Christmas.'

'But you wanted this deal?'

'Yes,' replied Toinette, 'very much. I wonder if you can ever really forgive me, but we must try to make things work.'

Corinne inwardly cursed her own blindness. A little more subtlety, a little more of her father's intuition, and

153

she could now be the outright owner of Marchand Enterprises instead of having to defend it from takeover.

'I'll tell you what I know,' continued Toinette. 'Count Ulrich von Stessenberg – I'd take the title with a pinch of salt, because it's not in the *Almanach de Gotha* – is either German or Austrian, though he's got American citizenship and he claims to have been brought up in Switzerland. But his accent isn't quite right. Anyway, he's got money. Lots of it. I was introduced to him by Laurent Dobry about six years ago. Stessenberg was in Paris looking for a base for a new holding company.'

'UVS.'

'Exactly. I helped him find some offices off the Champs Elysées, then out of the blue a couple of years later he offered me a thirty per cent stake in the company. I had the money and the shares were discounted. It was a very good investment. All I had to do was provide a presence for the firm in Paris.'

'What about the other seventy per cent?'

'It's held by two other companies – one Swiss, one British.'

'But he actually owns both, doesn't he?'

'Yes.'

'Now I get the picture. We tracked down the British firm, then came up against a brick wall. And you received orders directly from Stessenberg?'

'He would telephone when something important was moving on the Bourse and he wanted a slice of the action, but day to day business he left to his office in New York. It's not a hectic operation. He goes in for a few big deals – perhaps only five or six a year. He waits until he owns, say twenty to thirty per cent of a company, then he sells to the highest bidder.'

Corinne frowned. 'I see. He doesn't sound like he would be interested in taking over Marchand, so why won't he sell Yolande's stake back to me?'

Toinette shrugged her shoulders. 'I've contacted the New York office, but he's abroad and they have no authority to sell. Apparently he takes a keen personal interest in this particular deal. Now you've become his partner in UVS, put an offer to him directly. You can actually veto the sale of the Marchand shares, but then Stessenberg would probably force you out of UVS. The partnership is weighted very much in his favour. He can buy you out with three months' notice.'

Corinne sipped her drink thoughtfully. She had a feeling that Ulrich von Stessenberg's chain of companies led somewhere unknown to her, Toinette, or anyone else in Paris.

'I've got a question, Corinne.'

'Hmm?'

'About this salary – it's rather a lot of money just for attending a few board meetings.'

'Is that a problem?'

'I thought perhaps I could do a little to earn it. You really ought to adopt your father's views on corporate hospitality.'

Corinne had to concede that she was right. Jean-Claude Marchand had made many useful contacts through Toinette's skills as a hostess. If she wanted to start her famous corporate receptions and events up again, why not? It would keep her occupied and allow Corinne to get on with the nuts and bolts of business.

When Toinette had gone, Corinne cast an eye over Miles' report. None of the companies he suggested as possible predators now seemed to fit. There had to be someone else; someone who had engineered everything with Stessenberg's co-operation, possibly someone even involved in persuading Yolande to back Patrick's film. It was clear that UVS wouldn't sell the Marchand shares back to her because they were already earmarked for another buyer.

She called Miles and arranged lunch the following day to discuss the affair. He sounded delighted by her initiative, and that set off ideas and emotions that troubled her. She stretched out on the sofa with a copy of *Paris Match* to divert her thoughts, but there wasn't much in it; opinion polls, interviews with celebrities who didn't interest her, and a long illustrated report on the funeral of Henri Garnier-Dumont, a government minister her father had detested. She tossed the magazine aside, yawning. It had been another exhausting day, and she had been sleeping badly of late.

The telephone rang. Groaning, Corinne got up to answer it. Yves was on the line, sounding livelier than usual.

'How did it go with Toinette?' he asked.

'Really well. I've bought her out.'

'Fantastic!'

They discussed the pros and cons, then he casually mentioned that his mother had had another call from Philippe.

'What is it this time?' Corinne asked laconically. Philippe's long-distance eruptions into her life were becoming tedious.

'He's coming home. For good.'

'For good?'

'Yes. In a few weeks' time.'

'I see.'

'Apparently something has changed, some unforeseen circumstance,' continued Yves. 'It sounds mysterious, but he's promised to tell us everything when he gets here. I'll give you due warning if you want to avoid him.'

'OK.'

She finished the conversation hurriedly, her mind racing ahead. Yves didn't know about Philippe's daughter, he hadn't heard that rigmarole from Yolande at Christmas. But what was it she had said? An affair with the wife of a senior government minister, threatened arrest for tax fraud – and now, three and a half years later, it had all suddenly changed. Corinne rushed back to the sofa and seized the copy of *Paris Match*, tearing through the pages for the article on the Garnier-Dumont funeral. A picture of the president and cabinet ministers; Garnier-Dumont's brothers, sombre bourgeois in sombre suits; then the one she was looking for – the widow, Claire Garnier-Dumont, with the minister's young daughter, Isabelle. Corinne almost dropped the magazine. It was unmistakably Philippe's child. The resemblance was so strong; black hair, those vivid blue eyes, an alert, intelligent face. She even detected a turn of the head very similar to Marie-Christine's. A beautiful little girl. His daughter. *His* daughter.

She read the article quickly, skipping the paragraphs on Garnier-Dumont's political career for details of his death and his family. Philippe's decision to return to France must have been taken as soon as he heard of that fatal accident on *Vol-au-Vent* – from Garnier-Dumont's wife? Or the press? Corinne learned that Claire was thirty-three, had married Henri Garnier-Dumont when she was twenty-four, and gave birth to Isabelle three years ago. The probable date of conception only confirmed her worst fears. Philippe had been sleeping with them both at the same time. So that was all it was for him, all it had ever been. She knew that now. And yet she was still alive, still breathing. She wasn't going to throw herself off a balcony or go into a decline. In fact she was itching to punch his duplicitous jaw. Kick him where it would hurt, too. The bastard. He'd said he loved her, wanted to live with her, but it was just sex after all. How the hell had she let him mess her mind up for so long with plain old-fashioned sex?

Then the tears came. Long overdue tears, which she had never allowed herself to shed before. All illusions, all hope gone. The love she thought she could never recover from turned out not to have been love at all. She wasn't crying for the man she had adored, because in reality he had never existed; but for the woman she had once been, with a whole and loving heart and faith in happy-ever-after. Corinne sobbed until she was spent. And then, to her great surprise, came relief. Thank God she hadn't married him. Thank God. She had escaped. With a battered heart, true, but one that was free at last. He could never hurt her again.

'What are you up to, Miles?' Rupert Corsley stared uncompromisingly at his nephew, sitting on the other side of his desk in a plush penthouse office in Corsley European's headquarters on London Wall. 'I suppose it's something to do with that damned Frenchwoman you were sniffing about last year?'

'It is, actually. And don't insult her. Apart from being my friend and your client, she's John Albury's grand-daughter.'

'Well why didn't you tell me before? I'd have been a bit more polite when you rang with all that nonsense about pseudo Counts and the *Almanach de Gotha*. Albury's grand-daughter? Hmm, now I remember. His eldest daughter married a Frog. Ghastly chap. Ended in divorce.' He noticed Miles' chilly expression. 'Now what's wrong? You're not in love with her, are you? I thought she couldn't stand the sight of you – that's why Chetwode's handling the Marchand account.'

'Not any more. She asked me back.'

Rupert's resolute jaw dropped slightly. 'You sly bugger,' he said at last. 'I thought she was just a passing fancy. Everybody has one in Paris.'

'I'm sure Aunt Alice would like to know who yours is.'

'Now look here …'

Miles laughed at last, and his uncle stopped abruptly,

straightened his tie, and smoothed his iron grey hair. Though not conventionally handsome, he had an imposing air and looked more than capable of a Parisian fling.

'All right, let's get down to business. What exactly does your friend Corinne want to know?'

'She's bought a thirty per cent stake in a private equity firm called UVS, which owns thirty-five per cent of Marchand Enterprises. The head of UVS is refusing to sell his Marchand holding to her at any price. He calls himself a count, but he's not listed in any armorial directories. I'm looking for leverage on him to force a sale.'

'You mean you want some dirt?'

'The truth would probably do, Rupert. I'm sure he's a nefarious character.' Miles handed over a thick file containing all the information he had so far been able to gather on Ulrich von Stessenberg. Rupert put on his glasses and flicked through it.

'Well, he's got enough companies here to start his own exchange. I see the type. An opportunist stake-builder for corporate American raids?'

'Exactly.'

'Can he sell these Marchand shares to anyone else?'

'Not without Corinne's agreement now she's his partner in UVS. But he can force her out. She's not got much time.'

'I see. Ulrich von Stessenberg – what's his nationality?'

'Ostensibly American.'

'Ostensibly?' Rupert took off his glasses and gave Miles a querying look.

'It doesn't match his accent. I did speak to him on the phone to try to negotiate a deal over the Marchand shares, and he's definitely not a home-grown Yank. If you could find out his roots, I might be able to remind him of that dirty little bar he used to run as a drug store in Berlin – or whatever.'

'I must say, you have a vivid imagination.'

'Creative thinking. Isn't that what you prize in the bank's staff?'

'My dear Miles, I only look for staff who will help me run an efficient and profitable operation.' Rupert closed the file. 'Quite frankly, this doesn't look like one.'

'But there would be a good commission. However, if you won't help,' Miles took the file and stood up, trying to hide his disappointment, 'I'll have to look elsewhere. It's just that I've drawn a blank in Paris.'

'Frankfurt?'

'I've got Peter Muller onto it there, but he's found nothing, except that there's no such title as Count von Stessenberg.'

Rupert motioned Miles to sit down again. 'I see you're eating your heart out. Is she a looker?'

'Tell me what you think.' Miles showed him a photo he'd taken of Corinne on his mobile phone on New Year's Eve.

Rupert whistled. 'I see now why you froze out poor Olivia Denderby at Christmas. Your aunt's not too pleased about that, you know. What does she think of you?'

'She likes me. I came on a bit strong and she backed right off for a while. But we're moving forwards again now.'

Rupert picked up the file and looked through it slowly, then leaned back in his black leather chair. 'Perhaps I could help,' he said eventually. 'But I refuse to get personally involved in the deal. That's your job. Just make sure it pays, Miles. This is a bank, not a dating agency. I know you're my nephew and she's a beautiful girl, but don't think for a moment that I approve of conducting business affairs for anything other than profit. If there is an emotional dividend as well, I wish you luck.'

Miles tried not to smile.

'I have friends who could very well find the information you're looking for,' Rupert continued, swivelling his chair so that he was facing the window. 'It's delicate and possibly bends the Official Secrets Act, but I'll try my best. Naturally, I'd send anything to your apartment, not to the bank. Do what you can with it, and forget this conversation as soon as you leave the room. Do I make myself clear?'

'Yes, uncle.'

'How much time have you got?'

'Corinne will be forced to sell her UVS holding to him at the end of March.'

'Eight weeks. Well, it's not impossible. Now, to hard cash. How much did we make on the Masson takeover?'

They remained in discussion for some while. By the time Miles boarded his return Eurostar to Paris he felt confident that he would get the breakthrough he needed on Ulrich von Stessenberg. Rupert Corsley had been an officer in British intelligence for many years. His friends were well-positioned to make some discreet enquiries.

'Just what the hell is Rikki playing at, Althea? He's had those shares for months now. The whole deal's set up. Why won't he finalise? We were supposed to put in a bid for Marchand at the end of January.'

Hank Pedersen did not look relaxed, though he was meant to be unwinding in the comfort of his Malibu home. A mid-February weekend away from New York – time to be with his wife and forget Pedersen Corp's global strategy. But he was tense, irritable, and driving Althea mad.

'Sit down, Hank. Can't you just forget it for a day?'

He sat in a wickerwork armchair by the French windows, and gazed out at the garden. 'It's just that I've allocated the funds for the deal. The longer he takes, the more it costs. I hope he's on the level.'

'He's had a few hitches. Marchand's president has acquired thirty per cent of the company holding the shares.

He's going to freeze her out by Easter.'

'She's the sister of that Yolande you had here with Vic Bernitz and his crew yesterday, right?'

'Yes.'

'Let's hope she's as stupid as Yolande.'

'You're not very complimentary about my guests.'

'But she can't be switched on, honey. Sinking her fortune in a movie, and all because of some low-life like Dubuisson. What the hell does everybody see in him?' Hank was genuinely puzzled. 'He's a third-class jerk.'

Althea drew back. 'If it weren't for him, we'd have no deal with Rikki.' She sat down opposite him.

'But what does Vic see in him? Couldn't he have gotten Brett Gallway for the part?'

'The story required a European with sex appeal. Someone new. Dubuisson's got what it takes.'

'Yeah, hasn't he?' said Hank sarcastically. 'The guy had his lecherous eyes on every woman in the room. Yolande must be blind as well as dumb.'

'I'm surprised you noticed it,' remarked Althea, too pointedly for comfort.

He was silent for a while. 'Didn't you enjoy last night?' he asked at last.

'It would have been better if you'd taken the phone off the hook,'

'But honey, how did I know Carson was going to call? I'm sorry.'

He sounded really contrite, and she smiled encouragingly. 'I'm cutting the wire tonight. You never know, it might work. Dr Sidakis thinks we have a good chance if we keep to his regime for a few months more. I knew there wasn't anything physically wrong with you. Just too much work.'

'Come here.' He stretched out his arms, and she perched on his lap, tousling his hair as he kissed her neck and face. It was an improvement, but where was the zest?

162

He wasn't an incompetent lover, either, when he could make the effort; but with Hank, money still came before his wife. Althea knew it, too. It didn't help.

'I do want kids, honey,' he murmured. 'I want you to have them. It'll work out. Just be patient.'

'Do you have to go away for so long in May?' she asked. 'Can't I come?'

'Well, you could – but it wouldn't be much fun. Just shopping and the hotel while I'm in meetings. It's important, or I'd put it on hold. But we've got to look hard at our Pacific operations with all the change going on in China. Come along if you want. Althea?'

She slid off his lap, and was busily arranging some flowers in a vase to conceal her disappointment. He would never change. Still planning ahead, still wrapped up in business.

'I'd just be in your way.' She faced him. 'You go. I'll be OK.'

He seemed satisfied. Their lovemaking that night was uninterrupted, but somewhat lacking in energy. Hank flew back to New York the following morning. Althea decided to stay a little longer in California and watch Vic Bernitz making a movie. *Fast and Loose* had just started shooting, and the LA press was eager to get in on the action. A movie financed by a stunning Frenchwoman, starring her lover opposite Hollywood's own sex-symbol Jayne Herford – it was a paparazzi dream. Everybody was waiting for the inevitable fireworks. Althea felt it her social duty to pick up some gossip first hand before she returned to Manhattan. Vic had invited her to drop in at the studios anytime. It was an opportunity not to be missed, particularly as there might well have been no film if she hadn't found Patrick in Paris. It was all down to her. He had told her so himself, and she couldn't help noticing the glow in his eyes when he expressed his gratitude.

Yolande left her mobile phone on the bed, frowning, then wandered back into the lounge of the apartment she and Patrick were sharing in Beverley Hills. He was stretched out on the leather sofa, perusing the film script.

'Who was it?'

'Philippe de Rochemort.'

'Oh.' Patrick put down the script and sat up, making room for her beside him. 'What did he want?'

'He's going back to France soon. He wanted to know if I had any messages.'

Yolande brushed her eyes with the back of her hand, but if she was crying, she was trying not to show it. She picked up the script, looked at it unseeingly for a few moments, then dropped it onto the floor.

'Do you enjoy doing those love scenes with her?' she demanded fiercely. Yolande would never give Jayne Herford her name. It had been hate at first sight when they met.

Patrick pulled her into his arms and stroked her face. 'It's just work. I don't feel a thing when she kisses me. Not a thing.'

'Liar. I can see the pleasure on your face.'

'I'm just a good actor.'

'Not that good.'

She felt uncontrollably jealous, uncertain, confused. Hearing Philippe's voice had disturbed her, reminded her too forcefully of everything she had thrown away to watch Patrick smoulder in Jayne Herford's arms. Tears welled in her eyes and she tried to move away from him, but he tightened his grip.

'Yolande, how many times do I have to tell you that I want to be with you? I thought we were happy like this. Just the two of us.' She began to cry in earnest, clutching his shoulders and wetting his shirt. 'Who do you really miss, darling? Is it Corinne?'

'She hates me,' she said between sobs. 'She said she

164

never wanted to see me again. Because of you, Patrick. Because of you'

'But you mustn't let her wreck your life. Give it more time. She'll come round eventually.' He took a tissue from a box and wiped her eyes. 'Why don't you give your mother a call? You kept saying you would once we began shooting.'

It was a long process, cajoling her into a smile, then a kiss, then a declaration that she adored him, but Patrick was by now an adept in the art. She had been a nightmare lately; ever since that letter from Corinne's lawyers concerning the sale of her share of St Xavier and the Paris apartment. It remained unanswered. When it had come to signing an agreement, Yolande suddenly lost her resolve. There was no hurry, she had months to think about it, perhaps she could discuss it with her own lawyer personally when she went to Paris. But she wasn't going to Paris. It was a delaying tactic, a last straw she clung to ferociously because in her heart she didn't want to sign away her home – or her family. Patrick knew he could never break the bond, and now considered it might be for the best if she renewed contact, with her mother at least. It might stop her from darting those green eyes so disturbingly at him when he was in the throes of a delicious embrace with Jayne Herford, one of the sexiest women it had ever been his pleasure to play opposite.

Yolande rang her mother that evening, and was immediately invited to New York. Patrick kissed her fondly goodbye at the airport the next day, but rather enjoyed himself during her short absence. People were beginning to notice him. He was invited to more parties than he could attend. The women thought he was wonderful and photographers queued up to take his picture. It was just how he had always wanted things to be.

Chapter Eleven

The first Tuesday evening in March. Miles was relaxing in his Ile St Louis flat, cool jazz pumping out of his sound system as he idled his way through a batch of English newspapers. He was taking Corinne out for dinner again, and hoped she wouldn't still be engrossed by business. Their last date had been spoilt by her constant questions on the progress of his investigation into Ulrich von Stessenberg, which was pretty much at a standstill. Things were not looking good. Stessenberg had now made a formal offer for Corinne's stake in UVS, and she only had until the end of the month to launch a counter-offensive. The phone rang. It was Rupert, as crisp and exacting as ever.

'Miles? I need you in London tomorrow to discuss the Marchand business. Get a train tonight.'

'Can't we do this over the phone?'

'No. You'll understand why when you get here.'

'But I'm seeing Corinne this evening.' As soon as he said it, he knew he had dropped several notches in his uncle's estimation.

'For God's sake, it's her company we're bloody well trying to save! Think of some excuse. She's a woman, so she's bound to think you're having an affair, but whatever you do, don't tell her why I want to see you.'

'I hope it's worth it.'

'Planning candlelight and roses, were we?' snapped Rupert. 'I'm not sure it was such a good idea sending you to Paris. You've gone soft, my boy. My PA's booked you into the Landmark. Can't have you at home, or Alice will want to know all about it. I'll see you in my office at eight thirty tomorrow morning.'

'Yes, uncle.' Miles hung up. 'Damn.'

Oh yes, he had planned candlelight and roses. And a whole lot more.

Forty-five minutes later he arrived at Corinne's apartment, and was swiftly ushered into the salon by Toinette, who went off to fetch her.

'Miles is here.'

'Already?' Corinne was struggling with a back fastening on her dress. 'But it's so early! Will you lend me a hand?'

'Something has disturbed his sangfroid,' Toinette said, deftly undoing the fiasco Corinne had made of a set of hooks and eyes. 'Stand still for a moment, will you? There, that's better. This turquoise really suits you. Now, what about jewellery?'

She carefully picked through the jewellery case on the dressing-table, intent on creating the best possible impression. Corinne let her fuss. Her stepmother's taste was never less than impeccable. When Toinette had met Miles the previous month, her reaction to him had been remarkably similar to Grace's, much to Corinne's amusement. But they could push her at him all they wanted – until she was ready for a relationship, Miles Corsley would have to wait.

Once accessorised to Toinette's satisfaction, Corinne went into the salon with a warm smile, which died as soon as she caught sight of his face.

'Miles! What's wrong?'

She hurried across to him, and he grabbed her by the waist and pulled her hard against him for a long and ruthless kiss. She felt herself going under, giving way again, before her brain kicked in and she stiffened, pressing her hands firmly against his chest.

'What was that for?' she asked as he released her.

168

'I've already told you how much I enjoy kissing you – I thought you'd got used to the idea.'

'You caught me off guard, that's all. Let's try again.' She pressed her lips against his in a soft, tender welcome. 'You're early. I thought the table was booked for eight?'

He groaned as he held her close. 'Corinne, I'm afraid I can't take you to dinner. I've got to go to London tonight. Urgent business for my uncle. I'm so sorry.'

He caught the flash of hurt in her dark eyes before she covered it with a bright smile and stepped away. 'I see. Well, I wouldn't want you to miss your train. You should have phoned instead of coming over. I expect you'd like a drink.'

The fixed smile was worse than a slap on the face. So chillingly formal. Why was she still so unapproachable? Even now, when they seemed to understand each other so well? Corinne went over to the sideboard and poured whisky and soda.

'I was going to ask if you'd like to spend this weekend at St Xavier,' she said rather quickly. 'Will you be back by then?'

Miles cheered up instantly, then had gloomier second thoughts. The house would probably be full of other guests, which would kill any opportunities for intimacy.

'I should be able to make it,' he replied soberly. 'Thanks.'

She handed him a glass and sat beside him, forcing another smile. Philippe would be home this weekend. He was possibly at Rochemort already. Yves had given her plenty of advance warning, but she wasn't going to run away. It would help to have Miles there as a support. The thought that it might take their relationship to another level had entered her mind, but obviously not his. In fact he didn't seem at all pleased to be invited. She had evidently misread the signs. Again. She wondered if she would ever be able to understand men.

'If you've got something better to do, it's OK.'

'No, really, Corinne. I'd love to come. I'm just annoyed about this evening. Perhaps you and Toinette could use the reservation? My treat.'

'Well, darling,' said Toinette, sitting opposite Corinne at a table at Taillevent at eight-fifteen, 'I'm very disappointed for you. But since he's paying, we might as well have some fun.'

Corinne ran her eye down the menu, then looked up with a mischievous grin. 'My thoughts exactly.'

Miles Corsley quickly learned that no one stood up Corinne Marchand with impunity.

Philippe strode through customs at Charles de Gaulle airport with the minimum of fuss. He only had hand baggage, having sent his belongings home by air freight the previous week. Once clear of the crowd that had disembarked with him from an Air France jumbo, he looked about the arrivals lounge, trying to control his excitement. Only now that he was finally back on French soil did the homesickness he had shrugged off for nearly four years really hit him. It was marvellous just standing in the noisy confusion with staff who spoke French and French magazines on sale at the news stand. The sense of release from a protracted nightmare was overwhelming. Then he saw his brother. A little American girl was quite flabbergasted as they ran to each other and embraced.

'We got your things safely,' said Yves, once the hugging was over. 'Is that all the luggage you've got?'

'Yes. Now, let's go. I don't want to attract attention.' Philippe winked at the little girl, linked arms with Yves, and exited at top speed. It was early and they weren't in the VIP lounge, but he was taking no chances. He wanted to see his mother before Claire heard he was back in France.

They drove to Yves' small apartment on the Avenue de

Ségur in the 7th *arrondissement* so that Philippe could freshen up before the drive down to Burgundy. After a breakfast of coffee and croissants in the tiny kitchen, Philippe relaxed at last. He unbuttoned his collar as he sauntered into the bedroom.

'Do you want to sleep?' asked Yves.

'I'd better not, or you won't wake me for a week. That flight was fiendishly noisy.' He sat down in an armchair and stretched out his long legs, stifling a yawn. 'Nice pad. When did you get it?'

Yves sat on the bed. 'About six months ago. I don't use it much.'

'Cigarette?' asked Philippe, lighting one for himself.

'No thanks.'

'Still a health freak, eh? You're looking very well. So what happened to your old place on the Rue de Varenne?'

'It was too large. I was never there, so I sold it. Made a good profit.'

Philippe looked at him thoughtfully. The apartment on the Rue de Varenne had been furnished and decorated very much with Yolande in mind. Yves had obviously given up all hope of her now.

'I rang Yolande before I left. She didn't have any messages. Do you still love her?'

Ouch. Yves hadn't been expecting that. 'No point now, is there?'

'So you do.'

'Shut up. I'm supposed to propose to Gabrielle d'Emville.'

Philippe laughed loudly, and Yves felt as though nothing had changed. He had always suffered a little from being younger brother to someone so sophisticated. There was an eight-year gap between them, due to their mother having had three miscarriages before giving birth to Yves.

'So you'd marry a girl because you're *expected* to? For God's sake, think of yourself. You're the one who has to

171

sleep with her. Wasn't Gabrielle that little one with the brace on her teeth?'

'Yes.' Yves paused. 'She's fairly pretty now. Nothing compared to Yolande, of course.'

'Well, I shouldn't rush into anything. You're a handsome guy. You could have anyone.'

'Except the woman I want.'

Philippe raised his eyebrows. He was damned if he was going to see his brother shackled in an unhappy marriage just to satisfy their mother's desire for grandchildren. And the fact that Yves could even entertain the idea showed how depressed he was over Yolande. What a bloody mess. He'd have to see what he could do.

'How's business?' he asked. 'Flourishing, I imagine. Even I used to think twice when I saw the price of Château de Rochemort in the States.'

'We're doing very well. I bought some new bottling equipment last June, and we've had a couple of excellent years.'

'You still do the marketing with St Xavier?'

'Naturally. Corinne's delegated even more to me recently because of the takeover threat at Marchand.'

'How's she coping?'

'It's only a matter of time now before she regains overall control,' said Yves. 'She managed to pull off a deal with Toinette to block the owner of Yolande's shares.'

'I'm glad. Will she be at home if I call?'

Yves wasn't sure how to answer. Corinne hadn't expressly forbidden him to mention her movements to Philippe, but he had a feeling she would prefer to handle any communications her own way. 'She'll come down to St Xavier on Friday as usual.'

'OK, I won't embarrass you by further interrogation.' Philippe stood up and began to undress. 'Leave the bathroom door open while I shower, and I'll recount my global exploits in fifteen minutes' flat. I want a full account of Maman's arthritis and the specialists she's consulted on the drive home.'

'But aren't you going to tell me what happened so you could come back?'

'Patience, *mon enfant*,' Philippe threw off his shirt. 'Now be a good chap and get some clean clothes out of my bag. You'll see a box in the bottom. That's for you. It's some fancy new device for measuring sugar levels in the vat.' He tore off his jeans and headed naked for the bathroom, a tall, lean, muscular figure, moving like a panther.

Yves laid out the clean suit and shirt packed neatly in a suit-bag, examining the labels. Both tailor made. Typical Philippe. He hadn't changed at all. The same dominating manner coupled with a nonchalant charm few could resist. Just like him to pick up the latest piece of American gadgetry for professional winegrowers and offer it as a casual present. Yves had read about it in a trade magazine, and the price was far too much for his manager, who had nearly choked with rage at the thought of the Americans trying to teach him anything, let alone making him pay for the privilege.

He snatched a quick look at the present, then drew a chair up to the bathroom door and laughed for the next half hour. He'd forgotten just how amusing Philippe could be, and the telescoped account of his adventures with wine and women in Australia and California was side-splitting. How good it was to have him home again – he would be just the tonic their mother needed. Just the catalyst to make Yves realise that he too was a vigorous and handsome Baron de Rochemort, not necessarily condemned to eternal misery with Gabrielle or any other suitable girl.

Miles was surprised to find a smartly-dressed man of about forty occupying a chair in his uncle's office when he arrived at eight twenty on Wednesday morning. The stranger put down his coffee and stood to shake Miles' hand. He wasn't particularly tall, but was very powerfully built, fit, and carried himself well. Bright blue eyes slightly moderated the hawkish cut of his face.

'You must be Miles. Good to meet you.' Miles felt the firm grip and the strength behind it. 'I'm Grant Macdonald.'

'Regiment?'

Macdonald smiled. 'Not so illustrious as yours. But I'm in a different racket now. Coffee?'

He turned to pour, perfectly at home. Miles knew now why his uncle had been so mysterious. If the British security services were involved, Stessenberg's past must be even murkier than he had suspected. Rupert himself strode in ten minutes later to find them debating the team selections for the upcoming Six Nations rugby match between France and England like old friends.

'I see you've met,' he said, slapping his briefcase down on the desk. 'Ah, thank you.' He took a cup of coffee from Macdonald and scowled. 'Damn, don't tell me they still have white, two sugars on file?'

'Yes, sir. Sorry. I'll get you another.'

'It's black and no sugar.' Miles grinned as Macdonald poured a replacement. 'How are the mighty fallen.'

'Shut up, boy. It's too early and I haven't had nearly enough caffeine yet. Grant, perhaps you could fill my nephew in on your project.'

Macdonald resumed his seat. 'It looks like we'll be working together on UVS, Miles – and hopefully we'll both get out of it exactly what we want.'

Philippe couldn't play it cool when he finally arrived at Rochemort. For days he had been rehearsing what he would say to his mother, how best to break the news about Claire and Isabelle. But when the car drew up outside the entrance to the château's west wing, he ran out and

174

bounded up the grand marble staircase two steps at a time to the first floor drawing room where Yves had told him she would be waiting. She was sitting in an armchair facing the door. Struck by her fragile look, he almost fell at her feet to embrace her. Then he cried.

'Philippe, my darling.' Marie-Christine held him close, stroking his hair and kissing him as though he were a small boy.

'Maman, do you forgive me?'

'Of course. I love you. Now get up and be sensible. I can't walk very well.'

He watched with concern as she slowly pulled herself up, wincing with the pain. She was much worse than he had expected. He would have to get her to consult another specialist soon, though Yves had told him she was deaf to all persuasion. He put an arm around her and they stumbled across to the sofa, where they sat together for some time in silence.

Marie-Christine surveyed her eldest son with her keen blue eyes, noting his tired look and the odd flecks of grey in his jet-black hair. But he was still handsome, still the warm, lively Philippe who had made Rochemort such an inviting place before he left – virtually without warning – almost four years before. He held her hand fast, too overwhelmed for speech. His mother was the one woman he loved without reservation, and seeing her in this half-crippled state made him curse his years of exile, and even the years before it when he had fallen far short of being the kind of son she deserved. How was he going to tell her now why he had abandoned her?

'Philippe, don't squeeze my hand. I shan't run away.' She smiled bravely, and he hurriedly loosened his grip.

'Does it hurt?'

'A little, darling.'

'Arthritis? Or just my clumsiness?'

'It's damp today. That's when I feel it in my fingers –

but I'm all right. I still get around. You mustn't worry.'

'Maman, you can't go on like this! Yves has told me everything. You must have hip replacement surgery. You wouldn't even need a stick.' He put his arm round her shoulders and hugged her. 'You're still the most beautiful woman I know. I want you on my arm at Longchamp for the Arc this October.'

'Don't be silly,' she said sharply, trying to push from her mind the very fine figure she used to cut at Longchamp when his father used to escort her there, smiling at her in much the same way as Philippe was now.

Yves, having dawdled up the stairs to give them time alone, now appeared to announce that lunch would soon be ready.

'What do you think?' he asked, when Philippe slipped off to fetch her present.

'He's hiding something. I'm sure he's afraid to break it to me. Did he mention anything to you?'

'Not a word.'

They weren't enlightened during lunch, either. Philippe chattered gaily about New York, gave his mother a, beautiful diamond brooch from Tiffany's in the shape of the Statue of Liberty as a homecoming present, and caught up with news of all their neighbours and friends; but the confession he had so long prepared refused to be delivered. By the time dessert was served, he was yawning, and his mother packed him off to bed to recover from jet lag before he fell asleep at the table.

She remained with Yves in the dining room, gazing out thoughtfully at the cold grey sky. They made small talk for a while, then Yves went off to his office, and Marie-Christine back to her armchair in the drawing room. Everything seemed suddenly flat and cheerless, yet at lunch they had laughed. They both wondered how they had been getting by for the past few years.

Morning again, and this time it was sunny. Philippe glanced round his room twice to make sure he really was home – a well-proportioned wood-panelled room, both elegant and comfortable. His possessions were still in packing-cases in the adjoining sitting-room. He leapt out of bed, determined to get it all off his chest before he completely lost his nerve, and arrived at the breakfast-table armed with some emails from Claire, a recent photograph of Isabelle, and an apprehensive smile. It was so hard to explain. So painful to watch his mother's expression of disappointment after her joy the day before. But she had forgiven him, hadn't she? Yves just sat motionless in his chair, hardly able to believe his ears.

'This is Isabelle,' said Philippe, handing his mother the photograph. 'It was taken last month.'

She took it reluctantly and stared at it for several minutes, her mouth becoming a little less severe. 'She looks just like you. Doesn't she, Yves?'

He gazed at the photograph and smiled encouragingly at his brother. 'She's lovely, Philippe. I'm happy to be her uncle any time you like.'

That helped somewhat, but there was a great deal more explaining to be done. Philippe tried to skirt round the issues of abortion and divorce, but Marie-Christine was not to be sidetracked.

'So you had an affair with a married woman at the same time you were allowing Corinne to believe you would propose to her, you tried to persuade your mistress to abort your child, and when her husband took what I can only call a just revenge, you fled like a coward. Philippe, *mon fils!*' She gave him a look that made him wish he could disappear. 'Where was your heart? Your principles? And most of all, your religion? I tried to bring you up as a good Catholic. Apparently I failed.'

'But Maman, I couldn't marry Claire. Garnier-Dumont wouldn't agree to a divorce. I ...' His voice trailed off.

Now he realised what he should have done. He should have made a clean breast of it to his mother at the time. She would have been extremely angry, but she would have known what to do, and she wouldn't now be staring at him so reproachfully. He couldn't bear it from her.

'I'm sorry. Perhaps I should have stayed in America.' He stood up and turned towards the door.

'Darling, don't go. Please.' She stretched out her hand. 'We must try to put things right – if we can. Do you want your daughter?'

'Yes. Very much.'

'Have you seen her yet?'

'No. I shall soon. Claire wants me to.'

Marie-Christine smiled faintly, trying to encourage him. 'Tell us more about Claire.'

Philippe returned to his seat. Yves was looking at him expectantly, his mother was clearly doing her best to conceal her pain at the story she had just heard. How could he show Claire in a favourable light?

'Well, you must know what she looks like,' he began at last. 'We met at a dinner party. She was alone. I found her very attractive. She was desperately bored with her husband and she soon showed that she liked me. I didn't do much about it for a while, but our paths seemed to cross quite frequently. Then we became lovers. We kept seeing each other even after Corinne and I got together.' He caught the look on his mother's face. 'Yes, I know it was wrong. I tried to break it off, but by then Claire was pregnant.'

'Why didn't you use protection?'

His jaw dropped. His mother never discussed sex. But she seemed to want an answer. 'We did, but … um … well, occasionally we didn't.'

'Reckless passion.' She nodded. 'I suppose we've all been there. Where does she come from?'

'Le Mans. Her father's a doctor. Claire worked as

Garnier-Dumont's research assistant when he was just a deputy in the Assemblée. His first wife had died a few years before – cancer, I think. He wasn't very good at social events, and he wanted someone to boost his image. Claire was the ideal choice – intelligent, good-looking, and great with people. Why on earth she married him, I haven't a clue. They were certainly an odd couple. But it worked – on the surface, anyway.'

Marie-Christine nodded, and Philippe relaxed a little. She seemed sympathetic to Claire. 'Of course, when Garnier-Dumont became a minister, Claire was an extremely valuable asset to him. But she needed love, not political philosophy.'

'Do you love her?'

It was a question Philippe couldn't answer, even to himself. He still wasn't sure how he felt about Claire. She was sweet, wonderful, and very giving, and he had been extremely fond of her – but love? What did he really know about love?

Yves shifted in his seat, rather embarrassed. 'How did she keep in touch with you after all that trouble?'

'Email. But we had to be careful. Her messages were monitored. Letters sometimes too. We used a friend of hers in Le Mans as a go-between.'

'So you preferred to write to your mistress rather than your family?' asked his mother angrily.

'But I had to protect you! I was afraid Garnier-Dumont might try to ruin you. And we'd quarrelled so fiercely. I thought it best to keep right out of the way. But believe me, I missed you both so much. Every single day.'

Yves smiled, slapped Philippe on the back, and poured out more coffee while their mother sat silent and pensive, caressing Geraldine who was sitting by her feet.

'So what do you intend to do now, Philippe?' she asked at last. 'I don't mean about your private life. I leave that to your conscience.'

He winced and lit a cigarette, knowing perfectly well what she expected of him. 'Well, I want to remain in France. I have one or two business projects in mind. When I've chased up some old contacts in Paris I'll have a clearer idea of the future.'

'How much money do you have left?'

'Enough to start up a new company. But nowhere near the amount I had four years ago.'

Marie-Christine sighed, then rose slowly from the table. Yves helped her to the door. She turned to face Philippe before leaving the room. 'You can stay here for as long as you like, but I'd rather you didn't become involved in the business again. Yves is doing very well on his own. I'm sure you'll fall on your feet, darling. You know you always have my prayers.'

'Maman!' He started up and ran across to her. 'But won't you – don't you want to see your granddaughter?'

'Perhaps, Philippe, perhaps. When I've recovered from the shock. When *you've* decided if you want to be her father.' She kissed his cheek and left with Yves, who darted him a look of sympathy.

Philippe paced up and down the room, his tension increasing. It was over. He had confessed. But he had only opened up old wounds and unsolved problems. Snapping his fingers, he brought Geraldine to heel and went out to inspect the gardens.

Later that day he called Claire and told her he was in Burgundy. She asked him to visit her at Versailles the following Monday, when she and Isabelle would have returned from a weekend in Le Mans. Philippe accepted the invitation and went straight up to his rooms to unpack some toys he had bought for his daughter at FAO Schwarz in New York. Yves helped him to wrap them, but when he told his mother who they were for she was cool and uninterested.

'Bloody rain. Bloody office.' James Chetwode looked balefully at the dozens of unread emails in his inbox and the water dripping down the window pane, and coughed horribly. It was four o'clock on Friday and he had a feeling he would be trapped behind a desk until Monday morning.

'You can borrow my umbrella to get home,' said Miles sweetly.

'Home! I won't get through this lot for days. Could you lend me a hand?'

'No. I've already done half your work since I got back from London. You ought to be more careful where you take your girlfriends. It was hardly the weather for an outdoor shag, was it?' Miles stood up and put on his jacket.

James blew his nose. 'OK, OK. But she's that type of girl. Where the hell are you going?'

'I'm leaving. Corinne's invited me to spend the weekend at her country house.'

'I thought she dumped you. She must be desperate.'

'Keep up, James. I have business to discuss with her. We should make a good profit on this deal. I've finally got a meeting with Stessenberg, and I'm sure he'll play ball now.'

'So that's why you keep smirking. I was beginning to think you'd had Botox and it had gone wrong. You said Marchand was a hopeless case.'

'Rupert took it on board. The meeting's in London next week, so you'll have to hold the fort for a couple of days. You can take some leave when I get back.'

Miles strode out of the office. James swore.

Chapter Twelve

When Miles arrived at St Xavier just after eight on Friday evening, it was raining heavily, and the glow of lights from the ground-floor windows was decidedly welcome.

'I hope you've brought your wellies,' said Corinne, greeting him with a kiss at the door. 'The forecast isn't at all good.'

She led him straight upstairs to a large bedroom at the end of a corridor, comfortably furnished and well-heated. From its windows Miles caught a glimpse of the vineyards, at that hour just a black, damp blur in the distance.

'You've got your own bathroom. If there's anything you need, I'm just across the hall. When you've unpacked, come down to the salon. I thought we'd eat in about an hour, so you should have time to fill me in on the latest about UVS.'

A padding sound was heard, and Marius entered the room wagging his tail. Miles stroked him, too conscious of Corinne's beauty and their proximity to the huge bed.

'There's nothing new on UVS, I'm afraid,' he said, lying through his teeth. 'But Stessenberg's agreed to meet me in London next Tuesday. I'm hoping he'll be more amenable to negotiations face to face.'

'I really ought to come.'

'At this stage I think it's better if we don't let it get too personal.' He didn't want her anywhere near Stessenberg after what he had learnt from Grant Macdonald. 'Shall I dress for dinner?'

'Heavens, no. This is a break. The Rochemorts are coming for lunch tomorrow, and I have to go through some papers with my manager in the morning, but apart from that it's just you and me.'

When she had gone, Miles sat down on the bed, wanting her too much. Had she asked him here for business or pleasure? Just the two of them in this large, beautiful house; but she was so aloof, so reserved. He changed into jeans, then wandered along the corridor, admiring the pictures. The Avenue Foch apartment boasted a superb art collection, but he preferred the paintings here.

As well as landscapes, there were intriguing family portraits. Fabrice Marchand, who had bought the vineyard when the old monastery of St Xavier was sold during the Revolution, looked a canny old gentleman, dressed in period red velvet coat and high muslin cravat. His wife Yolande, on the opposite wall, was a sad, beautiful green-eyed aristocrat – the daughter of a marquis guillotined in 1793, as Miles learnt from an inscription underneath the portrait. Evidently not very enamoured of her bourgeois husband, notwithstanding their brood of children, who occupied a large canvas a little further on. Bearded Second Empire Marchands and their wives followed, then a quartet of scenes of workers in the vineyards at the turn of the century, and last of all, tucked away in an alcove, a modern portrait that kept his attention for some time.

'Miles?' Corinne sauntered along to him from the stairway.

'I was just admiring the paintings. This one of your sister is a very good likeness.'

'It was commissioned for her eighteenth birthday.'

'She's named after that rather sad lady back there, I see. They look alike too, don't they?'

'I'm afraid my sister inherited the temperament as well as the beauty.'

'Oh?'

They turned to go downstairs.

'Yes, it's quite a story. Fabrice Marchand would be called an entrepreneur nowadays, but they had less polite names for him then. He acquired Yolande de Charbuy for his wife in much the same way as he snapped up the vineyard of St Xavier. Her father had been a high-ranking courtier, and lost everything during the Revolution – including his life. I suppose his family were lucky to have survived, but they were reduced to poverty. Fabrice literally paid the Marquise de Charbuy for her daughter. We have a contract stating the exact sum. It was an elaborate deal – annuities, reversions, that sort of thing. He fathered six children on Yolande before she bolted with an Italian count while taking the waters at Vichy.'

'She left the children?' Miles enquired, following her through the hall to the salon.

'Yes. She disappeared completely. But in 1847 her eldest son received a letter from a gentleman in Italy claiming to be his half-brother. Apparently Yolande soon progressed from the count to a duke, by whom she had three more children. She died giving birth to the last.'

'And your sister? Do you intend to let her go the same way?'

They sat down together on a sofa. Corinne faced him, frowning. 'What she does is her own business. I don't suppose your sister cares too much for your advice.'

She was curious as to why he hardly ever talked about his family. His sister Caroline had been mentioned at the New Year, but in an aside, like a remote stranger.

'Hell, no! She thinks I'm part of the global capitalist conspiracy bent on the annihilation of the planet.'

'That's quite a responsibility.'

'I do my best.' He grinned.

'She'd hate me.'

'She'd envy you. She used to love fashion when she was a kid. Then she got an eco-warrior boyfriend at university, and it's been one lost cause after another ever since. I'm just waiting for Caro to wake up and smell the Fairtrade coffee. We even use it at the bank these days.'

'So what does she do?'

'Currently she's working as a volunteer teacher on a school project in Africa. She hasn't been home for two years.'

'Your parents must miss her.'

'They're both dead.'

'Christ, I'm so sorry.' She was appalled that she had assumed he came from a perfect family with adoring happily married parents; and she had rejected his sympathy over her father's death as a sham.

'It was a long time ago. Car crash. Caro was only thirteen. I think that's what kicked off her career as a perpetual rebel.'

'But you rebelled by being conventional?'

'Oh, I have my moments, you know.' He was toying with her hair, smiling. 'Especially where you're concerned.'

Corinne felt her heart thudding as he pulled her into his arms. This was just how they had been that October evening at his flat in Paris, and it had all gone horribly wrong. But she wasn't going to panic this time. For God's sake, she knew all about sex. And she was sure it would be wonderful with Miles. She used to be quite good at it once, before Philippe had shattered her confidence. But now, knowing he had had an affair while they were together, she felt even less sure of herself, even more afraid.

'Relax, Corinne,' Miles whispered. 'I just want to kiss you.'

He brought his lips slowly to hers and teased her gently into the kiss. His tongue flicked along her lips, then into her mouth. When it touched hers, she moaned and opened for him, wanting him to take, to stop her thinking, to kiss her mindlessly and desperately until she could give no more. He felt the change from fear to desire as she ravaged him with her mouth, hungry and relentless. She fell back against the cushions and pulled him on top of her, and they were exactly where they had been before. She could feel his erection, so hard and so ready, felt her own need, sharp and keen. And then the panic began. She wanted to scream at herself. No, it couldn't happen again. It couldn't. She wanted Miles. She wanted to give him all the pleasure she could, but her stomach was in knots of terror. Her hands fell away from him, her breathing grew ragged.

Miles raised himself off her. 'Corinne, are you all right?'

'I'm sorry. It's me. It's not you.'

'Tell me what the problem is – maybe we can fix it.'

'I can't. I can't.' Tears came to her eyes. 'I'm such a wreck.'

'No you're not.' He sat up and pulled her back into his arms, stroking her hair while she cried. 'You're lovely.'

He rocked her for a few minutes until she stopped crying, wishing she would tell him what had happened to her in the past to make her so petrified of her own libido. He had no doubt that she was very highly sexed. Her passion tore through him every time they kissed. But she just couldn't seem to trust her feelings enough to let go.

He turned her face up so he could look into her eyes. 'I want to make love to you.'

'I know. I want you to, but I just can't. Not now. I'm sorry, Miles.'

He kissed her. 'It's OK. I understand. Why don't we have dinner? I'm starving.'

She stood up, grateful for an excuse to extricate herself from embarrassment. Miles set the table and fetched the wine, and kept up a stream of inconsequential chat during the meal so that she felt almost normal again. Afterwards she showed him round the library, which housed family documents and an impressive collection of books on wine, built up over two centuries. They listened to the radio, locked on a station playing the latest hits, and then to French vocalists he'd never even heard of – Patricia Kaas, Alain Souchon, Patrick Bruel. Strange how much you could find out about someone from their taste in music. He discovered with surprise that the formidable Corinne Marchand had a very romantic streak and a great love of French popular song. They even danced a little, but the lighthearted atmosphere of Dorset on New Year's Eve was missing. Miles felt all the progress he thought he had made completely evaporate. She was undeniably charming, a perfect hostess, a lovely woman, but emotionally more remote than ever. When they said goodnight, she quickly pecked his cheek and slipped off into her room before he could try her lips. He heard her turn the key in the lock, and went to bed very dissatisfied.

Corinne cried herself to sleep, hating herself for being such a coward. What the hell was wrong with her? Hadn't she asked Miles here so they could sleep together? It couldn't be the thought that Philippe would be coming tomorrow. She had already decided how she would deal with him. What would Yolande do in the same situation? Take a chance, probably. Go to his room without a thought for anything but immediate pleasure. But what if when they got back to Paris it faded into a one-night stand, and she ended up hurt and used again? She couldn't bring herself to gamble with her feelings any more.

Marie-Christine took Corinne aside when she arrived at Le Manoir with Yves around noon the following day, her expression uncharacteristically anxious. She blurted out an excuse from Philippe, who had been included in the lunch invitation, and was about to hint at important revelations when she was stopped by Corinne.

'Don't worry. I know everything.'

'You *know*? About his child?'

'Yes.'

The baroness soon resumed her customary sangfroid. 'Philippe will probably be over later – if that's all right with you? It was a terrible shock to me, Corinne. The way he treated you!'

'I'm fine. Really.' Corinne linked arms with her and smiled. 'Don't you want to see Miles Corsley again? That Englishman you fell for last August?'

Miles now appeared, handsome, cheerful, and evidently poised to be the life and soul of the party. Marie-Christine breathed an inward sigh of relief. So Corinne had found someone else at last. Though she had only admitted it to herself, the effect of Philippe's return on Corinne had worried her the most. Now, perhaps, all their lives could be finally straightened out.

A lively meal followed, and if one or two at the table were hiding their deepest feelings, the casual observer would have been fooled. Miles, however, couldn't help catching a melancholy expression which now and then flitted across Yves' face, and when he and the baroness had gone home, asked Corinne about it.

'He's in love with Yolande. They were engaged.'

'What happened? Or shouldn't I ask?'

'Well, you shouldn't. But if you must know, she broke it off because of Patrick Dubuisson.'

'Ah.' He stretched out his legs, leaning back in his seat. 'And she sold her stake in Marchand because of him. Now I see why she's not a popular topic of conversation around here. By the way, who's this Philippe they kept talking about?'

'Yves' older brother. He's just returned from America.'

Miles wasn't interested in pursuing the subject, turning instead to a discussion he had had with Yves on the workings of the *appellation contrôlée* system, which provided a profitable source of conversation for fifteen minutes. But Corinne was clearly absorbed by something else, and when he asked if he could go out to the vineyards with Gaston Leclerc, she was only too pleased. Gaston had recognised him instantly that morning, and insisted on treating him to a grand tour. He liked Miles, and something told him that they would be seeing much more of each other in the future. Miles wondered why everyone except Corinne was being so kind.

Philippe borrowed Yves' BMW to drive to Le Manoir that afternoon, since he hadn't yet bought a car of his own. He was surprised to see a British-registered Range Rover parked beside Corinne's black MG in front of the house, then remembered his mother mentioning she had an English banker staying for the weekend. Evidently she was still trying to sort out the mess over Yolande's shareholding.

He nearly rang the main doorbell, then decided to use his old route into the house and walked round to the side entrance. The door was unlocked. He gently pushed it open and stepped cautiously into the passage, just as he used to tiptoe through it not to disturb Corinne's father in his office. Not that Jean-Claude had disapproved of Philippe – but he had always had a way of buttonholing him for a long chat when he was itching to be with Corinne. Now he was dead, and the silence in the house was deafening. No Jean-Claude, no Toinette, no Yolande; no laughter and cheerful voices. Where would she be? In the salon? Upstairs?

He was still hesitating when Marius suddenly emerged from Jean-Claude's office and began to bark.

'Marius!'

Her voice. Philippe froze. She was there, just metres away. Marius bounded up to him and sniffed him, then began to jump at his shoulders, his tail wagging, his tongue hanging loose. Philippe rubbed his back, glad of a welcome from some living creature at least.

'Marius, you silly dog! Come here.'

Corinne appeared at the office door, saw Philippe, and stopped dead. She called Marius again. The dog ran to her and was commanded to sit and be quiet. She shut the door and took two steps towards Philippe.

'Hello. Your mother told me you might call. Shall we go to the salon?'

'Hello, Corinne.'

He couldn't think of anything else to say, and stood rooted to the spot, staring at her. She was wearing a navy dress that suited her slim figure. Her hair was styled differently, in a longish bob, less ingénue than he remembered. Though she looked little older, there was a maturity in her expression which only accentuated her fine features and heightened her beauty. But she certainly didn't look friendly. He followed her to the salon in silence, and having shut Marius out, locked the door and put the key in his pocket.

'Philippe, what do you think you're doing?'

'I don't want to be disturbed.'

'Give me that key!'

'Come and get it.' He smiled, leaning against the door.

She sat down abruptly on the sofa, her dark eyes flashing angrily. 'Give me the key!'

'I will. After we've talked.'

Corinne had expected some change, but he was exactly the same. In looks, in manner – nothing about him suggested that he felt the slightest difference in their relationship or any remorse for the past. He sat beside her and gave her the key. She put it on a table nearby.

'So what do you want to talk about?'

'Us. How sorry I am. Corinne…'

'No! I hate you! Get off!'

But it was useless. She was in his arms and his lips were on hers. She struggled, but he just clasped her wrists and forced her down, his mouth pressed over hers, hungry, pitiless. Corinne could hardly believe it was happening.

Even as the tears started to her eyes she felt her body reacting to him. When their tongues touched, she lost her resistance completely. Her hands ran down his back and slipped under his jacket, pulling at his clothes, aching to touch his skin. How could he still do this to her? Make her want him, make her forget the years of pain he'd caused her?

Philippe began to kiss her neck, and his hand was on her thigh. Suddenly she was horrified. Her body was betraying her. She must be mad. How had she fallen into this old, old trap – now there wasn't even the shadow of love for him left in her heart?

'Let me go, Philippe!'

'But Corinne …'

'Bastard! Let me go!'

He was taken aback. She wriggled out of his arms and then slapped him hard across the face. Twice.

Stunned, he rubbed his cheek. 'I guess I deserved that.'

She stood up, glaring at him. Then the door handle turned.

'Corinne, are you in there?'

It was Miles. She hurriedly straightened her clothes and snatched the key from the table. 'Make yourself tidy,' she ordered Philippe. 'It's my guest.'

Miles registered several things as soon as he stepped into the room. Both Corinne and that devilishly handsome man sitting on the sofa looked embarrassed and dishevelled. The top two buttons of her dress were undone, and the tail of his shirt was visible below the hem of his jacket. The atmosphere was pulsing with sex. He found himself consumed with jealousy.

'Miles, you haven't met Yves' brother – Philippe de Rochemort.'

They shook hands, then Miles turned away.

'Won't you have a drink with us?' Corinne asked.

'No thanks. I've got one or two things to see to in my

192

room. I'm sure you've got plenty of catching up to do.'

He was gone, and she felt terrible. The expression in his eyes was unmistakable. He loved her, and she hadn't even realised it. And now Philippe had probably ruined her chances by his opportunistic attempt to revive the past.

She rounded on him angrily. 'Will you just go? I don't think there's anything for us to talk about.'

'Corinne, I haven't said a thing yet. Come back here.'

'Absolutely not.'

'Sit in a chair, then. I promise to behave.'

He stood up and tucked in his shirt, rather grateful for the intrusion. Things had got a little out of hand. He hadn't meant to lose control – just a few kisses by way of reconciliation. But the touch of her lips had made him wild. It had been a mistake to meet her here. The whole ambience reminded him far too much of what they had once had together.

Corinne left the door slightly ajar and went over to the sideboard. 'Do you want a drink?'

'Excellent idea.'

Philippe sat down and lit a cigarette, watching her as she poured two glasses of wine. He knew the meeting was going to be painful, but he had to pass the test with honour. He had other obligations now. They were together for over an hour. Miles did wander past the door once, driven by a tormenting curiosity, and heard snatches of a conversation in rapid, impassioned French. About a child, Marie-Christine, business disputes. So they must have had sex before he got back from the vineyards. That's why Corinne had been so anxious for him to go. He felt sick. He went upstairs with Marius, who watched him with soulful eyes as he began to pack his bag.

'I'm sorry for *everything*, Corinne,' Philippe said at last, so emphatically that she had to believe him. 'I know how you must feel. But I did love you. I never meant to hurt you. Please try to understand.'

'And Claire? Did you love her too?' Her tone was sarcastic.

'No. Actually, that's not true. Yes, I did. I loved you both.'

'You have absolutely no idea of what real love is, do you?'

'Look, I'm trying to be open with you. I know how it must look to you, but I can't lie to you again. When I fell in love with you, it was a bolt from the blue. I was already involved with Claire, and I was deeply attached to her. But I thought nothing could ever come of it because she was married, so I suppose I wouldn't allow myself to be in love with her. And that made it all the easier to fall for you.'

'Well, that was very convenient for you. God, Philippe! Didn't you think of anyone but yourself? You must have known someone would get their heart broken, but of course it wasn't you, so you didn't care. And to think I was in love with you. Horribly in love with you.' Disgusted, she looked at him as though it were for the first time. 'What a bloody fool I was.'

'But with excellent taste,' he said, the glimmer of a smile in his eyes.

She caught it and itched to slap his face again. But then, despite everything, found herself wanting to laugh. 'How much excess baggage did you have to pay for that ego of yours?'

'Had to charter a whole plane. It was damned expensive.'

The laugh came. He was utterly impossible. He always had been. She had thought she hated him, but found she didn't. Couldn't. No one could resist that wry grin of his, those appealing blue eyes, that fiendish charm.

'Oh, go away, Philippe,' she said, not unkindly, 'and leave me alone.'

'So you don't care,' he said in a quiet voice.

'You surely don't expect me to feel anything for you

194

now?'

'But when we kissed! Corinne, I felt it. You did too. Don't look at me like that! I know it's over – but that didn't stop me wanting you just now.'

'That was just sex,' she said coolly, but his words gave her a real boost.

'Have you had other lovers?'

'I don't suppose you were celibate while you were away.'

'No. But with you it was special. I wondered if you'd found it easy to forget.'

What did he want? She wasn't going to fuel his vanity by confessing she hadn't forgotten at all, and that until Miles no one had even come close to making her want a man the way she had just wanted him. He probably wouldn't believe her. Now she was near him, she could hardly believe it herself. Her heart was safe. As for the desire aroused by their kiss, that had been an instinctive reaction she thought lost beyond recall. And with it, Philippe had exorcised himself.

'I'm not discussing my private life with you.' She rose from her chair.

'I suppose we can still meet occasionally? As friends?' He stood up, suddenly feeling rather foolish.

'We can't really spend the rest of our lives avoiding each other. I'll see you around.'

'Can't you forgive me, then?' Their eyes met. 'You see, darling, we never said goodbye properly. This is it. I don't want you to hate me, that's all.'

'You ought to think of all the reasons why I should.'

Philippe moved towards the door. 'All right, if that's the way you want it.'

She let him go out, heard his quick footsteps crossing the hall, and then followed him. 'Philippe, wait.'

He stopped with his hand on the knob of the side door. She caught up with him, and they both went outside to his

195

car.

'When do you see Isabelle?' she asked.

'Monday.'

'Give her a kiss from me.'

Philippe cupped her face in his hands and kissed her forehead and both cheeks. He got straight into the BMW and she waved as he drove off. Yes, they would see each other again, but they both knew now things would never be the way they were before.

Afterwards Corinne sat for a while in the tranquillity of her office, trying to think of how she would approach Miles. Catching sight of herself in a mirror, she realised she looked and felt a mess. Nearly five-fifteen; they ought to have tea. She had arranged it specially, and Françoise had left everything ready in the kitchen before going off duty for the rest of the weekend. Corinne decided to freshen up and fetch Miles from wherever he had gone off to sulk. The library, probably. He had been poring over that contract between Fabrice Marchand and the Marquise de Charbuy all morning. She couldn't think why he found it so fascinating.

She went slowly upstairs and along to her room. The door to his was open. Looking in, she saw him sitting on the bed, Marius stretched at his feet.

'Oh there you are, Miles. I'm just going to change. Shan't be long.'

Miles didn't return her smile. He watched her go into her room, waited for the door to close. The bag was packed, he was ready to go. Should he just leave without a word, or make some excuse? He decided to speak to her – after all, it wasn't her fault she couldn't return his feelings. But he couldn't bear another night of torture, knowing she was only yards away; knowing now that she had a lover called Philippe de Rochemort.

He knocked on her door, but there was no answer.

After a few moments he opened it. Empty. She was in the bathroom. He could hear the shower. He went in to wait for her, and soon realised it was a mistake. There were photographs, books, little ornaments and knick-knacks; her clothes on the floor, the smell of her perfume, an old teddy bear with a jaunty beret sitting on the window still. It was so full of girl stuff, so full of her. And she was giving it all to a man who apparently only had to walk in after years of absence for her to spread her legs.

Miles hurt more than he had ever thought possible. By the time Corinne was out of the shower, his pain was jagged with anger. He had looked at all the photographs on her dressing table – of her with her parents at her graduation, on holiday with her grandparents and Yolande, full of life and fun, with those wonderful dark eyes sparkling, and it killed him inside. That's how she must look when she was happy, when she was with people she loved. She'd never looked at him that way. And he knew now why she never would.

The bathroom door opened and he whipped round in a flash. There she was, wrapped in a towel, staring at him in alarm.

'Miles, what on earth are you doing in here?'

'Saying goodbye. I'm leaving.'

'Leaving? Why?'

'Bloody hell, isn't it obvious?'

Why did she look so taken aback? And so damned sexy. Beads of water dripped down her neck, trickling between her breasts beneath the towel. His mouth went dry and he put his hands in his pockets so he wasn't tempted to grab her.

'Look, I'm really sorry about this afternoon, but Philippe and I had a lot to talk about. Let me make it up to you. I've got some homemade scones for tea and …'

'Scones! You think you can just offer me scones after you spent the afternoon fucking him? You've got a very

197

perverse sense of humour.'

His smoky blue eyes acquired an intensity she had never seen before, his mouth was set hard. She stepped towards him, wanting to hold him, but he moved back to the door.

'Don't bother to see me out, Corinne. And don't worry about UVS. I'll still handle it all for you. I'll call you with an update next week.'

'Miles, for God's sake! Stop!' She moved close and grabbed his arm. 'You don't understand. Philippe and I didn't have sex. I wouldn't sleep with him now if he were the last man on earth. But I had to talk to him.' His expression was unyielding. 'You don't believe me, do you?'

'No.'

Miles shook her off, stepped backwards. He would be gone. Gone. That couldn't be allowed to happen. She had to do something, keep him there, make him listen. She couldn't think of anything else, so she dropped the towel.

'I want you, Miles. Only you.'

He stopped dead, completely outgunned. She was absolutely stunning. More beautiful than he had even imagined, and he had done a heck of a lot of imagining. He took in the white, silky skin glistening with water droplets, the delicate hollow at her throat, the slender line of her shoulders, those delicious breasts, a lean stomach, and then the inviting curve of her hips and her sex. She stood proud, triumphant, with a smile in her eyes that told him everything he needed to know. He caught her by the waist and crushed her naked flesh hard against him.

'Corinne, *what* did you say?'

'I believe, Mr Corsley, that I just made a formal declaration of my interest in a merger with you.' She looked up. 'Is your offer still on the table?'

He seized on her mouth and her lips parted, drawing him in, tongues dancing in exploration until they were both breathless.

'I'm sorry for what I said, but …'

'Shut up, Miles.'

She didn't want words. She only wanted his arms around her, that beautiful feeling of being where she belonged, unafraid and free. He found that she was casually stripping off his shirt while her mouth devoured him.

He pushed her back towards the bed. 'You'd better be absolutely sure about this, darling, because I'm not going to be able to stop.'

'Make love to me. Please.'

Desperate need smouldered in her eyes. She threw his shirt to the floor, began undoing his belt. Then they fell on the bed, and he raced to get his remaining clothes off. When he slipped into her open arms it was like coming home.

'Darling Miles.' She said it on a sigh, then kissed him in a long, slow, deep assault that was total surrender and urgent desire. Her heart was racing, her skin damp with beads of water and sweat. 'I don't want to disappoint you. I'm a bit out of practice.'

'Corinne, you're lethal. You could make me do anything.'

And she could. No woman had ever made him forget himself so utterly. She was sex, beauty, all woman. His woman. His eyes feasted, then he trailed his lips down her throat, found her breasts firm and taut, the nipples already hard. He sucked and tormented her with his tongue, while his fingers stroked between her legs, felt her hot and wet and trembling. She started moaning, arching up to meet his hand, and he thrust his fingers inside her as she came in a sudden spasm and screamed. She bucked against him as he continued to drive her on, gasped as she felt a fresh orgasm building inside her.

'Oh God, Miles. Now! Now!'

Then he was inside her and it was frantic. She was so alive, so passionate, urging him on in as he plunged into her, fast, hard, desperate, driven to take and possess all she could give. She was his. It went through his brain every time he slammed into her, felt her gasp and shudder, pull him into her with an almost feral hunger. She was truly his. And as they climaxed together, he knew she had his heart and he'd never get it back.

'Corinne,' was all he could say as finally she grew still beneath him. 'Corinne.'

Later she couldn't remember if there was any part of her he hadn't brought to a shuddering orgasm. Every single pore of her body oozed with sex and satisfaction. He lay in her arms, nuzzling her neck and shoulders, loving the feel of her fingers in his hair and her heart beating beneath his head.

'Miles, you're marvellous.'

'You're no slouch yourself, darling. In fact, if I'd known just how hot you are, I wouldn't have been quite so patient.' He raised himself to look into her eyes. 'I was beginning to think you didn't want me. But it was him, wasn't it? What the hell did he do to you?'

'Said he loved me. Cheated on me. Ran off and left me without a word. Broke my heart.'

'Prick. But we aren't all like that.'

'I know. I did want you, Miles. Too much. But I don't do casual sex.'

He kissed her. 'Looks as though you're stuck with me, then.'

'So it would seem. Now that I am, I'd better make sure of exactly what I'm stuck with …'

Her eyes gleamed suggestively, her hands stroked down his back. She dragged his head down, brought her lips to his again. Found his tongue, tasted. She loved kissing him, loved making him feel every stab of desire, hearing him murmur her name as they fell ever deeper.

She pinned his thighs and rolled him over, straddled him, began to kiss her way down his body. She wanted him so much, it shocked her. She hadn't thought it possible to feel this overwhelming need to mate again, feel it pass through her yearning body to his.

'Let me make love to you, Miles. It'll be even better this time ...' her tongue was sending hot darts through every inch of him, 'now that I've remembered a few things.'

'Good God, woman. Can it get any better?' He was out of his depth, being carried away on her relentless tide of pleasure. He grabbed her, tried to hold on, get back control.

'Lie still. Relax. You're beautiful, darling. So beautiful.'

No one had ever called him that before. He let himself go and floated. She remembered things he didn't even know about. Admired and touched him as though his body was a banquet; feasted, found erogenous zones he never knew he had. Hands and lips caressed him expertly, thrilled him, built up waves of pleasure and urgency. She brought vivid sensation everywhere, played on every nerve ending, made him gasp and groan. And when he thought he couldn't possibly feel more, she lowered herself on to him, took him inside her, and rode him hard over the edge and into oblivion.

Miles glanced through half-shut eyes at the clock on the bedside table. It was nearly eight. Corinne was sprawled on top of him, contented and spent. He tipped her face up and laughed.

'Someone's rather pleased with herself.'

'You don't look too unhappy, either.' She stretched, nuzzled his neck. 'I'm ravenous.'

'We never had tea.'

'Shocking. I've failed abysmally as a hostess.'

'I think I can live with it.' He wrapped his arms around her. 'I'll cook if you like.'

'Can you?'

'Cheese on toast.'

'Wow, cordon bleu. I'm honoured.' She tried to get up, but he held her tight. 'Miles?'

He kissed her. 'I'm not letting you get away this time.'

'But I want to get up.'

'I didn't mean that.' He kissed her again, longer, deeper. 'I'm not letting you get away again, ever.' He looked into her eyes. 'Corinne, I love you. I need you with me. I never thought I'd feel this way about anyone. I can't go back to a life without you.'

'Darling, I'm right here. I'm not going anywhere.' She smiled impishly, as his words sank with delicious warmth into her heart. 'I really am stuck with you, aren't I?'

'Yep. Hope you don't mind.'

'No. Actually it's rather wonderful. *Je t'aime, mon amour.*' She kissed him and sighed. 'I love you, Miles. I do love you so much.'

Chapter Thirteen

Sunday morning. Yves scowled as he surveyed the black stubble on his face in the bathroom mirror. Time to make himself look debonair. Sunday was Gabrielle's day. The last time he had collected her, her father had dropped very unsubtle hints about their protracted courtship. He groaned as he switched on his electric razor. His mother was in the conspiracy too. They were all pushing him to marry Gabrielle – and the very idea killed him. Why was he even bothering to keep up the charade? Just to keep the peace, maintain the illusion that he was OK when inside he was an emotional wreck. He wondered if it was worth it. Peace at any price. Appeasers usually ended up having to fight.

Then Philippe wandered in and sat on the hard wickerwork bathroom chair, eyeing him while he finished his shave; almost like a farmer sizing up an animal at auction.

Yves glanced at him sharply. 'I'll be out of here in a minute.'

'No need,' said Philippe. 'I'm not in a rush. I want to talk to you, that's all.'

'Oh.' Yves faced him. Wearing only a towel he suddenly felt exposed and vulnerable. 'What are you staring at?'

'You, of course. You're a damn fine specimen. But I'm worried about you.'

'Why?'

'I'm wondering what you do when you need a woman.'

Yves just stared at the floor, wishing there was a trap door that would swallow him up.

'If you were getting it on with Gabrielle you wouldn't

look as though you're going to your execution,' continued Philippe coolly, 'and you broke up with Yolande ages ago. You don't seem to get out much and there's no talent here. So what do you do?'

'I work.'

'So that's why you make such good profits. I see now where I went wrong. But really, doesn't it get you down?'

Yves bit his lip. Trust Philippe to start a subject like this. He wasn't even like an older brother now; more like a concerned father, his eyes questioning, understanding, encouraging.

'Did you sleep with Yolande?'

'No.'

'Big mistake. She's the sort of girl who has to know she's wanted in bed. That's probably why she left.'

'It's none of your business,' said Yves tersely.

'Well I think it is. You look so bloody miserable, it's almost contagious. Now, why don't you stop being shy and tell me how you endure life without sex?'

Yves stared at Philippe, amazed. In only a few days his ne'er-do-well brother had detected a problem their mother wouldn't have guessed at in as many years. As long as he didn't complain and kept working, she assumed he was all right, trusting that Gabrielle would console him for the loss of Yolande – Gabrielle, who left him stone cold.

'Well?' asked Philippe.

'Sometimes when I'm abroad on business I go to clubs. You know what I mean. But I just can't go through with it. Women like that make me sick.'

'And in Paris?'

'I'm hardly ever there for more than a few hours at a time. Maman really needs me here now she's ill.'

'So when did you last have sex?'

Yves was appalled that he had to think about it. Must have been with Nathalie, a girl he'd dated briefly before he'd finally got together with Yolande. 'Almost two years ago.'

'Christ! It's a good thing I came home. First, Gabrielle – you don't even fancy her, do you?'

'No.' Yves perched on the edge of the bath, feeling more relaxed.

'Well you'd better do the decent thing and end it before she thinks she can't live without you. Then we'll find a woman who can appreciate your charms properly.'

'But Philippe, I ...'

'I know you still love Yolande, but she's gone. Surely you can't bear any more years like this?'

'No, but – well, I'm not like you.'

'Obviously not. But you always used to be able to keep the ladies happy in bed. Why on earth didn't you sleep with Yolande once you got engaged?'

'I wanted our wedding night to be the first time.' He became less tense. It was easy to talk to Philippe. When he was in a mood like this he was a good listener, and no one had listened to Yves for a very long time. 'The marriage was supposed to follow soon after our engagement, and I thought I could wait.'

'You honestly didn't think she was still a virgin?'

Yves gave him a withering look. 'You don't get it, do you?'

'Not at all,' agreed Philippe cheerfully, lighting a cigarette. 'I wouldn't have been able to keep my hands off her.'

Yves squared up, clenched a fist. Philippe just smiled. 'Idiot. I meant if I'd been you.'

His brother relaxed. 'Yolande is special, unique. And I wanted *us* to be special because I loved her so much. That meant waiting until she was my wife. Otherwise she would have been like all the other girls I've had – a meaningless shag.'

'She must have thought you were gay – or impotent. And if you love someone, it's never meaningless. You

205

moron.'

Yves sighed heavily. He didn't need Philippe to tell him that now. 'You don't understand how it was here after you left. Jean-Claude, Maman, even Toinette – desperate to get it all right. And I really wanted that for us too. But Yolande was away a lot on modelling assignments and she kept postponing the wedding. We had a few rows about it, but she came back each time. How long she'd been Patrick Dubuisson's lover before I guessed something was going on, I don't want to know. Two days after Jean-Claude's funeral she finally told me the whole thing was off. She went straight to Paris to do a fashion show and chase up Dubuisson – barely a fortnight after her father's death! I'll never trust a woman again.'

Philippe was momentarily reflective. Poor Yves. What a hopeless romantic. He sometimes wondered how he'd managed to have such a man for his brother.

'You must think I'm crazy to love Yolande after everything,' continued Yves. 'But I simply can't get her off my mind. At Christmas, when I saw her and Gabrielle together – God, it was hell. I'll never be happy with Gabrielle, but I haven't had the guts to tell her. She says she loves me.'

'You've got yourself into a hole listening to sensible advice, haven't you? Well, that's something I could never be accused of. I'm going to offer you a practical solution. Now, what sort of woman do you fancy? Tall? Petite? Blonde or brunette? What turns you on?'

'Philippe, I'm not going to be fixed up with some tart. Just forget it. I'm all right.'

'Do you really think I'd call up a tart? Don't you trust me?'

'Well what are you getting at?'

Philippe drew on his cigarette and exhaled slowly before replying. 'It's quite simple. All I'm proposing to do is restore your va-va voom. There are women – discreet, classy, perhaps slightly older than you've been used to – who'd be absolutely delighted to have you as a lover. They like little presents and flowers and secret rendezvous.'

'Married women?'

'Naturally. You'd be better off with someone who wasn't free as long as you're still hung up on Yolande.'

'I'm surprised you could even suggest such a thing after what happened between you and Claire.'

Philippe was silent, then he smiled. '*Touché*. But now I think what happened between us was a very good thing indeed – my daughter. You don't know how great I feel when I look at Isabelle's picture and know she's mine. I hope she likes me.'

'How could she resist you? By the way, when do I get to meet her?'

'As soon as I've sorted everything out with Claire I hope Isabelle can be introduced to her real family. Apparently the Garnier-Dumonts have never taken to her.'

Yves drummed his fingers on the enamel rim of the bath. 'Are you going to marry Claire?'

'I'll know the answer to that question tomorrow,' said Philippe, standing up. 'Now, I'll get out of your way. I'm sorry if I thought you more desperate than you are.'

Yves rose and looked him in the eye. The offer was still there. Could he accept it? Admit that everything Philippe had guessed was right? But a married woman, when he still burned for Yolande …

'Thanks for the advice,' he said. 'I'm going finish with Gabrielle today. About the rest – later perhaps?'

'Just say the word.' Philippe patted his shoulder, knowing it would take time. 'Are you taking Gabrielle out for lunch?'

'Yes.'

'Good. I'll try to knock some sense into Maman while you're gone. There's a specialist in Paris who's got a brilliant track record with hip replacements. I want her to let me arrange a consultation.'

He turned away, but was halted by a towel hurled expertly over his head. He pulled it away from his eyes and looked round.

'I'm glad you're home,' said Yves, grinning.

Philippe laughed and tossed the towel back. He had stayed away far too long.

Gabrielle giggled throughout lunch. At the clumsy waiter, her own jokes, and a woman sitting at a nearby table in Le Tastevin. Embarrassed, Yves ploughed through the meal in virtual silence. As they left he smiled apologetically at the woman, who looked angrily at Gabrielle but gave him a delightful smile in return. The sort of woman who could appreciate him properly? Late thirties, attractive, a full, firm figure, stationed opposite a man who looked decidedly gay. Surely not her husband. Just a friend. Perhaps she was a divorcee. Not a bit like Yolande. That stopped his reflections at once. He hurried out after Gabrielle.

'You didn't have to show me up like that,' he said sternly as they got into his BMW. It was always the BMW for Gabrielle; she wouldn't be seen dead in his muddy estate car. Yolande had never minded. She made any vehicle she sat in look like a supercar.

'Sorry, Yves,' said Gabrielle, still smirking. 'But really, that dress! And her husband – have you ever seen such a creature?'

He put his foot down hard on the accelerator and drove off, heading east out of St Xavier.

'Aren't we going back to see your mother?'

'No. I'm taking you home.'

'But I don't have to get back for ages! I wanted to talk to you. I'm thinking of applying for university.'

'That's a great idea.'

'My parents keep pushing me to make a decision, but

it's tough.'

'Not really. Just work hard for your *bac* and you'll be all set.'

'Do *you* think I should go to university?'

She sounded worried. He looked at her and noticed that her bottom lip was trembling. So she was trying to get him to propose and rescue her from higher education. He turned on the radio and kept his eyes on the road. When they drew near her home, he stopped in a lay-by. Gabrielle turned off the radio and waited for him to kiss her, her features now perfectly tranquil. Cold. Ugly in their immobility. He realised that he'd only ever managed to kiss her when he'd had a drink or two and kept his eyes firmly shut. Philippe had nailed it in one.

'Gabrielle, I owe you an apology. I feel I may have misled you. Although I'm fond of you, I'm afraid things aren't really working out. I don't think we should see each other again.'

She turned towards him, goggle-eyed, thinking it had to be a joke. Her father had told her to expect a proposal, pointing out that it was a very good match. Better than she could really hope for with her silly face and feather brain (she was doubtful she would even scrape through her *baccalauréat* exams). And Yves was handsome as well as rich, even if he did seem to have some weird hang-ups about pre-marital sex. She guessed her parents had warned him off, but she was going to tell him that she was quite willing to let him have her, there and then, in the car. She'd done it a few times with boys in cars already, and although she hadn't really enjoyed it, in fact found it all rather gross, it seemed to make them deliriously happy. She hoped Yves would get her pregnant; he was far too decent not to marry her then.

'So you aren't upset, Gabrielle? I was afraid you might be.'

'Yves, stop teasing me.'

209

'I'm not.'

Then the reaction came. First she pouted, then she yelled at him, and finally she began to cry. He felt an overwhelming sense of relief. At least he hadn't broken her heart. Bruised her vanity a little, but she'd get over it. When Gabrielle calmed down, she sulked, refusing to speak to him. He deposited her at her home and drove back to St Xavier a free man.

He was going straight back to Rochemort, then remembered that Philippe would probably still be trying to persuade their mother to consult that orthopaedic surgeon. He drove to Le Manoir instead.

'Yves! How lovely.' Corinne, beaming, almost jumped into his arms. 'Come and meet my new boyfriend'

'Boyfriend?' He couldn't process it. 'How? Who?'

'Miles, silly.'

He was flabbergasted for a second, but when he thought about it, things had been heading in that direction for some while. His mother had hinted as much after lunch the day before, but Yves had been so wrapped up in his own misery he hadn't paid attention. But he did all the right things; hugged and kissed Corinne, shook hands with Miles, and teased them about it for fifteen minutes, as was only proper. They were so happy, so much in love. He felt a sharp stab of envy, though he was very pleased for them both. Corinne had been having a tough time recently, and her love life had seemed as disastrous as his own. And he genuinely liked Miles – a straightforward guy who talked with equal authority about corporate finance, cars, rugby, and politics.

It was Miles who dragged him upstairs to ask some questions about the equipment being used in the pictures of nineteenth-century *vignerons*. Afterwards they moved along to the alcove containing Yolande's portrait. Yves loved it – the look of trust and tenderness, a smile uncorrupted by the lens of the paparazzi or the lips of

Patrick Dubuisson.

'I gather you were engaged to her,' Miles commented.

'Yes,' he said sombrely.

They walked back to the staircase.

'I wish she and Corinne would sort out their differences,' Miles continued. 'I don't suppose you still have any influence with Yolande?'

Yves laughed bitterly. 'Hardly. If I had, she'd be my wife now. Anyway, she tried to patch things up with Corinne at Christmas. It was too soon. When Corinne gets hurt, it takes her a very long time to recover.'

'I'd noticed.'

'I'm sure they'll work things out in the end. They were always very close.'

Miles didn't pursue it, and they began to descend the stairs. To avoid having to think about Yolande, Yves switched the subject to UVS and the Marchand shares, but found Miles strangely noncommittal considering the urgency of the situation. When he returned home he broke the news about Corinne's relationship to Philippe as gently as possible.

'I see. I suppose he must make her happy.' Philippe stood up and paced the room for a while, frowning. When he faced Yves again, he was his usual nonchalant self. 'So how did it go with Gabrielle?'

'It's over. She screamed a bit, but it was only her ego hurting.'

'Brilliant. I got results too. Maman has agreed to a consultation with Dr Kamekian. I'm going to arrange it while I'm in Paris tomorrow. And I've a favour to ask. You couldn't possibly let me borrow your car again, could you?'

Yves took the keys to the BMW from his pocket and dropped them into his brother's hand. 'Use it for as long as you like. I hope Claire and Isabelle enjoy the ride.'

Shit, the woman could talk for England, France, and California too. It was a wonder she wasn't hoarse. It was one of those things he hadn't found out until they started living together. Yolande's habit of spending hours on the telephone always irritated Patrick intensely, and today it was infuriating. They were expected for lunch with Vic Bernitz, Jayne Herford, and assorted movie insiders at Althea Pedersen's Malibu home. Another social success for him, another picture in the paper. But Yolande was chattering non-stop down the line to her mother, her dress half-zipped and her face still without a trace of make-up. Perhaps it hadn't been such a good idea of his to heal the rift between them.

He wandered into the living room and crept up behind her as she leaned against the wall by the telephone. She was just finishing the conversation, and nearly jumped when she turned and saw him.

'Patrick, you beast.'

He laughed, slipped his arms around her, zipped up her dress, then kissed the hollows of her shoulders.

'I thought you preferred to undress women,' she said. 'What's the hurry?'

'It's quarter to twelve. We're going to be late.'

'And is it so important?' Yolande stepped back, her eyes rather cold. 'Quite honestly I've seen enough of Jayne and Vic – and Mrs Pedersen – all week. We could have had a day to ourselves for once.'

'But the film, darling. It's good publicity. Anyway, what's there to do here on a Sunday afternoon?'

'I seem to remember when you would have liked to stay in bed with me.'

He drew close. 'We've got time. If you really want to.'

Yolande was always amazed by his constant readiness for sex. A hint, a few kisses, and he could be switched on like a machine, like the performer he was. But she wanted him focused on her alone, without consideration for time

212

or unwanted lunch invitations. It had been like that once – before they came to California.

Patrick kissed her lips and began to pull up her dress, but looking into his eyes she could tell his thoughts were elsewhere. She pushed his hands away. He responded by picking her up and carrying her into the bedroom.

'Put me down!'

'You wanted it, Yolande.'

He dumped her on the bed, pulled up her dress, yanked her legs apart and thrust inside her without preamble. She wasn't at all ready and gasped with pain as he pounded into her. It was the first time she hadn't enjoyed sex. The realisation that there was no love at all about it hurt more than the horrible sensation of being raked by his unrelenting cock. All he cared about was his bloody career. He grunted as he came – in record time – and almost immediately pulled out of her. Then he planted a kiss on her unresponsive mouth and got straight up to finish dressing. He hadn't even bothered to take off his shirt.

Yolande lay shaken and violated on the bed, wondering why they had never again reached that pitch of ecstasy she remembered from the night she had agreed to back the film. She had sold her stake in Marchand for him, alienated a sister she loved, and now they were together and their passion had dwindled to a tawdry three minutes before they went partying. Horrible. Degrading. She wanted to cry, but she was too angry.

He sauntered over to her, smiling. 'Coming?'

She glared at him. 'Did it sound as though I came?'

'I thought you were ready. Look, I'm sorry. Later, eh? I'll make it up to you. Now, are you going to get dressed for lunch?'

'You go on your own. I've got things to do here,'

'But Althea made a big fuss about inviting you. After all, without you there wouldn't be a film. And it's only a lunch. We can have all evening together.'

She sat up, semi-naked, beautiful, like a wild cat ready to pounce, her green eyes fixed on him reproachfully. He sat down beside her, suddenly contrite.

'Please come, Yolande.'

'I'd rather not. I've just had interesting news from my mother and I want to make some calls to France.'

Patrick lowered his eyes. He ought to give up the party and make slow, passionate love to her, then everything would be all right. She would once again be the sweet, carefree, fun-loving Yolande who had taken his fancy at Hervy. But he didn't want to. He had to keep his name before the public, go to all the promotional gigs Ethan told him to attend and work the most influential people in the room. It was no hardship. He loved the buzz, the gorgeous women, the huge mansions with ocean views and limitless cocktails. It was ridiculous of Yolande to behave this way, particularly given her investment in the whole project. He couldn't understand why she wasn't happy. They were together, which is what she had said she always wanted. Surely that was all that mattered. But she'd even started going to Belco's offices a couple of times a week and bringing home contracts and reports, whose turgid business prose, he was surprised to discover, she was actually able to decipher. Obviously she was more of a Marchand than he had realised.

'Look, darling, I really do have to go. They're going to have reporters from *Variety* and one of the cable channels there. We need the publicity, to build up expectations about the film. I won't stay long. And when I get back …'

He leaned down, pushed his head between her thighs and licked his way up to her vagina, slick and swollen from sex. She fell back on the pillows, arched up and moaned as his tongue flicked over her, inside her, sent spears of desire jarring through her. And growled in bitter frustration when he stopped abruptly and stood up.

'Patrick! Don't leave me like this!'

She was exactly where he liked her to be – at his mercy, begging for him. He smiled, bent to kiss her lips. 'Think of me.' He cupped her, teased her with his fingers. 'Think of all the things I'm going to do to you later.'

Then he left. This time she cried.

He drove to Malibu alone, in a brand new sports car with a personalised number plate which he had bought to look impressive on the set. Quite an advance on his old Renault. Soon it would feature in publicity photographs too; the image would be complete. Raybans, leather jacket, T-shirt, designer jeans, Ferrari – irresistible masculinity packaged in an irresistible format. It had taken Ethan Casavecchia all of two seconds to think of how Patrick was to be marketed. But Hollywood knew what it liked, and Ethan liked what Hollywood liked. It was a marriage of true minds. Patrick was a willing partner in the *ménage à trois*.

Althea Pedersen wouldn't have dreamed of treating Patrick as anything other than extra-special. After all, he was a rising star, and she liked to know the big names. But there was something else about him, too. An attention to women, a charming way of answering even the most innocent speeches with a gallant smile, a constant acknowledgement that she was feminine and he was acutely aware of the fact. It was such a difference from Hank's laconic love. Not that she had tired of her husband – she knew he was the only man she really wanted. But she was flattered by this clandestine, tantalising, safe flirtation.

'Where's Yolande?' was the question almost everyone asked as soon as Patrick arrived at the Pedersens' house.

He lied and said she was ill, then dutifully listened to their condolences. Lunch was a calorie-controlled affair, and he was glad he had stopped off at a drive-in for a burger en route. He made sure he conversed with the

215

reporters, flirting just the right amount with the cable journalist, who was a dizzy redhead with a great cleavage and bedroom eyes. But Patrick had other objectives. After the reporters had left, things got better. Vic, Jayne, and Ethan were engaged in a heated debate and did not wish to be interrupted, so Patrick and Althea took drinks outside by the pool.

It was warm and sunny, and they sat close together on a lounger, enjoying each other and the fresh sea air. Patrick wasn't sorry that Mr Pedersen had been detained by business in New York. Althea said it was an important deal he had been cooking up for a long time, though she failed to mention it was because Stessenberg had called to say he was soon leaving for Europe to buy Corinne out of UVS, and wanted to draw up a preliminary contract with Hank for the Marchand shares he would then be free to dispose of to Pedersen Corporation.

'I guess you're not much interested in business,' she said, smiling.

'No. I've always wanted to be an actor – ever since I can remember.'

'Do you have family connections with the movies? I'm sure I've seen you before somewhere.'

Patrick twirled his cocktail glass between his fingers. 'My mother was an actress at the Comédie Française,' he said at last. 'She encouraged me to go to drama school.'

'Oh. Well, I guess you've just got a classic French face. How's shooting going after that hassle with the scriptwriters, by the way?'

'Vic got them to do another rewrite. He had to. Jayne wouldn't say the lines. She wants Amanda to be a stronger role – no playing sidekick to a man. I don't mind. She has to say she loves me at the end.'

Althea laughed. 'Are we talking about the same script I read back in the fall? But I suppose Vic knows what he's doing.'

216

'The story did need tightening. And Jayne has really improved some scenes. I try to do the same.'

'How do you feel about the love scenes with Yolande keeping an eye on you?'

'Nervous.' Patrick leaned forward, putting his glass down. 'You see, Althea, when I have to hold Jayne like this,' he put his arms round her and pulled her close, 'it's embarrassing when Yolande's there. She starts coughing and walking up and down.' He could feel Althea breathing faster against his chest. 'Then when we kiss, it's worse. And when we have to do the sex scenes, it's going to be terrible.'

Althea looked up, rather nervous herself, and felt his lips against hers. Confident, demanding. She couldn't help but respond. She closed her eyes and slid her arms around his neck, enjoying his young, warm, vigorous kisses, his hand searching for an opening in her blouse, his sigh of pleasure as he touched her skin and began to negotiate her bra. The front fastening was very helpful. Her breasts were fuller than Yolande's. He eyed them hungrily.

'Patrick, no.'

He smiled as he slowly rubbed her nipples. 'Don't you like it?'

Yes, she did. More than she should. She gave herself up to his exploring hands and tongue, but when he started to unbutton his jeans, she panicked. No, she must cool it. What had Hank said about Patrick's lecherous eyes? She stood up quickly and fastened her clothes, while he lay back on the lounger, trying to get himself under control. It had been a perfect opportunity; but there would be others. He was sure of that. Now he had staked his claim, Althea was his anytime he liked.

They went back into the house and entered into a discussion with Vic and Jayne on another script change she had proposed. When they all said goodbye, Patrick kissed Althea's hand, then kissed Jayne's with extra gallantry. No one would have even guessed at their indiscretion. She began to think his acquaintance definitely worth cultivating.

'Corinne, it's me. Please talk to me. I just wanted to say how pleased I am about you and Miles. Mummy rang and told me.'

Corinne wasn't exactly brimming over with goodwill, but she was friendlier than she had been at Christmas.

'I suppose you also want to say *I told you so*,' she said dryly.

'Well, I was right, wasn't I? So come on, tell me what happened. You couldn't stand him. Don't spare the gory details.'

'Incorrigible brat! He just wore down my resistance with his charm, good looks, and general gorgeousness, of course. He's great.'

'You really are in love with him, aren't you?'

'You sound surprised.'

'I don't think I've ever heard you say that about anyone else. He must be special. I'm so glad. You deserve someone special.' And Yolande was more than a little pleased that she had been instrumental in kicking off the whole affair. 'There's something else I wanted to say. Can you get my shares back?'

'I think so. Miles is working on it for me.'

'About the apartment and Le Manoir …'

'I was wondering when you'd get round to that,' said Corinne crisply. 'My lawyers have been waiting for you to finalise for weeks. I'm having the contents valued soon.'

'Could you please put it off for a while? I think I'll come over in the summer, and it would be easier to do it on the spot.'

Corinne agreed. Long distance negotiations with a correspondent as poor as Yolande would be infinitely more difficult. 'By the way, Toinette's back at the Avenue

Foch. I had to do it to get a stake in UVS.'

Yolande could hardly complain, since it was all her fault. In fact she was surprised to find herself thinking how much more fun it would be at one of Toinette's parties than at Malibu. Pure heresy.

There was a pause, then Corinne said, 'I've seen Philippe.'

'Are you OK?'

'Yes, although he nearly blew it for me with Miles. I resisted the urge to slice him into small pieces, because I don't think Marie-Christine would have forgiven me.'

Yolande chuckled. That was her sister talking, not some frigid stranger called Corinne Marchand.

'Philippe's seeing his daughter tomorrow,' continued Corinne, 'and Yves has just broken up with Gabrielle.'

'Oh. How is he?'

'Not good. He misses you.'

And I miss you too, Corinne nearly added. She hadn't realised quite how much until she'd heard that wicked chuckle again.

Yolande had a twinge of conscience. Poor Yves. Perhaps he was fated not to find happiness with any woman. He asked for far too much, and gave so little. She knew she could never have lived up to his ideal.

'Well,' she said at last. 'I suppose I'll see you when I come over? Probably in August. Is that all right? I'm going to Dorset as well.'

'You know where you can reach me. How's the film going?'

'OK. Everybody tells me it's wonderful, anyway. I find it all rather tedious. They shoot some scenes so many times, I could repeat the entire script in my sleep. I'm trying to get to grips with the business side of Belco, but it's tough.'

'Christ, you *must* be bored.' And very lonely, Corinne thought. The idea of Yolande willingly trawling through company statistics was simply mind-boggling.

'I miss you,' said Yolande. 'Very much. Take care of yourself, darling.'

'You too. Goodbye, *petite fleur*.'

Yolande put the receiver down, relieved they could now talk again, delighted and touched that her sister had called her *petite fleur*. She saw hope for the future, but felt marooned. Stuck in the desert with Patrick, while everything she loved was happening in Europe. No modelling now, either. Perhaps she should get herself another assignment when she went home. She had started looking into Belco's operations in desperation for something to do on the days when she couldn't face the shoot, and had surprised herself by developing an interest in the company. After all, she owned it, and she wasn't persuaded that delegating all the management to Vic Bernitz, as he had repeatedly suggested, would be in her best interests.

The Belco office was a small low-rise affair on a distinctly unglamorous business park forty-five minutes' drive west of Hollywood, just south of Santa Monica Boulevard. It was kept afloat by an efficient production executive called Shelby Owens, accountant Troy Salzmann, a couple of assistants, and an intern from UCLA film school. Both Troy and Shelby had blinked behind their spectacles when Yolande had breezed in one day, asking sweetly if they would show her the ropes.

Troy had hardly been able to utter a coherent sentence for an hour, he was so dazzled by her smile, while Shelby had shown her to her desk with the air of a long-suffering teacher humouring a particularly capricious pupil. She'd doubtless reckoned it would take only thirty minutes for the impossibly beautiful Yolande Marchand to stroll out again and waste her time more appropriately shopping on Rodeo Drive. But Yolande had stayed, ploughed through accounts and company reports, asked intelligent questions, and took work home. She soon decided that profits on the back catalogue were too small and set Shelby and the intern to work on costings for a re-release of Belco's major hits on DVD and internet download. And, thank the Lord, ordered in real coffee and a daily delivery of doughnuts for the whole team. They all looked forward to Yolande's visits to the office now. She always had a smile and time for a gossip, even though she was the boss. She took the piss out of Vic Bernitz and Ethan Casavecchia. She continually surprised everyone by her instinctive grasp of business realities and her shrewd marketing ideas. It looked as though Belco might well have a future after all. They had decided that she was OK.

Patrick arrived back from Malibu to find Yolande busy emailing the office from her laptop. He was unsure of his welcome, but she logged out with a smile when she saw him and opened her arms. He complained bitterly of the miserable time he had had without her, and after he had atoned for his earlier sins by giving her two orgasms, amused her with a well-mimicked performance of Ethan daring to contradict Jayne Herford. Yolande noticed a mark on his neck, and he said he had been bitten by an insect in the Pedersens' garden. She believed him.

Chapter Fourteen

11 a.m. Only an hour before Philippe would arrive. Claire left Isabelle to play in the salon with her toys and went upstairs to change. The house seemed more bleak and empty than usual now there were no bodyguards about. A Versailles mansion with a large garden, it had once been the home of a Court official under Louis XIV. Henri had inherited it from his first wife, and relics belonging to her family still cluttered some of the rooms. They weren't Claire's style at all, but she hadn't had the heart to throw them out. She kept forgetting that the house was now hers and she could do what she liked. But nothing seemed as though it really belonged to her and she felt hemmed in by second-hand wealth. Henri had been a collector too; a bad one. She was haunted by the fruits of his ill-advised forays into auction houses and antiques shops – a disparate hoard of art and furniture united only in gloom. One or two pieces were attractive individually, but choked by the mediocrity of the rest. The whole house cried out for more space and light. Claire would have to see to it later, when she knew if she would be staying.

The problem now was how to dress for Philippe. She wanted to avoid looking intent on reviving their affair, so it would have to be something understated. Eventually she picked black Hervy jeans and a striped cotton sweater. Keep it simple. No make-up, only the faintest hint of perfume. She hoped he would get the message.

Philippe thought she looked absolutely gorgeous when he arrived promptly at noon. Claire ushered him quickly into the hall, then they stopped and just looked at each other. She could scarcely believe he was really there, handsome and smiling rather shyly, totally unchanged. It was as though they had parted only the day before. He dropped the large carrier bag he had brought and opened his arms.

'Hello, my darling.'

Claire found herself in his embrace, his fingers messing up her hair as he planted light kisses all over her face, then pressed his lips to hers for much longer than she had meant to allow. She had the sensation that the past was simply slipping away.

'Philippe, we mustn't.'

'Why mustn't we? You're more beautiful than ever, Claire.' He held her close, and she relaxed a little, her head against his shoulder. 'That's better,' he said, brushing his lips against her hair, liking the silkiness he had forgotten. 'How was Le Mans?'

'Fine.'

'Have you told them about me yet?'

'No.'

How could she tell her parents that Isabelle was his child, when he might walk out and never be seen again? It was a confession that would really hurt them. That she had had an affair would be hard enough to explain. That she had betrayed her background by loving a son of the noble house of Rochemort and bearing his child would be even more difficult for her Socialist family to swallow. They had been horrified enough when she had married Henri, though she had never been sure if it was because of his politics, the age gap, or his personality. Looking up, she noticed a couple of grey hairs on Philippe's temple and weariness about his eyes. Isabelle's eyes exactly.

'How long can you stay?' she asked. 'I've given Isabelle's nanny the day off so you won't be seen.'

He laughed and kissed the tip of her nose. 'I don't give a damn who sees me now. I can stay as long as you'll have me. Now, where's my daughter?'

224

She led him into the salon, where Isabelle, tired of her games, was sprawled on the sofa with her teddy bear.

'Isabelle, come and meet Phil …'

'No, Claire. I want her to know who I am.'

Philippe let go of her hand and went over to Isabelle, his heart thumping. He fell completely in love on the spot. He sat beside her on the sofa, longing to pick her up, but she was staring at him with a puzzled expression. They looked so much alike, and she seemed to know it. Philippe smiled nervously and picked up the bear instead.

'Hello, Isabelle. Is this your bear?'

'Yes. He's old.'

'How old?'

'Very, very old,' she said emphatically.

'Christmas present,' said Claire, sitting down in an armchair opposite them.

'Poor teddy, he's only got one eye.' Philippe examined him carefully. 'And you've been chewing his ears, haven't you?'

Isabelle giggled. 'Give him to me!'

Philippe handed over the bear, which she promptly dropped onto the floor.

'That's not very nice. You ought to kiss him better.'

'Don't want to.'

'Well, if you did that to me I'd really cry.'

Isabelle looked at him saucily for a few moments, then clambered up to him and put her hands up to his face. She smacked his cheeks, then tweaked his ears, and finally sat on his lap, laughing. Philippe caught her up in his arms and hugged her, then turned up her face and looked into her eyes. His daughter; his beautiful little daughter. He felt like crying for the years they had lost. Isabelle was surprised for a moment or two, then fastened her arms around his neck and planted a smacker on his cheek.

'Now you're better!'

Philippe smiled at Claire over the top of her head as he

225

picked up the teddy bear.

'He's called James,' said Isabelle, grabbing it. 'What's *your* name?'

'It's Philippe. But you must call me Papa, Isabelle.'

She frowned. 'Papa Philippe?'

'No, just Papa. I'm your papa.'

She looked across at Claire, who nodded, too overcome to speak. She would never have believed he could be so good with children – nonchalant, reckless Philippe, cuddling his daughter and taking every precaution to prevent James from suffering fresh indignity as he was dangled by his ear over the floor.

'I'm your papa,' repeated Philippe.

'Hello, Papa,' Isabelle said cheekily.

'Don't I get another kiss?'

'Give me a kiss! Give James a kiss! Give Maman a kiss!'

Philippe swiftly obliged. Then he swung her up onto his shoulders, and she spurred him with her little feet as they all went out to the hall.

'Claire, will you get the bag? I've brought a few things for mademoiselle.'

A riotous hour followed as the presents were ripped open and Isabelle tried to lay her hands on them all at once. A baseball cap, bat, and ball soon engrossed her attention. After a game of sorts in the garden, they sat down to a late lunch, and Philippe's questions were endless. He wanted to know about Isabelle's health, her nursery school, the names of her friends, what she liked to eat. Claire couldn't hide her amazement. Henri had never troubled himself over such details, but then he had hardly ever acknowledged that Isabelle was human.

'So you haven't got a pet?' Philippe asked his daughter when they were all back in the salon. 'What would you like, a dog or a cat?'

'A dog.'

'There are lots of dogs where I live. It's a big château in the country.'

'How big'?' she demanded.

'This big,' he stretched his arms out as wide as possible. 'And my dogs are *this* big.'

'Ooh' Isabelle opened her eyes wide. 'Is it a *real* château?'

'Oh yes. Do you want to see it? I'll take you.'

She nodded enthusiastically, and Philippe amused her with some stories about suits of armour that stalked the corridors at night, and a ghost who wandered around drunk singing songs every third Sunday at midnight.

It was quite a problem persuading her to go to bed after the day's excitement, and she had to be bribed with the promise of another story. But bath time came first, and that gave her another opportunity to play. She started splashing water energetically over her father, in spite of Claire's protests.

'She's behaving terribly, Philippe. I'm so sorry. Isabelle, no, no, no!'

Isabelle giggled and Philippe laughed, though the water had seeped right through his shirt. He hardly noticed it. He felt strangely elated. Proud to have such a child, thrilled when she called him 'Papa' – quite naturally, which somewhat intrigued him – delighted that she returned his affection.

And Claire was an angel. He could imagine the hell she'd had to put up with from her husband, but there hadn't been one word of reproach. She treated him as though it was only right he should behave as if he were at home. Seeing her in this domestic setting revealed facets of her personality he had never known when they were lovers, snatching an hour or two together as and when they could. He was struck by so much that had escaped him before; her patience, good humour, common sense, tenderness, and – now and then, when she thought he

227

wasn't looking at her – a certain melancholy which she quickly suppressed. Was he the cause? Or was she mourning Henri Garnier-Dumont?

'You'd better go to my room and dry off,' she told him, as Isabelle was being cajoled into her pyjamas.

Claire's room adjoined Isabelle's, at the end of a short passage. Fresh territory again for Philippe. They always used to meet in hotels or at his flat. He put his shirt to dry on a radiator, then wandered around, looking for clues about Claire.

It had been a splendid room once, with a fine moulded ceiling and panelled walls, but the original effect had been ruined by clumsy later alterations and layers of paint. The spirit had been lost, suffocated. The whole house was suffocating. There was a photograph of Isabelle with a smiling middle-aged couple on the table beside the double bed; obviously Claire's parents. They looked nice, respectable people. He wondered what they would think when they found out who had fathered their granddaughter. Philippe was relieved there was no picture of Garnier-Dumont, even if his unpleasant personality manifested itself in the decor. Had he and Claire slept together in that bed, or did they have separate rooms? Suddenly he had to know. He had always thought it didn't matter, that he didn't care. He'd left her in the lurch, he'd slept with other women both during and after their affair, he'd never fully returned the love she had given him. But he longed for it now. And he couldn't blame her if she refused to give him a second chance.

Claire came in from Isabelle's room and stopped when she saw him sitting half-clad by her dressing-table, glumly contemplating her jars of make-up. 'Aren't you coming? Isabelle's waiting for her story.'

She forced herself to look away as he stood up. He still had a body to die for, and she was horrified to feel a tug of desire deep inside again.

'Shall I get you a bath robe?'

'If it's one of his, I'd rather not.'

'He never used it.'

Philippe took the robe she offered him; a tight fit on the shoulders, but it concealed most of his muscular torso. He went in to Isabelle, now sitting up in bed determined to extract as many stories from him as possible. Eventually she was satisfied, and allowed herself to be tucked in and kissed goodnight.

'Can I really see your château, Papa?'

'Yes, darling.'

'Tomorrow?'

'No, that's a bit soon. In a couple of weeks, if you're a very good girl and go to sleep now.'

He kissed her and stroked her hair with a smile of such warmth and tenderness that it brought tears to Claire's eyes. She went back to her own room. Ten minutes later Philippe followed and found his shirt laid out on the bed.

'It's dry now,' Claire said. 'Is she all right?'

'Sound asleep.' He moved into the centre of the room. 'Do you know, I haven't had a cigarette for five hours. It's a miracle.'

'I gave up when I got pregnant.' She retreated to a corner.

'Claire, why are you cowering over there? Come here. We've got to talk.'

He put on the shirt and sat down on the bed, motioning her to join him. She remained in the corner, too conscious of his body, his piercing eyes, and her vulnerability.

'I'm so glad you came,' she said. 'But I didn't mean you to take it so far, Philippe. Isabelle's not used to having a fond papa.'

It only confirmed his suspicions about Garnier-Dumont. It was all his fault. He should never have left Claire to face it alone, never allowed his child to suffer the consequences. He was beginning to understand his

229

mother's attitude to the whole affair.

'Didn't you want me to love my own daughter?' he asked. 'She's marvellous. I adore her. I just wonder if you can ever forgive me.'

She forced a smile. 'Well, as we both agree that she's absolutely wonderful, there's nothing to forgive. I could never be sorry for having her. I suppose we ought to arrange times for you to visit her. If you want to, I mean. After all, you have rights, and I ...'

'Claire!' Philippe could bear it no longer. He bounded over to her and grabbed her shoulders. 'How can you say such things? Rights! I don't want rights! I want to see her every morning when she wakes up and tell her silly stories every night. Don't you understand, darling?'

'No, Philippe, no. It's impossible.'

'You said you still loved me.' He pulled her into his arms and held her fast, wanting her to kiss him. 'So why is it impossible?'

'Because ... ' She looked up, recognised the expression in his eyes, and tried to break out of his embrace, away from danger. 'Philippe, don't start it all over again. I can't, I just can't. Please, you must understand'

'Why are you crying? Because I'm trying to ask you to marry me? I want you to give me more babies to spoil.'

She was stunned into silence. It wasn't a hope she had ever allowed herself to entertain. How could he marry her? The eternally carefree and unshackled Philippe de Rochemort, who only had to click his fingers to get any woman he wanted?

'Claire?'

She looked up again, saw the glow in his eyes, and pulled his head down. Their lips met. Slowly, then with passion. Oh, it was so easy to fall into him again. Taste that mouth, stoke the heat building inside her, want him so much she forgot everything.

'Does that mean yes?'

She pushed him away, breathless. 'But …'

'Yes or no? Claire, I must know.'

'Do you love me?'

'Yes.' His turn to be surprised. He didn't even have to think about it. He just felt it. He belonged with her. She had finally given him a certainty he thought he would never know. And it felt so good. Kisses, hot, hard, devoured her. 'I love you. I know I don't deserve you, but I'll try to. Come downstairs, I want to show you something.'

He seized her hand and led her down to the salon to retrieve the carrier bag, now emptied of Isabelle's presents. At the bottom was a folder, which he handed to Claire, making her sit close beside him on the sofa.

'Open it, darling. No, I'm not mad. Open it.'

She took out two property specifications for wine-growing châteaux in the less renowned areas of Burgundy. Beautiful houses in need of modernisation, ample potential for development as hotels or conference centres, both with vineyards.

'What do you think?' he asked. 'It would be bloody hard work. The wines aren't brilliant, even though they're in *premier cru* villages. It would take us about five years to break even, let alone make a profit. But if we ran part of the house as a hotel, we wouldn't starve. Actually, this one, the Château Briteuil, isn't more than an hour's drive from Rochemort. Of course, if you can't bear the idea, I've got a couple of consultancy schemes that could work in Paris. But it's not what I really want to do and I'd probably be abroad rather a lot. Claire – you're not crying again?'

It was too much, too soon. She cried for a few minutes, sniffed, wiped her eyes. When he had kissed her back into a smile, she said she rather liked the look of the Château Briteuil.

'But how did you find out about these properties so soon after coming home?'

'I've been looking ever since I decided to leave America. A friend sent these to me in New York. They've not been advertised yet, so I've more or less got first option. Of course, you'll still have this house.'

'I hate it. I've been so unhappy here.'

'Let me make you happy.' He smiled as he pulled her into his arms. 'Come to bed with me.'

Claire hadn't thought she could feel so blissfully content. Locked in Philippe's arms, limbs entwined, skin to skin. Her heart was pounding, shock waves still rolled through her. And there was no rush to get dressed this time, no hurrying down back stairs and switching taxis on the way home. No need to hide.

'Mmmm …' she leaned up to kiss him. 'I could really get to like this.'

'You'd better.' God, she looked so sweet and sexy, all flushed and tousled and with desire lighting up her eyes. He rolled her onto her back, leaned over her, started to kiss his way down her body. 'Because, my darling, I need to make love to you again.'

Afterwards they talked for a long time. No recriminations, no bitterness. Only plans for the future, how to break the news to their families, when to go and view Château Briteuil. Philippe pushed for everything to happen as quickly as possible. Now Claire was his, he didn't want to risk losing the happiness he had found.

'But what about the media?' she asked. 'I don't think I can face all that.'

Philippe stroked her cheek. 'I won't let anyone get to you. That reminds me, Isabelle will have to take my name. Can we change her birth certificate?'

Claire found him early the following morning in his daughter's room, making her squeal with laughter by acting out scenes with her new furry toys in an American accent. She began to wonder what she was letting herself in for. Philippe kept insisting that he wanted more children. The Château Briteuil would be a very boisterous place indeed.

Miles walked out onto the steps of his club in St James's Square and glanced up. It didn't look as though it would rain. In fact it was just the morning for a brisk stroll. Forty-five minutes to spare before his appointment with Ulrich von Stessenberg. That gave him time to finalise plans with Grant Macdonald over a coffee before they were due at the Connaught. He walked up to Piccadilly, which he crossed with a throng of listless teenagers being herded along to the Royal Academy by a harassed teacher. Cars jumped the lights, scaffolding blocked the pavement, beautiful paintings sat serenely neglected in art gallery windows and the first trickle of tourists emerged from the tube to see the sights. It couldn't be anywhere but the heart of London.

He poked his head inside the Hervy boutique in Old Bond Street and emerged very impressed, then marched down Bruton Street and into Berkeley Square. Macdonald was waiting for him on a bench beneath one of the ancient plane trees, its winter branches bare and forlorn. He offered Miles a cardboard cup as soon as he sat down.

'Double espresso, as requested.'

'Thanks.' Miles took a welcome sip. 'So, what's the drill? Are you wired or have your guys bugged his suite?'

'That's not something you need to bother about. All you need do is soften him up, then let me rescue him when he thinks there's no other way out.'

'But it's OK for me to get the Marchand shares off him first? Once your lot gets hold of him, I imagine all UVS assets will be frozen.'

Macdonald smiled. 'Oh, we might play the markets for a little while. In a very controlled way, of course.'

'Not with my client's shares, you won't.'

'Of course not. You may restore them to Miss Marchand tonight, over dinner and … Well, you're a lucky man. She's gorgeous.'

'Damn you, you haven't had *us* under surveillance?'

'Not you, but we had to be sure about her since she bought into UVS. Don't worry, she came out clean. I'm a bit concerned about how much her stepmother knew, but we'll follow that up later. It's Stessenberg we need. Do you want me to run over any of the details again?'

'I've got it all. If I forget anything, just interrupt.'

'Right. Let's get him.'

Stessenberg had chosen to stay at the Connaught – the acme of discretion, tucked away in Carlos Place where only those in the know ever strayed from the better-known Mayfair thoroughfares. At 11.45 a.m. sharp Miles and Macdonald presented themselves at the hotel's reception desk. They were immediately directed to a suite on the second floor.

Stessenberg was alone. He greeted Miles with a brief, firm handshake. 'Mr Corsley, please come in. It was good of you to come to London.'

'Not at all,' said Miles, eyeing his host intently. He was attractive in a chilling way. His blue eyes were too light, but at the moment exceedingly affable. 'May I introduce my colleague – Grant Macdonald?'

Macdonald shook hands and quickly took a seat by the window, while Miles and Stessenberg moved over to a table on which there were several documents, a jug of orange juice, two glasses, and even a pen for Miles to sign the contract relieving Corinne of her stake in UVS.

'I hope you'll forgive me for asking for a quick settlement,' said Stessenberg, sitting down and motioning Miles to a seat opposite, 'but I have a great deal to attend to on this trip.'

'Setting up a new fashion label with Franco Rivera, aren't you?'

'May I ask how you know that?'

'My client likes to keep informed about the activities of her former employees. But that's not what we're here to discuss.'

Stessenberg smiled. 'No. I have the relevant paperwork prepared. Would you care to go through it?'

Miles placed his briefcase on the table and leaned back in his chair. 'Actually, no. My client won't sell her stake in UVS to you unless you sell your holding in Marchand Enterprises to her.'

'Please, Mr Corsley, don't waste my time. I've made it perfectly clear that I have no intention of selling the Marchand shares to Mademoiselle Marchand. You may assure her that I have no intention either of trying to take control of her company. She will gain absolutely nothing by these delaying tactics. I've offered her a fair price for her UVS holding, so we might as well sign. I thought we had a gentlemen's agreement.'

'That rather depends on your definition of a gentleman.'

'I really don't have time for semantics. I have a lunch engagement at one. Would you please review the papers? Otherwise I'll read them to you and then you can sign.'

Miles sipped his orange juice slowly. Stessenberg was one cool customer. He obviously felt secure. It would be rather pleasant to wipe that smug smile off his face.

'Before we get into more detailed negotiations, it might help if we got names correct,' said Miles, extracting a file from his briefcase. 'Now, Herr Graf Klaus-Ulrich von Altminden, what was it you wished to discuss?'

'Excuse me? I haven't the faintest idea what you mean.'

But Miles had caught a flicker of knowledge and annoyance behind that bland expression. 'Oh, but I think you have. However, if you need to jog your memory, I have something here that might help.' He took some papers from the file, one eye on Stessenberg all the time. 'You were born in East Berlin. Your father was …'

'Klaus von Stessenberg,' snapped Stessenberg, 'an East German civil servant. So what? That's how things were then. You had to survive. Now, I'd be grateful if you stopped this interesting chat about my family and read the contract.'

'Well, it is rather interesting that there's no record of any Graf von Stessenberg in armorial guides. No record of a Klaus von Stessenberg in the East German archives either – it's simply marvellous how thorough they are. But we do have a Graf Klaus von Altminden who had some rather questionable financial dealings with the Nazis during the Second World War. Managed to jump ship and persuade the Communists he could be useful. Dropped his title and married a Maria Stessenberg, settling down to a cosy existence in East Berlin working for the East German leadership. That's where you slipped up, Altminden. A little too proud of your noble ancestry, aren't you? It doesn't pay when you're wanted by security services across the globe. Why the hell couldn't you just change your name to Schmidt?'

'You're mad.'

Macdonald, watching from his seat, nodded at Miles.

Miles handed over an intelligence report, endorsed by both the CIA and MI6, and pushed it across the table. Stessenberg shot him a hostile glance and picked up the paper. When he looked up, his expression was ice-cold.

'This is of no relevance to our business. It's just family history. So, I wanted to use my father's title. That's not a crime.'

'No, of course not. Looks good on the headed paper, doesn't it? But, we started thinking, why didn't you just use your father's title? Why did you add his title to your mother's surname? Why, in fact, did you change your name?'

'After the Berlin Wall came down, I decided to launch my business. I didn't want people to keep associating me with the East, which they would have done had I been known as Altminden. My father was very well known in the DDR hierarchy. So I changed my name. End of story.'

Miles passed over the photograph of a man in the uniform of a Stasi colonel. He had kept it back on purpose. 'Not quite.'

Stessenberg glanced at it and looked up. 'Yes, I was a colonel in the Stasi. Not a crime either, as far as I'm aware. For your information, I and thousands of my colleagues lost our jobs after reunification, and our pensions are pitiful. I don't see what the fuck any of it has got to do with you.'

He was losing his cool. The swearing was a good sign. Macdonald got up unhurriedly and joined them.

'Rather a lot, actually,' said Miles. 'We know you worked for the HVA – foreign intelligence. Had masses of contacts throughout the Soviet bloc, the former Yugoslavia, and the Middle East. We know that you still nurture those contacts. That your business grew five hundred per cent during the wars in the Balkans and Iraq. That you are currently in constant communication with rather undesirable people in the Gulf and Afghanistan. I don't suppose you care where the money comes from or who gets killed with the arms bought with the profits you make. You just have to survive, don't you?'

'I invest money for people,' Stessenberg said. 'I make profits for them. And I'm good at it. Politics don't come into it as far as I'm concerned.'

'They do when you're investing money for terrorists,' said Macdonald smoothly, sitting beside Stessenberg, 'when that money has come from organised crime, stolen government funds, and drug trafficking. When the profits provide arms and training for terrorist organisations.'

'What the hell do you want?' Stessenberg sounded

237

weary, bored even. But there was a hint of fear in his eyes. He looked at the door, but Macdonald had him wedged in, and he knew he was carrying a weapon.

'A little bit of co-operation,' said Miles. It was time to go in for the kill. 'Then we might be able to discuss ways of keeping you out of jail. So if you'd care to look over *this* contract, we might be able to do business.'

He passed Stessenberg the document Corsley European had prepared for the sale of UVS' Marchand stake to Corinne. Below the market price, of course.

Stessenberg snatched up a pen and scribbled his signature on it.

'Thank you. I knew we could do a deal.' Miles quickly shoved the contract into his briefcase.

'I still want your client's stake in my company, Mr Corsley.'

'No problem at all,' said Miles, 'although you may find you won't have much of a company left. I'll leave you to discuss that with Mr Macdonald. Co-operation, Altminden, remember. It's his favourite word.' He stood up. Macdonald didn't need him now. 'There is one thing. Who were you going to sell your Marchand stake to?'

'I would have thought you'd have found that out by now. Look for an American corporation with Pacific interests. They're going global.'

Several names sprang to mind. A little research would surely uncover the predator. Not that it really mattered, but Miles was keen to piece the whole jigsaw together. He walked to the door.

'My bank in Paris will arrange the transfer of funds and shares with UVS in New York. It will all be settled by the end of the week. Thank you for your time.'

Stessenberg raised his glass of orange juice with a grimace. 'Not at all, Mr Corsley. I would say it was a pleasure, but my acting abilities don't stretch that far.'

'Don't let it spoil your lunch,' said Miles as he left the

room.

'Well?' demanded Rupert Corsley as he sat opposite Miles at a table at The Wolseley on Piccadilly an hour later. 'How did it go?'

'According to plan. I'll have those shares on Friday, locked in a vault in Paris.'

'Do you think he'll talk?'

'I'm sure Macdonald will be able to persuade him his interests lie in helping British Intelligence rather than being handed over to the Yanks. He certainly didn't look too keen on the idea of jail.'

'You look like a Cheshire cat, boy. Get over yourself. Wasn't all down to you.'

'I won't tell you then.'

'Tell me what?'

Miles' smile broadened even more. 'The emotional dividend – don't you remember?'

'Oh?' grunted Rupert suspiciously.

'Corinne's in love with me. Officially. She's absolutely wonderful.'

Rupert stared at him for a few moments, then slapped him on the back. 'Well done! Bring her home for Easter, eh? We'd be delighted to have you both. What the hell's that aftershave you're wearing?'

'*Hervy Pour Homme* – one of Marchand's new range. Guaranteed to make women weak at the knees.' Miles grinned again. 'Why don't you try some out on Aunt Alice?'

Rupert snorted, then he burst out laughing. It was a distinctly hung-over Miles who boarded a train to Paris that afternoon.

Chapter Fifteen

Tex Beidecker picked up the phone and dialled Yolande's number in Beverley Hills. It rang only twice before she answered.

'Tex, how lovely.' She was delighted to hear him. 'How are you? How's Mummy?'

'We're both fine. Your mother's gone to Edith Denbrake's birthday lunch.'

'That's brave of her.'

'I always send my woman in for the dangerous jobs. How are you?'

'Oh, all right. I'm heading down to the Belco office in a little while.'

'Filming getting you down?'

'A bit. It's not really my scene. But I'm trying to find out whether Belco has a future as a viable business. It's quite interesting, actually. Now that I've got stuck in.'

'Honey, I never heard that. I can't have people thinking my beautiful stepdaughter likes accounting. It'd ruin my street cred.'

She laughed. 'I doubt anyone would believe you anyway. They all think I'm playing games out here.'

'Let them think what they like. It's the bottom line that counts.' He was glad he had covered his own astonishment. Even when she'd been studying business, Yolande had never shown much interest in it. What the heck had triggered it off now? 'I've got some news for you. Corinne called me a short while ago. She's managed to buy back your stake in Marchand. Miles clinched the deal in London yesterday.'

Yolande gasped audibly. 'Do you really mean it, Tex?'

'Yes.'

'That's brilliant! Perhaps now she won't …'

'Keep up the vendetta?' he finished. 'Well, that's what I'm hoping. Your mother doesn't know yet, and I thought it would be good if I could fix a family reunion before she gets back. Are you doing anything special with Patrick for Easter?'

'His mother's coming over from France to see how the film's going.'

'Will you fly over to us, then? I'll try to get Corinne and Miles here too.'

'But do you think she'll agree if I'm there?'

'Listen, Yolande, this feud has got to end some day, and the sooner the better. If she can't make it you'll still come, won't you?'

'I'd love to.'

They chatted for a while and his craggy features crinkled into a smile as she rang off. Tex had always had a soft spot for Yolande. She was a sweet kid. He very much doubted that Patrick appreciated his good fortune and it really bugged him. Time now to try his magic on Corinne. He called the apartment on the Avenue Foch. Party noises were audible in the background as he waited for her to come to the phone.

'Tex! Has something happened?' She was surprised to hear his voice again so soon.

'I just had a thought. Perhaps you and Miles would come over to see us at Easter? I guess it's rather short notice, but you should still have time to book a flight.'

'Have you invited Yolande?' she asked.

'Yes.'

There was an uncomfortable pause. He held his breath.

'Well, I'm sorry, but we can't. We're going to stay with Miles' family in England. I haven't met them yet, and he's rather keen for me to be introduced to everybody.'

'Of course, honey.'

'Later perhaps? We'd love to come. We could probably manage a long weekend in May, if it would suit you.'

'Great.'

'I'll be in touch, then. Don't forget to tell Mummy the good news.'

She said goodbye and rang off quickly. Feeling deflated, he put the receiver down. The bitterness was still there. He couldn't understand why she couldn't forgive and forget now she had come out on top. Perhaps there was more to it than he knew, something between her and Yolande he could never fathom, being both male and American. But they frequently baffled their mother too. It was that French blood, he supposed. He settled down with a report and a cold beer and prayed that Grace would like take-out when she got home.

She was thrilled to be told of Corinne's success in recovering the shares, but was less happy with the outcome of Tex's telephone calls.

'Do you think Corinne won't come only because of Yolande?'

'I'm not sure, darling.'

'And Yolande?'

'Dead keen, poor kid. She's really fed up out there. She's trying to turn Belco Pictures into a profitable company.'

'Bloody hell,' said Grace, frowning. 'Things must be bad.'

He put an arm around her. 'I expect they'll reach a compromise before they start splitting up the family heirlooms.'

'I hope so.' She kissed him, trying to rally. 'Still, it'll be wonderful to have Yolande here, anyway. Edith told me Franco Rivera's over shortly to negotiate about a boutique, so that'll perk her up. I have a horrible feeling she and Patrick are drifting apart already.'

'I only hope it doesn't break her heart.'

'How on earth did we let it happen?'

'It's her life,' said Tex.

'But I'm her mother. A very bad one too.'

He grabbed her arms. 'That's bullshit. You've done a remarkable job with both those girls. Most guys my age are putting their kids into rehab. All you have to do is be a shoulder to cry on when their love lives go belly-up – which is perfectly normal.'

'I suppose you're right.'

'Always am,' he grinned, hugging her. 'Now, anything I missed at the party? Did Edith faint when you told her I wouldn't be coming?'

'No. I don't think she fancies you any more.'

'How dare she? After all the trouble I took to make her fall for me.'

Grace giggled. Tex had been running from Edith's advances for several years.

'Anyone else I ought to have seen?' he asked.

'Well, Hank Pedersen showed up for about ten minutes. He was in a foul mood, so I didn't say hello.'

'That's not like Hank.'

'Perhaps Pedersen Corporation's still feeling the pinch after a mere twenty per cent increase in profits last year.'

'Twenty *point five* per cent, Grace.'

'Oh, all right! He was in a mood anyway, and Althea apparently couldn't get away from California to smooth his furrowed brow. Now, darling, I really am starving. Take me out for a late lunch?'

'Wasn't there anything to eat?'

'Indeed there was. I took one look and fled.'

'Ethnic vegetarian?' he queried.

'Yes. Edith reckons it's doing wonders for her sex life, by the way. Want me to try it?'

He smiled, pulled her tightly against him. 'No need. But if you like we could order in and go to bed.' The kiss this time was much longer, laced with desire.

'In the afternoon?' She feigned shock. 'What about your work?'

'I'll finish it later.'

'We'll see about that.' Grace pinched his bottom and picked up the phone.

'Who was it?' Miles asked, sliding his hands around Corinne's waist.

'My stepfather. He invited us to New York for Easter.'

'Bugger.'

'Don't worry. I'll see if we can fix a weekend in May.'

They were by the telephone in the hall, out of sight of guests in the salon, and Miles was desperate to get his hands on her. They hadn't had a minute alone since his return from London, with business at the bank and then this impromptu celebration to attend. Was it really only yesterday he had persuaded Stessenberg to sign that contract?

Corinne groaned as the kiss became more urgent. 'Miles, darling, behave.'

'Can't we go somewhere?'

'Later. We can't desert everyone now.' Corinne nipped his neck. 'You can stay here tonight.'

'Who *are* all these people?'

'Mostly my father's old friends. Now come and tell Georges how you convinced Stessenberg. I hope you've got your story pat.'

Miles pulled a face, and they went into the salon, where the wine was flowing with the conversation. He had given Corinne an edited version of events which had been cleared by Macdonald, but even that wasn't something he could broadcast to the world at large. Everyone looked round as he entered. Several leading businessmen went out of their way to introduce themselves before Yves led him off to Georges Maury and Toinette, sitting in a corner and clearly bursting with curiosity. Corinne was pounced on by

Paul Dupuy and his wife, so Miles was left to battle it out alone in his suddenly hesitant French. Yves smiled encouragingly and refilled his glass.

'Well, Miles?' asked Toinette. 'How did you pull it off?'

Miles sipped his wine. 'I just persuaded Stessenberg it would be in his best interests to sell back to Corinne.'

'But how?' demanded Georges. 'I tried, Toinette tried, Corinne tried. Why did he suddenly change his mind?'

'You must have realised he was only holding on to the shares for a third party?'

'Yes, but we could never work out who.'

'When I got back to the bank this afternoon I had our research department look up a few things. Everything points to Pedersen Corporation of America. Once Corinne had been forced out of UVS, Stessenberg would have been free to sell his Marchand stake to Pedersen. Pedersen would then have put in a bid for the rest of Marchand on the basis of a thirty-five per cent holding.'

Yves whistled under his breath. What a narrow escape. Pedersen's asset-stripping tactics were legendary.

'My guess is that Pedersen went cold on the deal. They have big expansion plans in China, so that might account for it.'

'Did Stessenberg give you much trouble?' enquired Toinette. 'He's rather an enigmatic character.'

'Oh, he's not such a bad old stick when you get to know him.'

Corinne, who had been keeping an eye on things from a distance, managed to shake off Paul and drag Miles and Yves away to evade further questions. Georges and Toinette remained in their corner, perplexed.

'Did you believe him?' she asked.

'I'm not sure. It sounds far too neat. But I'm certainly not complaining. It's the best news I've had for over six months. If Corinne and Yolande would only come to some agreement, my mind would be perfectly at ease.'

Toinette took a cigarette from her case and lit up. 'It doesn't look too good with Yolande, I'm afraid. She's coming over in the summer so they can start haggling over the art collection.'

'Jean-Claude would turn in his grave.'

'Quite. I suppose I'll have to move again once it's all settled. Miles will obviously move in here, and I'd hate to be in the way.' She paused. 'I've had a letter from my husband.'

'What!'

'He's coming to Paris in April and wants to see me with his lawyer.'

'Would you like me to be there?'

Toinette patted his arm. 'I'd really appreciate it, Georges. I thought I'd seen the last of that bastard ten years ago.'

Georges sighed. Bernard Brozard was bad news. A washed-up professional skier, he had attempted to extort money from Jean-Claude Marchand once he found out about his relationship with Toinette. He'd cleaned her out when he'd walked out on her two years before that, not that it made a difference to the brutal way he treated her. Georges and Jean-Claude had rushed to the Avenue Foch in response to a frantic telephone call, to find Toinette slumped on the floor, battered and bleeding. A very nasty business. It had been hushed up, of course. Brozard had been served with a restraining order, and Toinette had been treated at a discreet private clinic. Fortunately Corinne and Yolande were away in England, and Jean-Claude made sure they never heard about it.

'I assume he won't be coming here?'

'God, no! He's going to stay at the Bristol, so we'll meet him there.'

'Must be doing well.'

'I expect he's finally inherited from that old uncle of

his in Geneva. That's all Bernard ever thought about when he was sober.'

'How did a rat like that ever persuade you to marry him?'

'I was overpowered, I suppose. He was so handsome in those days. His skiing career was really taking off, and everyone said he had world class potential. He loved me, and I was bored with life in Strasbourg. So I married him. Perhaps if he hadn't had such a bad accident he wouldn't have turned to drink. The treatment was horrendous – and extremely expensive. He just took it out on me.'

Georges shook his head and relinquished his seat to the financial journalist Laurent Dobry, who had been hovering on the fringes of the conversation. Toinette was another person entirely, then. Pretty, laughing, flirtatious; nothing like the mature cynic who took over in moments of reflection. He wandered over to Yves, who was standing alone by the door, having eluded Corinne's attempt to thrust him into company.

'What's all this about substantially increasing our stake in Elegance Hotels?' Yves asked for the sake of saying something.

'Still on the drawing board at the moment. I'll give you a full rundown next week. They'd like us to complete the deal we had on the table before Yolande sold out. Corinne's giving it serious consideration.'

'I see.' Yves put down his glass and prepared to leave. 'Think I'll shoot off. I've got a heavy day tomorrow.'

'Of course, Philippe's home! I'd quite forgotten. How is he?'

'Great. He's rather tied up at the moment, but he'll be making a few announcements later on.'

Corinne came over and accompanied Yves to the door, a little put out that although he'd been as polite as the occasion required, he had virtually ignored everyone. But she understood his reasons, and said nothing. Yves returned alone to his flat, and went to bed thinking of Yolande. He always did.

'Jesus, Althea, this place is turning into a hotel! I'm tired, I want to relax, and you've got that dumb movie crowd here again.'

'OK, Hank, OK. I didn't expect you back until tomorrow. I'll send them away.'

He slumped down on the bed, looking haggard, his suit crumpled and his tie loose. Althea forced a smile to hide her annoyance. Something must have happened to bring him back from New York on a Thursday evening. It couldn't be more inconvenient. Patrick was here without Yolande again, and they could have had the place to themselves when Vic and the others had gone.

'Shall I fix you a drink?'

'Please – bourbon and soda.'

'Why don't you freshen up and change into something comfortable, darling? By the time you're through I'll have gotten them to quit.'

'OK.' He stretched out a hand and half-smiled. 'Thanks, sweetheart.'

Althea went back to her guests. Only an intimate party, so there wasn't too much fuss. Jayne Herford had already left. Vic and his wife lived nearby and were about to call it a night, knowing that Hank in a bad mood was best avoided. Patrick, however, was not visible.

'He's out on the terrace,' said Vic in response to Althea's query.

'I guess I'll have to kick him out.' She smiled. 'I must get Hank back into the human race.'

'Good luck with that.' Vic kissed her goodbye. Not wanting to alert Juanita, Althea took a generous bourbon through to the master bedroom, where Hank was undressing for a bath. 'Your drink, honey. I won't be a moment. They haven't all left yet.'

249

'OK. I'm in no rush.'

She hurried out to the terrace. Patrick was wandering up and down smoking a cigarette, looking, she thought, distractingly kissable in tight jeans and T-shirt.

'Althea! At last. I need to talk to you.'

'Not now, Patrick. My husband's come home. The others have gone already.'

He groaned. 'Shit! This was my last chance until after Easter.'

'What makes you think you have a chance?' she enquired, her expression wry. At least he was open about it.

'You do. You're so sexy.' Suddenly she was in his arms, and his kisses were burning her lips. 'I want you, Althea. I always get what I want.'

She tried weakly to push him off, but his kisses were delicious. When he pushed his tongue between her lips, resistance melted. Sensing acquiescence, Patrick slipped his hand between her thighs, pulled aside her thong, stroked. She struggled, but her mouth clung to his desperately.

'Patrick, you must go!'

But her body was arching unbidden towards his. He was delighted to find her so hot and horny. She gasped as his fingers pushed up inside her.

'Althea, I want you now. Now!'

'But my husband!'

'Where is he?'

'Taking a bath.'

She found herself propelled through the French doors into the sitting room. Patrick ran upstairs and along to Hank's bathroom; sounds of splashing water and financial reports on the television. He returned to the sitting room, locked the door, and unzipped his jeans.

Althea watched, fascinated and unresisting. He was so gorgeous, so young, so dominant. Afterwards she didn't

250

remember how she had been overwhelmed, only the desire throbbing through her, the need to take him. He wanted her. He made her feel young again. He pulled her thighs apart and knelt on the floor, and began to do incredible things to her with his tongue.

'You're lovely, Althea. Beautiful.' His eyes bored into hers, enjoying her pleasure.

She had to bite her lips to stop herself screaming as he brought her to the edge. Then he plunged into her, and all that mattered was his inexorable rhythm until they came together in a suppressed howl of exultation. It seemed impossible that only a few days ago she'd been afraid to touch him. Now she was irritated by their remaining clothes and the inhibiting circumstances.

'You find it really hard to be quiet, don't you?' Patrick said, amused, hurriedly pulling on his clothes. When he was dressed, he held her fast in his arms, kissing her, whispering endearments. They had to fix another meeting, but he was going on location, then his mother would be visiting California. 'After Easter should be all right,' he said. 'Yolande will be in New York, I think. I'll call you as soon as the coast is clear. You can come to my apartment.'

Althea groaned with disappointment. 'I can't, Patrick. I'll be in New York too – for the whole of April.'

He swore savagely. 'When you come back, then. Althea, this is terrible. I want you so much.'

'Patrick, you really must go:'

But they had to kiss again, and when she kissed him, nothing else mattered. He was her lover. She realised now that she'd wanted this ever since their first meeting in Le Grand Véfour.

'Hank's going on a trip round the Pacific in May,' she murmured. 'I'll be awfully lonely.'

He caught on at once. Yolande would have to be got out of the way, but that wouldn't be too difficult to arrange. She was fed up already. He could surely engineer a scene at the studios and force her to storm off in a tantrum. He knew exactly how to push her buttons. He kissed Althea goodbye. Her husband was still soaking in the bathtub as he drove back to Beverley Hills. Patrick gloated over this added triumph.

Althea managed to pull herself together before she had to face Hank. She surprised herself with her own coolness as they sat together in the lounge after a light supper. His mood was no better than it had been when he arrived.

'So what's bugging you?' she asked at last. 'I've told you all my news.'

'You only stayed here to hang around with Vic's mob. What the hell do you see in these movie types?'

'They're fun. Oh come on, Hank, lighten up. I only stay here because when I'm in New York you're always tied up.'

'But you never used to like this place so much. It was always better in Paris, or London, or Timbuktu.'

'Don't forget I'm a Californian. Sometimes it's good just to hang at home.'

He frowned, sipping his drink. 'Well, I came back early because I found an unexpected hole in my schedule. Rikki von Stessenberg blew the Marchand deal.'

'*What*!'

'I thought that would get your attention. We don't get the shares. He's sold them to Corinne Marchand.'

She stared incredulously. 'But he drew up that preliminary agreement with you only last week! I don't get it. It must be a mistake.'

'No mistake, honey. Read this.'

He handed her a brief email from Stessenberg, stating baldly that UVS had sold its stake in Marchand Enterprises to Corinne.

'I managed to get a call through to his hotel, but he was out – or so they said. He's in Europe for the next few weeks. So I won't be able to give the son of a bitch the sock on the jaw he deserves.'

Althea sat silently opposite him, hardly able to digest the news. She was only too conscious that it had been her idea. Hank had every right to be mad at her. After all, Rikki was really her friend, not his. But she couldn't get upset about it, not now she had Patrick. It had been a game, and Hank had lost, but it wasn't likely to affect Pedersen Corporation's global well-being.

'What do you think happened?' she said.

'I guess they outbid me. Maybe they had some leverage on him because of that deal he's working on with Franco Rivera's new label. Rivera was designing for Marchand, wasn't he? I don't know. It just stinks, Althea.'

'Darling, I'm really sorry. Can you do anything about it? Sue him?'

He snorted derisively. 'Sue him? Are you crazy? What would be the point? Forget it. I'm just mad I even started the whole thing. We could have capitalised something worthwhile instead of chasing this mirage.'

'Go on, blame me. I put you up to it. Did you lose much?'

'Only my threadbare faith in human nature.' He smiled, then chucked her under the chin. 'But I've still got you, darling. Everything would have worked fine if Stessenberg had stuck to his end of the deal. I don't blame you at all. How can I, when you're the most wonderful woman in the world?'

He kissed her lovingly. She felt terrible. Fortunately he was tired, and fell asleep that night almost as soon as his head touched the pillow, leaving her to ponder on the fit of lunacy that had made Patrick Dubuisson her lover. Now he was gone, their ten minutes' passion seemed quite crazy and wrong. But delightfully wrong. She knew she would have to have him again. Her senses ached for Patrick's touch. She was nowhere near so indulgent towards Hank's snoring, and gave him a kick to shut him up. He just grunted before relaxing into snores again. The magic of Malibu. She had it all.

Chapter Sixteen

La Guardia was full of passengers heading off on Easter vacation when Grace met Yolande, who rushed headlong into her mother's arms and just clung for a few moments. They were soon ensconced in a limousine for the drive to Manhattan under a lowering sky, but Yolande didn't regret the sun she'd left behind. She was finally back on familiar turf.

'So Corinne and Miles aren't coming?'

'No. They're going to see his family in Wiltshire – not that far from Albury House.'

'I suppose it's my fault,' said Yolande gloomily.

'Of course it isn't.' Grace hugged her. Something was obviously going badly awry with Patrick. She'd never seen her youngest daughter looking so forlorn before.

'Have you met Miles yet?'

'Yes, on New Year's Eve. Corinne was extremely coy about it all. He's a lovely guy. I don't know why she was holding off. Everything seemed to move once Philippe went back to France.'

'Well, she must have got Philippe out of her system at last. I suppose it was because of his daughter.'

'His daughter!'

Yolande explained it all without mincing her words. Her mother was staggered. On the two occasions she'd seen Philippe just before he left New York, he hadn't given the least hint of being anything other than fancy-free. It had been rather galling to learn he had been living only two miles away for the previous eighteen months without her knowing. She had thought it must be because of Corinne, but Yolande's explanation threw a quite different light on his reasons for maintaining such an uncharacteristically low profile.

'Actually, I think he decided to go home because of his daughter. He seemed to want to be a proud papa.'

'Philippe? You can't be serious.'

Yolande shrugged her shoulders. 'Well, that was my impression. I had quite a conversation with him at the Hervy gala in October. I didn't tell you about it because it was all still secret. He's changed, though you'd never guess it when he's putting on his party face. But I'll bet his return had an effect on Corinne, even if it wasn't the one she expected.'

'Really, Yolande.'

'Well, I've tried everything to make it up with her. I only hope she's happy, even if she never wants to see me again.'

'Oh, come on, darling.' Grace hugged her again. 'It'll work out once she's settled down. She always takes her time.'

'I'm going home in August, anyway, so she won't be able to avoid me. I suppose we'll have to reach some sort of agreement over the apartment and Le Manoir.'

'You're not really going to sell out, are you?'

'I haven't got much choice.'

'But surely you don't want to break up the art collection? It's the work of generations. You *must* try to come to a sensible arrangement.'

Yolande stared out at the passing traffic, stroking her mother's hand. She didn't want to talk about it. All these rows – because of Patrick. Patrick, who had kissed her tenderly goodbye in the VIP lounge at Los Angeles that morning, saying he would miss her. But she had caught the flicker of a smile on his face before he turned away, and it couldn't be just because he was looking forward to his mother's visit. She wondered whether he was with Jayne Herford. But her mother must never know. No one must even guess. It was too degrading.

'Did you know that Franco will be in town just after Easter?' asked Grace.

Yolande brightened up at once. 'How lovely! Where's he staying? I suppose he's left Hervy now?'

'Yes – back in January. He's going to open a boutique on Madison. I think he'll have one on Rodeo Drive as well, so you'll be able to keep up the connection in L.A. There was an article about it all in last month's *Vanity Fair*, but there have been delays because his financial backer collapsed. In fact, Corinne is putting up the money for his label now. He'll be managed by Marchand.'

'What! When did all this happen?'

'Very recently. There's a strange connection somewhere with your shares,' continued Grace, 'but I'm not sure if I've got it straight. Franco was getting the finance for his label through Ulrich von Stessenberg. He owned that holding company you sold your shares to, didn't he?'

'Yes – but I didn't know that at the time.'

'Well, Stessenberg's company folded about a month ago. There's not been much about it in the press. Franco was in a complete hole, so he went to Corinne and she's launching him as an independent designer within the Marchand group.'

'So what's it got to do with me?'

'Apparently Stessenberg was building a stake in Marchand to sell to Pedersen Corporation – then Pedersen would have launched a takeover bid.'

Yolande was thunderstruck. Hank Pedersen, Ulrich von Stessenberg, Patrick's film. She had met Althea Pedersen and Stessenberg at the same time. But there was surely no link with Vic Bernitz and *Fast and Loose*. Or was there? Patrick, she recalled, had been deep in conversation with Althea Pedersen and Vic at the Hervy gala. Had Hank Pedersen manipulated the whole thing to get her to sell her stake in Marchand Enterprises? It was impossible. It had to be. Yolande shut her mind to the thought that she had been set up. She felt a big enough fool already.

The rest of the journey was given over to a discussion of the social engagements her mother had planned for her. It promised to be a fun fortnight. Grace knew everyone worth knowing in New York, and was determined to get Yolande back into the swing of things. If, as she suspected, the relationship with Patrick was disintegrating, something – or somebody – would have to be found to fill the void.

It was while she was waiting for a call from Patrick on Easter Sunday that Yolande caught up with the *Vanity Fair* article on Franco's new label. There was a full-page photo of him with his wicked lop-sided grin. Dear Franco. It would be great to see him again. Since settling in California she'd been deprived of friends on her own wavelength, and was only now beginning to appreciate the advice he'd given her about Patrick. She smiled when she remembered his seduction attempt in her car after that fateful meeting with Vic Bernitz at Gianni's, but the smile faded once she started reading about Stessenberg, who was also pictured, sleek and professional, in a Rivera suit.

Her thoughts kept straying back to that evening with him and Hank Pedersen's horrendous wife at Le Grand Véfour. And Patrick. Had he been part of a covert deal to get her shareholding in Marchand?

The telephone rang. She answered it immediately.

'Hello, is Grace there?'

It was Yves. Yolande just held the receiver by her ear, unaccountably affected by his voice.

'Hello? Hello?'

'Yves. It's me – Yolande.'

'How are you?' he asked after a pause. She could almost hear the lump in his throat.

'Fine.'

'Is your mother at home?'

'No. She's at church with Tex.'

She hadn't gone with them because she didn't do organised religion except for weddings and funerals, but she couldn't be bothered to excuse herself. Yves probably thought her morally bankrupt anyway.

'Shall I take a message?' she asked, rather put out by his silence. 'Is it important?'

'That depends. Wait – here's Philippe. He'll explain it all much better than I can.'

'Hello, Yolande! What's a beautiful girl like you doing so far away?'

'Reading,' she said primly.

'What a waste!'

'Are you at home?'

'Where else? It's beautiful here. Everything's marvellous. I'm getting married, by the way.' He swore that his happiness would only be complete if she promised to come with Grace and Tex to his wedding, which was being arranged for St Xavier in August. It didn't conflict with her plans, and she gladly accepted the invitation. What a relief that someone at home still liked her. Philippe talked a lot about Claire, and was quite ecstatic over Isabelle. He sounded so buoyant, she was envious. He was going to have everything she wanted with Patrick; everything that now seemed to be slipping through her fingers.

'What are you doing in the Big Apple, anyway?' Philippe asked at last. 'Tired of the movies already?'

'Patrick's mother came to stay. I've hardly had a minute's peace since I got here. Mummy's been dragging me out to parties.'

'How very decadent of her. Don't forget to tell her she *must* come. I'm putting Yves back on. Look forward to seeing you, my darling.'

She heard a slight altercation, then Yves was on the line again. 'Are you coming to the wedding?' he asked, more

259

for the sake of saying something than because he was interested in her answer. At least, that's how it sounded.

'Yes.'

'That's good.'

'How's your mother?'

'Philippe's arranged a consultation for her with a top surgeon, so I'm hopeful of progress at last. He's rather taken over since he got back.'

'I expect you could do with a break,' Yolande said. 'Give her my love, won't you? I hope it all goes well.'

He thanked her and rang off, with barely a word of farewell. Yolande was hurt. There was no need for him to hate her, though they had broken up; they had been friends since childhood. He didn't possess even a fraction of Philippe's warmth and charm. Patrick's call came through fifteen minutes later, and his endearments were soothing. He flatly denied any knowledge of Pedersen Corporation's plan to take over Marchand Enterprises, swore that he missed her desperately, and his mother was sorry not to have seen her, and quelled her anxiety by stating that Jayne Herford was spending the holiday on her Montana ranch with Sam MacPherson, one of the supporting actors. Yolande thought it was silly to get wound up over nothing, and forgot her suspicions. When Grace and Tex returned, she was curled up on the sofa with a mug of coffee and the *New York Times*, several of its unread sections scattered on the floor. It was the most normal Sunday she had had for months.

Franco was hovering expectantly in the lobby of the Plaza Hotel, and almost knocked over two other guests in his haste to get to Yolande, who sauntered past the doorman wearing one of his dresses and a beaming smile. He hugged her tightly, and they kissed on the lips.

'*Carissima*, you look gorgeous. But where's the belt for this dress?'

'I never wear it. Don't you think it looks better without?'

He glanced at her critically. 'On you, yes. But it wouldn't on a shorter woman. Still, I designed this with you in mind. It matches your eyes.'

They linked arms. 'Is it all right if we lunch here?' he asked. 'I've got some samples in my suite I'd like you to look over.'

'Lovely.'

'Why didn't you bring Patrick?' Franco asked. 'I've got a few items he'd appreciate too.'

'He's not with me.'

'Oh.'

'Yes, definitely *oh*.'

When they were seated at a table in the Palm Court, he demanded an explanation.

'Don't misunderstand me, Franco,' she said, trying to play down the remark, let out in the rush of feeling at seeing a friend at last, 'we haven't broken up. But Patrick's so wrapped up in the film, all the fun we used to have doesn't even interest him now.'

'Shame. I was hoping he'd do my collection in Milan this October.'

'So you're going to be based in Milan?'

'Yes, but I'll have a boutique in Paris. Left Bank, of course. There's no threat to you titans of *haute couture*.'

Yolande laughed. 'Don't pretend you don't know how many ripples you're causing already, Franco. I'm just waiting for the scents and accessories. Are you really opening up on Rodeo Drive as well?'

'Of course. The Rivera style is going to be the only style this millennium.'

'I hope someone's told Armani,' she said.

Franco snapped his fingers, his eyes twinkling. 'Don't forget the Roman Empire split into two, Yolande. It could happen again. In fact, if your sister has anything to do with

261

it, I'm sure it will.'

'I have to say I'm surprised at her involvement. She was never that interested in fashion.'

Franco looked at her keenly. 'You underestimate her, Yolande. I did too, but I've got to know her in recent weeks. She has a very acute understanding of the business and a real gift for spotting future trends. She's been brilliant. I wouldn't be here now without her.'

'Oh, don't get me wrong. I'm her biggest fan. But she doesn't want me.'

He caught her hand and kissed her fingers. 'Idiot. She's got a photo of you on her desk.'

It was music to her ears. It was so good to talk to him. He made her laugh, made her feel necessary. When he asked her how Guy Monthély was getting on at Hervy, she realised how out of touch she had become. She didn't have a clue.

'I've heard whispers that Corinne's going to ask me back to work on Hervy's *prêt-à-porter* lines.'

'But won't that take away from your own label?'

'I'd have to keep the Hervy look, naturally, so there shouldn't be a conflict. My label's for a different market. Now, tell me all about *you*. It's forever since I saw you.'

Later, over coffee, she asked a few questions about Stessenberg, but gleaned little. Stessenberg had simply dropped off the map.

'Probably avoiding his creditors,' said Franco. 'They're said to be extremely unpleasant people.'

'So what's the deal with you and Corinne? Could you buy her out?'

'If I make good profits, yes. But not for years yet. You wouldn't believe the rents we've agreed on those boutiques. But I must have an upmarket image, or the whole concept will be useless.'

Upmarket his designs certainly were. Silk, satin, cashmere, beautifully cut to fit comfortably, yet flattering the natural lines of the body. Yolande tried on a couple of dresses, but was most taken with a beige summer trouser suit. Perfect for California.

'You can take it,' Franco said, hanging the garments she had tried back on a rail. 'Go on. It's a present.'

'You made it for me, didn't you'?'

He smiled, approaching her. 'Yes. I told you I was going to miss you, Yolande. You have no idea how much.'

She eyed him apprehensively, conscious that this time they were in a hotel suite with a bedroom only next door. He slipped his arms around her waist. 'Come and model for me in October.'

The invitation she had been waiting for – a lifeline out of Hollywood, back to Europe. Back to her career. But it would mean leaving Patrick for some while, and she was already planning to be away from him during August. She hesitated.

'Please, *carissima*.'

'I'd love to,' she said at last. 'Thank you, Franco.'

'There are other ways of saying thank you,' he replied, holding her tighter.

'I know you want to be upmarket, but don't you think your price is just a little steep, darling?'

He had to laugh.

'I'm not going to sleep with you, Franco.'

His lips drew closer.

'Please don't.'

'Why not? We've got hours.'

'But I have a boyfriend.'

More laughter. His mouth hovered over hers. 'Just a kiss, then.'

She didn't have a chance to say no. Perhaps it was a longer kiss than she intended, and his hands did begin to stray, but she left ten minutes later with the trouser suit in a box and a definite engagement for his Milan show. He promised to do his utmost to attend a cocktail party her mother was holding the following evening. Franco was quite convinced that by the autumn Yolande would be free of Patrick and more receptive to his caresses. His career as an independent designer would certainly start with a blaze of publicity. When Yolande Marchand stepped onto a catwalk, everyone else was eclipsed.

Claire kept trying to tell herself to behave as normally as possible, not to be nervous. But it was impossible. Everything was happening too quickly. She was only just getting used to the idea that she was going to marry Philippe, when she was faced with this formal visit to his family. The little he had told her of Marie-Christine wasn't reassuring; she was religious, she hadn't been interested in Isabelle. Innocent little Isabelle, strapped into her child seat at the back of the BMW with some of her toys, continually asking when they would reach Papa's château.

'Relax, darling,' Philippe said, giving Claire a smile. 'Everything will be fine. After all, my mother did invite us, and she doesn't send out invitations lightly.'

'I bet you asked for one.'

He laughed, pressing his foot on the accelerator. Claire had forgotten what a good driver he was, how calm and capable, notwithstanding the heavy traffic. People always seemed to give way when they saw Philippe in their mirrors.

'Must we stay for the whole holiday?' she asked.

'Of course. I want to take you down to see Briteuil straight after Easter.'

'But suppose your mother really doesn't like us? I won't be able to bear it, Philippe.'

'Don't be silly. She'll adore you. And my brother will be there too, and he's on our side.'

Claire fell silent, looking out at the brown, cheerless landscape. It was almost like January still; not a sign of spring. She and Isabelle began a game of counting red cars to pass the time, but it was over all too quickly. They came off the A6 just south of Beaune, and then sped down winding roads flanked by vineyards, through villages whose names were a roll-call of the very best of Burgundy. Isabelle pressed her nose to the window, wondering where this fairytale castle was. She knew what it would be like; all turrets and towers, with a wizard up in one of the chimneys and a princess who sometimes came out of a lake in the gardens.

And then they had arrived, and both Claire and her daughter gasped at the loveliness of the place. A perfect sixteenth-century château – without a moat, true – but as if from a fairytale nonetheless. Though large, it was symmetrical and pleasing to the eye, surrounded by gardens laid out in formal terraces and parterres. The lawns and lake were concealed at the rear of the building.

Yves came out to meet them on the magnificent horseshoe steps leading to the main entrance. Claire hung back a little nervously, but Philippe carried Isabelle up to his brother, smiling broadly.

'Well, Yves, here they are – the two women in my life. Come on,' he shouted back to Claire. 'He's won't bite.'

She joined them, laughing, and was surprised by Yves' resemblance to Philippe. He was even a little bit taller, looking fit and relaxed in corduroys and a polo.

'Hello, Claire,' he said, stepping forward and kissing her on both cheeks. 'Welcome to Rochemort. Had a good journey?'

'Say yes,' interrupted Philippe, 'it's his car.'

She laughed again, and everything seemed easier. Yves wanted to kiss Isabelle, but she refused to look at him, her hands clutched tightly around her father's neck. Claire took her from Philippe and tried to coax her into a smile, but Isabelle was suddenly shy and wouldn't even speak.

Yves shrugged his shoulders. 'We'd better go inside, or she'll catch cold. I got Marie to make up a bed for her in your sitting-room. Is that all right?'

Claire wondered at which end of the long cold gallery that opened off at the top of a marble staircase she would be sleeping. It was vast. Philippe's stories seemed to be borne out by the suits of armour they passed, and Isabelle began to look about excitedly. Claire found herself hoping she wouldn't be relegated to a distant tower as an unwanted concubine.

'This is the oldest part of the château,' Philippe explained. 'Uninhabited, but tourists like it. We live in the west wing, which is more modern – Louis Quinze, actually. Now, Isabelle, there's the ghost – there! In the armour.'

She squealed in fright, then giggled. 'Where's the wizard?'

'Cooking his dinner. He'll come and see you later.'

Yves was bemused. He could never have imagined Philippe in this role, and yet he seemed quite at ease. He felt a sharp stab of envy. This was how it should have been for him and Yolande; yet here he was, playing host to his philandering brother, who hadn't done anything to deserve such a lovely wife and daughter.

Claire was relieved to reach the west wing, hung with eighteenth century pictures and tapestries. Though stately, it was warm and clearly meant for habitation. A large golden Labrador bounded up to them as they passed into the corridor leading to their rooms.

'This is Geraldine. She produces all our puppies,' Yves said, rubbing her ears. 'They're getting quite big now. Perhaps Isabelle would like to see them later?'

'Yes!' came the enthusiastic answer.

'Aren't you going to say hello to Uncle Yves now?' asked Philippe. 'He's my brother.'

Isabelle stared at Yves for some seconds, then smiled and proffered her cheek for a kiss. But that wasn't enough. He took her in his arms and hugged her, smiling shyly at

Claire, who suddenly felt sorry for him. There was something in his manner, a sadness that matched the ancient grandeur of the château, and she knew he was very unhappy. Yves left them outside their rooms, telling them that lunch would be ready in half an hour. Claire felt the butterflies start in her stomach. She would have to meet Philippe's mother – the formidable baroness.

'So you'll be sharing my bed,' he said, opening the doors. 'I wondered about that. Isabelle will be in here. Let's see what he's done for her. Good heavens, Marie's brought the whole nursery in here! Never mind, she'll be very comfortable. Now, we'd better hurry. The bathroom's just the other side. Then there's Yves' room. Maman is at the other end, so she doesn't have to walk too far to the stairs. We came the long way round, as you might have noticed. There's a much quicker way in from the back.'

Claire sat down on the bed and looked around, while Philippe lifted Isabelle up to get a view through the window. It was a lovely room; spacious, but cosy and inviting, with period Louis Quinze furniture and a romantic scene by Watteau over the fireplace. The sitting-room converted for Isabelle must obviously have been a dressing-room originally – suitable for a lady, with its lilac colour scheme. Claire began to breathe more comfortably. She had already jumped the first hurdle. She was accepted in his ancestral home as the mother of his child and his future wife. And she loved him to distraction.

'Well, Yves, what's she like?' asked Marie-Christine when he appeared in the drawing-room.

'Good looking, well-mannered, and very chic.'

'I see.'

It was neither approval nor disapproval. Yves wondered if his brother had done the right thing by bringing them here so soon. His mother was still very hurt that Philippe had kept the affair secret for so long.

Geraldine wandered in and stretched out on the carpet at his feet.

'So the marriage is definite?' she asked at length.

'Yes. They seem very happy. I'm sure it's right – for both of them.'

She looked at him sadly. 'I'd hoped to be welcoming *your* fiancée, not his.'

'Please don't go into all that again. I'm glad it's over.'

'But …' Then she stopped. His expression was too intense. 'So it's *still* Yolande?'

She sighed, gazing past him. It was hopeless. Yolande would never come back now. He would just stay here, mouldering away with regrets and what might have been. Philippe was right; she needed to get herself mobile again, then she wouldn't be so dependent and Yves could get out more and find someone new. Gabrielle had been a mistake, but he could have said so before. She only wanted to see him happy, not force him into something he didn't want. Was he afraid of her? Her confidence as a mother had been severely dented in recent months. She realised that only now was she beginning to understand her sons, when for years she thought she knew them both inside out.

Claire and Philippe each held one of Isabelle's hands as she dawdled her way past the family portraits in the corridor leading to the drawing-room. She seemed delighted with everything, though a little disappointed that the wizard hadn't yet materialised. Philippe told her to be a good girl because she was going to meet her grandmother who was a sick lady and couldn't walk very well. Isabelle didn't pay attention. She marched boldly into the room and headed straight for Yves and Geraldine, two familiar beings in vast, unfamiliar surroundings. Her parents waited out of sight behind the open doors.

'Come to me, Isabelle,' said Yves, opening his arms. She wasn't afraid of him now, though drew back a little when Geraldine bounded up and wanted to play. Yves sat Isabelle on his lap, watching his mother's wary face. He worried that she hadn't asked about her granddaughter. What if she rejected her? How could she fail to love this beautiful, cuddly little girl, who looked very much as she must have looked at the same age?

Marie-Christine stared at Isabelle's black hair as she leaned down to pat Geraldine, then caught the deep blue eyes and that full, firm mouth. It could have been the daughter she had always wanted but never had. She smiled, indicating a seat beside her on the sofa. Isabelle slid out of Yves' arms and ran across to her.

'Do *you* know where the wizard is?'

'That depends. We have rather a lot of wizards here.'

She raised her voice for the last sentence. Philippe gave Claire a smile, and they went in. Marie-Christine looked round briefly, then turned back to Isabelle to explain that the wizard was having his dinner, and would doubtless come out of his hiding-place in the kitchen when he had finished.

'But Papa says he lives in the chimney!'

'He does sometimes. He lives everywhere. You've got to watch for him.'

'Oooh – are you scared?'

Isabelle scrambled up onto the sofa, anxious to hear more. Marie-Christine talked about the wizard, stroking her granddaughter's hair, enjoying her alertness and wide-eyed interest. She gave Philippe a look which more or less admitted that she'd been conquered, and both he and Yves breathed a sigh of relief.

Claire hung back, her fingers interlocked with Philippe's, conscious that his mother had so far ignored her. She had never doubted that Isabelle would be accepted, but she remained unsure of her own welcome with this very elegant woman, who though clearly in pain, retained more than the vestiges of good looks and an

269

integrity of manner that was unmistakable. It was Isabelle who precipitated their introduction by deciding to sit on her grandmother's lap. Marie-Christine winced as the girl began to climb onto her knees, and Claire rushed over to remove her.

'Isabelle, darling, why don't you sit here with me?' She sat on the sofa next to the baroness, nervous and embarrassed. 'I'm terribly sorry, madame. Philippe warned her, but she doesn't understand.'

'That's all right. I'd love to hold her, but with this arthritis – perhaps when I've had my operation, it will be easier.'

Marie-Christine smiled reassuringly. Her keen eyes took in a great deal; Claire's nervousness, her delicacy, and a sweetness of personality that came through even in these difficult circumstances. She knew they were going to be friends.

'Congratulations, Claire. You have a lovely daughter.' She turned to her son. 'You don't really deserve it, Philippe, but I give you permission to hold the wedding here. We could do with a party. Now, let's get the kissing over, and then we can eat. Isabelle looks rather hungry – don't you, *ma chérie*?

Lunch was a protracted affair, taken in formal splendour in the panelled dining room, and Marie-Christine went out of her way to be kind. Yves was subdued, but the others kept the conversation flowing. Claire had obviously scored a hit with his mother, and when a silence threatened to descend, Isabelle soon created fresh talk with her insatiable enquiries about ghosts, wizards, and princesses. He loved to look at her, but he felt out of it, and after the meal he was sent off to show his niece the dogs and the gardens while Claire and Philippe had a private conversation with Marie-Christine. When he returned, a sleepy Isabelle in his arms, they had arranged everything; the wedding, a visit to that château Philippe was planning to buy, and accommodation for his mother in Claire's house at Versailles when she went to consult Dr Kamekian in Paris. Their collective happiness was over-powering, and feeling miserable, he excused himself from an evening of intolerable cheerfulness by claiming he had urgent work to do.

That night Claire revelled in a new sense of freedom with Philippe. He really was hers now; no need for any more lies. She was in a fair way to being in love with everything connected with the name Rochemort – except Yves. At first he'd been so friendly, then she'd felt an impenetrable wall of ice around him.

'Philippe, is something wrong with your brother? Or maybe it's me. I just feel that he doesn't want me here.'

He stirred in the bed, pulling her close in his arms and kissing her. 'Of course he does! But the poor guy's got a broken heart, and seeing us planning a wedding probably didn't help.'

'Really?' She raised herself in his arms, interested.

'He was engaged to Yolande Marchand, and she jilted him. I don't know if he'll ever get over it.'

'Yolande Marchand! The model?'

'The very same. We've known her from the cradle. Her family home is just the other side of St Xavier. Yves adores her. He always did.'

It was too intriguing a tale not to be told, and it rather suited their romantic surroundings. Claire was sympathetic, and resolved to be extra attentive to Yves the following day. She thought he was like a chivalrous lovelorn knight from medieval days. He would look just right in one of those suits of armour with a lady's favour on his arm. The fairytale atmosphere was becoming infectious.

Chapter Seventeen

'Toinette, what's this party for?' demanded Corinne, sitting by her dressing-table at the Avenue Foch. 'You've been in a mysterious mood all week.'

Toinette leaned against the door of Corinne's room, smiling. The rest of the apartment was alive with activity, Francoise to-ing and fro-ing with temporary catering staff to the dining room.

'To celebrate my divorce.'

'You're joking!'

'It sounds unbelievable after all this time, doesn't it? I had no idea one could be divorced so quickly. But I saw my husband a fortnight ago, and he'd already got proceedings well under way. We've been separated for so long that I ought to be free very soon.'

Corinne was stunned. Toinette had tried to divorce her husband years before, but had met with so many threats and outrageous demands that she'd abandoned the idea. What a difference it would have made to her father. He had always wanted to marry Toinette.

'I don't suppose congratulations are in order?' she asked, her voice subdued.

'I know your father would have been happy. Brozard never agreed before because he wanted to sabotage our relationship. Of course, now he wants to remarry himself, it's all different. But one should always celebrate freedom, and I intend to do just that.' She paused, eyeing Corinne anxiously. 'I've invited Philippe and his fiancée, by the way.'

'I see.'

'Well, everyone needs to get used to the idea of their

marriage, and she could do with some support. There were horrendous rumours floating about last week after Philippe announced that Isabelle was his daughter.'

'So I heard.'

'She's a sweetheart. Have you seen her?'

Corinne hadn't yet met Claire and Isabelle, though she'd seen Philippe a couple of times since he announced his engagement. The prospect left her undaunted. She stood up. 'Is Yves coming tonight? I wanted a word with him about Elegance Hotels.'

Toinette led the way to the dining room to put the final touches to flowers and ornaments on the table. 'I did invite him, but he said he was going to visit his mother at the hospital.'

'Surely he could have gone this afternoon?'

'Actually, I'm relieved. He's so miserable he really depresses me. It was bad enough when he was going through that farce with Gabrielle, but it's even worse now.'

Corinne grimaced. 'The power Yolande has …'

'It's a shame we can't bottle it. Our perfume sales would go through the roof.'

Corinne laughed and went to answer the door. It was Miles. He put a bouquet of flowers on the hall table, then crushed her against his chest.

'Miles, you're creasing my dress.'

'Who cares.' His lips were demanding, hers immediately responsive. 'That's better. God, I missed you. I've never hated London so much in my life as during the last three days. Have we got a spare half hour?'

'And here I was planning to let you ravish me all night.'

'Hmmm.' He kissed her until she felt light-headed and then pulled back. 'I don't suppose it would be asking too much for some food? Real men find it hard to ravish on railway sandwiches and flat beer.'

She led him off to the kitchen, where Francoise scolded him for eating some chocolate biscuits, though he assured her it wouldn't spoil his appetite for the substantial buffet in preparation. Corinne had briefed Miles about Philippe and Claire to avoid any awkwardness. Her gut feeling was that Philippe wouldn't have told Claire about their affair, and when they were introduced his deliberate way of casting Corinne as a friend and neighbour from childhood left no doubt as to the conduct of future relations. Claire greeted her warmly, quite free of embarrassment. Corinne was agreeably surprised. Trust Philippe to land on his feet again.

'So when do you two walk up the aisle?' Miles asked, keeping a tight grip on Corinne's waist.

'The end of August,' said Philippe decisively. 'I do hope you'll come with Corinne? Perhaps we'll set an example.'

Claire nudged him reprovingly, noticing Corinne's desperate look of appeal across the room at Toinette. Miles just held her tighter. He was surprised to find it a rather attractive idea. But he somehow found himself deftly detached from the group by Toinette to be introduced to some fresh arrivals, and Corinne asked Philippe for news of Marie-Christine, who had undergone her hip operation the previous week.

'She's doing extremely well. The consultant is confident of full mobility, but of course she'll need physiotherapy and some sort of support for a while.'

'That's marvellous. I can't tell you how pleased I am. We've been waiting for this for years,' she added, turning to Claire. 'I don't know how Philippe managed to persuade her. No one else could.'

'My superior charm, of course.'

Claire smiled at him affectionately, and Corinne saw how it had all happened. Claire really was attractive; not just in looks, but in her whole manner. Philippe seemed to appreciate his good fortune, and though Corinne felt he could never deserve such a wife, it would certainly be an ideal marriage for him now. She discussed their plans for the Château Briteuil, which they were in the process of buying, and asked them to bring Isabelle to see her soon.

Claire was favourably impressed, and looked at Corinne's retreating back for some moments when she left to rejoin Miles.

'So that's Yolande's sister. I see now why Yves is so upset.'

Philippe lowered his eyes, relieved the meeting had passed off so well. Corinne was a born diplomat. 'You're worried about Yves, aren't you?'

'Yes. I don't think your treatment is right for him.'

'Oh. And what do you know about it?' he asked, kissing her lightly on the lips. 'Been having a heart to heart?'

'Not exactly. But we had a long conversation about life in general.'

'And what's your verdict, doctor?'

'His symptoms show no signs of abating, and I think you've made a wrong diagnosis.'

'Really!'

'You think it's just sex, but that's not the whole story, Philippe. He's an emotional type.'

'I know that. But I was hoping that if he got back into circulation he'd see that there are other women out there who could make him happy.'

Claire shook her head. 'He's obsessed with Yolande. Couldn't we get them back together?'

'My darling, short of kidnapping her and carrying her down to St Xavier by force, it's impossible. Because she's also obsessed – with that rat-bag Patrick Dubuisson.'

'I wouldn't be too sure it will last. I saw an article about him last week to publicise this film he's making, and not a word about Yolande, even though she's backing the film. They ran a photo of him in a clinch with Miss California.'

'I might have guessed,' he said. 'I give up! Let them both be miserable and wreck each other's lives. It's not our responsibility.'

Claire allowed the subject to drop. Perhaps she shouldn't interfere. Yet she still had a feeling that no amount of prompting by his family would help Yves to find a replacement for Yolande or jolt him out of his depression. From scraps of gossip, she gathered that he was widely considered a loser for having let Yolande go and an even bigger idiot for moping about it.

Yves had spent a couple of hours with his mother as usual. Late April, and he could hardly believe the transformation. Philippe hadn't been home even two months, yet life had already changed completely. His mother was recovering well from her operation and could walk without pain. She would be able to leave hospital in a matter of days and it had been decided that she would convalesce at Claire's Versailles home, to be near her physiotherapist. The new arrangements meant that Yves found himself spending most of the week in Paris, and he was well aware that his family had a hand in the unwanted invitations to parties now flooding in from all quarters.

Driving back to his flat, he debated whether or not to go to a cocktail party later in the evening hosted by Jacqueline Lenormand, whose politician husband had recently sprung to ministerial prominence. One of those affairs where by dint of cramming as many people into as small a space as possible, sociability was compulsory. Probably a political crowd, with a sprinkling of journalists. Yves remembered being introduced to a rather lovely reporter at Jacqueline's last party – Anne-Louise Chevagnac. She had been interesting. He decided to go.

The Lenormands had an apartment on the Ile St Louis,

and Yves was greeted by serried ranks of official-looking cars as he cruised along the Quai de Bourbon, searching for a parking space. It promised to be a tedious couple of hours, but he deserved a drink for manoeuvring into the narrow gap between a Volvo and a Mercedes, while a taxi driver who had deposited other Lenormand guests nearby watched beady-eyed, willing him to reverse into a bollard.

'My dear baron, how good of you to come! How's your mother? Tell her I'll visit as soon as I can. For me? How kind. Such beautiful flowers! Do come and meet everyone.'

Yves half-listened to Jacqueline's effusions. She always said '*My dear baron*' very loudly, so quite a few people looked round. He found it amusing. She was an ungainly middle-aged woman with a certain charm, not at all in harmony with the slinky low-cut gowns she always wore. He followed her dutifully into her small salon, and was immediately lost in the crowd. These things were managed so much better on the Avenue Foch.

The usual Lenormand set – conservative politicians, one or two media types, a fair number of businessmen, and an assortment of women – at this stage engaged in energetic girl talk on the hard chairs lining the walls. Yves managed to pick up a couple of canapés and a glass of wine, and dodged a purposeful-looking man who would probably want to discuss the latest initiatives on unemployment. He headed towards the women. One or two smiled invitingly. Then he saw Anne-Louise, and promptly occupied the vacant seat next to her.

'Hello. I don't know if you remember me? Yves de Rochemort.'

'Of course.' She gave him a mischievous look, and he realised her eyes were green like Yolande's. But she had blonde hair, and a totally different cast of features. 'How are you, *my dear baron*?'

It was a wicked imitation, and he laughed. 'You look

bored.'

'Seen it all before,' she replied. 'I'm supposed to be gleaning some valuable insights into Lenormand's policies, but I had to give up the ballet to come here, and so far the talk isn't much compensation. Nor is the food for that matter.'

'Perhaps I could ...' He hesitated, trying to remember his moves. Be bold. Let her think he made a habit of this sort of thing. 'Perhaps I could take you to dinner later?'

She seemed rather surprised. After all, they barely knew each other, and his romantic failures were no secret. 'That would be lovely.'

Dinner and – well. He couldn't deny he found her very attractive and his body was screaming for action. They chatted for a while about her job, which she said she greatly enjoyed when it didn't involve evenings like this.

'I'm off to New York next week,' she said.

'For long?'

'Three weeks. Debate on sub-Saharan Africa at the UN.'

A flashgun popped in front of their eyes.

'Go away, Marcel!' she snapped.

Yves looked up, annoyed. Marcel Froment's pictures usually appeared in all the scandal-sheets. So much for discretion. Inviting photographers to her parties was one of Jacqueline's bad points. To avoid further intrusion, he took Anne-Louise's empty glass and went off to refill it, hoping the photographer would have disappeared before he got back.

Yves found it difficult to get through the press of people to the buffet. He was cut off by a group of men, who were deaf to any suggestions that they might move. Then he heard one of them mention Yolande's name. He strained his ears to listen. Yes, it was definitely her they were talking about. His heart began to thud.

'You haven't got a hope, André. She's been the

exclusive property of that actor since she left Hervy.'

Yves felt his hackles rise, and pushed forward to hear the rest. He recognised André Hamel, a stocky, dark man in his thirties, the editor of a fashionable weekly journal.

'She never used to be so exclusive. I had her before she even knew Dubuisson,' said Hamel. 'About the time she got engaged to be married, in fact. Never had such a great lay. '

Yves felt something within himself snap; no self-control, no polite heartache now. Just sheer, overpowering rage. He dropped the wine glass and grabbed Hamel's tie, forcing him round so they were face to face. Everybody suddenly fell silent and backed away.

'How *dare* you talk about any woman in such a disgusting way? Yolande wouldn't have looked twice at a heap of shit like you! Maybe this will teach you to brag about your imaginary lovers in future.'

Afterwards no one quite remembered how it happened, but Hamel appeared to fly across the room, sent sprawling by the punch Yves planted expertly on his jaw.

'Come on, get up and fight.'

Hamel moaned, and a bevy of women hurried over to help him.

'Leave him!' ordered Yves.

They scattered. Nobody recognised this Yves de Rochemort as the butt of their malicious gossip. His blue eyes were ferocious, his lips curled in scorn, he towered over Hamel.

'Come on, Hamel, get up!'

'Yves!'

It was Jacqueline, absolutely frantic. Her reputation, her sophistication, all threatened by this 'most unfortunate misunderstanding'. 'For God's sake, *my dear baron*.'

There was a muffled laugh from Anne-Louise Chevagnac.

'Get up! Get up and repeat what you said!'

Hamel held his hand over his mouth, blood running down to his chin, very reluctant to risk another blow. Yves stood over him, ready to haul him to his feet, while Jacqueline kept pulling his jacket and begging him to calm down. He shook her off, then turned and faced the spectators.

'What the hell are you gawping at? Maybe you didn't hear what he said. Why don't you repeat it, Hamel? Go on! *Who* was it you slept with while she was engaged to me? Or did you just dream up the whole thing?'

Hamel cowered by a chair, dabbing his mouth with a handkerchief. 'It was a lie. I withdraw everything.'

Yves unclenched his fist. 'I knew it was. If I ever hear you – or anyone else – insult her again, you know what to expect.' He turned to Jacqueline. 'Forgive me, madame, but no man could allow that slander to pass unpunished.'

'Yes, of course. I'm so sorry. It was all a terrible mistake, I'm sure.'

An uneasy air of studied normality returned as Hamel got to his feet and was led off to a bathroom to bleed in peace. Yves found people making way for him as he searched out Anne-Louise.

She appeared to find the whole episode a welcome diversion. 'You were superb,' she said.

He was silent, suddenly acutely embarrassed. What a scene. What an unutterable mess. He would have to leave.

'Are you coming?' he asked. 'I'm hungry.'

As soon as they were through the door, the whole salon erupted into a storm of gossip. It was the most exciting party the Lenormands had hosted for a very long time.

'I hope Yolande appreciates it,' Anne-Louise said, as they got into his car.

'I doubt it,' Yves said tersely. 'I've been a total idiot.'

'It was sweet of you.'

'I'm sick of being sweet.' He turned and grabbed her. 'I

281

want you, Anne. Just sex. I don't do love any more.'

She didn't know when she had ever seen such intense blue eyes, or felt such naked lust burning through her veins. 'Neither do I.'

'Takeaway and back to my place?'

'Sounds good.'

He leaned in, crushed her mouth beneath his, tasted her, branded her, ran his hands down her body. Then dropped her back into her seat, gasping.

'Seat belt,' he said.

They picked up a couple of pizzas, but as soon as they were inside his flat, the boxes were dropped to the floor. Anne found herself in arms of steel, a hot mouth devouring her, hands stripping her, clothes tangled on the floor. He was so sexy, nothing like she'd expected. And gorgeous, too. Long, lean, his chest covered in black hair, his face even more handsome now he also looked dangerous.

Yves buried his face in her hair, rubbing his hands up and down her back, her buttocks, pulling her into him. He was impatient to be inside her, but he needed to slow things down. This was going to be a one-night stand Anne-Louise Chevagnac wouldn't forget. She was tugging at his trousers, kissing his neck, wanting to give him what she felt they both so desperately needed. But it wouldn't be a pity fuck. Nobody whose body was starting to throb the way hers was under his hands could say that. She looked up at him, startled, when he suddenly pulled away.

'What's the matter?'

A vision of Isabelle had flashed through his head. 'Condoms.'

'I'm on the pill.' She struggled with his zip. 'What's wrong with your trousers?'

Yves smiled. 'Allow me.'

He pushed her hands aside and swiftly removed them, and her eyes widened. He was very impressive. Yves pushed her down onto the bed and lowered himself on top

282

of her. She quivered in anticipation as he started to kiss her, touch, slowly explore. He was so generous. It was all about her. Her needs, her desires. It had been so long. Too long. He had beautiful creative hands and the most sensitive lips, which seemed to know her body's every point of pleasure. She was panting, shaking, begging for him when he finally entered her, inch by delightful inch.

He kissed her when he was fully inside and smiled. 'You're sure you don't want to change your mind?'

'Shut up, Yves, and take me!'

She'd go mad if he didn't. She thought she'd go mad when he did.

Yves let out a long sigh of satisfaction. Anne was lying in the crook of his arm, nibbling his neck, her hand gently stroking his thigh. He felt himself getting hard again.

'Mmmm …'

'You were …' She raised herself to look at him. Eye to eye. 'Absolutely amazing.'

'My pleasure,' he said, and meant it. 'We both needed it. So who's the bastard who broke your heart?'

Oh, he was sharp beneath that cool exterior, she thought. Maybe not sharp enough, though. 'My husband,' she replied levelly.

'What!' He shot out of her arms and sat up. 'You're married!'

'Technically, yes. But we've been separated for a year now. That's why I don't wear a ring.'

'Going to get divorced?'

'I suppose so. It's not what I want, but – oh God, I don't know. We just can't seem to talk anymore. He's a financial analyst. He got a job in New York. I was meant to join him after three months, then he told me he'd met someone …' her voice trailed off.

Yves felt her pain and pulled her back into his arms. 'I know.' He kissed her gently. 'Believe me, I know.'

'You still love her, don't you?'

'Always. And you still love him.'

'Yes,' she replied with a sigh, snuggling against him.

'So are you going to have it out with him when you fly over there?' he asked, stroking her hair.

'That's the plan. My last chance to see if we can work things out.' Her hand slipped back down his body caressingly, while her mouth sought his. He was such a good kisser and for the moment his lips were hers. She took the sweetness he offered and forgot her pain.

Yves slid his hand between her legs. She was getting very aroused again, and so was he. She shuddered as his fingers stroked in and out of her. 'So this is the first time you've had sex since he left?'

'Yes.'

'You've got a lot of catching up to do.'

'I know,' she said, pushing him to his back with devilment in her eyes. 'I hope you weren't planning on getting any sleep tonight.'

'Well, well, you're quite a celebrity today,' said Philippe, tossing another paper onto the pile. 'You must have packed a pretty powerful punch.'

Yves sat opposite his brother in the salon of Claire's home, gazing in incomprehension at the pictures of his attack on André Hamel. Now it seemed like a bad dream. He wasn't really properly awake. Had he really had Anne-Louise five times last night? They had kissed goodbye only three hours before. She seemed like a dream too. A good one. He shook his head and rubbed his eyes.

'Are you all right, Yves?'

'Never better.'

'Hamel says you must have been drunk and he's no intention of pressing charges. You, drunk? What did he really say about Yolande?'

Yves told him, and Philippe's expression hardened. 'I'd

have given him one too if I'd been there.'

'I made him retract in public – but I don't suppose that's been reported?'

'Let me see. Editors get so selective about these things. We're keeping them in business at the moment. First Claire and me, now you in a fight. It ought to do wonders for the family name. I bet you'll get record prices for the wine.'

'I ought to. Last year was magnificent.'

Philippe continued to rifle through the papers. '"At last – the truth" By A-L C. Do you know him?'

Anne-Louise, of course. So she'd decided to cash in too. But the report was weighted entirely in Yves' favour. Philippe's mind was racing ahead. He discussed the subject with Claire later that day, and as a result, an envelope containing a selection of newspaper cuttings was couriered to the Beideckers in New York.

Yves decided that the only way to quell the rumours was to brazen things out. He called on Toinette that afternoon and was surprised by the warmth of her welcome. When he visited his mother afterwards, she dismissed it all as the inevitable consequence of Jacqueline inviting blood-sucking journalists to her parties. Yves returned to his flat reflecting that had he only punched Patrick Dubuisson the previous year, Yolande might now be his. It was a tormenting thought. He picked up the phone and rang Anne-Louise.

'Yves, please don't be cross about the article.'

'I'm not. How many days before you leave for New York?'

'Three.'

'Care to spend them with me? Dinner included this time.'

'I'd love to.'

'Amanda, I love you …'

'Oh, oh, mmm …'

Yolande could bear it no longer. She stood up and began to prowl behind the cameras. The rest of the studio was empty except for Vic Bernitz, Ethan Casavecchia, and the make-up artist and the camera and sound guys. This was an intimate love scene, and Jayne Herford had insisted it be shot in privacy. But it wasn't private enough. Suddenly she got off the bed where she and Patrick were lying semi-clad, snatching up a sheet for cover.

'Cut!'

Vic and Ethan bounded out of their chairs.

'Get her off the set!' yelled Jayne. 'Just get her off, or I'm not going through with this scene.'

'But Jayne …' Vic began.

'Quit the buts. Either she goes or I do.'

Furious, Yolande marched up to her. So Jayne wanted to make love to Patrick on camera without the inconvenient presence of his girlfriend. 'No one tells me where to go! You wouldn't be here at all if I hadn't put up the money for this film.'

'You're such a jealous bitch! Can't you let Patrick out of your sight for five minutes?'

'With you? Do you think I don't know what's going on? Get out! Now! I'm closing this picture down. I won't be made a fool of any longer.'

'Yolande!' Vic was instantly at her elbow. 'Please, come and talk to me. We'll sort this out. Jayne didn't mean it. It's difficult doing these scenes. Patrick, come here.'

But Patrick wasn't in the mood to play peacemaker. He grabbed Yolande by the arm and hauled her off to a dark corner, shouting at her in harsh, rapid French. The others just watched in helpless incomprehension.

'You can't pull out now, Yolande. There are contracts, remember? You agreed to back this movie and I'm going to make sure you do!'

'I can do what the hell I want! I know all about you and

286

Jayne'

'It's not true, and you know it. Just ask Sam MacPherson. I don't think he'd be overjoyed by your insinuations about Jayne and me. For God's sake stop behaving like a spoilt baby. I'm an actor. It's my work. Fuck off and let me get on with it!'

'Patrick!'

'I mean it. If Jayne wants you off the set for this scene, you go. You're driving us both mad. I'm not having an affair with her and I've no intention of starting one. Now fuck off, you stupid bitch!'

'You bastard, Patrick! I never want to see you again!'

She turned on her heel and fled, fighting back the tears. Patrick remained immobile, but Vic and Ethan pursued her, pleading with her, trying to calm her down. They knew very well it was legally almost impossible for her to withdraw her capital, but it wouldn't do to let her go off in such a temper. She just told them both to go to hell before she climbed into her car and drove off.

Jayne Herford downed a cup of coffee while Patrick smoked a cigarette. They then performed the scene uninterrupted. Vic thought it so good there would be no need for a retake. Once dressed and feeling calmer, they talked about Yolande.

'Is she always such a firecracker?' asked Jayne.

Patrick shrugged his shoulders. 'She's Yolande Marchand – what do you expect?'

'I'm glad no one else was around. Sam wouldn't like it getting out to the press.'

'I tried to explain that to Yolande, but she wouldn't believe me. Anyway, I'm sure *she* won't talk. She's too proud. That's her problem.'

'Where's she gone?'

'Who cares? She'll come back.' He turned to leave. 'See you tomorrow, Jayne.'

'See you.'

When Patrick got back to the Beverley Hills apartment, there were signs that Yolande had made a hasty departure. Some of her clothes were still in the wardrobe, but she must have taken at least three suitcases. That beige suit Franco had given her at Easter was still hanging in its cover, untouched. Patrick fingered it pensively, then looked about for a note. Surely she had left a note. He searched everywhere, without success. Perhaps she intended to ring up when she arrived wherever she was going. New York, probably. She'd almost certainly run home to Mummy.

He lay on the bed, elated and depressed at the same time. May 6th Hank Pedersen had to be on that Far East trip about now. Yolande wouldn't be back for at least a fortnight – three weeks if he was lucky. He picked up his mobile and called Althea Pedersen at Malibu. His luck was in. Her husband was out of the country. She told him to drive up straight away. Patrick bounded off the bed and left at once. That scene at the studios had been perfectly timed and excellently staged. He was quite sure his affair with Althea would be an award winner.

Chapter Eighteen

'Ten days and not a sign of life,' said Vic Bernitz. 'I don't like it, Ethan. I don't like it at all.'

Ethan Casavecchia dipped a finger into his Piña Colada, grinning suggestively at Vic's gorgeous daughter Tiffany, who was wearing an apology for a bikini. He brought the finger to his lips and slowly licked it clean. They were lounging by the swimming pool at Vic's house on a hot Sunday afternoon. All it needed for the day to be perfect was for Tiffany to straddle him with her perfectly toned thighs and rub sunscreen all over him. But Vic would keep talking about Yolande. Why he wanted her back was a mystery. Everything had been going just great since she had stormed out of the studios. Patrick had been a perfect dream to work for, smiling and good tempered.

'Are you listening?' Vic asked, digging a finger into his ribs.

'About Yolande? Sure, sure. She's a hell of a girl.'

'She's a hell of a rich girl, and she's still got our publicity budget tied up in Belco Pictures.'

Ethan's eyes narrowed behind his glasses, and he began to pay attention. 'Ah.'

'Now, let me give you another one. Can you figure out how we're going to lay hold of it? Only Yolande can authorise payment. And we need it now. The time's just right for a publicity blitz. I've spoken to the distributors and we're pushing for an earlier release than scheduled – probably November. We can cash in on the Christmas market.'

'No way!'

'Why not? We should be in the cutting room by

September now we've got the technical stuff sorted out.'

'But why can't you just call her? Last I heard she had a cell phone.'

Vic leaned forward in his chair, exasperated. 'Her cell's dead. I don't have any other contact info. Nor does the Belco office. Just find her. Fast. I guess she'll be with friends some place. Keep ringing round till you locate her. Then leave it to me.'

'OK, Vic. Will do.'

'Now! I'm busy.'

With a rueful glance at Tiffany, Ethan beat a speedy retreat into the house and hunted for some glossy magazines. Who did Yolande know well? Then he had a better idea. He put a call through to Patrick.

'Ethan Casavecchia here.'

Patrick groaned, then put a silencing finger over Althea's lips. 'What do you want?'

'Do you know where I can find Yolande?'

'What for?'

'We need to talk to her about the publicity budget.'

Althea started nibbling Patrick's neck. He shot her a warning look.

'Well, I haven't heard from her – but try her mother in New York.' Patrick quickly recited the Beideckers' ex-directory number and slammed the receiver down as soon as he could put an end to Ethan's chatter. Then he took it off the hook again. 'No more interruptions now.'

'What was that about?' asked Althea, stroking his chest.

'Vic wants some money from Yolande.'

'Oh. Do you think she'll come back?'

'Probably. I don't expect I'll have her, though. Not now I've got you. Althea, I could eat you …'

'Why don't you,' she murmured, and sighed as his mouth started trailing down her body.

What a fabulous way to spend the afternoon – in bed

with Patrick. Privacy guaranteed. They had decided that her house was too risky with Juanita around. It was absolute bliss here; no one to see them, nothing to do except have endless, glorious, mind-blowing sex. Of course Yolande would never come back. There was nothing left for her now.

Yolande had indeed gone to New York, but she hadn't given her mother and stepfather a clue as to why; just turned up out of the blue, sure of the offer of a bed. Her ostensible excuse was the need to oversee financial transactions connected with Belco that had to be finalised in New York, but neither Grace nor Tex believed her.

'It's Patrick,' said Grace. 'Something's happened.'

'I hope it's not a baby.'

That set maternal alarm bells ringing furiously. Grace imagined various unpleasant possibilities before she had the courage to ask Yolande directly. The answer was a categorical denial delivered with a flash of green eyes that put paid to further questions.

'Are you staying long?'

'I don't know,' said Yolande, shrugging her shoulders. 'It depends how long things take. Am I in the way?'

'No, darling, of course not. Corinne and Miles were supposed to come for a weekend, but they're tied up in France. Corinne's buying a controlling stake in Elegance Hotels.'

'Just like Papa – no sooner over one crisis than planning another coup.' Yolande sighed. She longed to see Corinne. She wanted Paris, her old friends, and familiar places. 'How's Marie-Christine, by the way? Tex mentioned something about her operation.'

'She had it done in April, and everything's fine now. She can even walk without a stick. Philippe wrote with all the details. I'll get you the letter.'

It wasn't through oversight that enclosed with the letter

were several newspaper cuttings about Yves' fracas with André Hamel. Yolande was absorbed by them for a good half-hour. Surely Yves didn't still love her? He'd been so offhand on the phone at Easter. But why had he punched a man on the jaw over her? She stared at the pictures of him looking proud and angry. Extremely handsome too. Anger suited him. It gave him the spark she felt he had always lacked. But when she got to details of the quarrel, she was furious. Hamel, an insignificant journalist, claiming he'd slept with her – well, not in so many words, but the insinuations were clear enough. She couldn't believe her reputation was so bad.

'Mummy?'

Grace looked up. 'Yes?'

'Is this all true?'

'I'm afraid so. Corinne called me about it. She was very upset.'

'I'll sue him! How *dare* he! I only met him once. I've never even kissed him, and there they all are talking about me as though I were a slut. Who would be best to handle a libel suit?'

'But darling, what would be the point? He's only *alleged* to have made and retracted some derogatory remarks.'

'You know damn well what that means.'

'But it's all hearsay, and witnesses would vanish if you took it to court. They'd drag the whole of your private life through the press. Yours, Yves', perhaps even your father's.'

'But he can't get away with this!'

'He didn't,' said Grace.

Yolande became very quiet. 'No, I suppose not,' she said at last. 'A gallant baron came to the defence of my honour. But it still stinks. It makes me wonder how many other slimeballs I've had the great pleasure of sleeping with.' She was close to tears.

'Yolande, please don't cry.'

'Well, wouldn't you feel the same?'

'But you must realise you're bound to be a subject for gossip. It's not exactly something new.'

'I ought to thank Yves. Perhaps I'll ring him up. Is he in Paris or Burgundy at the moment?'

'If his mother's still convalescing with Philippe and Claire, he'll probably be at his flat.'

Yolande made a move towards the telephone, then stopped. 'And you said Corinne was upset?'

'Yes.'

'Perhaps she does care about me a little, after all.'

Grace waited a while to see if Yolande would in fact pick up the phone, but there was no further action. So she was still besotted with Patrick, too proud to acknowledge that Yves had strength of character that Patrick didn't; too blind to see that he loved her. Grace went out. It was all so maddening, but she decided to wash her hands of it all. Yolande would wake up one day. She only hoped it wouldn't be too late.

Yolande toyed with the idea of calling Yves for several days, then dropped it. Her mother would report back to him anyway. That would be enough. He would know she appreciated his friendship, even if she didn't love him. It was all due to that ancient code of chivalry that he seemed to follow; honour, duty, family. But not love. Certainly not passion. He'd thumped Hamel out of wounded pride, that was all – because she'd been *his* fiancée. If Gabrielle d'Emville had been slandered, he would certainly have done the same thing. Yolande managed to talk herself into a philosophical view of the incident, and continued to sit by the telephone, even though she had invitations everywhere. She was annoyed with herself for having lost her mobile phone at LAX in the rush to escape – and with it her entire contacts list, since she never bothered with an address book. But Patrick knew where she was. He was bound to call and say he wanted her back soon. He had to. She was unbearably lonely without him.

The call came, but not from Patrick. A long, rambling appeal instead from Vic Bernitz, asking her to return to California.

'What about Patrick and Jayne?' demanded Yolande. 'Or is it over already?'

'Hey, come on, baby, you know there's nothing in it. Jayne asked me to apologise for snapping at you like that. She's fixed up long-term with San MacPherson. Patrick's just been a good boy, sitting at home on his own waiting for you.'

Her spirits soared. 'Really?'

'Sure,' said Vic. 'His ego's a bit too fragile for him to ask you back, but I know he's missing you like mad. Now, I've got a little plan. You come back quietly, I'll pick you up at the airport and then you can give him a surprise. What do you think?'

She agreed enthusiastically. Good old Vic. He knew how to handle everything. It was arranged that she would catch a flight early Sunday morning, have lunch with him at the Beverley Hills Polo Lounge, then go on to meet Patrick at their apartment. He would be back from jogging then. She could hardly wait. The call over, Yolande went straight out to buy Patrick a present, a silver pistol lighter engraved with his initials.

It all went according to plan. Yolande stepped into the VIP lounge at Los Angeles looking, Vic thought, like a million dollars. She even hugged him when he sauntered up to her, grinning broadly. His wife Babs joined them with Ethan for lunch , where talk soon came round to the publicity budget.

'I'm going all out for an earlier release this fall,' said Vic, casually pulling some papers out of a briefcase. 'So we'll need advance publicity spread out over the next four months.'

Yolande smiled. 'You want some money. You could have sorted that through Troy or Shelby.'

'Yes, but I need your autograph. And hell, we need you. I hope you won't mind doing a few interviews when we kick the campaign off?'

'I expect I could manage one or two. Give me a pen. Where do I sign?'

Ethan goggled. What a painless way to get a woman to part with her fortune. He wished he knew Patrick's secret. Still, it was a sure-fire investment, and Yolande probably knew it. Word on the lot was that *Fast and Loose* was set to be a major moneyspinner. Business accomplished, gossip and jokes took over, Vic being the most entertaining. He hurried the dessert up a little in order (as he put it) to reunite Venus and Mars. Yolande was driven to her apartment thirty minutes later.

'Need a hand with your bags?' asked Ethan when they arrived.

'Would you? That's terribly kind. They're not too heavy.'

He picked up the two suitcases, told Vic to wait, and followed her through the entrance to the block. They got into the lift. Ethan came right into the apartment with her, dumping the suitcases thankfully in the lobby. Darkness. She switched on the lights.

'Would you like a drink? I'll just go and get Patrick. He must be asleep.'

'No thanks, Yolande. I'd better go. Vic's waiting.'

She went along to the bedroom as he turned to leave. Ethan heard her open the door.

'Patrick? Darling, it's me. My God! What the hell are you doing?'

Ethan doubled back, took one look over Yolande's shoulder and ran. This was not going to be a one-man job.

For a few seconds, Yolande remained stock still, her

eyes riveted on Patrick and Althea Pedersen. Naked. Rutting like animals. In her bed.

His behaviour for the last two months instantly became appallingly clear – that scene with Jayne Herford at the studios, his indifference, the deterioration in their sex life. And he wouldn't say a thing. He just sat up, shielding that woman she had never liked, staring at her provocatively. Yolande picked up a vase on the dressing table and hurled it at him.

'You cheating bastard!'

Althea cowered in terror. The vase smashed against the wall above her head, and fragments fell on the pillows. Yolande then picked up a bronze statuette and advanced, eyes blazing. Patrick took one blow on his arm and shoved Althea off the bed.

'Althea, get out! Quick!'

He sprang up and seized Yolande while Althea fled, snatching her clothes from a chair. Then he prised the statuette out of Yolande's hand and slapped her several times across the face; hard, vicious blows, meant to hurt. She began to cry, but she was too enraged to feel the pain. She tried to claw his face, writhing violently as he grappled with her. He crushed her in his arms, pressing both her hands into the small of her back, and she began to bite his chest.

'You bitch!'

Patrick pushed her down onto the bed and sat on top off her, pinning her arms under his knees. She twisted from side to side, kicking her legs, hurling insults at him, hoping to push him off and retrieve the statuette, lying on the floor a few feet away. Patrick caught her by the neck, and suddenly she froze. His fingers were pressed against her throat, flexing threateningly over her vocal cords. Leaning over her, he looked so vicious she could hardly recognise him.

'Patrick – no! No!'

'Don't worry, I'm not going to kill you. It wouldn't look good on my CV. I'll give you five minutes to get out of here, and I mean for good. Understand?' He smiled maliciously, enjoying her impotence. 'You're washed up, Yolande. I got bored with you a long time ago, but I needed the money. Go back to your prissy baron! He's perfect for a stuck-up bitch like you.'

She managed to free one arm and hit him across the face, then decided to attack where it really would hurt and squeezed his balls as hard as she could. Patrick roared with pain, and struck her violently on the head. Yolande saw the room in a blur, there was a sick feeling in her stomach. Another blow, then another. She hit back at him again but missed. Anything to get him off, to stop that thumping on her skull …

Then suddenly it was over. She lay dazed and gasping on the bed, Vic Bernitz leaning over her anxiously.

'Jesus! Yolande, can you hear me? Ethan, leave him and come here.'

'But Vic, suppose he …'

'I'm going out.' Patrick groaned as he staggered from the room. 'Have her gone before I get back.'

'The bastard!' said Vic once he was out of earshot. 'Yolande, whatever happened? Here, come to Vic.'

He cradled her in his arms, rocking her to and fro like a baby as she sobbed. Ethan came over with some towels soaked in cold water, and applied them carefully to her temples. The door slammed a few minutes later as Patrick left the apartment. They managed to get Yolande into the lounge, where she lay on the sofa, convulsed with sobs, unable to answer their questions. Why did they need to know so much? She wanted to die.

'I'd better call the cops,' said Ethan, picking up the phone.

'No!' she shouted. 'No police. This must never get out. Just help me. Oh God.'

'We are helping you, honey,' murmured Vic soothingly. 'How are you now?'

'I'll be all right. But my head. Everything hurts so much.'

Ethan found some painkillers in the bathroom cabinet and brought them in with a glass of water. She struggled to get them down her throat.

'You're going to have bruises,' said Vic. 'I'll take you back to my place. Babs will get our doctor.'

'No, no.' She tried to sit up, hating even the room. It was so full of Patrick. 'There's only one thing you can do for me, Vic. Get me home – please!'

'To New York?'

'No. France! Please, Vic. I can't stand it here. I can't bear it. I …' She started sobbing, and it was painful to hear.

'But the movie! Don't you want to …?'

She clutched her head. 'You've got the money. You don't need me.'

Vic gazed at her, pity mingled with a total lack of understanding. So Patrick had knocked her around, but that was no reason to quit the movie business.

'Just do as I say. I hate Patrick! I hate the film! I'll hate you too if you don't get me home.'

'OK. If that's what you want. I'll deal with the Belco office, but we'll keep in touch. You're going to make a pile on this one, baby.'

She didn't care. 'Will you get me a cognac?'

'No. You've got a mild concussion. Have some more water.'

She gulped it down, but when she tried to light a cigarette, her hands shook so much that Vic had to do it for her. Yolande left California on a flight for Paris that evening.

Ethan took some trouble to explain to Vic exactly what he had seen in the bedroom, but not a whisper of the afternoon's events reached the press. It was the kind of publicity *Fast and Loose* could certainly do without.

'Yolande!' Toinette shouted with surprise as a devastated Yolande, wearing dark glasses and a hat, stepped into the salon of her Avenue Foch home. Françoise was beside her, patting her arm excitedly and asking what to do with her luggage.

'Put it in my room, please.' Yolande collapsed onto a sofa.

'My God, you're all bruised! Whatever's happened? Let me call Doctor Limon.'

'No, Toinette, please. I meant to say hello.' She stretched out a hand. 'I feel awful. Sorry.'

Toinette sat down beside her, alarmed. Yolande took off her hat and glasses, and the tell-tale marks on her face were clearly visible beneath her make-up. Her lovely eyes were red and swollen, the skin around them blue and purple. She looked as though she'd been crying for hours. Toinette dragged her into an embrace and just held her close.

'So it's over with Patrick?'

Yolande nodded against her shoulder.

'And these bruises?'

'I – I had an accident. A fall. '

She started to cry. Toinette cuddled her, stroking her hair. So Patrick had beaten her; after all she'd done for him. But she'd be too proud ever to admit it.

'When did all this happen?'

'Yesterday. I came straight back. I never want to see Los Angeles again.'

'You ought to go to bed, darling. You look terrible. Shall I get you something to eat? A drink?'

'No thanks.'

'Does your mother know?'

'No.' Yolande suddenly broke from Toinette's arms

and stood up, drying her eyes with a very crumpled tissue. 'Where's Corinne?'

'At the office.'

'I want to see her. I'll go now. I need some fresh air.'

'Yolande! You can't. You must rest. Françoise will make up your bed. Go and lie down.'

She shook off Toinette's restraining hand and bolted out of the apartment, down the stairs, past the ancient concierge, Monsieur Boniface, who was sulking because she hadn't greeted him with her usual sunny smile. She stumbled out onto the street, oblivious to everything except her own grief. She could never sleep in that bed again. The last time she'd slept there had been with Patrick, when she'd agreed to back the film. She loped unevenly along the pavement, her eyes full of tears. Beautiful Paris on a beautiful day. It would be perfect if she didn't feel so ill. Her whole body ached from sleepless hours on that jumbo jet – hours in which to turn black and blue. When she had finally managed to shut her eyes, Patrick's fists seemed to dance around her head.

A tourist stopped and tried to ask her the way somewhere, but she kept going. Down side streets, using her old route to the Hervy salon and Marchand's head office on the Avenue Montaigne. Past familiar shops, restaurants where she used to dine, a news stand where she was well known. She crossed the street to avoid an interrogation from the Tunisian lady who ran it. Her legs felt increasingly shaky, her vision blurred by tears that brimmed over in spite of her efforts to check them.

Then she was there. The Avenue Montaigne, busy with traffic on a warm May afternoon. Yolande quickened her pace to get to her sister's office. She didn't have the patience to walk to the traffic lights. Looking around briefly, she stepped off the pavement. A small van appeared out of nowhere, honking its horn furiously. She ran. Not fast enough. The screech of the brakes as the driver tried to avoid the impact brought the security guard hurrying out of Marchand's reception. Only minutes later Corinne learnt that her sister was lying badly injured and unconscious in the road outside. She went with her in the ambulance to the emergency department of the Hôtel Dieu – the hospital where her father had died.

It wasn't until late evening that Yves heard the news, and then in the cruellest way possible. He was alone at Rochemort, and had made good use of the lack of interruption to work on tax returns and urgent export documents. After a light supper, he switched on the television news. The same stale items. He was about to switch off when a picture of Yolande came up.

She was in intensive care in Paris: serious accident, unexpected return from America, her sister at her bedside, in a critical condition... Thank God he was alone. He cried – loud, harsh sobs which shook his whole body. He hadn't cried like this since his father's death when he was only a boy. When he had recovered from the shock, Yves rammed some clothes into a backpack, jumped into his car, and sped off. He arrived at the hospital just as Yolande was being wheeled out of the operating theatre.

Chapter Nineteen

'So you had the showdown while I was out of town,' re-marked Hank Pedersen, lolling on the sofa, his hands behind his head. 'I always miss the fun.'

Althea fidgeted nervously with the bracelet he'd given her on their last wedding anniversary, looking out through the French windows to the garden and the blue Pacific beyond. He was staring at her in a way that made her feel acutely uncomfortable, and his voice had an edge to it she'd never heard before.

'Well, Althea, aren't you going to fill me in on your movie pals? It must have been quite a circus.'

'You seem to know all about it. I can't really add much more than the media.'

Hank sat up, his eyes still fixed on her. 'And here I was hoping for some first-hand juicy details. It sounds as though Yolande has been smashed up pretty badly, poor kid.'

'Yes.'

'But what was she doing in Paris? And why's Patrick Dubuisson here instead of at her side? I guess I shouldn't ask, but you know me, sweetheart – insatiably curious.'

'If you really want the lowdown, ask Vic. He's getting all the reports. She'll be OK. There was some rumour she was paralysed, but it wasn't true.'

'And *Patrick*?' He pronounced the name in an affected French accent. 'Why don't you tell me about *Patrick*?'

He stood up and walked over to her, his expression intense and angry. She backed away as he approached. Surely he didn't know. Nobody knew.

'What's wrong? You're not afraid of me, are you? Just

your husband, baby. That shouldn't scare you.'

'Darling, are you OK?' She backed further away. 'You don't seem yourself.'

Hank stood there, looking not only angry, but disappointed, and somehow that made her feel worse. 'So you're gutless as well as faithless, Althea.'

She was absolutely silent. He knew. She couldn't think of a single thing to say. Hank turned away and sat back on the sofa.

'I guess you're wondering how I found out,' he said calmly. 'Well, I have asked Vic. He tried to brush me off, but that sidekick of his was less discreet. I gather there was such a brawl between Dubuisson and Yolande he's been traumatised. A bit of a wimp, that Ethan.'

Althea's hands were trembling. She sat down, still saying nothing.

'I'm not speaking just on my own account,' Hank drawled on, his voice strangely calm and disembodied. 'When I think of what's happened to Yolande. Jesus, what you've done to that girl! You and that bastard Dubuisson! She must have been happy once – before you cooked up this movie deal. I guess you couldn't wait to get your hands on him, could you? You just duped me about buying Marchand. But you'd checked out his assets in Paris first, hadn't you, huh? Althea, what have you got to say?'

'No! Hank, believe me, I didn't – I wanted you to get Marchand. I never meant things to turn out this way. But I couldn't help it.'

'You couldn't *help* it!' he thundered. 'There's just one word to remember for assholes like Dubuisson. No! How come you forgot such a vital part of the English language?'

'Hank, please! I can explain.'

Then she stopped. No explanation came. Now he had put it that way, she couldn't even begin to understand how it had happened, how she'd schemed and lied, been so pitiless towards Yolande, even continued the affair with Patrick after the news came through of her accident in Paris. And for what? A month or two's sex. They both knew it wouldn't last. Althea had made it clear from the start that she had no intention of leaving her husband, and Patrick certainly had no plans to settle down. Suddenly she realised that she would also be a casualty in this game of selfish pleasure.

'I guess I'd better go,' she said, trying to keep her voice level.

'Go where?'

'Does it matter? You can reach me through my lawyers. I shan't contest the divorce.'

'Divorce!' He bounded to his feet. 'What divorce? Althea, are you crazy? We haven't even talked this thing through. Or is it the chance you've been waiting for? Do you love him?'

'No, no.' She looked up at him. 'I love you.' Her voice broke. 'But you must hate me. I don't blame you for it. And we have no kids, nothing to hold us together.'

'Come here.'

Then she was in his arms, sobbing against his shoulder. Tears of shame and regret. She felt she could never look him in the face again. 'Hank, I'm sorry. I'm so sorry.'

Why was he being so gentle? It made her feel worse. He ought to get mad, shout, tell her to go to hell. But he just held her close, running his fingers through her hair.

'I guess I'm partly to blame,' he said at last. 'I neglected you too long. I didn't realise how bad you felt about it. But I never cheated on you, never. Hey, come on, sweetheart, stop crying. We're going to change everything. Starting with a vacation – a real, long vacation. Want to come? Just the two of us.'

She cried. She confessed. She was forgiven. But the wound remained inside; a distrust of her own character that would take a long time to heal. When Althea thought

305

of Yolande, she hated herself. But then hadn't Patrick initiated the whole affair? No, not entirely. She'd led him on. She'd thought she could flirt with danger and not get burned. Not hurt Hank. Not put her entire happiness on the line. How could she have been so stupid? She and Hank left Malibu for a holiday in St Bart's two days later.

Patrick listened to Althea's voice on the end of the line in ego-shattered silence. Leaving with her husband? Never wanted to see him again. Don't even think about calling her. It was fantastic, Patrick, now fuck off. He'd never felt so used and humiliated.

He was stranded until the film went on location to Mexico. He wanted to get away from LA. The girls were less friendly since the news of Yolande's accident had been splashed all over the press. A new town, a new country – and a new woman. Meanwhile there were interviews to be given for this publicity campaign Vic had started. Patrick had promised interesting revelations about his background, though questions on his private life were not allowed. Ironic, really, because for the moment his private life was non-existent.

Vic told him that Yolande had been transferred to a private clinic on the outskirts of Paris, where she apparently entertained vast numbers of friends in her room. Her mother had begged him to go and visit her straight after the accident, but he could hardly interrupt his schedule with Althea for the girl who had almost wrecked the affair. Yolande meant nothing at all to him. He was haunted by a vague twinge of conscience at having hit her, but she'd asked for it. Anyway, she would clear a handsome profit on *Fast and Loose,* which was already billed as the movie of the year, and her injuries were much less serious than at first feared. Patrick was quite convinced she would be all right. She's served her purpose in his life. It was time to move on.

Grace smiled at the duty nurse as she made her way along the corridor to Yolande's room. Another fine June day; another morning to be pleased with her daughter's progress.

'How is she?'

'Physically – coming along very well. But she's moody again today, Madame Beidecker.'

'Boredom, I expect. When do you think she'll be allowed out?'

'At the end of the month, the doctor says. The bones are mending well now, and we'll be increasing the physio soon. But her nerves – well, perhaps she'll be better when she gets home. Some days I feel I just daren't speak to her.'

Grace went into Yolande's room – bright, cheerful, and festooned with 'get well' cards. Not really like a hospital room at all except for the machinery at the head of the bed and that pervasive clinical aroma. Yolande was sitting up, reading a book which she tossed aside with a look of relief when her mother appeared.

'I've brought you some more magazines, darling,' said Grace, kissing her. 'Corinne says she'll come this evening, and I think Toinette will be in this afternoon.'

Yolande smiled wanly. With her long chestnut hair loose over the pillows, she looked pale and sad, but still beautiful.

'Do you have to go on Monday, Mummy?'

'I'm afraid so. But I'll be back again soon. We thought you'd like to convalesce in Dorset. Corinne and Miles will be there on holiday, and Tex will come and join us. It will be fun.'

Yolande looked unenthusiastic. So it was one of those days when no one seemed able to cheer her up, persuade her that she would soon be fit again and that life was still worth living. Her depression was obviously connected to Patrick, but Grace had no details of the quarrel, and she

307

was afraid to ask in case it was too disturbing. She'd been quite horrified by his flat refusal to come and visit Yolande immediately after the accident.

Grace pulled the magazines out from her bag and put them on the table. 'There's something about Franco in one of them, but I can't remember which. By the way, he's promised to come and visit you again next week.'

'That'll be great. Is he really going to do *prêt-à-porter* for Hervy?'

'I think it's more or less fixed. He's coming to finalise everything with Corinne and Georges – when they can spare the time from the Elegance Hotels deal. It's going to be a complete takeover by Marchand.'

Yolande managed to discuss the topic with more interest than she felt, then they turned to her situation. She hated the subject. The doctors had told her she'd been extremely lucky to escape with compound fractures to her left leg, arm, collar bone, six cracked ribs, and a ruptured spleen. The van had caught her left side as she had stepped into the road. She'd been in a coma for five days, so had no knowledge of the internal bleeding, the operations to screw her shattered leg back together and fix her arm. But she was on the mend now. It no longer hurt her just to breathe, and although she hated the casts and the pulleys and having to get a nurse to help her with every little thing, there was no reason to suppose she couldn't even resume a modelling career after physiotherapy and a few months' rest. But she felt she never wanted to step onto a catwalk again. That part of her life was over.

'I promised to do Franco's Milan show in October. I'd better tell him to find someone else.'

'But you ought to be fine by then. I shouldn't rule it out yet.'

'Oh, do talk about something interesting. Who's been invited to Philippe's wedding – or more importantly, who hasn't?'

'The usual suspects,' said Grace, not liking the way Yolande had switched subjects. They could never seem to talk about things that really mattered these days. 'Tex and I hope to make it. And Philippe's counting on you being there.'

'What do you think of Claire?'

'She's very sweet. Far too nice for Philippe, but she adores him. And he's really happy. Who would have thought it?'

'I don't think I've known him happier. Isn't she bringing Isabelle in to see me again today?' Yolande's expression brightened. 'They're all besotted with her, but I can see why. Even Marie-Christine seems to prefer her to Geraldine.'

Grace laughed. Then she thought of Yves – another taboo. Yolande hadn't been told of his frantic desire to see her on the night of the accident, and though he now visited her regularly, he always made sure he was accompanied by someone else. That way there was no embarrassment, nothing beyond general conversation. It was clear to everybody that Yves was deeply in love – clear to everybody except Yolande, of course. She seemed to rank him somewhere outside her intimate circle of family and friends, and it pained Grace to see it. If she could have got hold of Patrick Dubuisson, she would have cheerfully wrung his neck.

When Grace got up to leave, Yolande suggested they had a more serious chat the following day about her future plans. She needed to talk, but it was so hard. And she hated being alone. Though she had books, radio, and television, nothing took her mind off the humiliation of California if there was no one there to deflect her thoughts. At first she thought she had a broken heart, then she realised she felt too angry – furious because she hadn't got even with Patrick. Never would now. He had cast her aside like a piece of rubbish. The lies and deceit still took her breath away. How had she been fool enough to believe him? To love him for so long? To sink nearly all her money in his film? She couldn't come up with an answer she cared to acknowledge.

Claire was adamant: Yves had to go. Yolande would be so disappointed not to see Isabelle once more before she went to stay with her grandmother at St Xavier.

'But I can't …'

'Please, Yves. I really must stay. We think we've got a buyer this time, and you know how important it is.' She bent down to Isabelle. 'You'll go with Uncle Yves to see Yolande, won't you, darling?'

'Yes!' Isabelle nodded energetically. Since seeing Yolande's picture on the front cover of *Paris Match*, she had decided this was an acquaintance definitely worth cultivating.

Yves gave in. He left Claire's Versailles home ten minutes later with Isabelle, her teddy bear, some flowers, and a great deal of apprehension. Life had settled back into a familiar pattern, with him being the one everybody relied on again. And he liked to be useful. But he needed to be wanted, and wanted by Yolande. He and Anne-Louise Chevagnac had called time on their fling when she left for the States. She'd phoned him a couple of times from New York after Yolande's accident, worried about him. It seemed as though she was working things out with her husband and Yves was glad for her. She deserved it. There hadn't been anyone since. Yolande was as firmly locked in his heart as always, and now he saw her regularly it was killing him.

It was when he reached the Péripherique that inspiration came. Of course, he could take Grace or Toinette as armour. He drove straight to the Avenue Foch. Grace was out, but Toinette was delighted to see both him and Isabelle.

'Well, I was going to the hospital this afternoon, but now you're here you could take this book for me. Tell Yolande I'll definitely be in tomorrow morning. Actually, Yves, there's something I want to show you.'

She beckoned him into the salon and picked up the latest issue of the *Sunday Times* magazine. Miles had bought it on his last journey back from London, his attention caught by Patrick Dubuisson, leather jacketed and smiling, on the front cover.

Toinette settled in an armchair with Isabelle on her lap. Yves took the magazine, staring at the picture. Then he sat down and read the interview, frowning over one or two unfamiliar words.

'So he's Marc Quiberon's son!'

'You can see the resemblance now, can't you?' Toinette said, trying to rescue an earring from Isabelle's grasp. 'I always wondered where I'd seen that expression before. He's very like him.'

'I must have seen all Quiberon's films, and I would never have guessed – but of course, I haven't met Dubuisson.'

Yves scanned the article again, tight-lipped. So the 'unknown' Patrick Dubuisson was the son of one of France's film legends; a star who would undoubtedly be proud of Patrick's imminent success had he not died twenty years previously from a drug overdose. Already separated from Geneviève Dubuisson before Patrick's birth, he had apparently never even seen his son.

Dubuisson explains with a charming shrug that he has only chosen to reveal his father's identity now because he didn't want to trade on the Quiberon image to get a role.

Yves gave a derisive snort.

One thing is certain – he's got them all talking in Hollywood and he's sure of a warm welcome in Britain when his first major film is released in October.

'Was Quiberon married to his mother?' he asked.

'No. She was an actress too. I've been looking up a few things since I read the article. It all checks out.'

Yves placed the magazine face down on a table. He longed to grind Patrick's smug face into it. 'So why did he need Yolande's backing for this film? He must be worth a fortune.'

'Wrong. Marc Quiberon had three legitimate children and he was virtually penniless when he died. Drugs, fast cars – you know.'

Yves stood up. 'Do you mind if I borrow this?'

'You're not going to show Yolande? I don't know if she's able to take it.'

'Toinette, I've had enough. I don't expect her to say she loves me. But I must know if I have a chance – if she'll ever get over it.'

'Well be careful, please. I'm pretty sure it all ended very badly.'

'Isabelle! Hello, *ma petite* ...' Yolande stretched out her right hand, smiling as Isabelle entered her room. 'Where's your maman?'

Yves followed his niece, carrying a bouquet of flowers. 'Hi, Yolande. I'm afraid Claire couldn't come. And Toinette says she'll be in tomorrow morning. Damn! I forgot that book she asked me to bring. Hope you don't mind.'

'That's OK. I've got enough literature here to keep me going a lifetime.' She tried to sound poised, but she felt acutely embarrassed, lying prone and bandaged without a hint of make-up, totally unprepared for his visit. 'Thanks for the flowers. They're beautiful.'

'Like you.'

She flushed, then turned to Isabelle, who was doing her utmost to climb up onto the bed. 'Sweetheart, you won't be able to get up here.'

'I will!' shouted Isabelle.

Yves picked her up and held her out to be kissed, sitting on the bed to prevent her becoming too boisterous. Yolande covered her nervousness by asking Isabelle about James, one-eyed and nearly one-eared now, but still her favourite bear. Yves watched, too conscious of Yolande's body next to his own, the contours of her breasts beneath her silk pyjamas, her glorious hair spread over the pillow. He wanted to touch her. This was the first time they had been so close since their break-up the previous July.

'Isabelle, don't be rough.' He clasped his niece firmly round her middle as she attempted to get closer to Yolande.

'Oh leave her, Yves.' She stroked the girl's cheek. 'You're going to see your grandmother at Rochemort, aren't you? How do you like Papa's new château?'

'I'm going to have a dog,' announced Isabelle. 'A big yellow dog! And a suit of armour!'

Yolande laughed, and chatted to her until she got bored. Yves then lifted her down onto the floor and let her play, but he remained sitting on the bed, gazing at Yolande. So lovely, so perfect. He could hardly believe she'd had a scorching affair with Patrick Dubuisson.

'Why do you keep staring at me?' she asked.

'I haven't had a chance for a long time.'

'Well I'm glad you waited. I was like a bomb site when I came round from surgery.'

'I know. I was there.'

'You were there!'

'I only caught a glimpse of you. Everybody seemed to think it best that I kept out of the way. I drove straight up from Rochemort when I heard about your accident on the news.' He took in the warm response in her eyes, a little glimmer the old Yolande who had loved him, and his spirits lifted.

'Thank you, Yves. And while I'm at it, I'd better thank you for punching André Hamel. It looked like a

313

marvellous right hook.'

He smiled. 'I remember all the boxing lessons you used to give me when you were little. But you've got such delicate hands ...'

Gently he took her hand, then pressed it to his lips. She felt two burning kisses on her palm, and automatically moved her fingers to caress his cheek. They were both surprised by the contact. She dropped her hand back onto the bed, and Yves covered it with his own.

'How much longer will you be here?' he asked.

'A couple of weeks. Then I'll rest at home for a fortnight before I go to England.'

'England!' he echoed, dismayed.

'Only to convalesce. I'll be back in time for Philippe's wedding.'

'Have you anything planned after that?'

Yolande laughed wryly. 'I've given up making plans since this accident. But I really ought to do something sensible. Finish a degree, perhaps.'

'Are you sure that's what you want now?'

'No. But I don't seem to have done anything with my life at all so far.'

'You've made a lot of people happy, and there aren't many of us who can say that.'

There was a silence. She sensed that he wanted to say something else, but he just sat there, his blue eyes fixed on her face, his hand pressing hers. The warmth was comforting. 'What are you doing for the summer?'

'Being a fool as usual.' Yves laughed. 'Philippe's roped me in to help with the Château Briteuil restoration. He says he needs my advice, but it really means sorting out the gardens. They're in an appalling state.'

'Wasn't it Victor de la Haye's home? I remember staying there once when I was very young. Like something out of *Sleeping Beauty* – a fortress with a jungle around it.'

'Exactly. But it has potential. Philippe's found an old

plan of how the gardens looked in the seventeenth century. They were designed by Le Nôtre.'

'Le Nôtre! I suppose he'll trade on the royal connection?'

'Of course. It will be a palace in all but name. Actually, I think it will make a first-class hotel, and the wine's not half bad, either.'

Yolande smiled. How pleasant to talk to Yves like this again. She couldn't help remembering the good times they had had together. Her fingers curled around his firm, reassuring hand, like they used to when she was a child and he had been her hero. They must be friends. She was glad to see him now, pleased there was no one else today to inhibit him.

Somehow it wasn't the moment to raise the spectre of Patrick. Yves knew he wouldn't be able to take revelations about the affair, even if Yolande offered any. It was still too painful – for them both. They chatted instead about Miles and Corinne, of Marie-Christine, who was making astonishing progress, of the film business, books, wine, of everything but themselves. Isabelle interrupted from time to time, and noisily consumed a peach and some grapes from the fruit bowl on the bedside locker.

'She's got juice all over her clothes,' said Yolande, when it was time to leave.

'Damn. Claire will give me a telling off. She's strict.' Yves took a tissue Yolande proffered and mopped the juice from Isabelle's cheeks and chin while she wriggled furiously. 'You messy girl!'

'James was hungry!'

'Well he can't have any more. Now, kiss Yolande goodbye.'

She obeyed with gusto. Yves set her down and stood by the bed, finding it difficult to believe that he'd been sitting with Yolande for an hour and a half.

'When are you coming again?'

'I'm going to Canada on business tomorrow. You'll be out of here by the time I get back. Perhaps we can meet before you go to England?'

'Yes, of course. So I shan't see you for a while.' She sounded a little regretful. 'Take care of yourself, Yves.'

He leaned over to kiss her cheeks. Instinctively she slipped her hand around his neck and pressed her lips briefly to his right cheek and across to the left. But his mouth closed over hers, warm and possessive. His tongue parted her lips, teasing, probing. She felt a shock of pleasure through her body and responded, dragging his head down. Oh, it was good. But it bewildered her. He never used to kiss her like this. Why now? When she was a smashed-up wreck? As though she'd been scalded, she dropped her hand and pushed him away.

Yves drew back, smiling. 'Get well, my darling.'

Then he caught hold of Isabelle's hand and made for the door, just remembering to pick up the bag containing the *Sunday Times* magazine Toinette had given him. When they had gone Yolande burst into tears.

The smile on Corinne's face faded abruptly when she sat beside Miles on the sofa in the salon at the Avenue Foch and caught Patrick's face dominating the front cover of the magazine on the table.

'I hope it's strong,' she said to Toinette, who was pouring coffee. 'I'll take it black.'

'Yves told me he didn't show it to Yolande.'

'Probably wise,' added Grace. 'She's not having a good day.'

Corinne scanned the article quickly, her expression grim. There wasn't a single word about Yolande. She obviously didn't exist at all for Patrick now, yet it was she who had launched his career. Callous pig. Her mother and Toinette both gazed at her anxiously. One of the weirdest things to come out of it all was their friendship. They had got to like each other after sharing the apartment for several weeks; both deeply concerned about Yolande, both eager to promote family harmony, bound in some inexplicable way by the shadow of the man they had loved.

'Well I'm not surprised,' said Corinne, putting the magazine down. 'I never cared for Marc Quiberon anyway. '

'Better keep that quiet,' laughed Toinette. 'There used to be queues round the block in Strasbourg when one of his films came out.'

'It just amazes me that I didn't spot the resemblance when Patrick was staying with us in New York,' said Grace. 'Now I think of it, even his voice is the same.'

Corinne sighed and picked up her coffee. She heartily wished that Patrick Dubuisson would disappear off the face of the earth. 'I suppose I'm the one who's got to tell Yolande?'

'I think she'd take it better from you,' Grace answered. 'I'm afraid to mention his name to her, and she never brings it up herself. '

'Looks like you're lumbered,' said Miles to Corinne. 'While you're about it, why not find out if we can put the brakes on the release of his film? We ought to get back at him somehow.'

Corinne shook her head. 'We'd be shooting her in the foot. They've already got Yolande's cash. And it looks like a financial winner. I've had a few conversations with the manager at Belco's office, and they've got a distribution deal with a major studio. I think her best revenge would be to make as much money as possible out of the bastard after what he's put her through.'

As it happened, Yolande reacted very calmly to the article, only looking slightly pained by the photographs. That hateful apartment in Beverley Hills – she suddenly remembered she had left Franco's trouser suit there. She wasn't surprised by the revelations. Patrick had always been extremely mysterious about his father. It was clear now that he had simply been waiting for the right moment to trade on his name. Keeping it secret for so long was just another of his deep, selfish strategies.

She handed the magazine back to her sister. 'Bin it.'

'What really happened?'

Yolande took a deep breath. She thought of the way Yves had held her hand and kissed her, then of Patrick – that vicious, angry face, his insults, his fists beating against her head. A sob caught in her throat.

'Darling, was it that bad?' Corinne stroked her arm. 'Don't talk about it if you don't want to. I just thought it might help.'

'But you'll hate me for being so stupid, Corinne. I nearly destroyed the company.'

'I don't want to hear any more about that. When I saw you there, lying in all that blood,' she shuddered. 'Now that nearly destroyed me. I only wish you could put it behind you so we can get back to how things used to be.'

Yolande tugged her down and hugged her. Thank God she still had Corinne. Despite everything, she had never once said *I told you so*, or reproached Yolande, or said it was all her own fault for being such a selfish bitch. Instead she was there to offer love and comfort and help pick up the pieces – as she always had been. Yolande realised now how little she had truly valued her sister. Perhaps it was time to come clean and give her the whole story – and hope that she would still be able to forgive her.

The facts came out haltingly, and covered more than just recent events in America; everything from the day Yolande had first met Patrick at Hervy. Corinne listened, prompted occasionally, tried to work out what it now meant for Yves, and began making comparisons with her own dealings with Stessenberg and UVS. One name stood out – Althea Pedersen. It hit them both at the same time. She was the only link between the film and Pedersen Corporation's attempt to take over Marchand. Yolande felt terribly guilty. Althea Pedersen had almost wrecked Marchand, she'd stolen Patrick, she was virtually responsible for her lying in this hospital bed – and she still couldn't work out how closely Patrick had been involved in it all.

'I found them in bed together the second time I returned from New York,' she concluded, her voice strained. 'Patrick and I had an awful fight.'

Corinne was outraged. 'He *beat* you?'

'Yes. I'm afraid I started it. But I hardly knew what I was doing. Vic and Ethan rescued me and got me on a flight home. I just wanted to see you.'

'Please don't cry.'

'I'm sorry, Corinne. I'm really sorry.' Yolande fought back the tears. 'It's all so *sordid*. Yves was wonderful to me this afternoon, and I just can't bear it. I've treated him appallingly. And you. And everybody else who's been good to me.'

'But we love you.' Corinne, though still trying to absorb the tale, smiled reassuringly. 'Once you're out of here you'll feel so much better. The main thing is to get you back on your feet. Don't worry about anything else. And this university idea – I'm not too sure you'd enjoy that, would you?'

'But I want to use my brain – even though most people don't think I've got one.' It was good to see her smile again. 'I couldn't stand going back to modelling now.'

'You were enjoying getting to grips with Belco, weren't you?'

'Yes. I never thought I would. But it was *mine*. My responsibility. And I wanted to make it pay. Is everything ticking over? I haven't checked my email for a week.'

'Shelby Owens rings me if she's got a problem. She

emails every other day to see how you're getting on, too. I don't think you need worry. She's got her head screwed on the right way.'

'She's pretty cool,' Yolande said. 'Do you know, the only thing I miss about LA is that poky little office on that ghastly business park? At least the people there were real. Even though the coffee wasn't.' She shuddered at the memory of her one and only dreadful cup from the vending machine.

Corinne laughed. 'In that case, how about a business course and a job when you're better?'

'Sounds interesting. Where?'

'In London. You could do a short marketing course, then you'd be working for me here, if you could bear it. We want someone to make Elegance Hotels live up to their name. The image needs a complete makeover. It's just what Papa planned – luxury hotels, the finest wine, clothes, perfume, and cosmetics – all under his name. You'd be doing it for him, too.'

And when Corinne put it like that, Yolande felt a thrill. Time at last to see if she too had the Marchand touch.

Chapter Twenty

Franco Rivera walked through the doors at Harvey Nichols and out on to Knightsbridge feeling very pleased with himself. It was a wet, cold mid-November day, but there was sunshine in his heart. Everything was going extremely well. His October show had been hugely successful, his boutiques were all up and running, and his name was being mentioned in the reverential tones usually reserved for designer legends. Franco had only been to Harvey Nichols to inspect Hervy's latest *prêt-à-porter* collection for men – his designs, their label. Corinne Marchand, delighted with the new lease of life Hervy had enjoyed since branching out into ready-to-wear, had offered him a lucrative five-year contract. He had accepted. He still had great affection for Hervy, and her generous support and hard work in launching the new Rivera label had earned her his lasting respect and loyalty.

The Rivera boutique on Beauchamp Place, brand-new and distinctly Italian, was a different proposition altogether. Corinne had been careful to ensure there was no conflict with the Hervy brand. Franco's name was etched in lower case in gold paint on the window, which contained a single item from his winter collection. Oblivious of the rain and the crowds jostling along the narrow pavement, he stood back to admire his work – a funky crimson evening gown, shimmering in rich satin. He decided to go in and frighten the assistants a little before letting them know who he was, just to keep them on their toes. He'd rather enjoyed the chaos he'd caused by a similar ploy in New York.

Then he saw her, walking down the other side of the

street wearing a black Hervy trenchcoat and a silk scarf, oblivious of the stares she was attracting from passers-by. She never seemed to realise how beautiful she was.

'Yolande! Yolande!'

Franco dashed between cars and taxis, reaching the opposite pavement with only inches to spare. He caught up with her, smiling broadly.

'That, darling, will certainly put up your life insurance. London drivers have no respect for genius.'

He laughed and pushed back her umbrella to kiss her. They were blocking the pavement, so Yolande slipped her arm through his and pulled him into a shop doorway. He kissed her again. She hugged him hard, laughing as the rain dripped from the shop awning and ran down their faces.

'*Carissima,* how are you? What are you doing in London? Have lunch with me?'

'Good idea. I'm starving. For goodness sake, Franco, stop kissing me.'

Within a remarkably short space of time they were divested of their wet coats and sitting opposite each other in a restaurant just a few doors down from his boutique.

'I still haven't forgiven you for pulling out of my show,' said Franco. 'You've broken my heart.'

He was smiling all the time, his expression far from melancholy. Yolande laughed. Franco always made her laugh. 'I read all the rave reviews, so don't pretend you didn't manage very well without me.'

'But Yolande, I had it all planned. The complete seduction. A little hideaway – de luxe, of course – a box at the opera, superb food, sublime music. And you in my arms in the moonlight.' He waved his hand in a theatrical manner, as she did her best to keep a straight face. 'The world's greatest love story. Only it never happened. How can I possibly forgive you?'

'Because you love me.'

They both burst out laughing. Franco caught hold of her hand and kissed it.

'Yolande, you're adorable. Seriously though, when are you getting back on the catwalk?'

'Never. It was great while it lasted, but it's time to move on.'

'But it's not as though your accident has made a difference. You're as beautiful as ever. You could still make millions.'

'It isn't always about money,' she said.

'That's easy for you to say – you've always had money.'

'Well in that case we agree that the money can't lure me back. You left yourself wide open to that,' she added, as his face fell. 'And if you could see my scars, you might reconsider as well. Not to mention the fact that I'd never fit into any of the clothes now.'

'You look gorgeous.' He surveyed her with hungry eyes. She had filled out a little, but it only made her look even more seductive. 'Are you in much pain?' he added, concerned.

'I live with it. It's not too bad. But leaving all that aside, the accident did make a huge difference. It gave me time to think. I'm starting a new career. When I finish this marketing course, Corinne's got a job lined up for me in Paris.'

'An *office job!*' he almost exploded. 'Help, I need a drink.'

Yolande obligingly poured him some wine, smiling. She could see the thoughts going through his head, as his face was an open book, and it was clear that he was trying to work out what he could do to entice her to Milan and into his bed. But she had really enjoyed the change of direction over the past two months, and her tutors were impressed by her commitment and professionalism. The course was thorough and demanding, and Yolande had risen to the challenge magnificently. She had no intention of throwing away all her hard work by an ill-considered liaison with Franco.

'So when do you go back to Paris?' he asked.

'I'm popping home for occasional weekends at the moment, but I'll back for good after Christmas. I've got exams to get through first.'

Franco drank deep and sighed. 'I see the British premiere of *Fast and Loose* is next Tuesday. Are you going?'

'Possibly.'

Yolande had in fact been on her way to buy something for the premiere in Franco's boutique when he had appeared, though she was still doubtful about using the tickets Vic Bernitz had sent her. It would mean encountering Patrick both on screen and in the flesh. The media hype about him had been overwhelming since his disclosure about his father. Patrick Dubuisson was well on his way to becoming the eighth wonder of the world. And she despised him.

'I didn't think it would last with you two,' said Franco, as though he could read her mind. 'Still, you're bound to profit from the film by the look of things. I was worried it would be a total disaster.'

His brown eyes gazed earnestly into hers for a few seconds, and they both remembered that meeting at Gianni's with Vic Bernitz – and the car ride afterwards. Dangerous thoughts. Yolande began to pay serious attention to her lunch, and Franco fell silent. She couldn't deny that she was very fond of him. He would always be a good friend. But there could never be anything more between them, least of all now she had decided to forsake the entire male sex.

Their visit to the Rivera boutique after the meal restored the gaiety. Franco had the assistants in a spin, demanding to see various items, then criticising them harshly and sending them back. Yolande finally gave the game away by collapsing with laughter. Then the battle began over payment for the evening dress and matching bolero jacket that she chose. The jacket was essential – the scars on her upper arm were still too fresh for her to feel comfortable uncovered. Franco wanted to give her the dress, but she refused.

'No,' she said firmly, placing her credit card on the counter. 'You're supposed to be running a business.'

He shrugged his shoulders, defeated. So she was still unattainable. He wondered who could really make her happy. She was smiling, she radiated irresistible charm and glamour, but he sensed an underlying unease that nothing could quite dispel.

The outfit was paid for and packed in a large carrier bag with 'franco rivera' in minuscule gold lettering printed down a single white vertical strip. On the other side the legend was 'Milan – Paris – London – New York – Beverley Hills'. Not bad for a business start-up. Franco felt a proprietary thrill as he escorted Yolande outside.

'I'm flying back to Milan tonight, so we'll have to fix our next meeting for Paris. I'll give you a call when I'm sure of a date.' He put his arms around her.

'I'll look forward to it. Thanks for lunch, Franco. It was lovely to see you. I'm thrilled you're doing so well. Take care of yourself.'

'You too.' He kissed her firmly on the lips. 'Give Patrick what he deserves on Tuesday. And remember – I'm always here for you.'

Yolande kissed him goodbye and turned away. He watched her disappear down the street, savouring one last whiff of her perfume – 121, a sensuous fragrance from the new Hervy range. She always left him with a longing which, unfulfilled, somehow translated itself into inspiration. The outline of a dress came to him even as he trained his eyes on her retreating back, and he dashed into the boutique to draw a rough sketch. The design became one of the highlights of his Milan show the following year.

Yolande loved London in the rain, especially when it was growing dark and the pavements glistened in the light thrown out by shop windows, while people relaxed over cardiac-arresting pastries and steaming lattes in the coffee houses. Bustle, movement, the sort of excitement and anticipation she remembered from Christmas shopping trips with her mother when she was very small. By six o'clock she was tired, loaded down with presents to take back to France, and speeding along Kensington Gore in a taxi to her grandparents' house in Campden Hill Road. She was staying with them during the twelve weeks of her course, and one bag contained special thank-you gifts. Amongst the others was a collection of nineteenth-century watercolours of the Thames – an offering for Marie-Christine, who was celebrating her sixtieth birthday the following weekend. Having missed all the festivities the previous year, Yolande was looking forward to them. It was bound to be fun, especially now Philippe was home; he had such a genius for parties. Her life was getting back to normal at last.

'Quick, Yolande!' shouted Lady Albury, who was on the telephone in the sitting room as she entered. 'It's Yves.'

Yolande dumped her shopping bags and took the receiver. 'Hi, Yves. How are you?'

Fine. How was the retail therapy?'

'Ruinous.'

He laughed. They chatted for a few minutes about nothing in particular. They had got used to speaking to each other again without constraint and he rang at least twice a week. Lady Albury had looked sceptical when Yolande had told her they were just friends.

'I really wanted to know if you'd come with me to the

Confrérie dinner at Vougeot next Saturday,' Yves said at last. 'Can you get away?'

He was an active member of Confrérie des Chevaliers du Tastevin, the winegrower's association that did much to promote Burgundy's reputation, of which Jean-Claude Marchand had been a prominent member. An invitation to a dinner at the Château de Vougeot, the association's headquarters, was not to be missed. Yolande hadn't been to one of these grand *haute cuisine* affairs since accompanying her father to one when she was seventeen.

'I'm going back to Paris with Miles on Thursday, so I ought to be able to manage it,' she said. 'It's supposed to be a long weekend for home study, but I'd love to come. I've just bought a birthday present for your mother. Will she be home?'

'She's spending the weekend at Briteuil. Philippe and Claire have organised a party for next Sunday. You're invited, of course.'

'I'd better get all my work done on the train, then,' she said, wondering how she would fit everything in.

They chatted a while longer, just because Yolande wanted to, and he rang off after making arrangements to pick her up from Le Manoir the following Saturday evening.

'He's making progress,' remarked Lady Albury when Yolande hung up. 'You haven't gushed over anyone like that for ages.'

'Granny!' She sat down beside her on the sofa. 'I don't gush.'

'Well it sounded like that to me. Watch it, darling. He's sure to get ideas.'

'About what?'

'You, of course! Can't you tell he's as crazy about you as ever? God knows why, the way you trampled all over him.'

Yolande looked at her in surprise. 'But he was never

327

crazy about me at all. Yves isn't like that. We're friends, that's all. Like we used to be before that ridiculous engagement.'

Her grandmother shook her head. 'You'll regret letting him slip through your fingers one of these days, Yolande. He's simply obsessed with you.'

'Obsessed! Oh come on, Granny. Just because he rings me now and then, and we happened to be engaged. But that's all in the past.'

'Believe me, there aren't many men who would run to a woman's sickbed like he did – a year after you'd jilted him. And he doesn't call now and then. It's a regular thing, and you know it. I expect he spends the rest of the week hoping you'll have the decency to call him back.'

'You've got it all wrong,' said Yolande. 'He gets bored on his own, so he likes a chat.'

'And have you ever asked yourself why a gorgeous man like Yves is *still* on his own? You shouldn't lead him on again if you aren't interested. Now, let's see what you've got. Did you buy something for the premiere?'

Over tea they talked about Yolande's meeting with Franco, but her thoughts kept wandering. She had danced (or tried to dance, since she had still needed a stick) with Yves at Philippe's wedding, and nothing much had happened. He'd kissed her, but hadn't said anything, hadn't pushed for anything more. It was like old times. How could he be obsessed with her? She had never thought he was really in love with her, even when he asked her to marry him. Oh, he loved her, she knew that. But that was different – it was like a heartbeat that would always go on, always bind them. Not the blinding heat of passion when you were *in love*. He was so formal, so restrained. It was all too much in keeping with the arranged marriage both their families had wanted.

But they were friends again now, and she had been in love with him once, a very long time ago. A little girl's love – admiration for his strength and good looks, conceit that he had chosen her when he could have had so many others. When they used to kiss she felt hardly anything. Then she remembered the way he'd kissed her at the hospital, that time he came with Isabelle; hardly the kiss of a friend. She had felt heat then, and hunger. And he was still single. Perhaps her grandmother was right. Yolande decided to be extremely careful the following weekend at St Xavier. It wouldn't do to give Yves false hopes now she had finally straightened herself out. She had to think of her career.

'Yolande, are you sure you want to go to this premiere?'

'Absolutely.'

Miles looked at her thoughtfully as she sat opposite him in the Alburys' comfortable sitting room. She was dressed to kill. Long chestnut hair swept back from her face, figure-hugging black dress, endless legs encased in black silk, three-inch heels, a flash of diamonds on her ears, and a small silver cross studded with emeralds around her throat.

'You know Dubuisson will be there.'

She touched the cross, smiling. 'Why do you think I'm wearing this?'

'Superstitious, aren't you?' Miles laughed. 'But you won't need it. I'll be there if he tries anything on.'

The doorbell rang. 'Must be the taxi,' she said, getting to her feet. 'It feels odd to be taking an evening off. I've not been going out much – too much work.'

'Join the club. Corinne's already got the furniture for your office. Better get a break in before it really kicks off.'

'Oh, I will. Ten days at St Xavier and then it's New York for Christmas. What about you and Corinne?'

'Christmas at my uncle's, then we'll join you in New York. Honestly, it's going to be impossible to get round to all our relations when we have children.'

Her head swivelled. 'Children! Have you told Corinne?'

They moved out into the hall. 'Mmm … ah, no. But you know how I feel about her. There's never going to be another woman I'd want to have my children.'

'So you're going to propose?'

'Don't you dare breathe a word.' Then he looked worried. 'I just don't know what I'll do if she says no.'

Yolande patted his arm in sympathy. 'She'd be mad if she did. Just take a chance.'

'I hope you're right. Got your handbag?'

She giggled. 'I see she's got you well trained.' She held it up. 'Check.'

'Tickets?'

'Check.'

'Credit card, mobile phone that you'll forget to switch off, powder compact, lipstick, comb, keys, tissues, and all the other useless stuff you females cart around.'

'Check, check, check, check, check, check and check – you horrid man.'

'I'll take that as a compliment. Now, come on, or we'll be late. It's a good thing I happened to be over, or you'd have been without an escort. Met anybody tall, dark, and handsome recently?'

'No. And I don't want to.'

'Strange girl,' said Miles good-humouredly. 'Think of all the legions of tall, dark, handsome men you're making suicidal. My colleague is going mad over you. I haven't had a decent day's work out of him since he met you.'

Yolande vaguely remembered James Chetwode, who had tried to monopolise her at a party Toinette had thrown to welcome her home from hospital, and she laughed. Tall and dark he might be, but handsome he most certainly was not. He had, however, cracked some very funny jokes, most of them quite lost on the French guests.

Miles kept up the banter during their drive to Leicester

Square, hoping to boost Yolande's spirits. He couldn't decide whether she was putting on a bold front or was now quite calm about meeting her movie acquaintances. She'd sworn that she hated the whole lot of them when she was lying broken and bandaged in the emergency ward, and the very word 'Hollywood' made her wince. He couldn't forget Corinne's anguish, and having by now got to know Yolande rather well, shared it himself. She was such a lovable character – sometimes so mature and dry, then quirkily naïve, emotionally vulnerable, given to impulsive acts of generosity, and always ready with an infectious chuckle when something caught her sense of the ridiculous. *Just like Papa*, Corinne said. *Just like Papa*, Yolande would say about one of Corinne's business manoeuvres. They really were an extraordinary pair.

It was great that they were reconciled, and it would be even better if Yolande would put Yves out of his misery. Miles reckoned he would have a perfect opportunity this evening to size up the competition. Everyone had been shocked by Yolande's total lack of interest in men in the past few months – for a girl who had had men draped around her for the best part of eight years, she was in danger of turning into a nun. It could only be Patrick who was holding her back.

A damp and very bleak Tuesday evening, typical of London in November, but Leicester Square was awash with TV floodlights and an eager crowd was waiting outside the cinema to see the celebrities arrive. Miles was rather disconcerted by the heavy security, paparazzi, and reporters, but Yolande sailed past them all with barely a word, pausing for just a second to have her picture taken.

'God, it's like a madhouse,' he said. 'You didn't mention the Queen was coming.'

'She's not. It's Jayne Herford they're waiting for – the Queen of Hollywood.'

He wasn't a film buff, and the name hardly registered.

'Shall I lay down my cloak for her?'

'She'd love it. She expects men to fall at her feet. Now, let's see who's here.'

They went in. A crowded lobby, ushers organising the crush, some of the cast and crew already lined up to greet the French Ambassador, who had been prevailed upon to be the guest of honour in lieu of royalty. That was Ethan Casavecchia's one publicity failure. He couldn't understand why you couldn't hire a British queen or princess at short notice. So it had to be the French Ambassador, to promote the film's European dimension in the macho form of Patrick Dubuisson. The substantial European funding from Yolande Marchand didn't even make the billing.

'Yolande! Wow, you look fantastic!' Vic Bernitz approached at speed, looking slightly over-large for his dinner jacket. He gave her a bear hug and kissed her cheek. 'I'm so glad you could make it. We've got profits to discuss some time. You just won't believe it. And I'd like to run anther project past you.'

'Meet my financial adviser,' said Yolande, smiling. 'Miles Corsley – he's a banker.'

Miles shook Vic's hand rather stiffly. So it was going to be one of those evenings, with all differences forgotten in the general euphoria over the accumulation of dollars. He liked Ethan even less, but Sam MacPherson seemed a pleasant enough young guy without an inflated ego. He sauntered up to them shyly and pumped Yolande's hand with genuine pleasure.

'Yolande! It's so good to see you again. I was real sorry to hear about your accident, but you look fantastic. I hope you got my flowers?'

'I did, thank you. It was sweet of you. Are you with Jayne?'

'Nah. I've teamed up with Donna this evening. Jayne will be along in a while with Patrick. Ethan thought it would come across better if they made a couple for the press.' He raised his eyebrows expressively. 'I know my place. Why don't you come over and say hi to the others?'

They followed him and spent several minutes chatting to the supporting cast. Miles felt decidedly superfluous, but made the right noises and looked impressive. He recognised some of the names, but he was damned if he was going to kow-tow to any of them. They in turn seemed rather awed by him.

'Is that your new boyfriend?' Donna Jenkins, a petite and perennially cheerful character actress whispered to Yolande.

'My sister's, actually. I borrow him sometimes, but she doesn't charge me interest.'

Donna laughed uproariously. 'Well, I'm glad you're still able to make jokes after that smash. It was so horrible. We all felt for you, you know. Particularly as Patrick ...' she dropped her voice conspiratorially, '... acted so goddamn mean. I got suspicious when Althea Pedersen suddenly vanished with her husband after hanging around the studios so long. They've sold their Malibu place now. But Patrick didn't seem to mind. When we were in Mexico he was acting like some frigging Valentino.' She hastily cupped a hand to her mouth. 'I'm sorry. I always talk too much.'

'I'll live,' said Yolande. She took Miles' proffered arm and moved on.

Then there was a huge roar from outside and a general increase of tension in the lobby. Jayne Herford, sizzling in red, swept in first. The dress was eye-popping, with a low plunging neckline and no back at all (as far as Miles could see when she turned to embrace Vic Bernitz). Patrick followed a few steps behind her and shook hands with a few dignitaries. He looked across the lobby and started visibly when he caught sight of Yolande. She stared at him coolly.

'What a rat,' commented Miles. And then he could

have kicked himself for being so tactless.

Yolande just shrugged her shoulders. Jayne had now spotted her, and made a point of greeting her next, hurrying over with a twenty-four carat smile.

'Yolande, how great to see you again! How are you now? Your boyfriend? No? Well, *hello.*'

Miles held out his hand, but American royalty was in an affable mood. His cheek received a peck from the hottest lips in Hollywood. He looked utterly bemused, and stood silent as Yolande and Jayne chatted for a couple of minutes as though they had always been the best of friends.

When Jayne had moved on, Yolande gave him a wicked grin. 'You can breathe out now,' she said.

'You said she didn't like you,' he remarked.

'They don't give her awards for nothing, you know.'

He smiled and pressed her arm as Patrick drew nearer, lingering in conversation with Donna Jenkins, but looking at Yolande out of the corner of his eye. At length they were face to face. Patrick paused close to Yolande. Handsome in a rough way, Miles thought. There was no mistaking his sex appeal, but he somehow looked cheap and seedy in a dinner jacket. Patrick gave Yolande a half-smile, barely turning up the corners of his mouth, but his eyes suddenly glinted suggestively.

'Hello, Yolande,' he said in French, leaning forwards to kiss her.

She stepped back, her head high, her green eyes cool; disdainful even. Patrick faltered a little, waiting for her to respond.

She turned to Miles. 'I wonder how long before the ambassador arrives?'

Patrick couldn't conceal his annoyance. He hesitated for a moment, as though he was going to say something else, but was quickly pulled away by Ethan, who made a fuss about getting him in line to greet the ambassador, whose limousine was just pulling up outside.

Yolande relaxed. The worst was over and she had triumphed. Now she had seen him again, been so close that they had almost touched, she couldn't understand how Patrick had held her in thrall for so long. She hadn't felt anything but contempt. No recollection of their love, no memory of their passion; just pity for a man who didn't even have the sense to know when he was no longer welcome. As far as her emotions were concerned, he was dead.

Miles thought matters boded well for Yves, and patted her shoulder. 'Well done.'

The ambassador received a much warmer reception than Patrick. He had been a friend of Jean-Claude Marchand, and spent a few minutes in conversation with Yolande after giving her a hearty embrace.

'I hope you'll spend more of your time on this side of the Atlantic now, my dear. Beautiful flowers cannot bloom in the desert.'

She smiled at this diplomatic insult to California, assuring him that she intended to base her future career entirely in Europe. Had Vic Bernitz been able to understand French, he might well have been worried.

The film itself was something of an anti-climax for Miles after the real-life drama in the lobby, but he had to admit it was good. Patrick Dubuisson most certainly could act, the script was snappy, the music memorable, the sets and stunts quite stupendous. He took special note of the bedroom scenes. When Patrick finally got his way with Jayne, superb as the rebellious, independent Amanda, Miles looked round to gauge Yolande's reaction. She sat beside him quietly, her features immobile, though her fingers curled and uncurled around the clasp of her handbag. That was the only sign of tension. Miles mentally awarded her another point and turned his eyes back to the screen. Quite a performance, even if edited and blurred by the special lighting effects. Things suddenly didn't look so good for Yves after all.

Yolande said very little during the journey back to Kensington, though she remarked with surprise on the crowds still waiting to see the stars emerge from the cinema. *Fast and Loose* was a closed chapter in her life. Like Patrick. The following day she was busy with an assignment and glanced only briefly at the film's press reviews. Comment from all the important critics was very favourable. The film was going to be a major success. It suddenly struck her that she would probably make rather a lot of money out of it. She almost wanted to laugh.

Chapter Twenty-one

'You look just like Yolande de Charbuy with your hair up like that.'

Corinne smiled at her sister, who was sitting in her room at St Xavier putting the finishing touches to her make-up. Yolande looked closer in the dressing-table mirror and grimaced. 'I suppose you're right. Not very promising, is it?'

'Oh I don't know. She found happiness in the end.'

'But it didn't last,' said Yolande, picking up a diamond necklace from her jewellery box. 'Shall I wear this?'

Corinne moved across the room and helped fasten the necklace, then rested her hands on her sister's shoulders. 'This is a lovely outfit. Franco's?'

'Yes. I got it the day I bumped into him in Beauchamp Place. I was going to wear it to the premiere, but then I thought I'd save it for tonight.'

'It's obvious he keeps his best designs for his own label, but I shouldn't complain. So how was it? Miles said Jayne Herford kissed him.'

'Much good it did her. He didn't bat an eyelid.'

'And Patrick?' Corinne had had Miles' version of events, but she still wasn't sure how it had affected Yolande.

'Oh, I'm OK. Honestly. Don't worry. He had the bloody nerve to try to speak to me, but I cut him.' Yolande paused, then leaned back against Corinne. 'Darling, I really need to talk to you. I probably owe you some money.'

'For what?'

'It must have cost you a pile to buy back my shares

from Stessenberg.'

'Don't be an idiot. I'd have had to pay you for them, anyway. We didn't lose on it in the end. Now come on, or you'll be late.'

'But I've caused so much trouble. I want to make it up to you,' said Yolande standing up. 'You see, I think I may well make quite a lot of money on *Fast and Loose*.'

Corinne couldn't help laughing at her worried expression. Who else but her little sister would get upset about that?

'What's so funny?' asked Yolande, mystified.

'You! You're simply the craziest person I've ever known.'

'But couldn't you use some of it to invest in Marchand? I'm serious, Corinne, really. I never expected to see a penny out of it.'

Corinne's laugh died instantly. 'You're joking.'

'No I'm not.'

'You mean you backed the film solely because of Patrick?'

Yolande lowered her eyes. 'Yes. They insisted it would make good profits, but I really didn't expect more than to break even. You must think I'm a total airhead, but at the time – well, as it now looks certain I'll get a good return on the investment, it's only fair that you benefit.'

They looked at each other for a few moments. Corinne shook her head. 'No, Yolande. Thanks for the offer, anyway.'

'But why not?'

'It's very, very generous of you, but I'd never be able to think of it except as blood money.'

'I know what you mean.' Yolande thought gloomily of her accident, Patrick; the horrible way it had all ended.

'Are you going to keep Belco Pictures?'

'I don't want to long term. I'll have a meeting with Troy and Shelby, see if they have some ideas. It shouldn't be too difficult to line up some buyers on the back of the film.'

'Why don't you get Tex involved? He'll come up with a strategy for you. Now, do hurry up. Yves will be here any minute and we want you gone so we can doze off in front of the TV. I need some rest before Briteuil tomorrow. It will be the Rochemorts en masse.'

'Exhausting,' agreed Yolande, following her out of the room. 'But you really shouldn't miss dinner at Vougeot.'

'We went last month, and my waistline's only just recovering. Gaston will be there. I told him to look out for you. And don't worry about when you'll be back, because we shan't wait up.'

Yves had already arrived and was chatting with Miles in the salon. He looked up eagerly when they came in. Yolande made the somewhat mortifying discovery that he looked far better than Patrick in a dinner jacket. He kissed her cheeks and pulled her down to sit beside him on the sofa.

'I love the dress,' he said, his eyes appreciative. 'Did you buy it specially?'

'Yes.'

Suddenly she was lost for words, and looked away. Why he seemed so much more handsome now than she remembered was mystery. It was Yves, for God's sake. She'd known him all her life. But there was something different in his manner; a confidence and maturity that gave him an edge she hadn't felt before. He certainly lost no time saying goodbye to the others and getting her into his car. They drove off at speed, and when they had passed through St Xavier into the open country he glanced at her pensive profile.

'You're very quiet, Yolande. Didn't you want to come?'

'Of course I did.'

'Good journey home?'

'You don't really want all the details on my homework, do you?' she said, rallying. 'How are you?'

'What do you think?'

Provocative question. He smiled as she looked at him quizzically. The ball was in her court for once. Why was this casual chit-chat proving so difficult?

'You look very well,' she managed tamely.

'And you? Any trouble from your injuries?'

'Not much. The physiotherapy was pretty intensive and I swim quite a lot – that helps.'

There was a short silence, then they talked about her course, her job, his mother's birthday party. Finally, when they were within ten kilometres of Vougeot, he brought up the film.

'So you went to the premiere after all. Miles told me it was quite a do.'

'It was rather star-studded,' she said, her voice suitably blasé, 'but then premieres usually are.'

Yves laughed. 'I gather he was kissed by Jayne Herford. Did you have any luck?'

'With Jayne? Yes, as a matter of fact.'

Impasse. They drove on in silence, Yves keeping his eyes trained on the road. But he had to know about Patrick. Miles hadn't been exactly forthcoming on the subject.

'Dubuisson was there, wasn't he? Was he surprised to see you?'

'I really don't know. We didn't speak.'

Why do you need to know? she thought. What the hell does any of it matter now? She watched him, but his face gave nothing away and it annoyed her. The evening hadn't even started yet and she was already feeling jittery. She wasn't used to Yves making her nervous.

'I'd rather not talk about him. As far as I'm concerned, he doesn't exist.'

It was much more than Yves had hoped for, but he kept a tight lid on his feelings. The note of irritation in her voice cheered him. It was a flash of real feeling, the first he'd had from her in a long time. He looked round and saw that her arms were folded tightly across her bosom. 'You're cold, Yolande.'

'This jacket's a bit thin.'

'You should have told me before.'

The road was empty, so he pulled up, got a blanket from the back seat and wrapped it carefully around her. She was touched by the attention.

'Thanks.'

'I've just noticed that you don't smoke any more,' he said when they were moving again.

'I rather lost the habit while I was in hospital, and now I don't seem to enjoy cigarettes at all.'

'Like Philippe. He's so busy working, he hasn't got time. But I remember when I asked you to give it up once, you refused.'

Once. When they were engaged. He said it so casually and it hurt. It sounded as though he didn't care, and Yolande wasn't used to being considered unimportant, least of all by Yves. But why should she expect anything other than this friendly, superficial chit-chat? They had come out to enjoy themselves, and the number of cigarettes she did or didn't smoke was as trivial a topic of conversation as the circumstances required. She resolved to show a little more spirit, and amused him the rest of the way with some insider gossip on Hollywood. He learnt far more about famous boob jobs and face lifts than he had ever wanted to know.

A long line of cars greeted them when they got near to the Clos de Vougeot, all crammed with smart guests attending the dinner. They drove slowly down the approach road through the vineyards to the twelfth-century Cistercian abbey, now the headquarters of the Confrérie des Chevaliers du Tastevin. It was a large building, but plain and unornamented; not at all like the flamboyance of

Rochemort. The car parked, Yves tucked Yolande's hand under his arm and led her into the huge banqueting hall that had once been the abbey's cellar. Long rows of tables for the five hundred guests were laid out beneath the huge rafters. People were filling the hall, and a local choir was on a platform ready to sing songs about wine. There was a sprinkling of celebrities and a noticeable media presence.

Yolande felt people staring at her, and involuntarily clutched Yves' arm. It was harder than she thought stepping back into her own world, where everybody knew them both and had seen all the stories about her accident and Patrick. She gritted her teeth and tossed back her hair.

'Still turning their heads, aren't you?' Yves remarked, guiding her to their table. 'Just be sure you laugh in the right places when I make my speech. Ah ... here we are ... Excuse me, madame ...'

He pulled out a chair for Yolande next to a chic brunette in her early thirties, then went off to speak to officials on the platform. Yolande looked about to see if she recognised anyone. There had to be some people she knew here. She spotted Gaston Leclerc with his wife and sons in a distant part of the hall. Then a flash. Hell. Photographers. She turned her head, smiled slightly, and hoped they would soon be satisfied.

'Any comment on Patrick Dubuisson?' shouted one.

'Never heard of him,' she replied, still smiling.

The chic brunette laughed and introduced herself as Clarisse Beaufort, an actress. 'It's odd how women who've known Patrick always forget his name afterwards,' she said. 'So you're Yolande Marchand. Your photos don't do you justice.'

Yolande shrugged her shoulders. 'You know Patrick?'

'I worked on a TV programme with him a couple of years ago. I have to say, your escort tonight is *hot*.'

Yolande had never thought of Yves as *hot*. Still, each to her own. 'He's a member of the Confrérie. We're both winegrowers.'

Clarisse's interest was aroused, and by the time Yves came back, accompanied by two middle-aged bespectacled men in Confrérie robes, they were deep in conversation about the merits of various Burgundy vintages. Yolande broke off to renew her acquaintance with the men, who had known her father well, and soon the evening's festivities were under way.

Yves was most attentive until called upon to make his speech, though Yolande felt he could have been less gallant to Clarisse. He leaned just a little too close to her, laughed at her jokes, paid her compliments – *flirted*, damn him. She took a long hard look at him and had to agree that Clarisse had a point. He was positively sizzling. But when he had been hers, he'd barely been tepid and she'd tossed him aside. It was too late now for what might have been. Yolande bestowed her own battery of charm on an elderly gentleman to her right, who clearly thought he had died and gone to heaven. They sang the songs together, and he was delighted that she knew all the words. The dinner, as always, was superb, though for some reason she had no appetite.

Yves' speech, introducing new members to the Confrérie, was quirky and funny, and got generous applause – not least from Clarisse Beaufort, who continued to monopolise him until the dinner ended.

Miles checked and rechecked the table. Candles, roses, silver cutlery, napkins. All present and correct, in perfect symmetry. The wine was open and left to breathe, and the Champagne was on ice. Something was missing. Music. He rifled through the CDs by the stereo and opted for classical, then headed back to the kitchen to the sound of Chopin. And hoped the meal was as easy to prepare as Yolande had assured him it would be. She'd left it all ready with full instructions for heating and serving.

Corinne wandered in a few minutes later dressed only in a bath robe, her hair wet from the shower.

'Hmm, that smells good, darling. I thought you couldn't cook.'

'Jury's still out. I thought it was about time I treated you to *fusilli à la Corsley.*' He turned to her, and his mouth watered. 'Come here, woman.'

'Since you ask so nicely.' And she was in his arms, being kissed senseless and thinking she wasn't hungry after all and it would be much better if they simply went to bed where she could have her way with him. 'Miles, let's eat later.'

He tore his lips away. 'Not possible. This is all timed and I synchronised watches and all that technical stuff. Why don't you go into the dining room? And please, darling, put something on. You're distracting me.'

She winked and sauntered out, and when she reappeared fifteen minutes later was dressed in a midnight blue skin-tight dress, cut low back and front and ending several inches above the knee. Her long legs were in matching silk stockings, and diamonds glittered in her ears and around her neck.

He stared and swallowed hard. 'Oh hell.'

'Well,' she crossed to him, hooked one leg around his thighs and pressed her body against his. 'I wouldn't want to distract you.' Her hand found the bulge in his trousers. 'Would I?'

'Corinne, for God's sake. I'm trying to cook you a romantic dinner.'

'Is that why you put on Chopin?'

'Don't you like it?'

'It's fine. I'm just in the mood for something a little more … racy.'

His blood was pounding, his head swam with her perfume while she seemed to wind all around him like an octopus. And her hand. Dear God, her hand. And then the

344

microwave stopped with a loud 'ping' and he jumped like a guilty schoolboy.

Corinne collapsed with giggles. '*Fusilli à la Corsley?* Yolande cooked it, didn't she? And you just heated it up.'

'I … um … well, yes. But I'm sure it's good.'

'I know it is. She's a damn good cook when she puts her mind to it.'

'Why don't you go on into the dining room and I'll bring it through?' Although it was the last thing he wanted to do with her body plastered against him.

'Why don't you tell me what this is all about?'

He took her shoulders and stood her a little away from him so he could look into her eyes. They were both suddenly serious.

'Corinne, I want to give you a little more romance to show you how I feel. We've been together for several months now, and we don't seem to have done any real courting.'

She was confused. 'Courting? How very old-fashioned.'

'Darling, I *am* old-fashioned. I love you. I can't live without you. But we just keep jumping from bedroom to boardroom and there isn't enough time for us. This evening was supposed to be special. Slow. Romantic.'

'And I've spoilt it all by trying to seduce you. Oh Miles, I'm sorry.' She stroked his cheek gently. 'I love you. I can't live without you either. I don't need courting to know that.'

She found herself jerked into his arms, his lips burning hers.

'In that case,' he murmured between kisses, 'why don't you make an honest man of me?'

She pulled back, stared into his eyes. 'Miles?'

'Marry me, Corinne. Please. I promise never to cook for you again.'

She laughed then through the tears that suddenly came

to her eyes, then flung her arms around his neck. 'Oh darling, yes. Yes!'

He lifted her off her feet and carried her out of the kitchen and towards the staircase.

'What about dinner?' she asked, kissing his throat.

'When you ambush your fiancé in the kitchen like that it means he has to make love to you. Immediately.'

She sighed contentedly. 'Hmmm. I hoped it might.'

It was a stony-faced Yolande who climbed into the car at Vougeot after midnight for the journey back to St Xavier. She pulled the blanket around her shoulders, waiting for Yves to make his final goodbyes – probably to punch Clarisse Beaufort's number into his mobile – and slumped back in her seat. Perhaps she could sleep, then they wouldn't have to talk. She wished she hadn't come. He had made such a point of inviting her only to ignore her the whole evening.

Then he was beside her, and the engine started. 'Had a good time, Yolande?'

'Wonderful,' she said grimly.

Yves smiled in the darkness. So the medicine was starting to work. He didn't say much on the way home, and Yolande closed her eyes, feeling angry. She kept seeing him with Clarisse Beaufort, an entirely different man from the Yves she knew – suave, supremely confident, and far too handsome for her peace of mind. He had made a fool of her. Revenge, she supposed. He had waited all this time for his revenge. She dozed off, and was woken only by the sound of gravel beneath the wheels.

'We're home,' he said, as they came to a halt.

She threw off the blanket and stumbled out into the raw night air. Pitch black. Cold November. She wanted to cry. Yves slammed the car door behind her and draped his jacket over her shoulders.

'That's better. You're shivering. How about a drink to

warm up?'

Her eyes had adjusted to the gloom. She realised they weren't at her home but the Château de Rochemort. She just stared at him, puzzled.

'Coming in?'

'I'd better. It's bloody freezing out here.'

They went inside, through the entrance to the west wing, which was heated and welcoming. Yolande gave a contented sigh as the warmth spread into her chilled bones.

'I'll just check that Marie has locked up,' said Yves. 'Why don't you wait in the salon? Two doors on from my office. I won't be long.'

The salon was smaller than the draughty first-floor drawing room favoured by Marie-Christine. It looked as though it was Yves' private sitting room. Yolande slipped off his jacket and hung it on the back of the door, then sank down gratefully into the comfort of a modern sofa. Strange, she'd never been in this room before, though she thought she knew the château inside out. It had definite appeal; homely clutter, light-blue walls, dependable oak furniture, a cosy atmosphere. There were wine magazines on the coffee table and various measuring implements along the top of a cabinet which housed a stereo system and CD collection. A portrait of Yves' father hung on one wall, facing a post-Impressionist landscape that featured Rochemort's fabled gardens. On the mantelpiece there was a photograph of a beaming Isabelle with Philippe and Claire on their wedding day.

A very private room, really. Yolande picked up a copy of the *Revue des Vins de France*, flicked over the pages, then dropped it, yawning. She went across to the CD cabinet to check that Yves didn't already have the Rachmaninov piano concertos she'd bought him for Christmas. He loved classical music – unlike Patrick, who had listened to nothing but hip-hop and rap. Yolande herself had eclectic tastes, and liked anything from Mozart to the most recent pop so long as it had a good tune. Tucked in amongst some Schubert and Brahms symphonies she found a Jacques Brel album, and decided to put it on for old times' sake. They always used to sing 'Ne me quitte pas' at the end of the holidays, when she and Corinne had to return to London for another term at the Lycée. Then she thought perhaps it wasn't such a good idea after all, and sat down, just as Yves appeared at the door carrying a tray. His eyes wandered immediately to the Brel CD, which she hadn't quite managed to push back into place.

'Shall I put it on?' he asked, setting the tray down on coffee table.

'If you like.'

The familiar lyrics had an effect on them both. Yves sat beside her and poured liqueur – Marc de Bourgogne, distilled from the skins of his own grapes – into Baccarat crystal glasses engraved with the Rochemort arms. Yolande had to admire his style.

'We sold quite a few cases last year,' he said. 'It seems to be getting a favourable reaction.'

She sipped the drink cautiously. Some distilled burgundy was veritable firewater, but this was definitely a first-rate liqueur. 'It's extremely good, Yves. They'll be putting it in chocolates next.'

'Why not?' He smiled, leaning back on the sofa cushions. 'So what do you think of my salon? I converted it from an old storeroom. I'm sorry it's a mess, but I've only just moved things in.'

'It's coming along very well.'

Ne me quitte pas, il faut oublier ... Why did that song have to intrude? Yolande stared into her glass, wondering why he had invited her in to rub salt into her wounds with this nostalgia. He was even more subtly vindictive than she had imagined. And why was it upsetting her anyway? Weren't they friends now? Couldn't friends listen to old records over a drink and be civilised?

'Actually, Yolande, I'm doing up some more rooms and I thought you could help me with the colour scheme. Would you mind? You're so good at that sort of thing.'

Je ferai un domaine, Où l'amour sera roi, Où l'amour sera loi, Ne tu seras reine, Ne me quitte pas, ne me quitte pas, ne me quitte pas ...

She nodded and he fetched an interior designer's catalogue from a bureau in the corner. But all he could hear was Brel's inimitable voice, singing everything that he wanted to say to Yolande. Forget the past. Forget our hurts. Don't leave me. I'll build you a realm where love will be king and you will be queen. Don't leave me ...

They pored over the catalogue for some minutes, neither paying much attention to what they were doing. She felt the warmth from his body next to hers on the sofa, kept looking at his strong beautiful hands turning the page, caught her breath when he turned suddenly and his face was only inches from hers. Eventually she opted in desperation for severe, symmetrical red and gold patterned wallpaper.

Yves put the catalogue down. 'Another drink?'

'No thanks. I've revived now.'

'I suppose it is rather warm in here. You could take off your jacket.'

Yolande looked at him warily, but his expression was innocence itself. And she was getting hot – hot and bothered. What the hell was he doing to her? She removed the jacket and sat back on the sofa.

Yves nearly lost his control then. Everything he had ever wanted, so close. He wanted to kiss her shoulders, that little hollow in her throat, the scar running down her upper arm, her proud lips turned down in a sulky pout. It was the pout and slightly haunted expression in her eyes that made him think that just a little more indifference would bring her to his arms. He picked up the catalogue

349

again and thumbed through it, making one or two empty remarks about the designs.

Yolande lost her patience. 'I really can't help you any more, Yves. It's your place, so do what you like. Why do you want to change everything, anyway? It looks fine as it is.'

'For a bachelor. But as I'm planning to get married, I thought I'd better get a few rooms ready for my wife.'

Her hands suddenly trembled, and she was glad she had put down her glass. She needed a packet of cigarettes, something, anything, to keep herself busy. He was going to get married, he was making the place beautiful for his wife. It sliced through her. She had lost him. And she loved him. She had never loved him or wanted him so much in her life. He'd found some other woman to fill the place she had always been sure she held in his heart – even after she had left him.

Everything suddenly became startlingly clear. Hadn't she been jealous as well as surprised by his courtship of Gabrielle d'Emville? Jealous of Clarisse Beaufort this evening? Upset because she hadn't been receiving the attention she expected from him? She couldn't blame him for breaking it to her this way. She'd hurt him so badly. It was naïve to suppose he wouldn't want to get his own back. But she wasn't going to give him the satisfaction of letting him see how devastated she was. *Get your coat, Yolande, wish him well, get out, don't look back.* She didn't even want to know who could have brought about such a change in him. She choked back the tears, her face turned away from him as she retrieved her handbag and jacket.

'Well, I hope you'll be very happy. And … thanks for taking me out tonight. It's been … quite … an evening …' The tears began to flow unchecked. 'I think I'd better go home.'

'Yolande!' He leaned forward and caught her in his

arms, turning her so he could see her face. Her beautiful green eyes were bathed in tears. She was crying. For him at last. 'I thought perhaps I was wrong about us. Please tell me I'm not. Say it, my darling!'

She gulped then and looked into his eyes; brilliant blue eyes, as intense and tender as they had always been. Full of love and hope. He was hers. *Hers.* How could she have been so blind? So utterly stupid? And how dared he trick her into admitting her feelings? She launched herself at him, furious.

'You pig! Making me think you've got someone else!'

He grinned devilishly, pulling her close. 'It worked, didn't it?'

Oh, it was wonderful to be in his arms again, feel his heart pounding against hers. She flung her arms around him. 'Yves, I love you. I love you!'

Their lips met. Yolande felt his fingers trying to loosen her hair. She quickly took out the clips and shook the chestnut locks free, then his mouth was burning hers as it had never done before. Hot, passionate kisses, his tongue seeking hers, drawing her into him, driving her wild with desire. His hands caressed her shoulders, her breasts, her thighs. She could hardly believe it was Yves. Her whole body ached for him.

Quickly upstairs hand in hand, along the corridor to his bedroom. Nervous, she suddenly freed herself and moved away. She'd adored him when she was a child, miserably watched him go out with other girls, been thrilled when he had finally told her he loved her and asked her to marry him; but they had never even seen each other completely naked. Now she was a couple of feet away from his bed and there was no mistaking the expression in his eyes.

He moved close and rested his hands on her arms. 'Yolande, what's wrong? I want to make love to you.'

'But you ... we never ...' She was stammering. But her face gave it all away.

'My God, you didn't think I couldn't?'

'What was I supposed to think? You've never so much as kissed me like that before.'

'I want you now. I wanted you then. I've always wanted you.' He pulled her tightly against him.

She was shocked to feel a huge erection pushing into her belly. No mistaking that, either. And then the nerves were jangling again. 'Yves, I'm not that girl anymore.' The tears sprang into her eyes. 'You can't want me now. I'm scarred and ugly, and I've been an absolute bitch, and …'

'Don't you say that! Just let me tell you what you are.' He pressed a tender kiss to her lips. 'My Yolande.' Another kiss, just below her left ear, longer, deeper. 'Beautiful.' Her right ear this time, erotic, teasing. 'Tender, warm.' Her throat. Nibbling, licking.

Oh, he was so good at this. She felt a stab of raw lust right through her.

'Kind, generous.' Down between her breasts, tracing patterns on her skin with his tongue.

She moaned. What the hell was he doing to her?

'Funny, clever.'

Before she realised what was happening, he had unzipped her dress and slipped it off, unhooked her bra. His tongue and teeth teased and sucked her nipples, setting off fire between her legs. More, please, more … His mouth moved down, over her belly, then lower. Her briefs were suddenly gone, and he was stoking the heat between her thighs. Light, flickering touches.

'Adorable, charming.' He was pulling her stocking down, so gently, over the scars on her left leg. And then he dropped light kisses all along each wound. 'Sexy, desirable …'

'Oh Yves,' she said helplessly. 'Show me.'

He scooped her up in his arms and she was on the bed. His mouth came down on hers, crushing, demanding this time, and she responded with an urgent hunger she didn't know she possessed. She had to have him, hold him, love him, feel him throb beneath her hands. Clothes were tugged, sent flying.

'Dear God,' Yolande murmured when he lay naked beside her. 'You're enormous.'

'I'm all yours.'

Skin to skin, heart-stopping kisses, his hands and fingers exploring, detonating explosions throughout her body. She threaded her fingers through his hair, pulling his mouth back again and again, each kiss a fresh exploration; deep, wet, endless pleasure, and she couldn't seem to get enough. She reached down to touch him, but he pushed her hand away.

'You first.'

Yolande just melted into it. Such clever fingers, stroking. Just there, oh perfect, lovely ... don't stop. No, don't stop! Her legs were stretched wider, knees pushed back. Then his tongue. Oh my God, where had he learnt to do *that*? Patrick had never hit that spot. She writhed under him and moaned, panted, screamed as he pushed her to the edge, and then he plunged his fingers into her and played her like an instrument. His mouth closed over hers as she bucked and trembled and gasped his name.

And then he made her come again. And finally, when she thought she couldn't take any more, thought she'd die, he entered her and took her somewhere she'd never been before, where all that mattered was Yves and the moment and his body, heart and soul becoming a living part of her.

Much later Yolande lay cradled in his arms, almost unbearably happy but totally confused. 'I never knew it could be like that,' she murmured, kissing his neck. 'It was magical, darling. No one's ever made me feel that way before.'

'I always knew it would be magic with you.'

'Yves, can you forgive me? Truly forgive me? I've been so horrible to you.' It hurt her to think of the pain she'd caused him. 'I really want to make you happy. I love you more than I can possibly say. Oh God, I'm making such a hash of this. I want to apologise.'

'You're doing fine.' His voice was thick with emotion. 'There's nothing to forgive. We start from here. I love you, Yolande. I've never loved anyone else.' He kissed her, long and hard. 'I never will.'

'I've got something to confess too. I've been in love with you since I was five years old. Before I even knew what it meant. You were always there. Even when we quarrelled, even when we were apart. You always will be.'

He pulled her closer, and she clung to him. 'My darling. How on earth did I manage to lose you?'

'I thought you didn't love me. Didn't need me. Didn't really want me.'

He groaned. 'But I asked you to marry me! It's not something I make a habit of. And I've wanted to make love to you for years. Ever since you stopped wearing your hair in that ridiculous ponytail. How old were you then?'

'Thirteen.'

'Do you remember you said you'd have your hair down or cut it all off? I could have died for you then. But you were only thirteen and I was eighteen. So I waited. And you had that grungy boyfriend at the Lycée.'

'Pierre? He wasn't grungy.'

'He certainly was. So I waited. Then you went to university in the States. So I waited some more. But I wanted you all right.'

'But when we were engaged, why were you afraid to touch me? You never even kissed me properly.'

'If I'd kissed you how I wanted to, I couldn't have kept control of myself.'

She looked at him, then flushed with embarrassment as realisation dawned. 'Oh God. You wanted to wait until we were married. Yves, I'm so sorry. If you'd only just told me …'

He sighed. 'It's my fault. I was a complete idiot. I thought you understood that you were so precious to me, I wanted to make it mean something really special. A sign of my commitment. If you hadn't got sidetracked at Hervy we would have married sooner and then it would have all worked out.'

That was a very polite way of referring to Patrick. Yolande kissed him lingeringly. Some day she would earn his forgiveness – now she just took it with love.

'Do you know, my grandmother warned me about going with you to Vougeot? She said you were sure to get ideas.'

'Actually, I had a few before I asked you.'

She sat up. 'You know, I think I'm rather cross with you.'

'Mmm?'

'I need to make you pay.' She ran both hands slowly over the thick black hair on his chest and stomach, down his sides, and over his thighs, then massaged her way back up to his groin. He was such a gorgeous man, all rippling muscle and hard contours and he was fully erect again. She wanted more of him, much much more.

Yves smiled. 'Why?'

Her hands wrapped around his cock, stroking, fondling. She knew she could make him do whatever she wanted. Intoxicating power. 'For making me jealous. For making me fall in love with you. Twice.' She wanted to make him quiver, make him tremble. She lowered her head. 'And for making me wait all these years.'

He suppressed a moan as her tongue made contact. 'Wait for what?'

'For the pleasure of driving you mad.'

She didn't think she ever wanted to stop, could ever have enough, give him enough, show him that he meant all to her, that she belonged to him and never wanted to belong anywhere else. Every taste of him left her wanting more. And she gave more.

If this wasn't heaven, Yves didn't know what was. She was expertly tormenting him, thrilling him, emptying his mind of everything except the two of them and the night. When he could take no more, he hauled her up and took her mouth in a long kiss.

She lowered herself onto him, eager, aching. She couldn't believe how right it felt, how familiar to be filled so completely by Yves. And the dance began again.

'I forgot to ask you something,' he said.

She was in a fine rhythm now, hips pumping, breath catching. 'Hmm? What?'

'How soon can you marry me?'

'You want an answer right now?'

How did he expect her to think straight with him throbbing and pounding inside her, building up layers of heat and ecstasy?

'Darling,' he said, and thrust harder, 'it's what's known as pressing home one's advantage.'

'Name the day,' she gasped. 'Because I certainly can't even remember what week it is. Oh, Yves. … *Yves* …!'

And that was answer enough.

The following day Philippe saw it instantly, the moment they got out of the car at the Château de Briteuil and walked towards him. He gave Yves a huge smile and a bear hug.

'Nice work, Yves. *Finally.*'

Then he hoisted Yolande up in his arms, swung her round, and planted two kisses on each cheek. 'Hello, beautiful. I hope we're top of the guest list.'

'What guest list?'

'You're not going to tell me you and my slowcoach brother aren't planning a wedding at last?'

'How did you know?' she demanded when he put her down.

'You have the look,' he said, as they turned to enter the house. 'Both of you. I think it's catching. I saw the very same look on my own face in the mirror this morning.'

Yolande caught something else in his expression. 'Philippe! Claire's pregnant, isn't she?'

He stopped and held out his arms as they both jumped him with shrieks of delight. It was going to be one hell of a party.

Grace Beidecker held the phone closer to her ear. 'How was the birthday party, Corinne? Oh, good, good. Do give Marie-Christine my love. You're *engaged*? Darling, that's marvellous! Can I speak to him? Hello, Miles, my dear ... I'm thrilled ... Yes, June should be good. We'll block out our diaries. Oh, Yolande wants a word. Hello, darling. How was the dinner last night? You're *what*? *Seriously*? Fantastic! Do give him a big kiss from me. Yes, of course, we'd be absolutely delighted to ... so soon? Well, I understand ...'

Tex sauntered up to her as the call ended. 'What's the big story?

'Corinne and Miles have just got engaged. And Yolande and Yves are getting married in a fortnight.'

For once his composure was ruffled. '*In a fortnight?* They weren't even dating the last I heard.'

'Tex, please ... She wants you to give her away.'

'No kidding.' He gave her a comical look and tugged her into his arms. 'Those girls of yours will be the death of me, Grace. OK, you win. I guess that means we won't be staying home for Christmas after all. I knew I shouldn't have bought those new slippers.'

Other Accent Press Titles

For more information about **Eve Bourton**

and other **Accent Press** titles

please visit

www.accentpress.co.uk

Lightning Source UK Ltd.
Milton Keynes UK
UKOW04f1828291115

263780UK00001B/7/P